The Coming Rebellion

LEGENDS OF CORALIA

The Coming Rebellion

KATE JENKINS & MORGAN MOREAU

4 Horsemen Publications, Inc.
1497 Main St. Suite 169
Dunedin, FL 34698
4horsemenpublications.com
info@4horsemenpublications.com

Cover & Typesetting by Autumn Skye
Edited by Devora Gray

Library of Congress Control Number: Pending

Paperback ISBN-13: 979-8-8232-0370-8
Hardcover ISBN-13: 979-8-8232-0371-5
Audiobook ISBN-13: 979-8-8232-0372-2
Ebook ISBN-13: 979-8-8232-0373-9

Dedication

For David, whose imagination is bigger than
mine, and yet, still insists mythical creatures
aren't real, but aliens are.
For my mom for being our biggest Hype
Woman without ever reading our books.
For Shawn. You shacked up with my mom,
so yes, this is your circus, and we are your monkeys.
For Nom. I would say sorry for all
the pan-panic I've caused you, but I'm not.
For Morgan, my amazing coauthor and best friend.
You put up with so much.
For BTS whose music and drive have
inspired me every day.

~~ Kate

For Gavin and Avery who are ALWAYS
excited to see Aunt Yippee.
For Scarlett who anxiously needs me to get
her tennis ball from under the couch.
For Alane, Grey, and Katie. You know why.
And the Toms… who will never know.

~~ Morgan

Table of Contents

Cast of Characters

Agnes Aballe: Human. Queen's Maid.

Alba: Elf. Palace Servant.

Aphros: Nereid, King of the Nereid people

Rhoslyn Almeida: Human. Sister of the Earl Veitel.

Wrenn Almeida: Human. Earl Veitel.

Borin: Human. Guard.

Carac: Human. Guard.

Ceto: A Nereid advisor to Aphros.

Lord Garibald Crobán: Human. Minor Lord who favored the Merscale Trade

Tolan Dethenal: Half-human, Half-elf. Palace cook and for-pay arena fighter.

Jayden Drake: Nereid. Duke and Ambassador.

Lady Elrick: Human. Wife of Lord Elrick.

Lord Elrick: Human. New Captain of the Guard, Minor Lord.

Thomas Fletcher: Human with magic. Arrow maker and political activist.

Collette Venora Josselyn Gaillane: Human with magic. Former Queen of Coralia.

Gisela: Elf. Palace Servant.

Cremisius "Crem" Hawke: Human. Commander of the Queen's Guard.

Diana Hawke: Human. Palace cook.

Howle: A Veteran of the King's Guard.

Barris Ilthane: Human. Barron of Pontus Bay.

Jarin: Human. Guard. (Deceased)

Kenrick: A young guard.

Larent Leassitor: Shapeshifter. Mercenary.

Lynessea: Merperson accompanying Lord Barris

Nawalya: Elf. Mercenary.

Rowan: Human. Guard. (Deceased)

Rulf: Human. Guard.

Sadon: Human. Guard. (Deceased)

Sargarus: Human. Former King of Coralia.

Riken Saullet: Human. Baron of Wildrun.

Arian Tal'Dela: Elf. Mercenary.

Rion Thorax: Human. Furrier.

Zephraim Villot: Human. Earl of Norbrick. King of Coralia. Brother of Collette.

John Whyldon: Human. Captain of the Queen's Guard.

Azmarin Empire
Qvenall
Barcomb Mil
Myrefall
Coralia

L'orilan
Fyithas
Other Locations
Catillatio: The Capitol of the
Azmarin Empire
Pontus Bay
Galel
Nereid
Kingdom
Veitel
A'lierdeen
Wildrun
Farner
Branlin

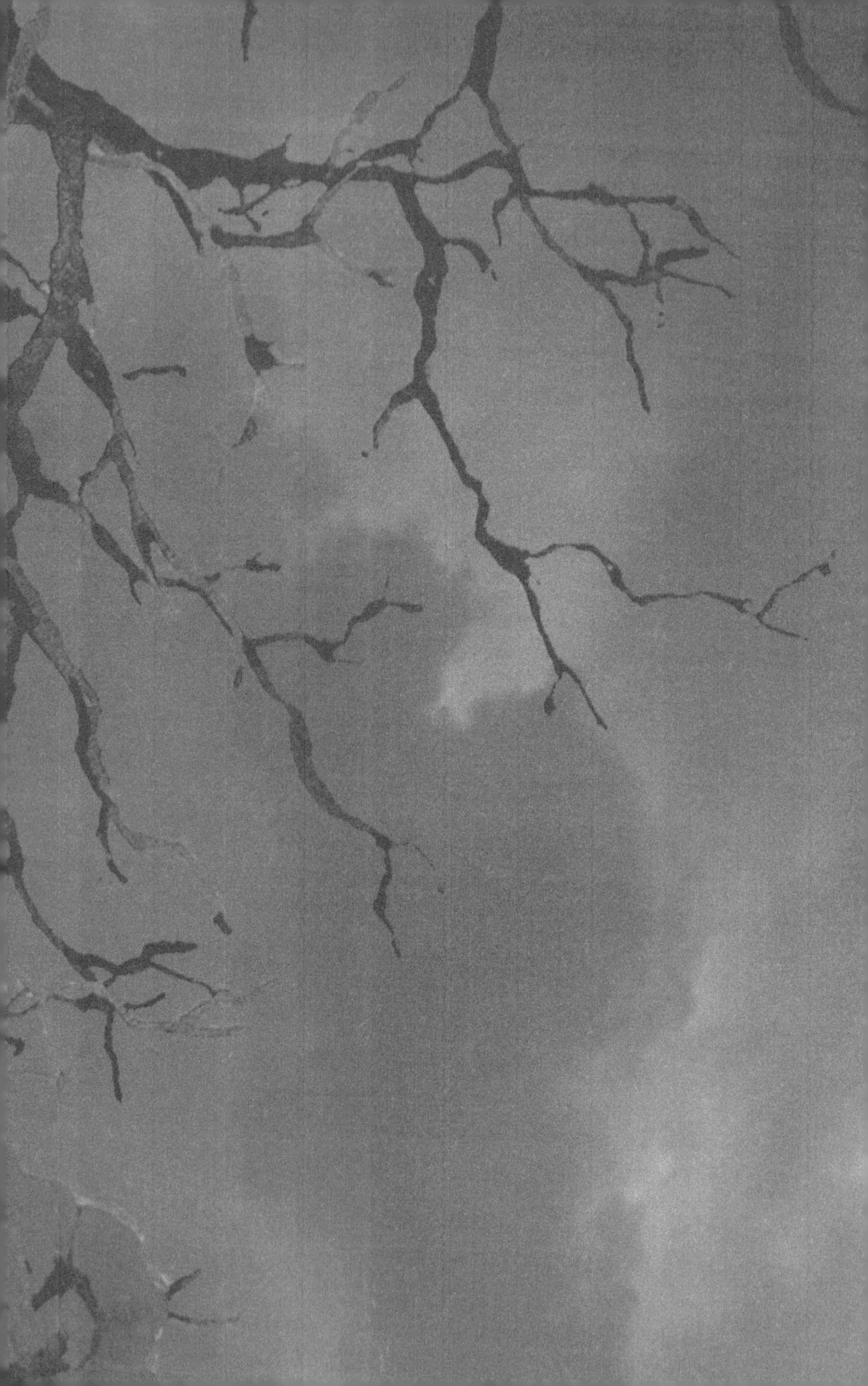

Chapter One

"Your Majesty!" Garibald Crobán bowed low, extending an arm to the side to keep balance. He quickly rose, despite his girth, and landed his gaze on the triumphant, bright green eyes of Coralia's new queen. "Where has His Majesty gotten to? I'm shocked to see your husband abandon your side on this celebratory day," he asked, pitching his voice to be heard over the music and hum of voices filling the room.

Rhoslyn held the place of honor in the royal dining hall which had been draped in tapestries of purples and greens in honor of the recent union between Zephraim's and Rhoslyn's families. She'd discarded the trailing coronation robes she'd worn at the Temple of the Seryne, the location the Mother was meant to have made the ultimate sacrifice, revealing the entirety of her pale silk overgarment accented by intricate pearls attached to the bodice. The simple dress suggested a humble innocence. The irony of marrying Zephraim in a place known for sacrifice had not escaped her.

Upon Rhoslyn Almeida's cinnamon hair sat a glittering crown consisting of linked gold circles. Emeralds dangled from the center of each loop, jewels she'd picked to complement her complexion and eyes. The lit torches along the banquet hall cast a warm glow around her, and she knew she looked every bit a divine-inspired ruler.

A striking contrast to their former queen who had preferred trousers and hunting attire.

Rhoslyn offered her hand to Crobán, and he brushed his lips against her knuckles. "Zephraim will be here soon." She removed her hand and gestured for Crobán to join her at the royal table laden with food and drink.

Servants dashed back and forth, refilling cups, removing empty trays and replacing them with dishes of succulent pork, bread, and glistening fruit. Crobán's jubilant smile left Rhoslyn wondering if he was more excited by the spread or the company. No doubt he would be visiting the fourteen tables scattering the banquet hall that night.

"What could keep His Majesty occupied on a day like this?" he asked and managed his bulk into a seat. He carried most of his weight around his stomach, so it was of little consequence to fit between the armrests. Pulling close to the table was another matter entirely.

"He received word that the traitor was spotted in the north." Rhoslyn kept her voice low and her expression neutral anytime she talked about Collette. Her gaze fixed on a couple at a distant table who appeared to be squabbling, if their wild gestures meant anything. "You can imagine his eagerness to address the situation."

A frown marred Crobán's round face. "It is most unfortunate that Collette managed to escape the palace." He shook his head, though his expression brightened as a servant filled his wine goblet. "What is His Majesty's opinion? Do you think she was actually spotted?"

Chapter One

"He thinks there is a real possibility," Rhoslyn said, giving no elaboration. She focused on her wine glass. "If she travels north, there is a complicated history to consider."

Crobán, like all the members of court, knew the history between Coralia and the Azmarin Empire to the north. A rocky history as of late, given the bit of courtly drama that arose when the former queen refused to honor a betrothal arranged by her late father. "Indeed. King Brath might desire to apprehend the traitor on His Majesty's behalf."

"That is the hope," Rhoslyn confirmed. There was also the distinct possibility that Brath would strike a deal with Collette but mentioning that possibility was not wise. At least, not when so many were around to overhear those concerns. Thankfully, Rhoslyn's pragmatism balanced Zephraim's dreamier tendencies, but there would be much to contend with from the court as long as Collette was on the run. "I assume you have advice you wish to give."

Crobán shook his head. "Nothing I haven't already mentioned," he began, then paused. He leaned forward, though his belly prevented him from closing much distance. "I worry that, with a little luck, she will be able to negotiate for royal support and an army," Crobán admitted. "We'd be no match in that case."

Collette's overthrow owed some credit to luck. So many different situations arose to provoke anger amongst the dissenters. Regaining power could come just as easily, not that Rhoslyn's expression showed concern. No, her face remained as neutral as ever. "I am not afraid of Collette. Nor is Zephraim." She motioned towards the crowd. "Do you think any of them would turn against us?"

"I see no reason for fear," Crobán said. "Nor do I think the court would prove difficult. They did play a role in putting the proper king on the throne. As for Azmarin? I would think the

neighboring states will quickly understand that His Majesty does not abide by high-minded dreams."

Rhoslyn snorted, then picked up her wine goblet before taking a long sip. "Collette was not high-minded," Rhoslyn insisted. "She was arrogant and foolish. She thought no one could touch her. Now, she's on the run, and she will be caught."

"Indeed," Crobán said, raising his goblet to toast the idea. "Forgive me for prying, but how is His Majesty feeling about the loss? I know she committed grave crimes against her family and yours. And the kingdom. However," he paused and took a daintier sip of wine, stalling, "she is his sister."

Rhoslyn gave another snort, and she leaned toward him so she could be heard over the celebratory swell of noise from their guests. "We both know family doesn't mean much when it comes to these things, Garibald."

Crobán nodded, though his brows knitted in worry. "I believe His Majesty would be open to suggestions and guidance from his wife when sorting through his lingering familial emotions, should she decide to give it."

Rhoslyn's eyes narrowed. "It does not matter what relation they once shared," she snapped. "That woman killed my brother and Zephraim's oldest friend. That alone, in addition to her insistence we abolish the Merscale trade, is enough to sever lingering ties. She deserves more than any punishment she is going to get."

Crobán nodded again. "Of that, I have no doubt, Your Majesty." He looked up as he and Rhoslyn were joined by another.

Lord Riken Saullet, the Baron of Wildrun, was a striking man: tall, broad-shouldered, dark-haired, and tanned from various outdoor ventures, leaving him the handsomest of the men joining the group. Rhoslyn's passive neutrality changed into a genuine happiness. She motioned for the man to take one of the empty seats at the table.

"Why am I not surprised to find you here of all places, Lord Crobán?" Riken bowed to Rhoslyn, their eyes briefly locking before he dropped his gaze. He took a seat. "Trying to flatter your way into our new Queen's good graces?"

"I'm chatting with Her Majesty," Crobán said, his annoyance evident in his thinly pressed lips.

Riken gave a small huff of laughter. "Thankfully, Her Majesty has better company to chat with now. Do not fret, Crobán. The food is just as plentiful elsewhere."

The dismissal was clear even if not stated, and Rhoslyn was thankful to not have to reiterate it. Crobán rose from his seat and shuffled off in the direction of Lord Elrick and his wife as quickly as his bulk would allow. The benign smile remained plastered on her face, and it took years of proper training and a good dose of self-control to avoid rolling her eyes or showing any sign of displeasure.

Rhoslyn had much to be displeased with. How had Collette escaped her prison cell so easily? Why had Zephraim done nothing to prevent similar catastrophes from happening again? How did the children of King Sargarus lack the fortitude to ensure Coralian victory? A true leader, a title Zephraim could hardly claim, would have already apprehended Collette rather than tolerate her running into the night with dirty elves, the brutish guard captain, and the Mother knew what else.

And all over fucking Merpeople. Those disgusting beasts. Alone, all of Riken's attention focused on Rhoslyn. "I apologize that I was unable to arrive until today, but I would not have missed your coronation for the world, Your Majesty."

Riken's eyes shone with teasing humor, and Rhoslyn's relief must have been present in her own. She'd few regrets in

life, but the possibility of hurting Riken in her decision to marry Zephraim had been one she'd most feared.

"I was beginning to think you chose to miss out on the festivities, Riken," Rhoslyn replied with genuine pleasure. She reached over and placed a hand on his forearm. "At least you've finally arrived."

"I rode my horse near to trauma to be here," Riken insisted with a laugh that felt forced. "I was surprised to find I even beat my latest letter here." He removed a sealed letter from his jacket and held out it out to her.

She plucked it from his hand, her eyes dancing over the brief contents signed with the decorative "R" he always placed at the end of his letters. She folded it back and tucked it away into a pocket.

"You shall have to tell me about your trip," Rhoslyn said. "Later, of course."

Riken chuckled and glanced around the crowded banquet hall before settling his gaze on the new queen. "I would be happy to go over my trip in detail with you in a more private setting. I know others will want your attention."

"We shall have to make an appointment to catch up," Rhoslyn said. Her smile turned unnaturally saccharine as she saw another approach. "Finally, Zeph! We were missing you."

Zephraim fell into the empty seat beside Rhoslyn, his red-gold curls weighed down under the gold crown that adorned his head. As always, he draped himself into his chair, looking more as though he was poured into the thing than as a tall, strong, and confident king he should have represented. Rhoslyn would have to do something about that.

"Sorry, my love. I needed to respond to the letters we received. It's the first real news we've had in weeks." Zephraim finally seemed to notice Riken, and he offered him a genuine smile which made him look boyish. "I'll admit, I didn't think I'd see you near this castle again."

"There was a time I thought a certain someone would find reason to ban me for life," Riken said with a knowing chuckle. "Since the fortuitous change in leadership, there was no question of my return."

"We certainly need good friends around for support and guidance," Rhoslyn confirmed, managing to keep her smile contained.

"Indeed," Zephraim agreed. "I'm just sorry Wrenn was not here to see it."

Riken and Rhoslyn exchanged glances at the mention of her brother. "It is a great shame," he said. "What do you say about escaping this party and getting a private drink in his honor, just the three of us? This rabble won't notice, and if they do, you're newly married. No one will ask questions."

Zephraim looked to his wife, an eyebrow raised in question. She nodded, and Zephraim grinned. "Let's go."

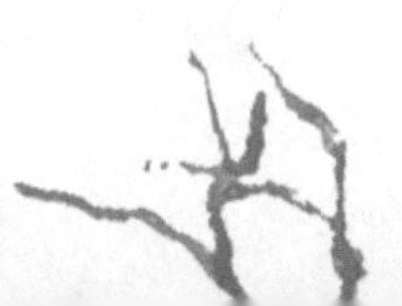

Chapter Two

Diana frowned as she pulled pastries from the oven. Were they sufficiently golden and attractive enough to please the discerning eye of their new queen? There had been many complaints about her food over the weeks following Queen Collette's overthrow, despite no actual examples being provided as to the faults.

Diana knew Rhoslyn was being cruel for the sake of it, probably because Diana made no secret of her fondness for Queen Collette. That alone was not a crime, so Rhoslyn sought to punish Diana in different ways. The young cook did her best to manage the criticism and her snarky tongue.

The coronation had required a lot of Diana and the kitchen staff for the past several weeks. While the whole thing was supposed to be celebratory, the days and weeks following the overthrow of Queen Collette resembled a slow, tedious funeral march. Some were choosing to be optimistic, but Diana believed in embracing reality.

She looked up as she heard someone enter the kitchen and spotted her husband. He was pale, and the dark circles under his eyes spoke volumes about his lack of sleep. He collapsed into a chair by the worktable, the back of his head resting against the stone wall. Diana wasn't certain he wouldn't fall asleep where he'd landed.

"You should go to bed," Diana said as she moved trays around the kitchen, pausing briefly to push her golden hair from her face with her forearm. She pursed her full pink lips into a scolding pout.

"I wish I could," Cremisus replied with a yawn. "But we both know the moment I lay down, I'll be called out again." He gave a deep sigh and rubbed the back of his neck. Diana noted he needed his hair trimmed. The rich brown hair he usually wore closely cropped had grown out into something longer and wavier. He looked much younger, despite the exhaustion.

Diana felt sorry for him. Queen Collette's escape had required numerous changes for the guard. Many had abandoned posts out of loyalty. The remaining few dregs had been promoted, and Crem suffered for his past role as Commander under Captain Whyldon.

"Let me make you something to eat, then," Diana said. She quickly gathered a plate of bread, fruit, and cheese to present to her husband, placing the items on the worn workspace. She'd get him a bowl of stew when she had a moment.

"Okay. Where is my real wife?" Crem joked through his exhaustion. "She is never this nice to me." He glanced at the plate of food. "Never mind. There is no meat. Clearly, it's you." He winked at her as he picked up the bread, tore off a piece, and popped it into his mouth.

"Keep on and, tired or not, you won't get anything else from me," Diana playfully admonished. Still, she walked over to her husband and wrapped her arms around him. Crem put his bread aside and leaned into his wife. "I got them out," he said quietly. "The elf family Rulf and Borin accused of being dissenters. I got them out."

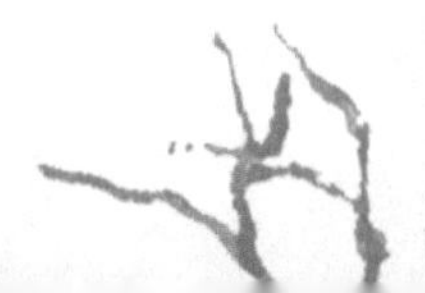

Diana nodded, knowing better than to verbalize a response. One never knew who was listening, even when it felt like they were alone. "Eat, and I'll get you some more when I'm done with these pies," she promised.

He nodded, pulling her close to press a gentle kiss to her lips. "I love you."

"I love you, too. More than anything. No matter how any of this turns out."

Crem gave her a soft smile before he retrieved his bread. He got about halfway through the meal before a page came looking for him.

"Commander Hawke?" the young girl asked, a sealed letter clutched in her hand.

"My husband is eating," Diana told the girl sternly. "Can this not wait?"

The girl shook her head and looked down as she mumbled an apology. "I was told to deliver this to the commander at once."

Diana sighed after meeting her husband's gaze. For weeks now, deliveries of letters from an unknown sender had found Crem. Each note detailed a person in need of help, and each time, Crem had assisted them. Diana half wondered if this was a trap, for surely the sender would come forward if they truly meant no harm. She knew Crem would subject himself to another dangerous mission, and there was no stopping him. "Deliver it to Commander Hawke, then," Diana insisted. She picked up one of the small meat pies she'd been cooling and handed it to the page. "And eat up."

The page's eyes grew wide at the offered hand pie, and after passing the letter to Crem, she eagerly accepted it. Her job done, the girl scampered off licking the dripping filling from a hand.

"All of them are getting too thin," Crem remarked, looking up from the letter he'd quickly skimmed. "And it's going to get worse.

Chapter Two

"I can see that," Diana remarked, shaking her head. She wondered, some days, if it would be wiser to leave this place. "It might be wise to start thinking even further ahead."

"It would be," Crem agreed. Another bite of food and he stood, handing the letter over to his wife for safekeeping. "Duty calls, my lovely wife."

Diana went to Crem, putting her arms around her husband again because she knew he was in serious need of rest and rejuvenation. There was nothing to do about it now other than protect the information coming in. "Try to find time for sleep," she instructed him.

"Even if I must pass out in the stables to get it?" he joked. "I will try."

"If you have to hide in the stables to cobble together a handful of hours to rest, you do it," Diana insisted. "Or I will take matters into my own hands."

"I could bury myself in the hay. No one would think to look for me there. Well, except the horses." He held her for another moment. "I will be back soon."

"You had better," Diana told him. "I'm scarier than anything you'll face out there."

"Yes, yes you are," he agreed. He gave her a final kiss and retreated.

Chapter Three

CH,

As you can imagine, Thomas Fletcher is officially a target. Guards have been skulking around his shop with increased frequency. Tonight, I hear they plan to strike. He will need an escort out of the city. I know you are more than capable, but I've sent along some help. Meet at the barn, then go to the coordinates listed below.

– A Friend

Crem gave a tired sigh as he left the warmth of his wife and the kitchen behind him. He did not want to be back out on the streets, but the letter was urgent, and if he did not intervene, no one else would. Rulf, Borin, and their little group had been targeting citizens since the overthrow, and the latest of the victims was Thomas Fletcher, the man who'd once spent hours outside of the palace criticizing Queen Collette. The letter indicated word of a planned attack, so Crem went.

Chapter Three

Fletcher had brought much of that attention on himself by continuing to speak out against the policies of the new royals despite advice Crem had given him in the weeks following the arrest and overthrow. Zephraim and Rhoslyn had less forgiveness about his antics than Queen Collette ever did.

Crem walked into the city, receiving none of the attention Diana and the true queen had when they crossed the same path. He was a man, and disgraced in his position though he was, he still didn't receive so much as a raised eyebrow. The city was already dark, though here and there the warm light from a tavern indicated groups who'd gathered to celebrate or commiserate.

He knew where the fletcher worked and lived, and he thought it likely the group targeting him would know as well. As he approached the fletcher's shop, he heard the voices of the rogue guard before he saw them. Crem rolled his eyes, seriously questioning how they could be stupid enough to think Thomas would still be there.

Turning down the street, he headed in the direction of the abandoned barn that had once hidden their queen. It was there that he found Thomas Fletcher.

Thomas looked up from his dinner as Crem let himself inside. He saw the arrow maker had done nothing to conceal his appearance, which was unmistakable given the cornsilk-colored hair that curled to his shoulders and his pale complexion. "Evening," he said after he swallowed a mouthful of potatoes.

"Evening," Crem replied. "That group of idiots is at your house."

"I heard," Thomas replied, glancing in Crem's direction. His light, grey-blue eyes shone with mirth. "I used to wonder why nothing was ever done about them."

"They are nobility. Anytime Whyldon tried to do something, their fathers or uncles would step in, tying the queen's hands."

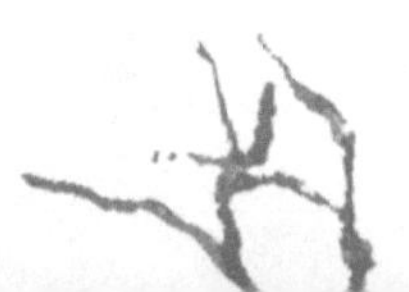

Crem checked to make sure the door was secured. "Have you thought about where you're going?"

"Galel or Branlin, if I stay in the country," Thomas admitted. Myrefall was far too close for Thomas's liking.

"I would avoid Galel for now. That's the first place Zephraim sent soldiers." When Thomas raised an eyebrow, Crem elaborated. "Whyldon is from northern Galel. Rhoslyn is from the southern area in the region. They thought it possible that Collette might travel there. Branlin would be the smarter choice."

"Then it looks like I am taking the long way to Branlin," Thomas said.

"Smart choice," Crem said with a nod. "Are you ready to go? I told your transport we'd meet him soon." Thank the Mother he still had people he could rely on even with the regime change, but he wondered who the escort might be.

"Absolutely," Thomas agreed. He took a final gulp from his drink then gathered his shoulder bag which contained everything he could bring into his exile.

The men exited the building and took to the streets, careful to avoid guards and blend in with the celebratory crowds. Thomas stepped around a snoozing drunkard and glanced back to make sure the man was breathing. "Did you ever imagine we would be conducting treason so openly?" he asked as they hurried along an alley.

Crem chuckled. "Is that what this is called? I thought it was 'ensuring the freedom of the people from tyranny,'" he said, quoting one of Thomas's many speeches.

"Both things are true, Commander Hawke," Thomas chortled. Like it or not, they have called themselves our rulers, and others in power have accepted it. That means what we've been doing is treason."

Crem glanced around. "They put themselves on the throne illegally and under forceful circumstances. This is not, and will never be, treason. No matter what they say."

"Our necks will fit in the noose all the same."

"We'll be lucky to get the noose if we are arrested and sentenced," Crem said darkly. "Riken arrived today. He's got very specific political beliefs, and he's friends with Zephraim and Rhoslyn. He's too much like the old king for my liking, and he could sway them."

Thomas frowned. "Zephraim lacks a spine of his own, but Collette is still his sister."

Crem's visage darkened. "Riken is a smart man. He will gather followers quickly now that Collette is gone. Once he has the court on his side, Zephraim will have little choice but to follow, no matter his inclinations."

They continued working their way through a crowd of people. Crem was thankful for his height as he could force his way through more easily than Thomas. A final turn, and Crem knew they would be at the meeting point soon. He sneered as he recognized one of the guards in the distance, drinking and carrying on with a joviality he hadn't noticed before the overthrow.

Thomas saw it as well, and he shook his head. "The smartest thing the true queen's supporters could be doing for themselves right now is fleeing the palace," he said. "But then, who else would fight back?"

"Many have left, but some don't have the option, at least not yet," Crem replied. "I plan on staying until they are all safe."

"You and your wife, then?"

"Yes, we will be the last to flee," Crem confirmed, although he wished he could compel his wife to do as much now. Diana was stubborn, and he could not deny the usefulness of remaining where she was.

"That's bravery," Thomas replied.

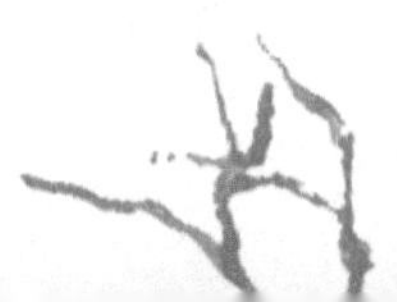

"Or stupidity, as my wife says."

"And yet she stays in the palace?"

"That was her choice, and she'd castrate me if I tried to forcibly remove her." He gave his companion an amused look. "I do have plans to make sure she's not implicated should I be caught."

"That must make it easier for you," Thomas said. They paused as they came across a man who seemed to have been waiting for them. He was exceedingly tall and broad shouldered, and his expression was concealed by a ginger-colored beard.

"Hello, Rion," was all Crem said, giving the man a nod. Thank the Mother this was a person he could trust. Once again, the letter sender had not led him astray. To Thomas, he said, "This is the man who will get you out of the city safely."

"Such faith in me, Crem. You never change," Rion said, chuckling lightly. He straightened and looked at Thomas. "It won't be hard getting out tonight, but with the crowds in the street, you never know."

"Need a distraction?" Crem asked, a half-smile on his face.

"Wouldn't hurt," Rion drawled. "We may not need much of one. The goons are out. Their drunken cheers are sufficient concealment."

"One of those goons roughed up one of the tavern girls. I'm fairly sure the owners and her brother will want to know where they are. That should help."

"Somehow, I'm not surprised," Rion replied, his brow furrowing in disgust. "You ready to go?" he asked Thomas.

"I am. The rogue guards were at my home when Crem showed up."

"Not surprised," Rion said. "I'll send word if I can," he told Crem. "If I know Joss, she's well-concealed for now."

Chapter Three

Crem reached out and placed a hand on Thomas's shoulder. "Take care of yourself, Fletcher." He nodded to Rion. "Be careful out there, especially if you run into Queen Collette."

"We will," Thomas replied. "We have too much to do."

"That we do. Well, time for a distraction." Crem waved and jogged off into the night.

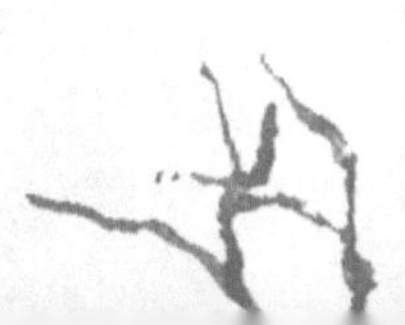

Chapter Four

Riken adjusted his grip on Zephraim's waist as they reached a hidden staircase, one he knew was used by the palace servants. The king's lean stature hardly mattered when he was unable to keep himself on his feet, and Riken looked forward to depositing the man on his bed. Still, he shot a grin towards Rhoslyn, who was on Zephraim's other side, helping to balance her incoherent husband. "This brings back memories."

"Very much so," Rhoslyn agreed.

The three of them had spent the evening in celebration, toasting to the crowned couple, reminiscing about their childhood, and honoring Wrenn, who could not be with them. Riken paid special attention to Zephraim, making sure he drank heavily throughout the evening. He craved the ability to speak openly with Rhoslyn, and an intoxicated monarch was the fastest way to achieve his goal.

"Did you ever imagine that one day, we would be here?" Rhoslyn asked.

They began ascending the spiral stairs, the stone steps poorly lit by the occasional torch. It was slow work, one mostly accomplished by Riken's strength. Rhoslyn's long cinnamon hair was down, free of jewels and other finery, and yet Riken found her the most beautiful thing he'd ever laid eyes on.

"Do you mean escorting Zephraim while he is so drunk, he'll remember nothing come morning?" Riken asked with a teasing smile. "And without Wrenn by our side? Yes, to both. I just thought it would be an angry husband, tavern brawl, or the drink that did it." His expression turned serious. "But if you are referring to you being married to Zephraim? No, I never thought that."

"Are you angry with me?" Rhoslyn asked after a prolonged silence, only interrupted now and then by the tap of their shoes on the stone steps.

"No," he said in a low, firm voice. "You are the most beautiful, intelligent, and cunning person I have ever met. I'm proud of you for doing what needed to be done. For you and this kingdom." He looked down to see her, his expression faltering for just a moment before he reigned it back in. "I just always thought that when you said your marriage vows, they would be made to me."

"So did I," Rhoslyn confessed, their gazes meeting. Riken shifted Zephraim's dead weight into a more manageable hold, and they resumed their climb. Rhoslyn continued, "I do wish this had turned out differently. As much as I planned and participated in the way things ended up, I will always regret what could have been."

Riken nodded and kept his gaze forward. "Regardless, this is the hand the Mother has dealt us, so we must move forward." He offered her a reassuring smile that didn't quite meet his eyes. "I will be here for you. In any way you wish."

They reached the king's landing, and after getting the directions from Rhoslyn, Riken hoisted the snoring man over his shoulder like a sack of potatoes. The move changed his mood. "I have to ask, with all he drinks, how satisfying was your wedding night? Surely, it could not have been worth all the times you left me wanting you?"

Rhoslyn let out a short laugh. "He doesn't usually drink like this. That honor belonged to my brother. But since you're being vulgar, are you expecting the same sort of response?"

He gave her a heated look. "Be as vulgar and descriptive as you want. Maybe I'll learn a bit about what you might like if you ever venture to my quarters."

"Some things … you need to discover for yourself."

Riken threw back his head and laughed, a deep rich sound. "I take it there is a possibility of that happening?"

"So presumptuous," Rhoslyn replied with a smirk.

"Always," he said.

They eventually found their way to Zephraim's chambers, and Rhoslyn pushed the door open and motioned Riken inside. Zephraim had taken over the space that had once been occupied by Collette, and the dark rich furnishings marked the change in leadership.

"Do you have your own rooms?" Riken asked as he dumped Zephraim on the bed. The king landed at an odd angle, and Riken's spiteful side debated leaving Zephraim like that before he straightened him out into a more comfortable position.

"I do," Rhoslyn said. "Although I'm sure Zephraim would have no objections were that not the case."

"I'm sure he wouldn't," Riken agreed as he removed Zephraim's boots. "And what are your plans for the rest of the evening?"

"Truly?" Rhoslyn asked with a knowing smile. "I was going to my own chambers and falling into bed. It has been a long day."

"Well, if that's what you wish." He bowed deeply, a playful grin on his face. "I wish you pleasant dreams."

Chapter Four

"So formal," Rhoslyn observed. "But have it your way, Lord Riken. Perhaps Zephraim would enjoy your company."

Riken laughed. "I would rather spend my time in your company, but if you'd rather have a quiet evening alone…" He paused as Rhoslyn extended her hand to him.

Riken followed her from the room. They barely made it into the corridors before he pulled her body against his and kissed her heatedly. Her slender arms went around his neck, drawing him closer, and Riken's senses were flooded with her delicate scent and soft skin. He wanted more and more of her. "Show me your rooms?" he asked in a husky voice.

Rhoslyn did not reply but kissed him again. When that kiss came to its natural conclusion, she took his hand again and pulled him in the direction of her bedroom.

Chapter Five

Jayden's last letter from Coralia, now worn and well-read, drooped as Aphros picked it up. He rose from his desk and began to pace as he considered his options. Far too much time had passed since the Nereid King had heard from his cousin, and despite Jayden's optimism, Aphros found himself increasingly contemplating what he needed to do. Had the Coralians turned on Jayden? Was he in danger? Was he even alive?

The bright blue and orange glimmering on his skin intensified as he walked past the window, an easy giveaway to his true nature. Nereids could only do so much to appear human, and he had no need to blend in just now. Was that the problem? Had Jayden succumbed to some danger because he hadn't blended with the humans?

He looked up from the letter as he heard footsteps, spotting Ceto, one of his advisors. "What is it?" he asked her.

"Jayden has arrived," she said as she pulled her long red hair into a messy pile on her head. If the dripping strands were any indication, she'd likely been in the sea. She was about a foot shorter than Aphros, her build more athletic than his leaner one.

Chapter Five

"Jayden is here?" he asked, astonished. "Is he well?" He absently pressed a hand to a statue residing between two windows. Carved from a white stone flecked with orange and coral, the statue represented the ancient sea goddess he only seemed to believe in during times of uncertainty. The matriarchal goddess of the Nereid people, the Goddess Galene looked over the office with sightless eyes.

"He is," Ceto confirmed to the Nereid king. "Tired from travels, but well. He is waiting for you in the great hall."

The proper palace resided beneath the water, where the Nereid people were safe and better able to defend themselves. However, a small cluster of islands had slowly built up over time, sprouting businesses and political offices that served their allies and welcomed visitors on dry land.

The building Aphros occupied was tall and themed in pale, nearly white decoration. Columns made of a rough, porous material supported half walls and a sloped, bright coral-colored roof. The interior held a workspace for members of court and a large meeting room for visitors. All of the rooms surrounded the entrance which the occupants referred to as the Great Hall.

When they arrived, Aphros took in his cousin. Thankfully, he looked well. "By the gods, Jayden," Aphros exhaled, running a hand through his own wavy brown hair. "Your silence has been alarming."

Jayden gave his cousin a tight smile. "It was rather difficult to write to you when I was fleeing for my life."

"Queen Collette turned on you?" Aphros demanded in surprise.

Jayden shook his head. "No, cousin. In fact, she put herself in danger making sure I escaped. One of the unsavory nobles was murdered, and those who stood to gain from the Mertrade turned on her."

A dark look crossed Aphros's features. "Ceto," he said to his advisor. "Can you have some food and drink brought up for Jayden? It seems we have much to discuss."

"Of course," Ceto said and left without another word.

"Come and sit," Aphros invited as he started towards the table just inside the meeting room. "Your story must be lengthy."

"It is," Jayden confirmed. He practically collapsed into a seat inside the meeting room. "I suggest we send out warnings to our people, encouraging them to return home. I know some tribes and families will refuse or can't, but we need to do what we can."

"We will," Aphros promised his cousin. Never again would they live through a terror like Collette's father, King Sargarus had created. Low estimates indicated that thousands of Mer had been lost in the last decade of Sargarus's life. "Tell me everything so I know best how to proceed.

For the next twenty minutes, the king listened intently as Jayden explained his experiences in Coralia, including the discussion he had with Queen Collette before he was sent from the palace towards safety.

"From what I picked up, she was accused of murdering a lord and torturing a Mer. I found both to be highly unlikely." Jayden shrugged. "She's in trouble, no matter how you look at it."

"Are you certain she's innocent of the charges?" Aphros asked.

"Yes," Jayden replied without hesitation. "She was earnest about wanting peace and ending the trade. Conversely, she was surrounded by people who made money on the trade, people who would do anything for economic advantage. There was no way I could doubt her sincerity."

"And she got you out of the castle before she left," Aphros repeated from Jayden's earlier statement. He paused as Ceto brought up food and drink. After thanking her, he issued orders. "Send out alerts to our people and all of our allied leadership.

Coralia's peaceful queen has been overthrown. Our people need to return to safety."

"Of course." Ceto bowed her head and dismissed herself.

"Many won't return," Jayden pointed out. "Your spy is there, of course. Perhaps they will aid in rescue efforts. You'll likely also get coded messages soon."

"Hopefully so. We need to know what is going on in Coralia." Aphros stroked his chin. He did not like all of the unknowns. "Did they arrest the queen? Is she even alive?"

"From the news I heard the few times I stopped to rest on dry land, she was arrested. The rumors say she escaped or was executed in secret by her brother."

"We should do what we can to find out," Aphros said after a moment. "If she is alive, and she can be helped, we need to know."

"I wish you would tell me exactly who your spy is. I would be happy to use the contacts I forged to gather information if I knew," Jayden said.

"I know," Aphros replied with a nod. "But the fewer people with information, the safer everyone is, especially if things go badly." He smiled at his cousin. "Eat up so you can go rest. The gods know you've earned it.

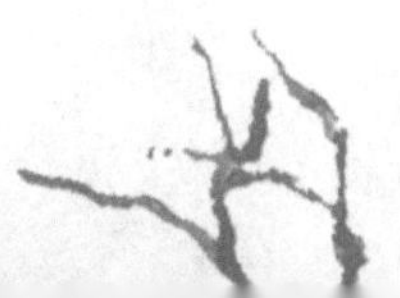

Chapter Six

The inviting scent of roasting venison wafted in Collette's direction, warm and inviting, and contrasted with the dark, cool surroundings of the forest. Stretching her legs in front of her, the queen smiled as she carded fingers through her carob-colored hair, her stomach rumbling with anticipation. She relaxed against the remnants of a long-fallen tree while Larent, their resident shifter, lay nearby on the ground, hands tucked under his head.

She'd enjoyed their talks before the overthrow, though it was hard to believe their meeting where he had dropped onto her balcony in the middle of the night only happened a few weeks before. Now in hiding, the restrictions that previously limited her familiarity were forgotten, and she met his crude observations and suggestions more bluntly than she had in Quenall. "So how many times did you bed Elrick's wife?" she teased.

Larent raised an eyebrow, his lips scrunching together in contemplation. "Ummm…" he said. He lazily ruffled his russet hair, thinking. "Five. I'm going with five."

"Even though she was bad the first time?"

"I'm a giving man, Freckles." A lecherous grin spread across Larent's face. "All you have to do is ask."

"Back off," Tolan interjected, lines of tension emphasizing his hazel eyes. He poked at the burning sticks beneath the fire, coaxing the flames to burn hotter. Collette smiled as she saw the glint of her mother's bracelet on his wrist. The item had been a good token at the long-ago tournament.

Larent smirked at Tolan. "What?" he asked innocently, casting a grin towards Collette. "I'm just trying to get to know her better."

Tolan didn't dignify Larent's claim with a response.

"Perhaps when getting to know Her Majesty, you should keep to respectful subjects," Whyldon said, focused on the blade he was sharpening. The guard captain's brown hair hung loosely around his shoulders, with strands of silver twinkling in the firelight.

"What's more respectful than treating her the same as I would anyone else?" Larent demanded. He jabbed his thumb in Collette's direction. "She would be mad if I decided to gloss over stories of my sexual escapades, or Nawalya's violence. I've seen her mad. No one wants that."

"Considering my exposure to the royal guard as a young girl, I think we're in safe territory." Collette raised her eyebrows, silently challenging Whyldon to argue. A soft scoff from in front of the fire drew her attention. She rose, walked to Tolan's side, and wrapped her arms around his muscular frame, smiling as his expression softened, his dark eyes focused on her. He pushed a strand of his long black hair from his face before wrapping his arms around Collette.

Whyldon paid no mind to the scene. "If you recall, Your Majesty, I was outspoken about the crude exposure you had to the guards when you were younger."

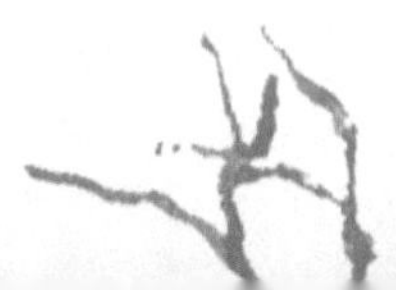

"I recall you buying Crem a courtesan on the way to Branlin and telling him he needed to empty his balls before you'd travel with him again."

Whyldon laughed. "I'd probably tell him the same thing now if he wasn't married."

"Wait," Larent said, sitting up and giving Collette a playful stare. "Courtesans are an option for this trip? No one told me." He flopped back down dramatically, causing Tolan to roll his eyes.

"You can buy all the escorts you want," Collette said. "The show you'll put on while acquiring their time will help break up the monotony."

Larent laughed. "While hiring an escort might break up the monotony, I would rather they pay me. I've pretended to be one once or twice. There was this time we were in—"

He stopped speaking as a rock hit the back of his head.

"Inappropriate tale," a soft voice called out from the forest.

Larent's head whipped around. "The fuck? You're all the way over there," he called out in indignation at Nawalya. "How did the rock hit me from that direction?"

"She ricocheted it off a tree," Arian said flatly, his deep blue eyes shooting Larent a disapproving look. "And she's right. Inappropriate story." The elf quickly tied back his wavy blond hair.

"I like inappropriate stories," Collette insisted with an amused grin. "And it's not like we have much else to do for the evening."

"It ends with a botched murder and that one—" Arian thumbed over at Larent "—having to escape naked."

Larent grinned as though running naked through the streets of a neighboring kingdom was a normal day.

Arian examined his supplies spread on the ground before him, shoulders tense. "As amusing as all of this is, we have better things to do. Coming up with a workable plan, as one example. Unless our queen feels like hiding in the woods for the foreseeable future?"

Collette pulled away from Tolan and resumed her former seat. She surveyed Arian's expression and body language. "I'm not saying playing in the woods wouldn't be fun, but we do need a plan that isn't hiding."

"Agreed," Whyldon interjected. "Given that we've been traveling north, the logical plan would be to proceed into the Azmarin Empire. We'd avoid crossing the mountains in winter, and we'd also avoid backtracking into Quenall. Azmarin comes with complications, though."

"Complications don't bother us. Come to think of it, we're usually the complication," said Larent.

Arian's shoulders seemed to lose some of their tension. "We've done some work in Azmarin, but none of us are that well known in the capital. What complications do we need to be concerned about?"

"I broke an arranged marriage with the Azmarin king," Collette explained with a shrug. "That should make him interested in the bounty on my head."

"You could always marry him," Arian suggested, packing away a vial in his leather pack. "I assume there is another reason you refused, other than the obvious." He motioned towards Tolan.

"King Sargarus made the arrangement," Whyldon replied. He turned his freshly sharpened blade in various directions, the fire glinting in the metal, and nodded to himself. "If we go north and our presence is discovered, we might find they sided with Zephraim. He always leaned in favor of his father's policies."

"Alerting the Azmarins might be the first thing Zephraim did after putting a bounty on the queen's head," Nawalya said as she strolled into the temporary camp. The mercenary looked

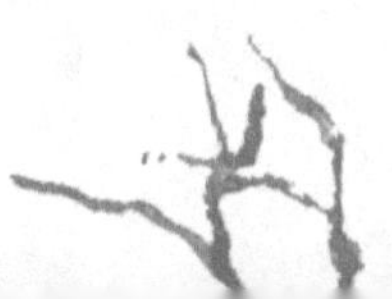

disheveled from her time in the woods, her long tawny hair, more curly than wavy, needed a good brushing. She dropped an armful of wood beside the fire before taking a seat between Whyldon and Arian. Arian offered her a water skin, and she drank deeply.

"Even if Zephraim hasn't reached out to the Azmarins, that doesn't mean we'd reach a bargain," Whyldon pointed out. "The Azmarins are proud people. I'd think their leader would be the proudest."

"As Whyldon said, we risk running into anyone who is on the lookout for Collette. We may not have much choice but to travel by way of the Azmarin Empire, even if we don't intend on entering negotiations for support or an army. Not this time of year, anyway," Nawalya replied. "The mountains of Galel would be a difficult journey for every person in this group."

"While I think we would be better off heading to Myrefall, crossing up through Galel, and from there, entering the Nereid Kingdom or Fyithas," Tolan responded looking over at Collette, "Azmarin is the most viable option we have."

"So, most of our options require us to navigate through Azmarin, over the mountain pass, or back through Quenall," Whyldon replied. "Azmarin is the safest and quickest path to any of those destinations."

"If we are going through Azmarin, we might as well try our luck," Collette said.

"Why Fythias?" Whyldon asked. "The Nereid King might be a potential option, but I don't know about the other."

"My mother talked about Fythias a lot," Tolan replied as he carefully removed a spit from the fire. "Fythias is a kingdom known for helping its people. They also stood against Sargarus more than once. I doubt they'd appreciate an overthrow by people who wish to reinstate the policies he favored. They may help us."

Chapter Six

"Then to Azmarin we go," Collette summarized. "From there, we can travel into Galel and figure out if the Fythiasians or the Nereid are our best options."

"Well, at least we have a plan," Arian replied. "Now let's eat."

Nana and Pops,

Sorry I haven't written in a while. Things in Quenall were busy and chaotic all at the same time. Most of that wasn't my fault. I wish I could say I had good news, but I think it's gonna be a long time before I can write again. Nawalya and Arian send their love. I miss you, be safe.

Larent

As the members of the camp slept, Collette found she couldn't rest. Insomnia had increasingly become a problem for her since they'd fled the capitol, and she didn't see her situation changing anytime soon.

Collette abandoned the warmth of the fire to find Tolan. He'd volunteered for the first watch and was quietly observing the area from the distant tree line. As she expected, his tense shoulders and knitted brows demonstrated his earlier agitation with Larent, and probably her, hadn't waned.

"Hi," she whispered, finding him a few hundred feet away from their camp.

"Hello, my queen," he said, giving her a soft smile. He wrapped an arm around Collette and drew her closer. "You should be sleeping."

"Probably. When I figure out how to do that again, I'll let you know."

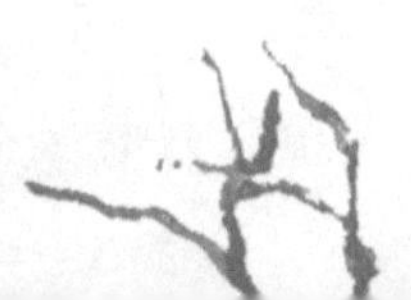

"Arian could mix something for you," Tolan pointed out, then cringed. "He'd probably be unpleasant about having to do so."

"Exactly," Collette said with a chuckle. She released her hold on Tolan but took his hand and began leading him around the perimeter of the camp. "He has other things to worry about. Not to mention how Whyldon would react." She let out an exasperated sigh imagining it.

"Spirits know we want to avoid that," Tolan said. "Sometimes I think Whyldon doesn't trust us."

"He claims he never trusted you," Collette replied.

"Well, of course not. I'm just a peasant making things worse for the Queen," he muttered, his expression darkening. As they walked, he ran his fingers along the bark of a tree.

"I don't think he's ever said anything about your social status," Collette replied. Whyldon well remembered his humble beginnings if the many talks she had shared with her guard captain over the years were any indication. He'd have no judgments against Tolan in that regard. "And even if he had, you know that's not how I view things."

Tolan shrugged. "He said as much to me before all this happened. How I'm a stain on your reputation and such." He shook his head. "Maybe he's right." Tolan hissed as the skin of his index finger tore, catching on a sharp piece of bark.

"None of this has to do with our relationship," Collette assured him. "What happened to me was because of my weak-willed brother. I won't have you thinking disparaging things about yourself." She brought their walk to a temporary pause, then lifted his injured hand and pressed a couple of fingers near the cut. She felt the warmth of her healing spell spreading down her arm, into her hand and fingers, and pouring onto Tolan. The cut healed over, leaving behind nothing but a pink line that would fade.

Tolan gave her a grateful smile as she healed his finger, though his slightly pursed lips suggested he found it unnecessary. "Be careful when you do that. You don't want the others to find out."

"Should I be worried about our companions learning of it?" she asked.

Tolan shook his head. "No, but I've never seen healing magic like yours before. I would hate for the wrong people to find out." He gently caressed Collette's face. "Lately, all I can think about is if I were of noble birth or claim, this wouldn't have happened," he said softly, going back to their original topic.

"Even if we had an army, victory would not be assured, and I'd still have to convince the nobility left behind, and the people, that I was the legitimate ruler." She leaned in and kissed Tolan, hoping to reassure him that everything was going to be okay. Then, she resumed their walk. "Right now, what matters is that we are safe, and we will figure out the best way forward."

Tolan nodded, though his expression remained downcast and distant. "I know you'll figure something out. It might not be legal, and Whyldon might hate it, but I know you'll fix this."

"I fear Whyldon might insist I refrain from participating in whatever plan we eventually form." She nudged Tolan along, so they began tracing the path he'd been taking before she interrupted. She smiled to herself when he took her hand in his, lacing their fingers together.

He laughed. "Apart from tying you up and locking you in a secure room, nothing is going to stop you from participating."

Collette couldn't help but chuckle along. "Even then, there is no guarantee. I did manage to sneak out of a castle full of my enemies. I'd probably be fine tackling a couple of ropes."

"True, and I'm still pretending I didn't see Nawalya teaching you lock picking."

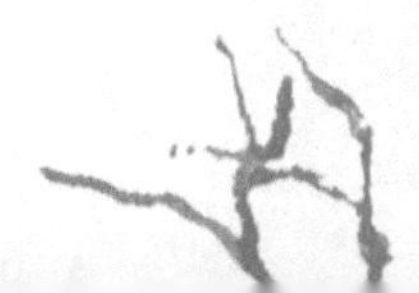

"She was astounded by my limited skill set in that area," Collette pointed out. She stepped over a bulky fallen branch. "I was told to rectify this in the future."

Tolan shook his head. "That's Nawalya. She believes in being prepared for anything. Though I wish I could have seen her face; that had to have been priceless."

"It was interesting. I think she took up my lack of preparedness with Whyldon after she told me what she expected."

Tolan considered that. "Spirits! I know she's been waiting for him her whole life, but when those two finally decide to stop dancing around each other, it's going to mean trouble for all of us."

"Why is it bad?" Collette asked. "They'd both be happier with one another."

"Nawalya sees you as a symbol of hope. A person too, but a symbol of hope all the same. Whyldon is just overprotective. I'm willing to bet he could convince her to help him lock you up somewhere safe while they handle everything."

"They can protest my involvement all they like, but that will not affect what I choose to do," Collette said. "Besides, it feels like we've already had arguments about what my involvement should be on a daily basis."

"Be careful with Nawalya. You can't handle her like you do Whyldon. She's very good at using guilt and threats when she feels she's right or needs to protect people," Tolan said. He scanned along the tree line and nodded to himself in satisfaction. "It's how she managed to keep Arian alive. Expect her to single you out for talks."

"I will," Collette promised. "I am good with people, despite the overthrow," she teased.

"Oh, I know you are." He pulled her close for a moment.

Chapter Six

She softly laughed and wrapped her arms around Tolan, pulling him against her warm body. He leaned down and kissed her, fingers toying with the ends of her dark hair.

When the kiss ended, he pressed his forehead against hers. "As much as I enjoy having a peaceful moment with you, we should walk you back to camp so you can try to get some sleep."

"I will try, once you trade watch with one of the others," Collette countered. Her fatigue did nothing to help bring on sleep.

"Okay," Tolan agreed quietly, and he kissed her again.

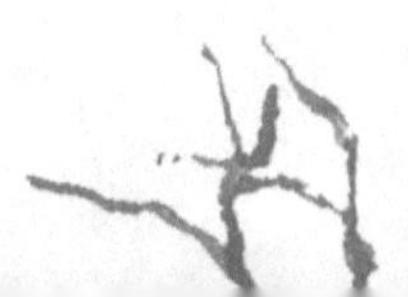

Chapter Seven

Morning came, cool and crisp, promising a day similar to all the prior ones since fleeing Quenall. They'd risen at daybreak, eaten a meager breakfast, and begun the process of breaking down their camp, replenishing supplies, and covering their tracks.

As Collette packed away her bedroll, she noted Arian standing at the base of the closest tree. He gazed up into the tall branches, his brows furrowed with serious concern.

"We both know staring at her won't help anything," Larent commented, his mouth full of the manchet bread he'd chosen from his pack for breakfast. Arian sneered at the sight of half-chewed bread, but that didn't deter Larent. "Whyldon will be back in a few minutes, Chuckles. He'll be able to get her down."

Arian must have agreed with some part of Larent's argument because he shook his head and moved away from the tree to help pack up the remainder of the camp.

Larent grinned over at Collette. "He's a fucking worrywart."

"He has a right to be," Collette pointed out. She fastened her travel bag, content with the size and shape of the bulk she would be carrying that day. "We are on the run. Not being able to get her to come down could be a problem."

"True," Larent acknowledged. "But then, if we're attacked, the attacker probably wouldn't see her."

He glanced at the clearing as Whyldon appeared, but Arian greeted him first. "All clear?" he asked.

Whyldon nodded. "The only signs of disturbance were made by our party. I erased our tracks." He thanked Collette who passed him some jerky to eat and tore a bit off with his teeth, glancing around as he chewed. "Where's Nawalya?"

Larent pointed up at the tree. "Arian wants you to get her down."

"If you can," Arian added. "At some point this morning, she decided to channel the spirits and walk the branches of the tree without alerting anyone. I can't draw her back." He took a steadying breath and nodded at Whyldon. "She responds well to you."

"I'll try," Whyldon said after taking another bite of the jerky. He approached the tree and looked up, apparently spotting her since he stopped walking around the trunk. "Nawalya," he called up to her. "Are you ready to come down?"

No response came from the tree. Arian grimaced as he focused on packing Nawalya's supplies. "Keep trying, please," he instructed.

Whyldon followed the command, calling up to Nawalya every few seconds. Collette began to wonder if they would be forced to stay in that spot, but no sooner did the thought cross her mind than the camp heard the stirring from above.

"Hello, there," came Nawalya's response, more dreamy and distant than usual.

"Hello," Whyldon returned, his own voice warm and calm. He'd always been skilled in fluctuating between firm leadership

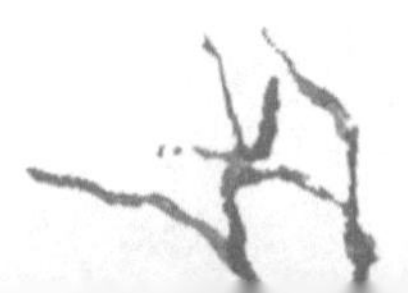

and calming strength. "We are packing up," he explained. "Do you want to come down?"

Nawalya did not respond at first, and instead looked off into the distance. Eventually, though, she nodded, and began the slow climb down. She stumbled slightly when she reached the ground, and Whyldon offered an arm to steady her. "Thank you, Captain," she said in a faraway voice.

"Of course," Whyldon replied. "Do you need anything?"

Nawalya cocked her head to the side, considering the question. "No, I'm okay."

Arian scowled as he finished packing Nawalya's things, though he remained silent on the matter. "I'd have thought Tolan would be back by now."

"Why?" Larent asked with a snort. "It's not like he's contributing anything."

"Foraging for supplies is a contribution," Whyldon pointed out as he helped Nawalya to her pack. She took over for Arian, though slowly. "We do need to replenish when we can," Whyldon added. "We don't know what we'll encounter. It's winter. We're going north. Supplies may be scarce."

"Is it useful, though?" Larent asked, causing Arian to roll his eyes.

"Larent," Collette warned, but she didn't get further in her admonishment as Tolan walked back into camp.

The scowl on his face and his clenched fists suggested he'd overheard Larent. "You're back on that bullshit, I see," he said and handed off the half-full pouches to Arian.

Larent let out a bark of laughter. "You can't even find enough berries to fill the bags. I think that speaks for itself."

Tolan growled and took a step towards Larent, who moved to meet him, a smug smirk on his face.

Collette moved to stand between them, hands pressed against their chests in a physical demand for them to stay apart.

Chapter Seven

"Can either of you explain how fighting is going to help?" she demanded. "If nothing else, this draws unnecessary attention, and I would like for us to avoid attacks and possible death."

Both men immediately withdrew, though Larent took the opportunity to shoot a vulgar gesture at Tolan before he went back to cleaning up the camp.

Tolan stayed by Collette, the anger still evident in his narrowed eyes. He took a deep breath, then looked at Collette. "Sorry," he said softly as he reached out to tuck a strand of hair behind her ear.

"You don't have to apologize," Collette replied, offering Tolan an encouraging smile. "I know this is stressful, and Larent isn't helping."

"I shouldn't let him get to me," Tolan said softly. "What else do you need help with?"

"I'm all packed up," Collette assured him. She cupped his face in her hands. "You know I could not do this without you?" she asked softly. "You are infinitely important."

"I'm here for you, always." He placed his hands on her waist and pulled her close for a kiss.

"You are," Collette whispered when the kiss broke. "Perhaps we should sneak off for a bit after we make camp tonight…"

Tolan smiled. "Assuming we find somewhere safe, absolutely."

"You think Arian would let us camp anywhere that wasn't?" she quipped with a grin.

"True," Tolan said, laughing softly. "But we might miss out on him tying Nawalya down in her blankets tonight."

"I think we'll just have to miss out." She kissed Tolan one more time and dropped her hands. "Cheer up. It's a lot warmer today. It will make the trip less miserable."

"The travel isn't the problem," Tolan said wryly.

"No, but the existing tensions aren't aided by the poor travel conditions," Collette said brightly.

He laughed. "You are not wrong."

"I know," she said with a laugh. "And it's one of the reasons you love me."

"Yes, it is." He gave her a small smile, and as he studied her face, Collette wondered if she looked as exhausted as she felt. "You are quite cheerful this morning."

"Given that we've made it this far, I've chosen to look towards the positive."

"I'm glad that's the reason. I was worried Arian gave you something. Or you found the red spotted mushrooms in the forest."

"We have to travel. I have no time for fun mushrooms," Collette joked.

"There's always time for fun mushrooms!" Larent shouted from behind them.

Collette laughed, and Tolan ignored him. "He's speaking from experience," he explained. "I've seen all three of them after they ate those mushrooms. Best. Thing. Ever."

"You should see me on them," Collette replied, laughing again. "Whyldon highly disapproved."

"I would love to see that," Tolan assured her. "When all this is over."

"Promise?" Collette asked, echoing words they'd shared numerous times before.

"Promise." He cupped her face, letting his thumb trail along her cheekbone.

"Are you two finished with whatever that's supposed to be?" Arian asked, motioning towards Tolan and Collette.

"We can be," Collette replied. "Is everyone else ready to go?"

Arian took a quick glance around the clearing. "Everyone looks ready."

Larent gave a jaunty salute.

Nawalya nodded. She was still holding onto Whyldon's arm, something Collette was willing to bet would continue for much of the day.

"Let's move out?" Arian asked the group at large.

Receiving nods, they gathered their supplies and set off.

Dear Thomas,

We do not know each other very well. Our time in Quenall was limited, and often interrupted, but I cherished every moment in your company. I find myself thinking of you often as I listen to Larent and Tolan bicker over Collette's attention or am forced to watch Nawalya and Whyldon make moon eyes at each other. I am, in fact, willing to say it is only thoughts of you, your courage, and your kindness that stop me from stabbing one of them, leaving with the queen, and walking away. I miss you and I hope you are well.

Yours Always,
Arian

The letter, unsent, remained at the bottom of Arian's pack.

Chapter Eight

Zephraim frowned as he sorted through a stack of parchment, mostly unsealed correspondence that demanded a response. He'd been acting king for just over a month, and already, he was weary of the work. There was a never-ending pile of requests to attend to, concerns raised by the nobility that couldn't be ignored, demanding his time and attention. Sometimes, he felt as though he might drown under the crushing weight of responsibility.

"How did you do it all?" he muttered to himself, thinking of his sister. Resting a hand on the top of the dark wooden desk, his finger traced along a shallow scratch he didn't know the origin of. He didn't remember seeing it or feeling it from the days of his father's reign but couldn't know if the fault of the blemish should be assigned to his sister or not. It wasn't like he needed something stupid to blame her for. She had been at fault for much more serious matters that could, in part, never be corrected. Nothing would bring back Wrenn.

Still, he couldn't deny that in moments like this, when he would have loved to be doing literally anything else, he had been hasty in his treatment of Collette. She might have been guilty of terrible things, but surely there could have been another consequence than where they found themselves now. Had an overthrow been necessary? Had he needed to gloat with cell bars between them? Had she fled because he'd been too threatening? These were answers he would never have.

He sighed and tossed the parchment back on the desk, tempted to leave it for later, when someone knocked at the door. "Come in," Zephraim called out without looking up.

Riken entered the office, a striking figure as always. He was dressed in muted tones that day, a striking contrast to the burgundy and gold Zephraim had chosen for himself. The king offered his friend a smile and sat back in his chair. "You have provided me a welcome reprieve by visiting," he shared.

"Issues with your paperwork, my king?" Riken asked in a jovial tone.

Zephraim shook his head, his red-gold curls swaying gently. "Does disinterest qualify as an issue?"

Riken chuckled and approached the desk, perching on the edge as he looked everything over. "I remember when I had to take over after my father's untimely demise."

Zephraim recalled those days, shortly after the assassination of the prior Baron of Wildrun. Riken had been overworked and half-mad with anger and grief. He was in much better spirits these days, thank the Mother. "I do recall you had much to handle."

"I did, and it was horrific at first, but over time, it grew more manageable," Riken agreed. "I am willing to assist you, however I might."

"As much as I would love to accept your offer, I feel as though I must take responsibility for this. I'd not be a good king to shirk responsibilities so early in my reign." Zephraim leaned forward again and picked up a random piece of parchment for emphasis.

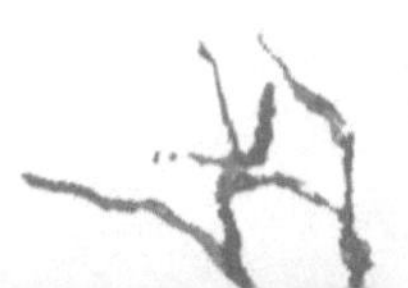

"Delegation is part of being a good king," Riken insisted. "If you dedicate all of your time to the paperwork, you might lack sufficient time for more dire needs." He held out a hand, and the king passed his letter over without hesitation. Riken smiled in acknowledgment. "I know the former ruler delegated much of her correspondence to others," he commented.

Zephraim sighed, thinking back to his sister. "You're not wrong, but she was also more familiar with the goings on in the kingdom. I feel as though I should be as well."

Riken paused long enough to read over the letter Zephraim had given him. He folded it when he was done. "I completely understand your reasoning, but I must suggest that some of what you have on your desk, including this letter, is full of pointless and petty disputes a king has no business involving himself with. This one from Lord Elrick discusses his pursuit of illegal use of Lord Barris's property."

Zephraim rolled his eyes. "I've no interest in that."

"I thought not. Might I suggest you hire a secretary or trusted advisor to review your correspondences and weed out the inconsequential requests? I know several reliable people you could turn to."

Zephraim laughed at the eager offer. "Is this how you got yourself banned from the palace last time?" he teased his old friend. "Of course, you are right. I need someone to sort through this stuff before I sit down to work. Rhoslyn disagrees with your stance, though. She feels I need to be more invested in this work."

Riken laughed this time, pressing a hand against his stomach. "Our queen has strong opinions, which makes her a perfect partner for you, my king. I can speak with her, if it pleases you, to see where we might align on advising you."

"You are welcome to it," Zephraim said. "She does not change opinions just because a close friend might view something differently."

"Oh, that I know. I look forward to the exchanges," Riken assured Zepharim. "I must also confess I have selfish reasons behind my offer. Working with you will keep me out of the way of the … eligible ladies of your court." He sneered a bit but shook his head and resumed a more pleasant expression. "If you are amenable, I am happy to take this, and any other items you feel should not be brought to your attention, until we get someone in place for you."

"I suppose you can do as you like," Zephraim decided. He wasn't going to complain if an old friend was willing to help him prioritize. "I do appreciate you being here, offering your expertise."

Riken reached out and rested a hand on Zephraim's shoulder. "You never expected the tragedy that happened, or for this burden to fall on your shoulders. I will be here to support you by any means."

"I don't think any of us anticipated things would turn out this way," Zephraim said reflectively. "And naturally, Collette's response to the arrest made things worse. Who knows what she's out there doing."

"Her decision to break out of jail, take members of her guard, and virtually disappear suggests that she disagrees with being arrested and losing the throne. I suppose that's understandable. She may try to gather allies, but I'm certain you've written to our neighbors to warn them already."

"I have, but you know how long it can take to receive correspondence, and that's before we consider what choices they may make." Zephraim doubted they had anything to worry about.

"Perhaps, for everyone's sake, including her own, Collette will decide to settle down somewhere with her half-elf lover,"

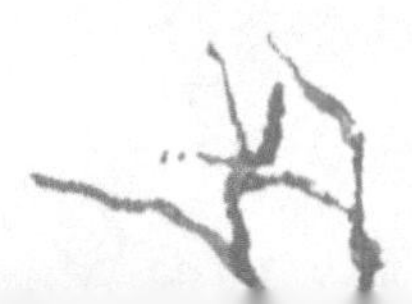

Riken suggested, sneering again at the mention of a half-elf. He couldn't imagine subjecting himself to something so disgusting. "She could have a peaceful, fulfilling life."

"Her lover was a rumor, even if I think the rumors were probably true," Zephraim pointed out. He leaned back in his seat and surveyed Riken. "And I doubt she is just going to settle. As often as she ran off to hunt or do other things, she took her job seriously." She had just done unforgivable things, and no amount of duty or dedication changed that.

"I tend to agree, but one can hope she does the wise thing," Riken replied.

Another knock sounded, and after being admitted by Zephraim, Lord Barris entered the room. Barris was a tall young man with golden skin and dark wavy hair. His ears were adorned with bright golden trinkets, and his hands and neck showed intricately designed tattoos. The second son of a favored duke in the court of King Sargarus, Barris had the misfortune, or perhaps fortune depending on perspective, of losing both father and brother in the Mer-Wars a decade prior. As such, he'd inherited everything.

Riken took the opportunity to rise from his seat on Zephraim's desk. "I shall leave the two of you to it," he declared and offered Zephraim a quick bow. "Is there anything else I can do for you, my king?"

Zephraim looked over his desk and shook his head. "No, I think I am doing well enough for now."

Riken smiled and turned to Lord Barris. "Always a pleasure." With that, he left the room, leaving Zephraim to check in with Barris.

"Hello, Barris. What can I do for you?" Zephraim said with more formality than he'd used with Riken. He liked the lord well enough, but they were not old friends.

Barris bowed deeply and straightened. He gave Zephraim one of his trademark smiles, bright as the sun and just as welcoming. "I hate to bother you, King Zephraim, but a few things came to my attention, and I wanted to discuss them with you before I proceeded."

"Of course," Zephraim said. He motioned towards the chair in front of his desk. "Please."

Barris sat and let his smile slip as he ran a hand through his hair. "My apologies for bringing this to you. It is a matter I would normally handle on my own, but I have been informed that Lord Elrick is trying to involve you in the matter."

Zephraim nodded. "Yes, I received a letter regarding a conflict between the two of you."

Barris sighed. "I shall be brief on my side of things. As you are aware, the sale and manufacturing of Merscale jewelry and specialty items was my land's specialty and main source of income. The product my people created was unmatched, not just in our kingdom, but across many others as well. We also produced our art without the egregious harm others cause."

"I recall your family business," Zephraim confirmed.

"Wonderful. The concern that has risen involves the potential reinstatement of the trade. Lord Elirck made it clear he intended to discover and profit from my family's processing secrets. I fear Lord Elrick plans to use your new position to force his way onto my lands and into my workhouses."

"Why would Elrick have any rights to your lands or workhouses?" Zephraim replied. "That's without even getting into the fact that I have made no decision on the matter of the trade."

"We both know he has no rights," Barris said. "But he's been overheard by many claiming that he will do as he pleases and that you will back him. I do need your intervention to protect my property. Additionally, I am sure you are aware of the

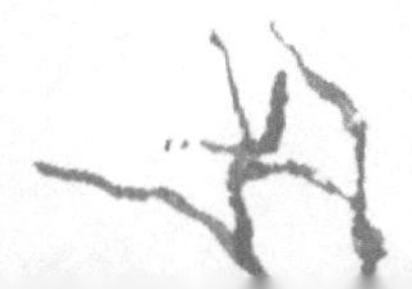

Mers who accompany me while I am in Quenall. They will need protection."

His tone was friendly, firm, and bright, but there was a hint of darkness to it that told Zephraim something had already occurred. "I will make sure he understands he has no access to your property regardless of any changes in the current status of certain laws."

Zephraim knew he had to make definitive decisions regarding the Mer issue, and soon. He wasn't going to be pressured into quick decisions, regardless. Zephraim regarded Barris for a time. The young lord's expression was hopeful but concerned. "You've more to say?"

Barris paused before answering, clearly distressed. "I never want to be the cause for discord amongst members of the court," he began. "However, I have to report that Lord Elrick attempted to assault Lynessea, the female Mer who travels with my party."

A dark look crossed Zephraim's face at the news. "You've witnesses?"

"A minor lord who is now owed a favor, and another of my Mer guards. Oh, and the head cook. She was passing by at the time."

"I see," Zephraim said and nodded. "I will take care of it. Regardless of what may be thought of the Mers, this one came with you, either in your employ or otherwise. Such an attack cannot stand."

"Thank you. I didn't feel right acting on this without your knowledge, but I will not have him get away with this."

"Of course. I will have my people deal with this expeditiously," Zephraim promised.

"I trust your judgment and your word, King Zephraim. I know this will be handled quickly and efficiently in a manner you see fit."

Chapter Eight

His bright smile was back, and Zephraim felt as though he had done a good job today.

"I shall take my leave." Barris bowed. "I'm sure I've used up much of your precious time."

Even as Barris left the room, Zephraim fell back in his seat again. He needed to speak with Cremisius Hawke."

Lord Elrick,

I understand it may be confusing to receive a message from myself and not our very busy king. He requested my aid in helping him with the less important paperwork, which is how I came into possession of your letter. The king expressed to me that Lord Barris's lands are his and his alone, that you are to cease and desist all actions to gain control or knowledge of his lands, and any further action will lead to disciplinary action, including fines on your land.

On a more personal note, having reviewed the reports we have received from your own lands, my advice would be to focus your attention there. I have found a disturbing discrepancy in the reported taxes coming into your land and the actual taxes you receive. If you continue your course of action, I will take my findings to the king. Your lands do border mine, and I would hate to have to take control of them.

Your humble servant,
Riken

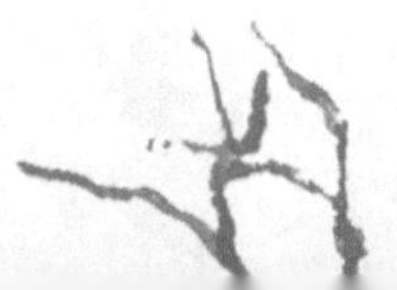

Chapter Nine

Tolan looked darkly at the hawk perched on Collette's shoulder. The hawk, who was actually Larent, played with her hair, doing everything he could to keep her attention. As they sat around the clearing, eating a quick meal and resting from a long morning of walking, Tolan wished he had a rock or something he could use to knock Larent from Collette's shoulder. That was not possible because Nawalya had already given him a nasty glare when he tried to reach for one.

"Fucking shifter," he muttered, his dark mood contrasting sharply with the bright, clear blue sky above them.

Arian gave a laugh. He'd been noticeably on edge since they'd been forced to leave the covering of the forest, but it didn't stop him from taking a dig at Tolan. "You're just upset that Larent is taking all of her attention again," he said from Tolan's side.

"He's not taking all of my attention," Collette insisted, though she laughed again as the hawk nuzzled into her hair, a feat made all the easier by the gentle breeze wafting through the carob-colored strands.

Arian cocked his head to the side, observing the shifter and the queen. "We would have an extreme tactical advantage if he could shift into other humans, not just different animals." He motioned to Larent. "But then, shifters would be hunted into extinction rather than almost."

"True," Collette agreed. "Of course, even if it weren't deadly, I'm not sure Larent could be serious long enough to accomplish anything," she teased her friend. Larent playfully plucked at her hair in response, gaining another laugh.

"That's another reason as to why it would be so dangerous," Arian said seriously. "A shifter who could imitate another person could cause all kinds of problems. Imagine if he pretended to be you."

"Let's not," Whyldon spoke up. He'd tied his long hair back to counteract the breeze and rummaged through his supply pack for an additional layer to add to his travel attire. Slowly, they'd all added protective layers over the past few days. "Larent has many skills. Subtlety and sobriety in serious moments are not his strongest."

"His break is over, anyway," Nawalya announced. Larent looked to Nawalya but did nothing to show argument. He gently pecked Collette's shoulder farewell and took off.

"Does he still hate flying?" Tolan asked.

"Yes, yes he does," Arian replied with a small malicious smirk on his face.

"He'll have to endure a little longer," Whyldon surmised. "We'll cross the border into Azmarin before dusk."

"How well do you know the king?" Arian inquired of the captain. He also opted to pull out his traveling cloak while they talked. "I know the capitol is still days away, but we need a plan."

"Not well," Whyldon said, then scratched his beard in thought. "The arrangement between Her Majesty and King

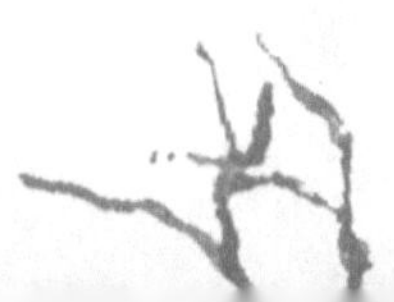

Brath was devised by Sargarus and Brath's father. I don't know if I was ever in the same room with him for more than five minutes."

"You missed nothing," Collette assured him. She was braiding her hair, something Tolan briefly debated doing for her despite the knowledge that Larent had been the reason it was down in the first place. "I had to go on a hunt with both. Brath disliked that I knew how to draw a bow."

Arian nodded, but Nawalya spoke up. "We have done a few jobs in Azmarin. I gathered that Brath dislikes strong women. I can see him taking issues with you knowing how to hunt." She moved to sit beside Collette and took over braiding. "We have also heard he can be greedy, but nothing too horrendous."

"Didn't Azmarin profit from the wars?" Arian asked.

"Yes," Collette confirmed. "And the marriage was supposed to strengthen the alliance, which would make future wars more profitable for all."

"Is there any way to use that alliance to enlist his help? You're not going to start wars like your father did, but there must be something you can bargain, other than your hand in marriage," Arian pointed out.

Tolan scoffed. He knew marriage was very likely the thing Brath would ask for.

"Sargarus promised them the land portions of the Nereid kingdom at one point," Whyldon said. "But that was Brath's father. Brath may be different."

Both Nawalya and Arian let out low growls, causing Tolan to side-eye both before asking, "What else do you think they might want?"

"Honestly, I have no idea," Collette said after a moment. "He could very well be like his father, and that might mean a proposed renewal of the arrangement. He could also be vastly different." She herself was nothing like Sargarus. "There is the possibility he'll still be offended that I broke the arrangement."

Tolan nodded. "Should we do advanced recon?"

"It wouldn't hurt," Whyldon said. "Once we arrive, we can't approach the palace. We'll need to find a safe place within the capital city and send out inquiries. Knowing what we are walking into is the safest path forward."

"Absolutely. And if the situation seems hopeless, we can leave without notifying them of our presence," Collette said.

"Arian and I should go in first," Nawalya determined. "We can secure lodging while Larent gathers intel."

"You may not like sitting back," Whyldon interjected before Collette could respond. "But the royal family might recognize you."

"It's the safest plan," Arian added.

Nawalya reached out a comforting hand to Collette, but then the hawk returned. Larent quickly shifted into his human form. "Coralian travelers are ahead."

"You, especially, need to hide," Whyldon said to Collette, ignoring the glare she gave him. Nawalya gently nudged Collette off to the side, instructing her to conceal herself in the grass. The others took less concealed positions, with Nawalya scaling a nearby tree, her bow in her hands and an arrow ready, while Whyldon knelt below, ready to strike. Larent shifted into his wolf form and crouched low on the ground near Collette.

Slowly, a group of merchants made their way along the road, their wagon heavy with a variety of goods from the kingdom. Tolan momentarily thought Larent had been mistaken until he spotted a guard in a worn, but distinct Coralian uniform that had been given to him at the palace.

The political refugees hid, staying in formation long after the merchants disappeared from view. Eventually, it was deemed safe to continue forward. "This tells me that we will need to

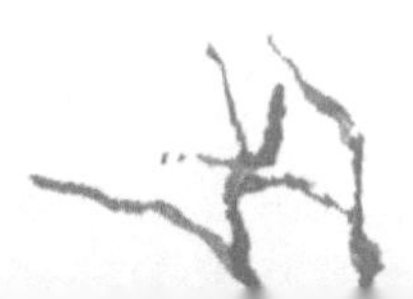

be extra cautious after crossing the border," Whyldon observed quietly as he brushed the debris from his hands and clothing.

"We will want to make camp outside the city, so anyone staying behind is safe while we scout," Nawalya said as she nimbly jumped from the tree, her bow over her shoulder.

"I don't know if that is the safest option or not," Whyldon said. "This far north, people aren't going to recognize any of us, including Collette, unless we run into people we actually know. Thieves and those looking to start trouble will likely be outside of the city."

Tolan tried to ignore the debate as he rejoined Collette. He meant to kiss her, but he saw the look of annoyance on her face. "What is it?" he asked.

"Let's desist with making plans on my behalf without consulting me, yes?" she said to Whyldon, Nawalya, and Arian.

Nawalya and Arian both froze at her words while Larent almost doubled over in laughter. His humor resulted in having to dodge a couple of bags the elves threw at his head.

"I told you," he announced cheerfully. "I told you, you'd have to plan with her and not around her. This isn't normal escort duty. She's a damn queen, and she's not going to take orders lying down, especially from us."

"We apologize," Arian said stiffly, the words causing a most painful sneer to form on his face. "We are used to having to work around those we escort, not with them. We will work on that." Nawalya nodded, and Tolan just shook his head.

"It's not even about me being a 'damn queen' as Larent put it," Collette replied. "I'm a person who is intelligent and capable. I don't need my hand held while other people make decisions."

"Of course not," Whyldon replied. "No one is suggesting that."

"Really? A group of people who would not recognize me still resulted in everyone acting as though I needed to be shielded from the world like a defenseless child," Collette pointed out.

"Again. We apologize," Arian interjected, thankfully cutting off a potential argument. "Often, when we do this type of thing, the people we oversee don't want to take part in our plans. They just want us to fix the issues so they can move on. In the years we have been mercenaries, you are the second person to want a say in the planning."

"Oh yeah," Larent said with a laugh. "Remember the noble who decided it would be best if we dressed as his concubines, and he wanted Tolan to be his 'wife?'" For the first time in years, Larent and Tolan exchanged a genuine smile. This happy moment quickly passed, and their scowls returned.

"We will do better and include you going forward," Nawalya promised Collette softly. "It's your life on the line, and you should have a say. But forgive us if we slip. Please."

Collette nodded.

"So, how would you like to do this?" Arian asked, his eyes sliding to Nawalya.

"Unless we see a decisive reason to avoid going into the city when we arrive," Collette said in favor of Whyldon's suggestion, "hiding is easier in a crowd, even if people might recognize me."

Nawalya and Arian nodded, though it was impossible to tell if they agreed or not.

Larent interjected, "Well, if no one has any complaints, I'm going to fly into the city, see what the current hair styles and such are so we blend in better. Unless there are objections?" He threw a flirty smile in Collette's direction.

"Go do your job," Tolan replied, and Larent laughed before shifting and flying off again.

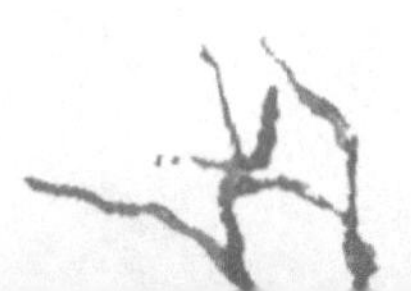

Chapter Ten

His Royal Majesty, King Zephraim,

I recently received your response, through your intermediary Lord Riken, regarding my concerns over Lord Barris' lands. I understand your decision, and in offering all due respect to that decision, I will cease my efforts. However, I seek an audience with you to discuss the trade. There is so much happening beneath our noses, which benefits no one. I am available at your request.

I look forward to your answer my king,
Lord Elrick

Walking down the cobblestone streets towards the merchant district, Crem kept his eye out for possible threats. Every so often, he would glance at the man walking next to him.

Crem had known Sunny "Call me by my first name, and I'll rip off your head and shit in it" Howle for the duration of his time in the guard. Howle was a mountain, towering over most men in the kingdom. His handsome dark skin and long, thick dark hair streaked with silvery gray always drew the gaze of those they passed. Not that the man gave two shits.

In his prime, Howle had been one of the old king's personal guards. Then, he'd taken an arrow to the knee. His responsibilities shifted to training new recruits for the guard, helping Whyldon prepare the group. He retired shortly after Collette took the throne. Although the older man had never confirmed it, Crem had always suspected that the motivation to leave the personal guard had more to do with Sargarus than his minor injury.

Howle had approached Crem several days after the queen disappeared, somehow knowing she had escaped rather than suffer long-term imprisonment or execution as so many expected. He'd also asked Crem exactly what he was going to do about the cum stain brother sitting on the throne. At the time, Crem believed it was a waiting game. Maybe Zephraim wouldn't be that terrible. Howle had laughed hard enough to cover Crem's face in spittle.

"Never lose that optimistic streak," Howle said before asking why he couldn't just kill the donkey-fucker now.

However crass Howle was, he had been invaluable once it became obvious the worst of the guards would be given free rein, and the letters from the mystery man started arriving. One such letter currently resided in Howle's hands, telling them of an elven merchant and his family who would be targeted soon. The merchant was a known supporter of Collette's, one who had been asking a lot of questions.

"So…" Howle started, looking up from the letter. "These letters have yet to be wrong?" he asked, his voice thick with a slight accent from being raised in Myrefall.

Crem shook his head. "Not so far, and before you ask, that's letter number eight. I think you were escorting a young Mer family out of the kingdom when the last four letters showed up."

Howle nodded. "Those piss ant guards are gettin' worse. We might have to take them out before long."

"I want to talk to Zephraim first. Maybe he will step up when I tell him his people are being arrested under false charges of treason. I mean, the victims are trying to understand exactly what has happened with the Queen. Zephraim's merchants are having their stalls and warehouses unlawfully searched and merchandise stolen. The pretty daughters of the poorer people are being harassed. That's not even the worst of it."

"That cum stain won't care. Ya said one key word there. 'Poor.' He doesn't give two shits about them, or Mers, elves, or anyone else who supports the true Queen. Mother knows I once told Sarg he should have pulled out when Zephraim was five and a mopey little shit, and it's still true today."

Crem laughed, shaking his head. He opened his mouth to ask a question and then closed it, knowing Howle would never answer anything that involved the old king. He decided to go back to the letters. "I still don't trust these notes."

"And you shouldn't," Howle replied with a snort. "Unknown, overly helpful letters from a mystery sender? That's definitely a trap meant to lure you into a false sense of security and then–" he moved his finger in a slashing motion across his throat. "It could be legit. Who knows anymore." The big man shrugged and stopped walking as Crem held out a hand.

In the distance, Rulf and his associates lingered around one of the houses. Half of them were visibly drunk, and the laughter and jeering from all of them told Crem they were up to no good.

"I told Collette she needed ta not let the nobles shove their unwanted kin at her. If there is one thing I wish she had listened to, it was that," Howle observed.

"Whyldon said it was on her list, but the Mers and elves had to come first."

Crem saw a look of distaste cross Howle's features. "Wouldn't have taken you as someone to dislike other races."

Howle shrugged. "I don't dislike them, but it's hard to work past a lifetime of conditioning. I grew up being taught to hate them, to kill them. I'm sorry to say it took a long time for me to see past that. I'm even sorrier there's a part of me that still reacts poorly, but I'm workin' on it. Maybe doing things like this will help."

Crem nodded and the two moved closer to the group, hoping they could hear their plans.

"Of course, the fletcher is still in town," Rulf bragged to a couple of the younger guards. "There's nowhere for him to go."

The boys had joined the guard after Collette's arrest, and though Crem did not know them well, he knew the way they gazed at Rulf, impressed and adoring, spoke volumes of the men they would grow into.

"Besides," Borin interjected, his deep voice slurred. "We'd have caught him on his way out."

Crem saw Howle cover his mouth to hold in a snort. Just last week, Crem had removed one of the bakers and his family right in front of this same group of guards. He nudged Howle when he failed at suppressing his amusement, causing Borin to glance in their direction.

"We ought to do something about that fletcher," Rulf grumbled after a moment. "I'm tired of waiting for him.

Crem tensed, not liking the way that sounded. He moved to take a step forward, to stop whatever madness they were about to come up with, only for a large, muscular arm to stop him. Crem looked at Howle incredulously, but the older man wasn't looking at him. All his focus was on Rulf and his people. Crem

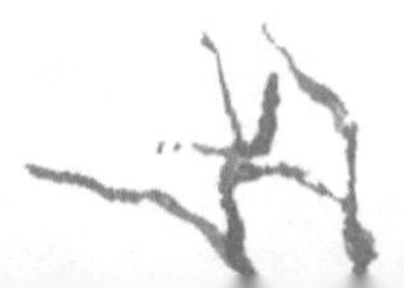

didn't understand why Howle didn't want him to stop this, but trusting the man, he waited.

"What do you want to do?" Kenrick, a young soldier asked, his dark freckles and large ears making him seem all the younger.

"We can start by taking down the potential hiding spots," Rulf replied with a devious grin.

Crem closed his eyes, letting out a long breath. There were only a few ways someone could take out a hiding spot, and none of them bode well. Feeling movement next to him, he glanced at Howle, who had a grim smile on his face, his arm still held out to stop Crem from moving forward.

They watched as Rulf and the others started in the direction of what had once been Thomas Fletcher's home. Once they were out of hearing, Howle resumed the conversation. "Whatever stupid thing they are about ta do, we can use this. You can take it ta the king, and I can rouse more people. I hate it, but we have ta let them do it."

As much as Crem wished he could disagree, he trusted Howle's judgment, so he just nodded. Making sure to stay out of sight as best as possible, the two followed. The journey took longer than it reasonably should as the path to Thomas Fletcher's old shop was situated in the merchant district. Neither Crem nor Howle had trouble hiding. The area was still crowded despite the time of day. In fact, Crem was willing to bet the guards were so preoccupied with their goal, the crowd levels wouldn't have mattered.

Once they reached the old shop, the two men stayed back, knowing that they couldn't intervene unless absolutely necessary. They found a wall near the alley to lean against, at first unimpressed as Borin gave a sound kick to the door. The booming sound might have been impressive to a child, but otherwise, the move seemed pointless.

"No reaction from inside," Borin reported to the group.

Chapter Ten

"Of course there's not," Howle growled, rolling his eyes at the ridiculousness of it. "I don't think they have an actual plan, but we can stay for a bit. We're close enough to the potential victims pointed out in the letters to give this more time."

Crem nodded, but he couldn't help feeling a little destruction of property wouldn't be the end of it. Rarely was his gut wrong, and when the first of the fires was lit, he knew he'd been right.

"What the shit!?" Howle growled out. "Don't they know how flammable these buildings are? The Queen hasn't been able ta update the roofing yet. This whole block could go up." He moved to run out and bash some heads, rational thought being replaced by blinding anger, only for Crem to stop him.

"This is the perfect cover. Go get the families out. I'll get the water garrison and make as much noise as possible. The more people who see this the better." He gritted his teeth and stared at the guards who had just started a fire in the middle of the city.

Back at the palace, Crem took a deep breath and then another, glad the corridor was empty as he prepared himself for the coming battle. Though there were no swords or arrows involved, there was no way to describe the discussion he needed to have. He could only hope Zephraim was willing to listen and not dismiss his claims outright.

That fear was logical, since the weeks since his ascension to the throne had proven, at best, Zephraim was easily swayed by those around him. Diana thought Crem would affect no change, that Zephraim would easily dismiss his concerns because Crem had no noble title to attach to his name. Diana was likely right, but Crem was determined to do what he could.

He knocked then entered when the king granted him permission. At least he was alone. Approaching the desk where the king sat, he bowed, though not as deeply as he might have for Collette. Not that Zephraim would notice. He was not concerned with details. "Your Majesty, I apologize for the interruption."

"Not at all," Zephraim said without looking up from a letter he was writing. "How can I assist?"

Crem swallowed hard and braced himself for what he knew would be a fruitless discussion. "I have come to voice my concerns about the current state of the guard and the actions of several of its members. There is currently no guard captain, so I am to bring these concerns directly to the ruler."

"I have not yet decided on a new captain," Zephraim replied. "Are you anxious?"

Crem knew his face gave nothing away. It couldn't with Collette gone and Riken back in the kingdom. "Less anxious than … concerned with the actions of some of the guards."

"And what concerning things are you here to make me aware of?"

"I assume Your Majesty is aware of the fire in the merchant district?"

"Yes, and I've heard a version of events from a reliable source," Zephraim said, finally looking up from his writing. "I'm sure your version differs."

Crem raised his chin slightly. "I assume your source told you the guards Rulf, Borin, and three of their associates are the ones that started the fire?"

"I have heard that an unknown group started the fire," Zephraim said as he surveyed Crem. "I've also heard that when Captain Whyldon was around, the two of you often blamed Rulf and Borin for a number of mischievous deeds."

It took a great deal of effort for Crem to avoid frowning. "Every one of those deeds were documented and had witnesses. In the case of the fire, I was patrolling the area and saw it myself, as did several townsfolk," he said firmly but in a way that could leave no offense. "The fire, however, is just my latest concern since it could have harmed many of your subjects."

"I will look into it," Zephraim said without much enthusiasm or interest. He raised a brow as he looked at Crem, his expression not quite accusatory, even as the following question was. "I suppose you have heard nothing from Captain Whyldon since his departure?"

Crem's face remained neutral, almost bored. He'd been asked this question numerous times since the night of the arrest. "I have not, and I doubt he would reach out to me."

Zephraim nodded once. "And you have no idea how Whyldon managed to escape the castle the night of Collette's arrest?"

Crem's response hinted at impatience. "As I have reported, I was with him only for a short time after the queen was arrested. While he seemed agitated, he was more concerned with the safety of the people and sent me and others on patrol to ensure there were no riots."

"Of course," Zephraim replied. "And your wife, the palace cook. She went into town that evening. What was she up to, again?"

"Diana had been unaware of the events and had gone into town in hopes of finding me at a tavern, celebrating your rise to the throne." There had been a concerted effort to keep both of them as safe as possible that evening and in the coming days, but Crem did not like the questioning of his wife.

"You have many convenient explanations," Zephraim said after a moment, but he seemed content for now and moved on. "You dealt with the conflict between Elrick and Barris?"

"I have spoken to both, starting first with Lord Barris. Then I informed Lord Elrick he has no rights to Barris's lands or workhouses. Lord Barris was grateful for the assistance and asked me to tell you if anything more comes up with Lord Elrick he will deal with it himself. Lord Elrick, on the other hand, vows to bring this to your attention personally. He said something about trade secrets being passed between friends and other very unflattering things towards Lord Barris's person. Nothing I could say would sway his decision and eventually Lord Crobán took him away. The report should have arrived for you last night."

Crem left out that Lord Elrick had also made threats against Barris's Mers, as Crem doubted the king cared.

"I will speak with Lord Elrick should he bring the matter to my attention or should he decide on action without granted authority," Zephraim stated. "Were there any other matters you needed me to contend with?"

Crem opened his mouth to tell the king about what was happening to the poor, the Mers, and the elves in his kingdom, of the arrests, the product stolen from his merchants, and the harassment of the women under his care. But as he looked at the king, truly looked at him, he knew Howle and Diana were right. This man was no king and cared little for his people. Feeling a small part of himself break, Crem replied. "No, Your Majesty."

Zephraim nodded again. "Thank you, then. I have work to see to."

Crem inclined his head and headed out. He needed to find Diana.

"I told you," Diana whispered to her husband. The two were in a corner of the kitchen, and although they were alone for the moment, one never knew if someone was lurking nearby. "He's not going to listen. He's not interested." Diana was angry. Zephraim had potential, regardless of his lack of rights to the throne. He just didn't want to make the effort, and too many people were pleased that he wasn't Collette to call him out for his lack of usefulness.

She crossed her arms and looked up at her husband. "I'm not surprised that he lacked concern for your accusations of who started that fire. I am surprised that he's not thinking about how much damage that fire caused."

"It's so much worse than that, love." Crem leaned a shoulder against the wall, the weariness in him more obvious than ever.

"Oh?" Diana was going to make sure he got sleep tonight no matter what.

"He implied Whyldon and I made up the numerous charges against Rulf and Borin over the last several years. I'm led to believe he's going to look the other way every time their behavior escalates. He does not care about this kingdom whatsoever." Crem took a deep breath and shook his head. "And now I'm going to ask something of you that I know you'll argue. I need you to leave the kingdom."

Diana scowled. "You're a crazy son of a bitch if you think that is ever happening," Diana said flatly and almost felt sorry when he sighed. "I'm not going anywhere. Not with you staying here, anyway."

"Why are you so fucking stubborn?" Crem asked her, though there was no heat to his words. "Zephraim asked about your actions the night of the arrest, and there was a gleam in his eye I did not care for. You are in danger if you stay here, and you know I cannot leave with you. Not while there are people in danger."

They both paused as the door on the far end of the kitchen opened and in walked a young kitchen worker whom Lord

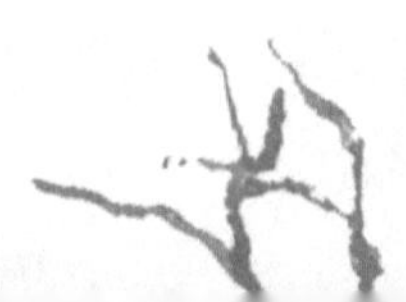

Crobán seemed to favor. Diana had no reason to suspect she would be a problem, but caution was vital these days. She took Crem's arm and pulled him towards the pantry where there was more of a sound barrier and resumed their conversation. "So your plan is for me to run away even though you're arguably in more danger?"

"Yes," Cream said, half-exasperated. "They will not hesitate to harm you if it means hurting me." He reached for her, pulling her into his arms. "It would destroy me if something happened to you. You are my whole world, Diana."

"Listen to me very carefully," Diana said, wrapping her arms around her husband's neck. "I'll not step foot from this kingdom without you. You cannot make me, and I will not be convinced to leave you here to face this alone."

He sighed again but nodded in acknowledgment. "Fine, if you won't leave, then we must do what we can to make sure people think there is a growing rift between us. It will help keep you safe."

"Argue with you in a more public setting? I can do that," she replied.

Crem huffed a laugh, though he rolled his eyes. "Just make sure that you remain vague about all of the politics so they can't make up a reason to charge you with treason. And, possibly send me to the barracks for the night every now and then."

"Leaving my bed cold, I see," Diana half complained, but she nodded. "If that's what is necessary. Give me tonight before I banish you to the barracks tomorrow."

"I can do that," he said, then lowered his head to kiss her softly. "It's not as though I have objections to sharing a bed with my wife."

Lord Elrick,

Chapter Ten

There are many decisions yet to be made regarding the sale of Merscales, though I anticipate initiating discussions on the topic at the next council meeting. Naturally, if there is something else, something more pressing that you wish to discuss in person, I have allotted time to meet with members of the court.

Zephraim
King of Coralia

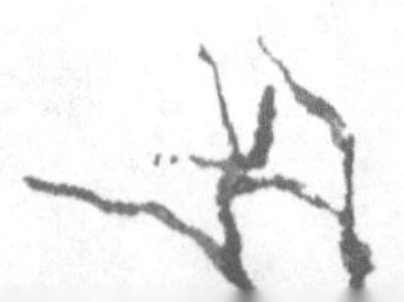

Chapter Eleven

Collette's party arrived in the Azmarin capitol of Catillatio four days later in moderately cheerful spirits. Even with the initial part of their plan on the horizon, Whyldon worried over Collette, who was not forthcoming with the expected negativity since the overthrow. In many ways, her actions suggested a leisurely journey rather than an escape. She'd also developed a worrying friendship with Larent, a man who supported her decision to dwell in a less serious mind space. He imagined there would be conflict with Tolan before long.

Fortunately, when the group reached the border of the Azmarin lands, Arian, Nawalya, and Larent disappeared for days at a stretch, hoping to gauge a possible reception of Collette. The rest of the group had taken up rooms at the Infamous Apple Tavern. Whyldon sat at a table in his room, casually eating bread and stew as he browsed news pamphlets they'd collected when arriving. There was little mention of the happenings in Coralia, save for a quick paragraph mentioning the overthrow. He was curious to know how the Azmarin viewed the situation.

He glanced over to Collette who was relaxing against Tolan on the other side of the room. With nothing to do, her attention was easily given to her lover, and Whyldon found that he had nothing to say on the matter. If she could find moments of happiness in the middle of this mess, he couldn't begrudge her.

He looked up as Arian knocked on the door before letting himself, Nawalya, and Larent inside. "I think it's safe to put in a request to meet with the king," Arian announced as soon as the door was closed and secured. "All the same, I would like to give Larent more time to scout exits from the castle in case things go wrong."

"Did you get the impression they might?" Whyldon asked.

Nawalya shook her head before taking the seat beside Whyldon. "Not at all. Everything appears safe, but we would like to be cautious."

"Caution is good," Collette agreed. "Especially when we still don't know if Zephraim has made contact."

"If everyone is alright with it, I'll head back in," Larent said.

"The sealed rooms might be a problem. Any ideas on how to get in?" Tolan asked in a doubting tone.

"The king is a falconer, or he's trying to be. I've seen his birds all over the castle. It seems their trainer works well but doesn't like to stay in their area. I'm going to see what leeway that can grant me." Larent paused and waved at his companions. "If no one has any other questions…"

"Go do what you can," Whyldon replied.

Larent nodded, shifted into a falcon, and flew out the open window.

Tolan watched the window for a moment, begrudging concern showing in his expression. "That shift was slower than before."

"We are keeping an eye on him," Nawalya said, her soft tone unusually sharp.

"He's been doing this kind of work long before we arrived," Collette pointed out. "Magic wears on people. He needs a break when he can get it."

"We know," Nawalya said, her tone soft again as she addressed Collette. "Changing into anything other than his wolf is very draining, but his change is taking less than a few seconds so he is … being argumentative about taking breaks."

"Sleep is one of the few things that help, which is why we've started taking his shifts at night," Arian added.

Collette nodded. "We may have to figure out how to let him rest for a few days, all the same. He's been doing a lot."

"Logistically, I don't think that will be possible until after we are done here," Arian answered.

"Then we need to figure out how to make it possible," Collette insisted. "It will be a bigger problem to contend with if he continues to decline."

"You mean when he passes out for a week or two like last time," Tolan said in a very frank manner.

"It was a week and a half, and it was his own fault," Arian retorted. "If he can get several full nights of sleep, he should be fine."

Collette shrugged. "It's not like things would be easier if he did pass out. Are you volunteering to hoist him over your shoulder if we have to make a quick exit?"

Arian nodded, though he scowled. Looking at Nawalya, he said, "No more searching, at least while we are here. We can't have you lost while working."

Nawalya tilted her head and raised an eyebrow, which was almost an eye roll for her. "I made the rules for our mission," she pointed out. "When was the last time, four days ago? Five?"

"Given that we are not going to be in hiding if granted an audience with King Brath, it may be beneficial to observe as much caution as possible," Whyldon said, breaking up what felt to be the threat of several arguments. He stood from the table and took position in the middle of the group, hoping to give off an air of authority. His experience with soldiers told him this subtle move often cut tension. "Collette is right about the performance aspect of what we will be doing. On top of everything else, we must give off the appearance of cool reassurance of our position. She is the rightful ruler, and we are her loyal subjects."

"You're right, of course," Nawalya replied, her expression thoughtful. "We have to look the part."

"That means we need to gather supplies, including clothing that doesn't look like we all fled the city in the middle of the night a month ago." Arian looked around the room. "Is there anything specific anyone would like?"

Whyldon shook his head. "I think they will expect us to look like we've been traveling. Nothing too ostentatious, I think. However, Her Majesty may need formal items if we are invited into the palace."

Nawalya made a face, pressing her lips together and wrinkling her nose.

"I will buy you something pretty, too. Stop with the face," Arian said, exasperated.

Tolan leaned towards Collette. "Nawalya collects pretty dresses that she never wears. Her collection is stunning."

"Where does she keep them?" Collette asked, amused.

"From my understanding, she stashes them at whatever place they are staying during missions. Then, when they aren't off being vigilantes, she takes them to their home somewhere near Pontus Bay. I'm not exactly sure where it is as I've only been there twice, and both times they blindfolded me."

"Blindfolding you might be fun," Collette said with a grin. "Another thing I'll have to see for myself one of these days."

"Maybe next time we're alone?" Tolan said softly.

"Maybe," Collette replied. "I feel as though we don't get nearly enough privacy these days."

Tolan had a feeling that was purposeful, especially with the look Arian and Nawalya exchanged at her words. He just wondered how much was Larent's fault and how much was their honest belief he wasn't good enough for Collette. "I'll fix that."

"I would like that," Collette told him quietly.

Tolan gave her a soft smile and pulled her close. "Anything else we need to handle for now?"

"Nothing off the top of my head," Collette replied. "I think we're going to have to accept that we are going into this thing in a vulnerable position."

Arian made a face and looked like he was going to say something, but Nawalya just shook her head.

Chapter Twelve

His Royal Majesty and Azmarin Emperor, King Brath,

I hope this letter finds you in good health and spirits. Due to circumstances beyond my control, I have found myself in your kingdom and would like to request an audience with Your Majesty to catch up and discuss the state of our alliance. I await your response.

Yours,
Collette Venora Josselyn Gaillane,
Queen of Coralia

A few hours later, Arian watched as Nawalya smiled softly at the captain and gently pulled him out of the room. She'd convinced him to go shopping with her before she showed him one of the hideouts in town, and Arian wondered how long it would be before they made their way back. He did not begrudge

Nawalya, his oldest friend, finding Whyldon, but it meant a shift in their dynamic that he wasn't comfortable with.

It also made him miss Thomas, a thought he refused to entertain even if the blond man featured more and more in his dreams. He hoped he was safe, but Thomas's pleasure in castigating the crown would put him in the path of danger regardless.

Reining in his thoughts, he focused on the queen. Tolan and Larent had been sent out in search of supplies, and this was the first time Arian found himself along with Collette since they'd pretended to fuck in the alley the night she'd been arrested. He was uncomfortable, to say the least. However, because the group agreed to split up for the afternoon, here he was, babysitting the queen.

"We have a safehouse in the city," he said quickly and with a slightly gruffer tone than he wanted.

"Do you think we'll need it?" Collette asked.

Arian shrugged as he checked his money bag. "Honestly, I hope we don't, but we didn't think you would be accused of murder and mutilation, and locked away in jail. Well, most of us didn't." The last part was said slightly lower and with a lot more snark.

Collette chuckled at that. "I didn't see any of that coming either if it makes you feel better. At least, not until it was about to happen."

"No one truly expects the bad things that happen. Those that do either ignore the signs because it's easier to stick your head in the sand and pretend, or they over-prepare for them." He shrugged. "Nawalya would tell you I over-prepare, but it's saved our lives more than once."

"In my case, a lot of the political strife remains verbal. An overthrow is usually not on the table, even when a wide cavern of opinions exists." Collette shrugged and stood to follow Arian.

"But I tend to agree with you. Being over-prepared is often a better way to exist."

Arian paused as he took in her words. "An overthrow wasn't something we had truly prepared for, not until after Wrenn's murder. We were, well—I was prepared for another eventuality—like your murder." He paused then added, "Truthfully, I had plans in place to cover for you when you eventually murdered someone, but you were nowhere near Wrenn Almeida when he was killed, so I was caught unprepared."

"Even if I'd the inclination to kill my enemies, Wrenn was just an annoyance. I still wonder who was behind that, though I have suspicions."

"So do we," Arian said darkly, violence lacing his body before he visibly shook it off. "Wrenn wasn't the one we bet on you murdering."

"Who did you think I would murder?"

"At first? Lord Riken, but after you banished him—smart move by the way—I thought you might go after Lord Crobán. The man is as slimy as they come, and while I know he believes himself too good to dirty his own hands, I think he had a hand in Wrenn's death. We know he was involved in the deaths of hundreds of Merpeople." He motioned for her to grab her cloak.

"Lord Crobán wouldn't be worth the effort," Collette replied as she obeyed his directive. "But he was, undoubtedly, involved with Wrenn's death. He became quite familiar with Rhoslyn in the weeks following my birthday."

"Crobán's murder wouldn't have been pre-planned. I guessed it would be in a fit of rage after he touched your shoulder or arm one too many times. I know you hated it when he used the tone that implied he knew better than you because of what's between his legs."

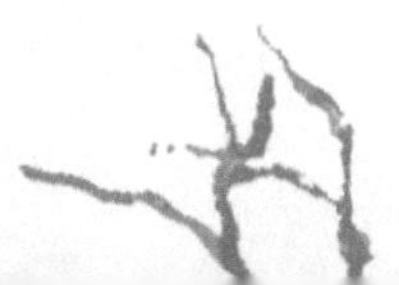

"He did like to touch," Collette reflected, shuddering. "I just wonder if he's managed to worm his way into Zephraim's good graces."

"More than likely yes, and if they recalled Lord Riken..." Arian gave another shrug. "We won't know until we hear news from the kingdom."

They left the room in silence, and Arian led her down the stairs and through the entrance of the inn. Once they were on the crowded streets, he began speaking again. "I have something I must teach you." He made a fist and knocked it against the palm of his other hand. One knock, then a pause, then four slightly faster knocks, then another pause followed by two more. "I need you to memorize this knock."

"Show me again," Collette requested, her humor left behind as she took on a studious disposition.

He did it once more after dodging around a man hauling lumber on a cart. He paused, distracted, as he realized they were passing an offensively ornate temple dedicated to The Mother. A bastardized religion created by the humans so they could pick and choose the qualities of the elvin traditions they liked, worshippers of the Mother always seemed clustered around the temples, clutching chests and throwing gold. Arian couldn't help but sneer. He motioned for Collette to continue forward.

"When we arrive, repeat the knock on the door, and it will get you to safety if something goes very wrong."

Collette nodded and repeated the motion for Arian's critique.

Arian smiled as she did it correctly. "One more time," he instructed as he led her up a street lined with expensive homes. Again, she obeyed, and Arian was satisfied.

He led them down the street, passing the large manors with little interest until they arrived at the fourth in line. "We're going to go to the door and use the special knock," he instructed. "Do not speak to whomever answers."

Chapter Twelve

"And who is going to answer?" Collette asked, brow raised.

"It should be one of two women. Either a rather pretty plump blonde, or her wife, a tall and handsome woman with copper hair. If we can come in, they will say 'It's such a beautiful day' without looking at us." He knew the code was complicated, but so far, she'd demonstrated enough intelligence, and he was pleased when Collette did as he bade and knocked out the correct rhythm on the correct door.

It took a moment before a woman with a shock of curly copper hair answered. Just as Arian said, the woman looked through them and said, "It's such a beautiful day." Turning back, she walked into the house, leaving the door open.

Arian motioned for Collette to go in first and shut the door softly behind them. He held up a hand for her to wait as they stood in a tastefully decorated hallway. He said nothing. Just stood there waiting for another few seconds before a melodic voice rang out. "Magda, will you please get my scarf from upstairs."

An older voice replied in the affirmative, prompting Arian to say, "That means the kitchen is clear. Let's go quickly."

Arian led her down the hall, through the dining room, and into a spacious kitchen. The mouthwatering scent of roasting duck and baking cakes filled the air as they made their way to the back corner where barrels were stacked. Moving the third barrel, Arian revealed a trap door which he easily lifted.

Instead of going down right away, he shifted another barrel, revealing a pile of letters. He stooped to pick them up, then quickly sorted through them, choosing a couple which he tucked away for later. The rest were covered again, and he turned his attention back to the room. He motioned for Collette to follow. Steps went down into a dimly lit but comfortable looking room.

Once inside the room, Arian's eyes adjusted to the darkness, and he saw Collette cross her arms as she looked around the space. The room was a decent size, with six beds lining one wall, what looked like a bathroom on the left side of the room, and two wardrobes. There was a second, more heavily barred door on the right. "So, this is the safehouse?" she asked as she looked around. Her willingness to observe and take in information boded well in Arian's opinion.

"It is, and you will come here if something goes wrong, and the group gets separated. We have a handful of places like this scattered throughout the city." He walked over to the door which had been open and unsecured when they came down. "If you need to use this space, make sure you close the door behind you and lock it. One of the ladies will move the barrels back."

He crossed the room and indicated a different exit obscured by the shadows. "This door leads to a tunnel that will take us under the walls and out of the city." He paused, debating, and then sighed before indicating the only other noticeable item in the room. "That wardrobe has some of Nawalya's collection of dresses, in case you were interested. Please don't comment on the color. I'm more than aware."

The comment must have piqued the queen's curiosity. She saw herself to the wardrobe, opening the doors with excitement. Several blue gowns were revealed, all of them perfectly matching the color of Captain John Whyldon's eyes.

"Oh," Collette said, causing Arian to close his eyes and nod.

"Again. I am aware, but at least her taste in dresses is exquisite," he commented as he started to unlock the door on the right. "It looks like no one's used this in a while."

"I'd hope there was not a need for hiding very often," said Collette. She closed the doors of the wardrobe and faced Arian.

"Depends on the job and who's working it. Sometimes these won't be used for years. Sometimes they're needed every day.

There was a time when many safehouses existed in Coralia, you know. Most of them have been discovered and shut down."

"Believe it or not, I am well-versed in many of the hide-aways that existed, and probably still do, in Coralia," Collette replied. "I'm under no delusions, nor am I naive."

"You are neither of those things. Your father on the other hand… He either didn't know about them in the beginning or chose to ignore them until it cost him too much to ignore. We were never sure." Arian cooked his head to the side. "Does your brother know about them?" Arian motioned for her to follow.

"That is a good question," Collette replied after a pause. "Zephraim was not terribly interested in anything I did as queen. He's not unintelligent, though."

"I will try and be optimistic that he doesn't know about the safehouses, but it would be better to tell Larent and he can be optimistic for me," he said dryly and closed the heavy door. Next to it sat a table with an old oil lamp. Fortunately, it had plenty of fuel to burn, and Arian got a small flame started. He started down the tunnel, the oil lamp held aloft so they could both see. "We managed to find a few Coralian tunnels that were promising. Hopefully, if your brother knows about it, he'll disregard them."

"I'm hoping he's not interested enough in tunnels to even consider them, let alone put in an effort to find them," Collette replied.

They walked down the tunnel before finally coming out into a sunny field beside a line of scrawny trees. Come spring, they would be taller and filled with sweet smelling flowers. Arian doubted they'd be around to see them.

"This is far enough from the wall to be safe, and it's a good meeting place if things don't go as planned. If things go wrong, we'll meet in the safehouse or out here. If you get to the clearing before any of the rest of us do, be smart and hide." He narrowed

his eyes when she opened her mouth to argue. "I've no doubt you have enough skill to protect yourself, but it's risky to take chances you do not need to take."

"You're right," Collette replied with a long sigh.

"I am," he agreed. "If we head back now, we can probably get back to the inn before Tolan and Larent manage to kill each other."

"It will be disappointing if that happens," Collette said with a nod. They began the walk back, this trek less interesting.

"Disappointing for you, maybe," he said with an evil little smirk.

"Are you suggesting you wouldn't miss the constant stream of bickering?"

Arian tilted his head in consideration. "They spend too much time squabbling when they really need to be silent, which causes me to spend too much time contemplating slitting both their throats. So, yes and no."

"I think it would be quite sad if that happened," Collette said after a moment. "We should endeavor to come up with alternative ways to handle the situation."

"I'll wait for you to become exasperated enough to ask me to stab them," he countered.

"That might be a valid response, actually," Collette said with a laugh.

Chapter Thirteen

Nawalya leaned into Whyldon as they walked through the market. Her hands wrapped gently around his left arm as she basked in being close to him. Her head was blessedly silent as they walked through the semi-crowded marketplace, her eyes darting from stall to stall as she took in their wares, breathing in his scent as she did.

Whyldon's relaxed expression and posture pleased her. He needed to relax and enjoy moments when he could.

"You know, this is the most normal I've felt since we escaped Quenall," Whyldon commented as they strolled.

"I'm glad. I know all this has been stressful for you," she replied softly.

"I think it has been stressful on everyone," Whyldon replied as they walked. "And I imagine it will continue to be so."

"Larent would tell you this is normal for us, but I agree with you." She gave a small laugh, then made an "oh" noise and dragged Whyldon to a stall where fabric, golden trinkets, and beautiful dresses were for sale.

Nawalya moved slowly but methodically through the dresses, twice holding a dress up in Whyldon's direction without waiting for him to give any opinion. Her excitement was palpable, and she would have to be diligent to only buy things she absolutely couldn't do without. Eventually, she settled on a beautiful pale blue gown, even though she didn't have an occasion to wear it. She happily handed over gold to the vendor, and then carefully folded the dress and wrapped it in spare cloth so she could tuck it into her pack. Satisfied with her purchase, she took Whyldon's arm and led him onward.

They walked in companionable silence; even with Nawalya's high spirits, she was content to enjoy the bright sun and her closeness to Whyldon. Still, she looked up at his handsome, tanned face, noting the concerned lines etched around his eyes. "You are worried about Collette," she observed.

"I usually am," Whyldon acknowledged. He sighed and shook his head. "She doesn't say it, but she is struggling. She keeps so much of it bottled up because she knows others have high expectations of her."

"I've observed that," Nawalya said. Despite all the loss Collette had suffered, she'd approached their impromptu road trip with a positive, carefree outlook many of lesser rank would never have considered. "It's not a new development, though. What's renewed your worry?"

"What is it you believe I am worrying about specifically?" he asked her.

"I'm not sure," Nawalya admitted. "Sometimes, when she's playing around with Larent, flirting with Tolan, or sitting around with us when we are making plans, you get this very concerned look on your face."

"I admit, I wonder how much longer she's going to be able to balance Larent and Tolan, given how much they dislike one another."

"I've been wondering how long it will take her to realize Larent has developed … feelings."

"She is rather intuitive," Whyldon said. "She hasn't said anything to me, but she likely already knows."

Nawalya tilted her head as they continued browsing carts and stalls. She approached a group of children and twitched her fingers in a specific pattern, smiling slightly when one of the older teens returned the gesture.

"I wonder why she flirts back with Larent," she dared. "Especially when Tolan is around. I suppose it's possible neither have told her the source of their animosity, but still. Do you think she enjoys the attention? The freedom all this has offered her?"

They passed a rather odious noble and frowned as he became far too familiar with a shopkeeper. She gently guided Whyldon closer, and with fingers light as air, she relieved the noble of his coin purse. It was dropped near another group of children soon after.

Whyldon said nothing, though she knew he'd watched the act of thievery. Nawalya even smiled as he continued their conversation.

"My understanding is that she's heard several versions of what happened between Tolan and Larent. As for her intentions? I don't know that what she is doing with Larent is flirting. She's always been very playful. I'm happy to see some of that showing again."

"Larent might consider it flirting," Nawalya pointed out. She paused and looked in the window of a shop, admiring the knives glimmering behind the glass. "I'm also willing to bet the summaries she has heard are drastically different from one another. She should ask Arian, if she wants the entire story."

"Perhaps she should," Whyldon agreed as Nawalya led him into the shop. "But perhaps it is an issue that she will need to work out with Larent and Tolan all the same," he said in quieter tones.

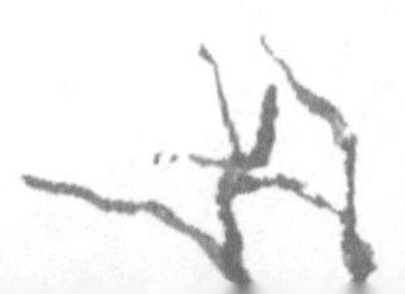

"I'm unsure how she would get them to talk considering they can barely be around each other without throwing insults or punches." Nawalya selected an iron knife with a polished bone handle. She knew Arian would love it, and since Larent would also need a gift, she picked up a leather-bound kit of woodworking tools. She paid the shopkeeper with a broad grin, and they left the shop.

"You could speak with her," Whyldon pointed out, resuming the conversation. "I do know she is unreasonably in love with Tolan. I doubt she has intentions of hurting him."

"It's her I worry about in regard to Tolan," Nawalya said, guiltily biting her bottom lip. Still, she persisted. "Tolan does not have the best track record, and I don't mean with Larent. I know he truly cares for her, but things happen."

She led him to another stall, this one advertising the sale of the medicinal and magical. As she looked over the vials, she started to touch certain ones. Making eye contact with the shop owner, she smiled and held up a blue potion. When he handed it back to her in a protective bag, it was heavier than it should have been. A quick glance inside showed a brand new lockpicking set in addition to the potions. Gifts for Collette acquired, she stepped away from the stall before stopping suddenly.

"I don't know what to buy you," she said slightly confused.

"You don't have to buy me anything," Whyldon said, his smile soft and warm. "I am getting to spend an afternoon with you. What more could I want?"

Nawalya pouted a bit, or at least that was what she was trying for, but she wasn't very good at pouting, thanks to Arian. "I am enjoying spending time with you as well, but I would like to buy you something," she said as she walked to one of the bread stalls and bought Tolan one of the sweet breads he liked.

Chapter Thirteen

"And what ideas do you have, since I know you will not be dissuaded?"

Nawalya stared at Whyldon for a moment. "Your cloak is looking a little worse for wear. I could replace that or get you a new whetstone for your sword." She made a thoughtful noise as she absent-mindedly grabbed another coin purse from a passing merchant, then handed it off to the next child she saw. "Or I could get you some of the stew from the baker that is tasty. You really liked Diana's stew."

"I hate to tell you, we all look like we have been traveling, and mostly on foot," Whyldon said with a gentle chuckle.

"I know, but a good coat can keep you warmer than a blanket on cold nights," Nawalya said, speaking from experience.

"The nights are growing colder and will become more so if we are here for long," Whyldon conceded.

Nawalya paused and pressed her lips together, reaching out with her powers to see if she might be able to see how long they would reside there before remembering herself and pulling back. Her sight wasn't foolproof. It could show her anything, and she was already seeing visions of Collette's death. She didn't need more uncertainty now.

Decided on Whyldon's gift, Nawalya led them this way and that before she found a seller with gorgeous leather coats. She picked her way through the options before settling on a dark charcoal-colored duster lined with what appeared to be rabbit fur. "What do you think of this?" she asked.

"It's quite beautiful," Whyldon said as he looked over the coat. He felt the leather between thumb and forefinger and nodded his approval. Nawalya clapped her hands together in excitement and urged him to try it out.

He obeyed and slid his arms into the well-made jacket. He looked quite handsome in it, and she was moved to run her hands along his shoulders and down his chest as though testing

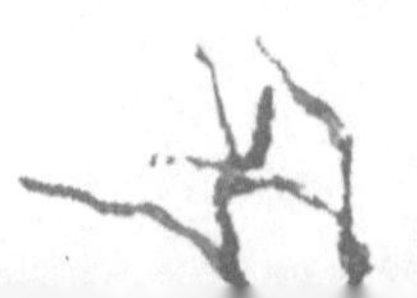

the fit. When their eyes met, there was no uncertainty of their deeper connection. She regretfully stepped back and handed over coins to the merchant.

She laced her fingers with Whyldon as they walked away, understanding what he meant when he said this was the most normal he'd felt in a long time. She felt that way too. "We have one more errand to run while we are out," she said, looking up at him. "I need to show you our meeting place should things go wrong, and we get separated."

"Which you mentioned before we started this journey," Whyldon said with a smile. "Lead the way."

Nawalya smiled again, raised up on her toes, and kissed his cheek. She came to a stop and tilted her head as she observed Whyldon's features. "She has your nose."

Whyldon's response was not immediate, and the firm press of his lips demonstrated he knew who "she" was. He finally nodded. "She does," he agreed simply. "And Adora's eyes."

Adora had been the young bride of King Sargarus, and despite the evils of his reign, Adora had been well-loved. She exemplified kindness, warmth, and charity, and to this day, Whyldon still heard comparisons to the Mother, the patron goddess of Quenall.

"I see," Nawalya said softly.

"It's probably best that we ignore the connection," Whyldon said very quietly. "She'd be in more danger."

"I have no plans to mention this to anyone else," Nawalya quickly promised. "I wouldn't have noticed if I did not watch you as closely as I do." She blushed slightly. "But I will say nothing. Not even to Arian."

"I appreciate that," Whyldon said, letting out a breath. "Of course, Arian might not keep secrets, should he ever learn."

"Arian wouldn't say anything, nor would Larent, but it's best if the people who know remain few and far between. As you said, it would put her in more danger, though she might be happier," Nawalya said. "Not having to be queen."

"She would be," Whyldon agreed. "She's never been treated especially well by many in the court, likely because Sargarus didn't treat her well. And the Mother knows I can't blame her. Being at the palace was not my plan. At least, not until she was a reality."

He sighed and prompted them to start walking again. That was the smart move, and Nawalya gently directed them while he spoke. "Collette has inherited a lot from me, including my inability to walk away from a problem she thinks she can help repair."

"I cannot imagine treating your children the way Sargarus did. Taking everything the king is guilty of into account, the way he treated Collette, and even Zephraim, should have shown people how much of a monster he was," Nawalya said hotly.

"Sargarus had a worldview that did not include kindness or love, not even for his children," Whyldon explained. "He practiced a great deal of negligence with both Zephraim and Collette during their early lives. Only when Collette became useful in negotiations did he become interested."

"That man never should have been allowed to rule. Did he not have a brother or another sibling?" she asked, unable to remember.

"He did, but he was the oldest of the legitimate children. He had the legal right to rule, and he had support."

"You would think one of the younger siblings would have attempted to remove him once his nature showed. I would have killed him, had I the chance," she declared.

"I did have the chance," Whyldon said, not a hint of remorse in his voice.

Nawalya froze, wide-eyed at the words. "You killed the king?"

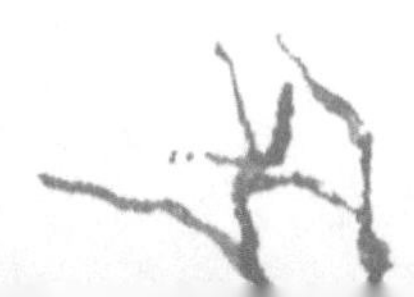

Whyldon nodded. "He took a riding crop to Collette when she refused to marry Brath. I was angered, as you can imagine."

They grew quiet as they turned onto a street of fine homes that were so unlike anything Nawalya would have for herself. Flashy and enormous, she could not imagine any real warmth in most of them. Still, they had their uses, and the one she wanted was an excellent safehouse. As the intended home appeared in the distance, Nawalya took the opportunity to show Whyldon the knock that would get them inside. He was a quick study, as she knew he would be.

They were let into the home by a blonde woman who did not meet their eyes, and Nawalya showed Whyldon to the kitchen and down into the hideaway. Once down the steps, she muttered to herself, "I'm tired of waiting," before turning to launch herself at Whyldon, her lips finding his in an impassioned kiss. Pulling away, she looked up to meet his gaze. "Apparently, I find the idea of you killing that monster extremely attractive."

"Apparently," Whyldon echoed, as he pulled her against him for another kiss.

Chapter Fourteen

Larent waved at a pretty shopkeeper with thick waves of auburn hair as he and Tolan made their way down the cobbled street. The day was sunny, the city nice, but Larent's company was more than enough to sour his mood.

"Let me guess, you've fucked her while her husband was out, right?" Tolan sneered and regretted it immediately. He didn't have to be so hostile to Larent.

"Nope, but I would," Larent quipped, his voice a little too cheery. That was never a good sign. "I mean, she's pretty enough, but if it doesn't involve a job, why would I?"

"Because you fuck anything that moves," Tolan returned. "You have ever since I've met you."

"That's a fucking lie, and you know it. If it's not for a job, I rarely sleep with people I don't—" Larent cut himself off and took a deep breath through his nose.

"Yeah. We can pretend that's true," Tolan retorted.

"You're only saying that because you can't stand how Collette looks at me sometimes. As if she knows I would be a much better fuck than you." He gave a derisive laugh. "I'm already more useful to her out of bed. Maybe she's finally wising up and looking for your replacement."

Larent let out a harsh rush of air as Tolan slammed him into the stone wall of the nearest building. The continuous comments and jabs about his lack of suitability for Collette had finally made him snap. "I am so sick and tired of your mouth," Tolan growled out as he slammed Larent against the wall again.

"You love my mouth, especially when I'm on my knees. You used to beg for it," Larent replied, smirking.

Tolan shook the other man, his anger growing. "Shut up! Shut your damn mouth. I get that you're angry at me, but it's been years. Grow the fuck up and get over it."

Larent laughed. "You're such a worthless piece of shit."

"I am not worthless! Collette knows it, and so do I." He faltered a bit on the last part and Larent, of course, caught it.

"You want me to grow up and get over it? I told you I loved you, and what was your reaction? To bed me and abandon me while I slept." Larent gave a bitter laugh. "That's the thing, Tolan. You are worthless, and it's got fuck all to do with your birth rank or any of the shit you get yourself worked up about. You're fucking worthless because all you do is kill, use, and leave. You did that before we were together, and you've done it ever since you left me. You'll do it to her, too." Larent pushed against Tolan's hands, but Tolan held firm, keeping him in place. He knew Larent wanted to stay in Collette's good graces, which would prevent Larent's claws from coming out.

"You didn't love me. You don't even know what love means," Tolan growled out. "You had never been in love before, and you mistook lust and our connection for more than it was."

"No. You don't get to invalidate my feelings, you fucking asshole." Larent pushed against Tolan's hands once more, then stopped struggling. His eyes shot to Collette's bracelet on Tolan's wrist, and the wolf leered. "I know Collette wanted to tell everyone she was in love with you. I also know you told her no, again and again. You refused to let her publicly acknowledge your relationship, and I don't think it was to protect her. I think it was so you could bail when the time was right, when this got to be too much. Just in time to avoid facing the consequences again."

Past the point of anger, Tolan balled up a fist and raised it in the air.

"Hit me," Larent dared him, his voice a jeering taunt. "The others might get why, but she'll be so fucking disappointed in you when I come back with a black eye or worse."

For a second Tolan saw red, but he forced himself to take a deep breath and drop his fist. Larent was right. He couldn't hit the shifter, no matter how much he wanted to.

Taking another deep breath, he loosened his grip on Larent only to find himself slammed against the opposite wall, a clawed hand wrapped around his throat. Larent pressed up against him, closer than the two had been in years. Tolan's keen awareness of that closeness was only heightened when he realized one of the shifter's legs rested between his own. He swallowed hard as a new emotion smothered his anger. Something deep and raw.

Larent pressed closer, so close that it would have been nothing to brush their lips together. Their eyes locked, and Tolan licked his lips with anticipation. Something Larent must have noticed as his gaze focused on his mouth.

"This is familiar," Larent breathed out in a harsh, husky whisper. "You used to love it when I held you like this. When I fucked you hard, Nawalya and Arian asleep in the next room. Maybe that's why you're throwing me around so much. Not because you're upset, or because you think I'm right, but because you desperately miss my cock." He paused, as though considering the options, and his eyes traveled back up to meet Tolan's. "Sorry for you, I'm no longer interested." He tightened his grip for a second and felt Tolan catch his breath, both in terror and arousal. "Throw me around like that again, and I will fucking gut you."

Larent turned from him and stalked down the alley. "Let's go," he eventually called back. "I have to finish showing you the safehouse."

Tolan took a steadying breath and brushed himself off. Only then did he feel prepared to follow after Larent, hoping he didn't come off as overly eager. The two walked in silence towards the safehouse. Larent showed him the knock only once, knowing Tolan wouldn't need to see it a second time, thanks to their long history.

"Why were we paired up together?" Tolan finally asked once they reached the house.

"Because Nawalya wanted to spend time with Whyldon and Arian didn't want me alone with Collette," Larent bit out before knocking. They were quiet as they were let in and quickly walked through the kitchen. Pulling away the barrel, Larent tilted his head to the side. "Arian's already been here." He opened the hatch to go down into the safe room and stopped as a distinct female groan reached his ears. "That's Nawalya..." he said, looking at Tolan in abject horror.

They remained in place, debating what to do. Only when a masculine grunt echoed from below did Tolan issue a directive. "Close it, close it, close it," Tolan mouthed in a panic. Larent obeyed and hastily returned the barrel to its correct location. That done, the two stared at each other again.

"Upstairs window is the emergency escape," Larent croaked out.

"Let's use that instead," Tolan agreed, feeling as flustered as Larent sounded. "I assume the layout of... down there is the same as always."

"Yep," Larent responded, and he motioned for Tolan to follow him toward the emergency exit. Their silence, this time, was not due to unresolved anger.

When they burst into Collette's room at the inn a quarter hour later, their frenzy hadn't died. Arian quickly rose from the table, hand on his blade. "What's wrong?" he demanded as he moved quickly to the door and investigated the hallway. Collette remained seated on the bed, legs crossed as she leisurely browsed the pages of a book.

"I need to wash out my ears and scrub my brain!" Larent declared dramatically, waiting for Arian to secure the door before throwing himself at the elf in a dramatic fashion, his arms encircling Arian around the shoulders.

Tolan, his own face slightly white in general horror, made his way to Collette. "Whyldon and Nawalya were having sex in the safe room," he explained with slightly fewer dramatics.

Arian snorted and pushed Larent off. "You're still alive which tells me you didn't walk in on them."

"Yes, but now we know what Whyldon sounds like when having sex!" Larent cried out.

"And we know what you sound like having sex, so what's the problem?" Arian asked.

"I'm not Whyldon or Nawalya!" Larent said.

"I don't exactly want to know what the two of them having sex sounds like, together or otherwise," Collette said with a snort of laughter. "But was it that traumatizing?"

"Yes!" Tolan and Larent said at the same time.

Larent threw himself into a chair. "I mean, we knew what Nawalya sounded like already, but Whyldon? I will never be able to make eye contact with him again."

"I'm in hiding with children," Collette said, amusement sparkling in her brown eyes.

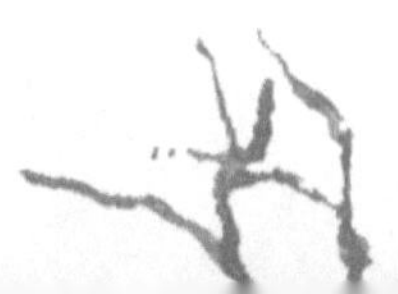

"Can we not talk about sex with Nawalya or Whyldon please?" Tolan asked.

"He's just jealous because he hasn't slept with Nawalya. Neither have you, for that matter, Freckles," Larent said with a grin.

"Larent, shut up," Arian demanded in a dark tone.

"I was just going to tell Freckles about you and Nawalya," Larent insisted with a cheeky grin. "Imagine this. Baby Arian and Baby Nawalya…"

That was as far as he got before Arian roared and launched himself at Larent, who had moved close enough to the door to be able to throw it open and dive behind it, using it as a shield between himself and a homicidal elf.

"Bye!" he yelled as he took off down the hallway, Arian hot on his heels.

"What was that about children again?" Tolan asked.

"You don't think that display was childish?" Collette asked him.

"I think that was Larent letting off steam after the two of us were forced into close proximity for too long and somehow didn't kill each other," Tolan said. "It could also be to distract himself from what we heard, or he could just be stirring shit up for fun. It's Larent, so who knows." He cuddled up next to her. "How was your time with Arian?"

"It was an hour with Arian," Collette replied as she leaned against Tolan. "Efficient, mostly silent."

"Sounds like Arian." He pulled her closer and took the opportunity to press his nose against her sweet-smelling hair. "They won't be back for a while. I could lock and bar the door," he offered, a husky growl in his voice.

"Weren't you traumatized just a moment ago?" she asked, her tone teasing.

Chapter Fourteen

"I still am, but how often do we get time alone in a room with a bed?" he asked, nuzzling her neck. "Besides, if I was going to replace those horrible sounds with anything, I would like it to be you screaming my name."

"Then go lock the door so I can help you recover," she said and pulled him in for a heated kiss, only nudging him to make sure they had privacy when they broke apart.

Tolan stood and in short order had the door locked. "Where were we?" he growled and pounced on her.

Chapter Fifteen

Collette Venora Josselyn Gaillane, Queen of Coralia,

It would be my honor to host you in my palace tomorrow. I look forward to seeing you and discussing the future of our kingdoms.

Sincerely,
His Royal Majesty, King Brath

It was dinner time when the letter arrived, and Collette unsealed the envelope with a hastiness she normally didn't feel. She skimmed the page. The long, narrow, constricted letters made it necessary to read a little slower, but a second read through confirmed the invitation. "We're in," she declared, passing the letter across the table to Arian.

"Simple and straight to the point," Arian said with approval. Somehow, the efficiency of the letter appealing to Arian didn't surprise Collette. "We just have to hope everything else is just as simple," he added as he handed the letter to Nawalya.

She shook her head, sighed, and leaned away from it towards Whyldon. Whyldon, in turn, snaked an arm around her, which Nawalya took as an invitation to rest her head against his shoulder.

Giving her a dark look, Arian reached into his pack and pulled out a bottle with purple liquid in it. He handed it over with a look Collette had come to learn meant he'd be obeyed, or he'd force it down Nawalya's throat. "Eat and then get to bed," Arian said in a voice that was only marginally warmer.

"I'm fine," Nawalya insisted softly. She uncorked the potion, drank it with a grimace, and went back to her plate.

Arian watched her for another minute before turning back to Collette. "What time should we leave tomorrow?"

"Early, I'd imagine," she said. "We are guests, and he knows that I am in need of some assistance. So, after sunrise and before noon, I'd think."

"Sounds good," came his terse response.

"We should do what we can to mitigate signs of struggle on our part," Whyldon suggested after finishing a gulp of ale. "You especially," he directed to Collette.

"You mean he won't like my dusty, worn boots?" she asked with a playful grin.

"He probably would be less enamored with them than you are," Whyldon returned, eyes crinkled in amusement.

"I can help with some of that," Nawalya said. Her own pack hung on the back of her chair, and after retrieving it, she pulled out a package and handed it over so it could be passed down to Collette. "It shouldn't take much alteration," she said and waited expectantly for Collette to open it.

Not seeing a reason to object, Collette unwrapped it to find a beautiful blue dress. She couldn't help but remember the

conversation she and Arian had shared about her collection earlier in the day. "This is beautiful, Nawalya. I can make it work."

Nawalya smiled in response, and she began passing out parcels to each member of the group at the table with renewed happiness.

They settled back into their meal, and Collette was happy to avoid further talk of plans or eventualities. Going into this without any good idea of their reception should have worried her. For now, it did not.

The inn was quiet and dark, though lanterns dotted the hallway for those who needed to leave their rooms for whatever reason. Larent used the meager light to his advantage as he crept along the hall, listening for anyone who might surprise him. Even with the obligations they had the following morning, he and Arian had plans that night, separate though they were.

He stopped briefly outside of the room shared by Whyldon and Nawalya, pleased that they both slept. Nawalya needed an untroubled evening, and Whyldon's easy sleep meant that he had not spent the evening coaxing Nawayla into a peaceful rest.

Quietly, Larent continued, passing several doors until he was in front of the one occupied by Collette and Tolan. He paused to listen, and like before, noted the occupants were already asleep. He briefly considered letting the queen rest, but thought better of it, knowing Tolan wouldn't be disturbed by his knocks. The man was a heavy sleeper, and it took much more to rouse him.

He tapped the door a couple of times and quietly celebrated as new movement sounded from inside. When the door opened, Collette appeared, her eyelids heavy and her long hair down and mussed from sleep. Lady, she was beautiful.

He grinned and held a finger to his mouth, then motioned for her to follow him. To his surprise, she did. He let himself back into the room he shared with Arian, then closed the door once Collette had joined them.

The elf was dressed in leathers Larent knew Collette hadn't seen before, all black with dark buckles, which would be difficult to spot at night. He was pulling his blond hair back into a ponytail, so the light color would be hidden by a cloak. There was a small grappling hook and rope hanging on his left side, potion bottles on his right, and knives tucked everywhere.

Spotting letters on the bedside table, Larent picked them up. "I knew you'd grab a couple." He skimmed the first one but the second had his face darkening. "Shit. You've got a plan for this?" he asked Arian.

"The first target is easy," Arian said. "He should be at the tavern listed on the note. Timed right, I will catch him before he can hurt someone on his way home." He looked to Collette and nodded, which was much nicer a greeting than Larent had expected from him. "Your Majesty."

Collette, who stood by the door with her arms crossed, didn't ask him to elaborate, but she nodded in return.

"What about the other?" Larent prompted.

"The second target is harder. He lives in the wealthy quarter near the market. He'll have guards."

Larent sighed. "We could just leave this for the next group who passes through."

"We could," Arian agreed. "But it could be months before anyone else comes, and I don't feel comfortable leaving women, children, and anyone who looks vaguely elfish to suffer at his hands."

Larent nodded. "Time frame?"

"Two hours, two and a half at the most. If I'm not back—"

"I'm coming to get you," Larent said in a tone leaving no room for argument.

"Fine," Arian said.

Larent's eyes went to Collette. "No complaints? Not gonna stop him?"

Collette's brow rose. In a deadpan, she said, "No. Wait. Stop."

Arian actually smiled, though briefly, then quickly rechecked his supplies before slipping out the window.

"Well fuck," Larent breathed.

"Was there a reason I needed to come see this exchange?" Collette asked, causing Larent to look back at her.

"I thought you'd be interested to see a little deeper into what we do when we aren't escorting," he said. "Are you?'

"I am," she admitted. "But now I'm wondering what happens if he gets caught."

Larent believed her, noting the furrowed brow and slight frown. "He won't get caught," he promised. "But if he does, I'll go get him out. A lot more people will die, but we'll get out, and no one will be able to identify us. In a worst-case scenario, they won't be able to link him back to us. There are people out there who handle such things."

An explanation given, Larent got on the bed and stretched out, patting the empty space next to him.

Collette crossed the room and took a seat on the bed. "So, imagine he is seen, and recognized, or you are. Then what?"

"He will be wearing a mask to better conceal himself," Larent explained. "He won't have slipped it on until he was outside. All three of us have them. They aren't foolproof, but they are another layer of protection." He gave her a wry smile, wondering how she'd react, and when she gave her answer, he was a little surprised.

"Okay. I'm just going to say this. You realize all of this sneaking around and secretive stuff the three of you are involved in looks very suspicious, right?"

"Yup." Larent popped the "p." He surveyed her for a moment, then decided to be frank with her. "We are here for you, and we support you. We will protect you until our dying breaths. I swear we will. I will. But to be honest, Freckles, I've been wondering why you trust us as much as you do." He had to look away, knowing his eyes showed something very open and raw with his confession. "You know so little about us, our lives and motivations. Yet, you've willingly put your life in our hands. You've got to know that even though we try our best, we aren't good people. Despite that, here you are in a room alone with me." He shook his head. "I could hurt you. I mean, you've seen the wolf, and yet you're still here. I don't understand it."

"I have my reasons," she said, though her words came slower than he'd expected them to. She met his gaze, and though it was hard to look her in the eye, he thought he saw something in her expression, something unguarded and honest. And just maybe, a little yearning. "If we're talking about the basic facts and you intended to hurt me, you've had ample opportunity. How many times have you and I been alone? How many opportunities have the three of you had to hurt me or Whyldon?" She tilted her head. "Would you prefer I be afraid of you?"

"Lady, no," he breathed out roughly. The very thought of her being afraid of him caused a pang in his chest so acute that he had to consciously choose to not rub it. "You are so different from everyone else. I just want to understand." He reached out and brushed a strand of hair behind her ear.

"How am I different?" she asked, the question further surprising him.

Larent shifted closer to her. "Do we want to start with how smart you are? How kind, compassionate, and beautiful? Or I could begin with the more important ways?"

"And what are those?" she asked.

"You're selfless to a fault," he began. He loved that about her, but he also knew that, eventually, it would be to her own detriment. More than it already had been.

"And?" she asked. "A lot of people are."

"No other ruler would have put Jayden Drake's life above their own. You're not afraid of me or what I can do, and the number of people who aren't afraid of me could be counted on one hand. You treat Nawalya like a person, even knowing what she can do. You're kind to Arian despite his being a prickly fuck. We won't even touch on how you handled Thomas Fletcher."

"Thomas Fletcher was funny and not always wrong."

"True, but most people wouldn't have tolerated him. Or trusted the help he offered the night you escaped." She didn't argue it, so Larent continued. "One of the other things that's struck me is that instead of rage-plotting the murder of your brother, you're mourning his loss. And yes, before you ask, it's obvious. You also made the hard decision to leave your kingdom instead of engaging in a bloody battle. Arian and I would have brutally murdered those who stood against you, if that was what you had wanted. You're just so inherently good and kind when the way you were raised should have made you anything but."

When she didn't respond, Larent wondered if he'd said too much. His words might have been too overwhelming for her to accept. He knew everything she was dealing with, everything she had to consider. At least, everything that seemed obvious to him.

"You actually see me," she quietly observed.

"I do," he confirmed a little too eagerly. "I don't understand how others can't when you're so open and honest about yourself and with yourself. I know I'd do anything to keep you safe, shady or not."

"Why?"

"Because you're worth it," he breathed out. A new kind of longing cemented itself in Larent, just as strong as his earlier pull toward Tolan had been, but different and inspired by completely different parts of his soul. He wondered what it would be like to reach for her, to pull her to him, to show her the kind of adoration she deserved. Was this wishful thinking, or was she leaning towards him, wanting the same thing?

His temptation to touch her would have won out had a crashing, followed by raucous laughter, not sounded from below. He looked down, his face feeling a little heated. "Sounds like we're missing out on a party," he said.

"It does," Collette agreed.

He felt the weight shift on the bed and looked up to see that she'd stood. That was probably for the best.

"I should probably go back to bed."

He forced a playful grin on his face. "You sure? You could stick around and ask more questions about our shady dealings."

"As much fun as I know that would be," she said, her voice sincere, if a little reflective, "we have a very long, mysterious day ahead of us. There will be ample time for you to tell me about your shadiness later."

"That I will," he agreed. "Go get some sleep, Freckles. I'm gonna wait up for Chuckles."

"Maybe he won't be gone most of the night," she said before she reached out and rested a hand on his shoulder, giving it a gentle squeeze. "Get what sleep you can."

"If he's gone too much longer, I'll go after him," Larent promised. He reached up, put a hand on hers, and gave it a squeeze back.

"Goodnight, Larent," she said and let her hand drop.

"Night, Freckles." He watched her until the door closed, listening as her light steps faded back to her room. He bowed his head again, letting out a sigh of frustration. "Stupid fucking wolf." Closing his eyes for a second, he pulled out his figure of the Lady and sent up a silent prayer for Arian before going back on watch.

Chapter Sixteen

"Are you certain you want to do this?" Whyldon asked as they approached the castle, Collette on horseback while the rest walked, flanking her sides. Arian had deemed the distinction necessary, and the effect provided a little more ceremony than they had been accustomed to in the past weeks.

"About as certain as I've been about anything else we've done so far," Collette replied. The alterations she'd made to Nawalya's dress had worked well, and she looked every bit the regal queen. The blue was very becoming to her complexion, and her hair, though simply styled with a few decorative plaits, looked neater and more refined than the loose knot she'd kept it in while on the road. She'd arrive to King Brath's meeting perfectly groomed and presentable, free of the dust and grime from the streets. As they drew closer to the palace, she was thankful for the shallow support her appearance gave her.

"Don't worry," Nawalya said. She reached over and took Whyldon's hand. "Worst case scenario, we have to get back on the road sooner than we planned." Her tone was bright, and Collette hoped she was actually optimistic rather than comforting.

"I don't like this," Arian grumbled. "What happens when he decides to hold you prisoner until Zephraim can ride up with his soldiers? There's a bounty on your head."

"She managed to break out of prison on her own before," Larent said.

"I did," Collette replied. "I could probably figure it out again."

"See? Freckles isn't dainty. She's got this," Larent said with a grin.

"Yes," Arian quipped sarcastically. "I'm concerned over how dainty she is. That's the issue."

"You're just upset because she asked you not to stab anyone," Tolan muttered.

"And you're bitchy because you're just supposed to stand there and look pretty," Larent quipped.

"Shut up," Arian snapped irritably. "Can we get through one day without you two fighting?"

"Please," Collette added, gently pulling the reins of her horse and bringing him to a stop. They had a good twenty-minute journey ahead of them, but this nonsense needed to be settled now. "Believe it or not, this is more than a little nerve-wracking, and I can't keep calm while you two snipe at each other."

"Sorry," they said at the same time, studiously avoiding eye contact with one another.

"Thank you," she said and let out a breath. "Any other arguments anyone wants to get out before we continue?"

Arian opened his mouth to say something, but before words could appear, Nawalya placed a hand firmly over his mouth and gave him a look.

"Ignore Chuckles. He's going to complain no matter what we do. Might as well see this to the end. I mean–" Larent motioned towards Collette, gesturing to all of her. "You look amazing in that dress."

Chapter Sixteen

"An opinion you should probably keep to yourself, when we arrive," Whyldon said, letting out his own sigh.

"I'm beginning to think you don't like me, Captain." Larent said cheekily.

They arrived at the palace without fanfare. The castle was older, surrounded by a wall of dark, porous stone. It seemed foreign to the wet, inland climate of Catillatio, but Collette wasn't there to judge the architecture.

After crossing a long, narrow bridge, the security gate was raised, and the party welcomed onto the grounds. Guards, nobles, and palace courtiers, all dressed in silvers and vivid golds, greeted them with genuine enthusiasm which only served to put Collette more on guard. She nodded to the crowd in acknowledgement, then briefly froze as she spotted a familiar face: King Brath.

Brath had always been a tall man, though he'd bulked up in the seven years since Collette had last seen him. He was, as he had been, quite handsome. Smiling at her, his straight white teeth teased a predatory nature beneath the friendly facade. His dark blond hair was longer and wavy, and reminded her a little of Arian's. The dark green eyes lacked the sullen elf's warmth, and this was all the more emphasized by the sharp angles of his nose and chin.

Collette didn't miss the subtle changes in formation from her companions. Arian's disinterest didn't disappear as he moved to join Whyldon, and Larent kept the smile on his face even as he stepped closer to Collette.

Tolan eyed the king and his guards as he offered his hand to Collette so she could dismount. It was a gesture they both knew she didn't need, but Collette appreciated the slight squeeze of his hand. When she was on her feet, Tolan gave a shallow bow then took control of the reins.

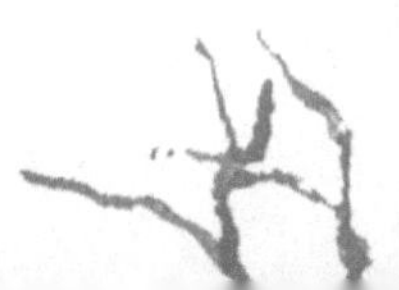

"Greetings, Queen Collette," King Brath welcomed. He inclined his head in a sign of respect before closing the distance between them. Placing hands on either side of her arms, he offered a kiss to both cheeks. He let his hands linger for several seconds longer before finally dropping to his sides. "I must say, you're even lovelier than I recall. I cannot wait to see how becoming you are after rest from your long travels.

"Thank you for your warm welcome, King Brath," Collette greeted, the placid smile she wore to disguise her true feelings of anxious disgust expertly placed. "And thank you for your compliment. Fortunately, the journey north was quite pleasant. My party," she motioned in the general direction of the five, ''provided good company and entertainment. I could not have asked for more."

"Indeed, they must have," Brath agreed. "If I recall, you have always held your companions to a high standard."

Collette nodded. "I cannot disagree with that assessment."

"If I recall, even I was not deemed worthy," King Brath added.

"I am simply grateful that you were not negatively affected by the rumblings in my kingdom such a union would have ensured," she said. "We have been fortunate."

King Brath agreed, his lips pressed into a thin smile. "Still, I cannot help but wonder if the coup would have happened had we followed through with your father's arrangements. Surely, a strong, supportive army would have crushed the uprising."

"I find it best to avoid speculation about things we can never truly know," Collette countered. "I prefer to deal with the realities of the situation."

"Then let us deal with realities," Brath responded. "Are you still unmarried?"

Several seconds of silence followed while Collette quickly put together a lie. She didn't have to say anything though, as Larent stepped forward.

"Happily, her Majesty is taken," he said with surprisingly genuine warmth.

Brath frowned, clearly not having expected the answer. His jaw worked as he considered the news, and his handsome features suddenly brought a cow chewing cud to mind for Collette. She smiled back at Larent, and she hoped her wild surprise at what Larent had just done wasn't obvious to Brath. She would have to have strong words with her friend when they were alone. "Yes," Collette confirmed. "This is my husband, Larent, Prince-Consort of Coralia."

"I see," Brath finally said. "Congratulations." He said nothing else to her but turned to one of the senior members of the court, a designation marked by the unmistakable presence of Merscales glittering from her sleeves. "Lady Marine, please see Her Majesty and her party to their chambers. I am sure they are in need of rest and good food."

"Of course, Your Majesty," Marine replied, dipping into a shallow courtesy. Collette took in the slight woman, pale skin with hair so blonde, it was nearly white.

His orders given, Brath turned back to Collette. "We shall meet this evening to discuss the details of your situation, and what we might do to resolve it, yes?"

"I look forward to it, King Brath. In the meantime, thank you dearly for the hospitality you have shown." She offered him another smile, doing her best to ignore the ugly red spreading across Tolan's cheeks, and allowed herself to be led inside.

"Is there anything else you need at this time?" an eager young man dressed in fine silver and gold threads asked. He was young, perhaps fifteen, but he seemed happy and well-fed. That was potentially a good sign regarding Brath's rule.

Arian shook his head. "We're fine," the elf assured the boy, and Larent was tempted to make up some excuse to leave. He thought better of it, knowing it was best to get this over. So, when the door closed behind the young man, Larent locked it, and leaned against it, crossing his arms protectively.

Arian stopped in the middle of the room, breathing slowly and deeply, his usual method of trying to keep calm. Nawalya took up a place between them, copying Larent's stance against a tapestry covered wall. Larent rolled his eyes as the two exchanged looks.

Finally, Nawalya spoke calmly. "Did you step up in order to anger Tolan or because you didn't think Tolan would step up?"

"He wasn't going to step up," Larent replied. "I waited. I counted to twenty before stating she was married, and I damn well gave enough room for him to step in and claim to be her husband. It's not my fault he didn't."

Nawalya put her hands up. "We aren't saying it is. We also aren't mad. We just wanted to understand your reasoning."

"Are you worried Tolan is going to attack me? He touches me, and I'll throw him out of the nearest window," Larent said with a huff, his shoulders slumping. "I had to do something or that ass would have tried to force Collette into a marriage. You saw how he put his hands on her out there."

"Yes, Brath would have forced the issue." Arian confirmed. "And please, for the love of the Spirit, don't throw Tolan out a fucking window."

"You take all the fun out of life," Larent muttered in the growing silence.

"Are you in love with her?" Nawalya asked after a moment, causing Larent to jerk back hard enough to hit his head on the door.

"What? Lady, no," Larent responded quickly. "I mean, she's great. She's beautiful, smart, funny, damn good with a weapon, quick on her feet…" He opened his mouth to say more before trailing off, his eyes looking down at the floor, a frown forming on his face.

Nawalya gave Arian another glance.

"I'm not in love with her, but I do feel … connected to her… drawn to her. But it's not love. I will not make the same mistake I did with Tolan. Never again." Larent said firmly, causing Nawalya and Arian to approach him.

Nawalya put a hand on his chest and Arian a hand on his shoulder. "You didn't make a mistake with Tolan. Love is never a mistake, Larent, even when it ends badly. We just see how you look at her, and if it's not love we feel like it's something that could be love, if allowed to grow. That concerns us. Not because it's wrong, but because she's with Tolan, and we all know how much of a mess everything is between the two of you," Nawalya said gently.

"Spirits, if you and Tolan could work out your shit, I would say woo her together. The queen seems likely enough to enjoy that," Arian said dryly.

"I almost kissed him yesterday, and I feel so fucking stupid because of it," Larent confessed in a near whisper. He leaned into Nawalya who wrapped her arms around him. "Fuck, later that night I almost kissed her." He gave a bitter laugh. "I have feelings for her, and they grow by the day, but I'm still drawn to him, and I hate that. I don't want to care for either of them, not when they are so clearly in love with each other. Sometimes I lash out at him because I want…" He sighed and shook his head. "I want, and I can't. I just can't."

Nawalya held Larent tighter. "We will figure this out," she said softly.

Larent snorted. "I hope you can figure it out in the next few minutes because they placed me in a room with her, alone, with only one bed."

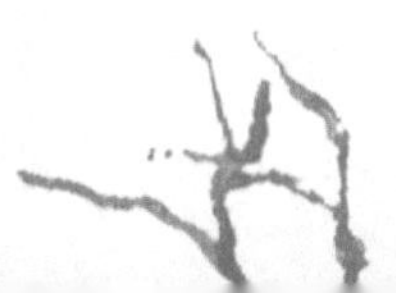

Arian smacked Larent's head. "Sleep on the floor, and keep your hands, mouth and toes to yourself," he said firmly.

"I love how you add toes, like that's one of my kinks." Larent laughed weakly. His face was still pressed into Nawalya's shoulder.

"I'm just covering all the bases," Arian said. "You're too creative for anyone's good."

"Too true," Larent pulled himself away, wiping his face. "I'll behave. Just figure out a way to make it so Tolan doesn't maul me or vice versa," he said heading for the door.

Lady Marine happily lead Collette, Tolan, and Whyldon along a long corridor lined with paintings and lanterns. The décor gave the older castle a warm, welcoming atmosphere. It struck Tolan as strange since Brath had seemed anything but warm. He frowned as he recalled the way the king's hands had lingered on Collette's arms, the move intentional and possessive. It had almost been enough to distract him from Larent's declaration. Almost.

The men accompanied Collette and the attendant to her assigned room under the guise of carrying her sparse luggage and to make sure her companions knew where to find her should she require anything of them. He managed to avoid rage-stomping into the room, even though he knew his anger and frustration must have laced every line of his body.

"This is it," Lady Marine said, motioning around the opulent guest suite Collette had been given.

Tolan could see the entrance into the bedchamber from the door and a separate living area with an ornate desk. He carried Collette's bags to the wardrobe and started unpacking as her attendant expected. Under other circumstances, he knew he'd have been curious to see more of the space. Right now, he was just angry.

"Does Her Majesty require anything else?" Lady Marine asked.

It was Whyldon who spoke up. "Not at this time. We will help her settle so that she might rest for a bit."

"Good. If she does change her mind, the bell can be rung, and someone will come up." Tolan saw Lady Marine gesture, but as she was not in Tolan's direct field of vision, he didn't see exactly where.

The door closed not long after, and he abandoned his show of unpacking to look at Collette. He didn't have a chance to speak before she began.

"I know you're angry," she said.

"I am more than angry," he said in a level tone. "I am going to murder Larent." He began pacing the room, feeling helpless and enraged by his inability to fix the situation.

"Why?" Collette implored. She fell into a plush chair placed in the living room, admittedly looking drained in a way he hadn't expected. "He saved my ass back there."

"You didn't need saving," Tolan argued. "You were more than capable of navigating that situation with diplomacy and tact. He didn't have to declare himself your husband." The last part of his retort was quiet, and Tolan knew he needed to rein in his temper. He wasn't mad at Collette.

"I'm not saying this is the ideal solution, but did you want me to have an argument about whether or not I would marry Brath?" Collette asked him.

The wind wasn't completely taken out of his anger, but the rational part of his brain pointed out that she was right. Tolan, however, wasn't listening to the rational part of his brain. "You would have found a way out of this without a public argument, and we could have come together to figure this out. What he did was impulsive and meant to undermine our relationship—something he's apparently allowed to do again and again."

Collette didn't have the opportunity to respond, as Whyldon took the opportunity. "Without minimizing your relationship with Her Majesty, I would like to point out that in the long run, Larent's actions matter very little. I know what he did is frustrating, but it solved a problem." He looked at Collette. "I did not like how Brath put his hands on you."

"I didn't like it, either," Collette said. "There was a very real threat in those actions."

"Larent's actions matter a lot," Tolan interjected. Why was no one understanding him? And when had Collette become so comfortable with the wolf? Letting his anger simmer, he redirected, knowing he was coming off poorly. "You should not be alone with the king if you can help it."

"I plan to avoid it where possible," Collette said. "It would be the height of stupidity."

"Exactly," Tolan agreed. He sighed, not really wanting to say the next part. "Someone should tell Larent to watch his back. If Brath means to marry you, he seems the type to remove anything he deems a problem." And truthfully, as angry as Tolan was with Larent, Tolan didn't actually want to see the shapeshifter dead.

"I will pass on the message," Whyldon said. He looked at Collette and frowned. "Are you going to be okay?"

"Yes," she said. "I'm just tired, and my head hurts. I'm sure I will be fine by this evening. Afterwards, we should all reconvene to discuss options."

"Of course," Whyldon said. He stood from his seat but paused to put a comforting hand on her shoulder. "Let me know if you need anything."

She offered him a tired smile. "I will." Seemingly satisfied, Whyldon excused himself from the chambers, perhaps to go find the others.

"I should go. After all, your husband is the one who gets to share a room with you," Tolan said bitterly, then with a sigh, apologized. "I'm sorry. This isn't your fault, and I don't mean to take it out on you."

"But you are," she pointed out. "And I have no more control over Larent's actions than you do."

"I know, just like I know he's not really trying to come between us. It just seems like every time I turn around, he's there with you. Or he's saying or doing something to belittle me, and I'm so angry about it." He sighed again, and walked over to where she sat, opening his arms to her. The regret over his behavior in the last fifteen minutes couldn't be put into words, especially with her looking so worn down.

Thankfully, she didn't tell him to leave or ignore him. She lifted herself to her feet and went into his embrace, wrapping her arms around him and pressing her forehead against his shoulder. "I love you," she whispered to him. "Until my dying breath, I will love you, but I need you to trust and support me."

"I love you, too." *But I don't think I'm worthy of you.* The thought stung, but it was true, and he didn't know how to reconcile it with himself.

"Then trust me," she requested. "Nothing Larent says or does will change how I see you or my plan to spend my life with you."

"I do trust you," Tolan insisted.

"Okay," Collette replied. She held onto him for a while longer. "I'm going to go lay down and see if I can ward off this headache. Do you want to come with me?"

"I want to, but I should go. We don't know who is watching this room, and we don't want to cause suspicion." He leaned

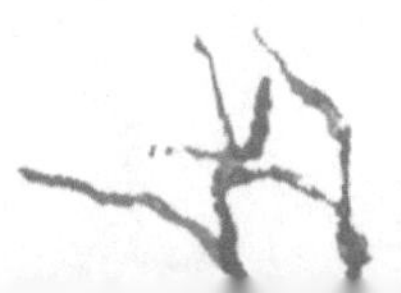

down and gently kissed her lips. She kissed him back, soft and slow, and even when the kiss broke, she pulled Tolan to her for a few more seconds.

"We won't be here long," she reminded him.

"I know," he replied softly. "But for as long as we are, I will miss you every second we aren't together." He lingered a moment longer, then made himself pull away to step outside of her chambers. Closing the door, he looked around. Not spotting anyone, he allowed himself a moment to lean against the door, face buried in his hand.

He should have stepped up, and he had no justification for having not done so. He also knew Larent had waited for him to do as much, and he had to admit to himself that his lack of action was the source of his anger. He'd thought Collette would somehow manage the situation, that she could talk her way out of the problem. She was good at that. She was skillful with words. Still, he should have stepped up. Much like he should be doing more to help. With a sigh, he pushed off the door, hand playing absentmindedly with his necklace. As he sought the others, he wondered what more he could do.

Chapter Seventeen

The evening meeting with Brath was pointless. Not only did they not address the overthrow in Coralia, Brath seemed content to drink and interrogate Collette about her days since fleeing Quenall.

After intense focus on her marriage to Larent, something Collette expected, the surprising questions came when she was asked to explain the role of each of her companions. Whyldon's presence had been an easy explanation. He was her guard captain and longtime advisor. There could be no doubt that he'd followed his queen while she sought to reclaim her rightful place. Using that basis, Arian had been assigned the role as a member of her guard, a position he had pretended to serve in while in Quenall. Tolan's build and protective nature also led to him being assigned a similar role, which left Nawalya to pick up the slack as her lady's maid.

Whyldon wasn't certain how much of their story Brath believed, but he refrained from making any open challenges. Like always, Whyldon let Collette take the lead and offered advice when asked.

He and Collette spent the next morning walking the palace gardens, and he was amused to note that her preference to be out was just as evident in Catillatio as it had been back home. The gardens were smaller than the ones at the palace in Quenall and both more and less organized. The path between rows of plants ran in a long rectangle, and occasional paths dissected the boxed shape. Whyldon imagined it made it easier for palace staff to tend to the garden in warmer months. The plants themselves seemed less curated, more random and left to chance. Come spring, the garden would appear lush and overgrown with colorful plants. Right now, everything looked dead and brown, with a few scattered exceptions.

"How are you feeling after yesterday?" he asked as they strolled along the worn paths.

"Honestly, I think we are wasting our time," she admitted. "I just don't think we have a way of making a graceful exit yet."

"Is that what you would like?" Whyldon asked. His tone was soft and concerned but neutral enough she would not feel compelled to act. "I'm sure we could come up with a plan if you think it's time to move on. This isn't your only option."

"I know it's not," Collette said. "And it might not be a bad idea for an exit strategy to be made for many reasons." She just hoped she didn't end up behind bars again.

Whyldon nodded. "In that case, I will talk with the others to form plans for a variety of scenarios. In the meantime, I would suggest you determine how much elusive bullshit you're willing to tolerate from Brath. He's non-committal at best, and he doesn't view your arrest as particularly alarming."

"Why would he?" Collette said. "At least in the short term, what impact does it have on him? It will take months for Zephraim to figure out his next steps, assuming Rhoslyn Almeida doesn't do it for him." She shot Whyldon a look, her eyes narrowed in pretend anger. "And you wanted me to get along with her."

"At the time, I didn't know she was plotting your overthrow, in my defense." Whyldon gave her an amused look. "Going forward, I could assume the worst of everyone you encounter and act accordingly."

"Who knows," Collette quipped back. "That might better serve me. There is something rather suspicious about my guard captain."

"No doubt," Whyldon agreed with a solemn nod. "He has befriended a couple of mysterious elves as of late. And a fugitive queen."

"And how could you trust someone who keeps those friends?" Collette asked. They turned the corner of the garden heading back in the direction of the main hall. It was just as well. The king had invited Collette and Larent into a morning of games. She'd need to get ready.

"Do you think it's worth all of this effort?" Collette asked him after a minute.

"What specifically?" Whyldon asked.

"Is our being here worth the uncertainty and danger? We don't even know if I have any real support back home." She looked forward as she spoke, which came as no surprise to Whyldon. Collette's ability to conceal was enviable, even if he knew his daughter well enough to see when she was using it.

"I think you had more supporters than not," Whyldon said quietly. "They didn't have the money and armies of your dissenters, but they were there, just as we were."

Collette smiled at this and nodded. "I suppose I should focus on remembering the rules of that asinine game Brath wants to play."

Whyldon nodded and motioned for her to proceed first into the castle.

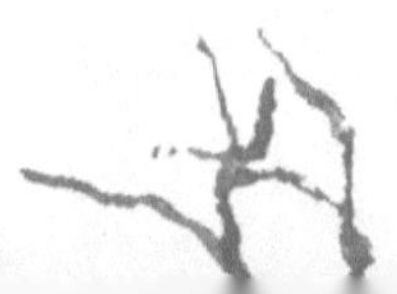

Larent placed his hand on the small of Collette's back, his thumb making small circular motions as they stood, watching members of Brath's court prepare for the game. He had no idea what it was called or how to play, but the sheer mention at the morning meal had everyone excited. He was interested in how this would turn out.

He smiled at Collette, playing the dutiful, doting husband of the queen. He knew she was stressed and doubted the effectiveness of their visit, but he made sure she knew she was supported and never alone. Besides, he loved it when he could get her to smile, and that task grew a little more difficult each day. "Okay," he whispered as clubs were handed out to each of the participants. "Tell me about this game again. I see the clubs and the balls, but are we meant to hit the ball at the small animals or through them?"

"What?" Collette asked with a laugh. "There can't be real small animals used in this game."

Larent grinned, happy to have achieved his goal. "No, there are. Lady Marine told me this morning at breakfast," he insisted. "Aren't you the queen? You should know these things."

"Well, if such a game exists, you're shit out of luck," Collette responded. "We don't play it in Coralia, and my suggestion to you would be to watch and mimic."

Larent chuckled and inclined his head, so it looked like he was whispering in her ear. "I'm willing to bet I can cause enough general chaos for them to cancel the game within ten minutes."

"Imagine, you causing chaos," Collette teased, her tone playful, though quiet. "Would it be better to do that, or for me to lament that my dear husband doesn't have a background in this particular game?"

Larent did not have a chance to answer.

"Good morning, Brath," Collette said as the king approached as well-adorned as he'd been the night before.

"Good morning, Collette," he replied with a nod, looking thrilled to be surrounded by people, drink, and sport. "I'm so glad you are here to enjoy this fine morning with us."

It was a fine morning. The weather was mild enough that they could enjoy the sunshine without shivering, and with the gardens in the distance, the little courtyard was a perfect place to meet. Larent studied Brath and couldn't help but think Brath posed a little too perfectly and his excitement over the fine morning was about how nice his golden hair looked in the sun.

"I'm excited to have been asked to join," Collette assured him. "As is my husband."

Brath looked to Larent and offered him a curt nod. "Of course, we are delighted for you to join as well."

Larent struggled to avoid snorting in response and managed to offer an amused smirk. That was enough for Brath who turned his attention to the group.

"We will be departing for the game field. If you will follow me, we can get started."

Brath didn't wait for responses and began walking. Larent knew as his guest of honor, Collette should have followed closely behind, but he didn't complain when she hung back. He offered his arm which she took, and they began following the group. "Since I still plan on creating chaos, I have to ask, how many men do you think you could fight off?"

"In what timeframe?" she asked as they strolled past a group of what appeared to be new recruits practicing their archery skills. The oldest of them might have been sixteen.

"The ten minutes it takes for me to get the game canceled, of course."

"Oh, I hope it's more than five. There's no sport in it, otherwise," she said.

Laughing, Larent leaned down to whisper something, only to pause when the sound of releasing arrows caught his attention. Something immediately registered as being off, wrong even, and he barely had time to think as he wrapped his arms around Collette and quickly spun them to the left and down to the ground, taking the brunt of the fall just as an arrow appeared where his head had been a second ago.

"That was a bit too close," Larent said, jumping up and holding out a hand for Collette to take. He glared at the training guards. They had gathered around a young boy who'd gone pale and rigid in fear.

"What's happened?" Brath called out from a distance, though he moved quickly back to the scene. His gaze locked on the archery practice, and the corners of his lips turned down. "Are you trying to kill my guests!" he demanded of the boy.

"I'm…" the boy began but froze.

"You're what?" Brath roared. "Useless? Careless? Guilty of attempted regicide? Do you realize what you could have done?"

"It was an accident," Collette intervened. "Larent is fine, aren't you?"

"Of course," he said, catching on. "And so are you, thankfully. No harm done." He gave Brath what he hoped was a reassuring smile. Something about Brath's anger struck him, but he pushed the thought aside.

"I would feel better if you would both be seen by my physician, all the same," Brath insisted.

"That is not necessary," Collette said. "Larent and I will retire back to our room, but nothing else need be done." She looked over at the young soldier. "Should I speak with him and assure him we are fine? I would hate for anything to happen to him over a mistake."

Brath's surprise showed in his widened eyes and the drop of his jaw. "You don't wish him to be dealt with?"

"For a mistake I made myself when first learning to shoot? Of course not," Collette said. Her expression took on a concerned note. "You wouldn't dream of retaliation?"

Brath huffed, his lips swelling with the effort. "If it is your wish, the boy will not be punished."

"Thank you," Collette said with genuine sincerity and relief. "We shall meet again tonight at the banquet, perhaps?"

"Of course," Brath agreed. "Please, go rest and recover. If you need anything, let one of the staff know."

Goodbyes were made, and Larent put a protective arm around Collette. He pushed their way through the crown and back towards the castle. Catching Brath's look of anger, Larent promised himself to look into it.

When some distance was put between them and the crowd, Collette said, "That wasn't an accident, and that soldier was not responsible."

"No, he wasn't, but for whatever reason, he will take the fall. There was no way he shot that arrow." Inside the castle, Larent directed them to the staircase that led to their suite.

"I don't like this," Collette said as they walked. "They were aiming for you. The shot was too perfect."

"I know, but this isn't the first time someone has taken a shot at me. Normally, when things like this happen, it's a jealous spouse or upset family member. I've never had a king angry enough to target me."

"You think Brath is behind this?" she asked.

"Don't you?" Larent asked her. Staircase reached, he motioned for her to go first. They began the short, winding climb. "He's not just angry about our declared marriage. He feels jilted. Even if there is some small chance he's not behind what just happened, I'm proceeding with a lot more caution from now on." As they reached the landing, he took her hand and led them to their shared chambers. His intent was to look after her before he found the others.

When they entered the suite, he had her stand beside the door as he made a quick sweep of the room, and on finding nothing concerning, beckoned her further inside. He gave her a warm smile. "I'm okay, Freckles," he assured her. "No new holes."

"I still don't like it," she said as she settled in one of the chairs. "This is what happens when you volunteer to be my husband, a thing to remember in the future."

Larent raised an eyebrow at her statement but ignored the feelings it conjured. "I will keep that in mind, even though it's not enough to scare me away." He paused and decided to lighten the mood. "So, I got us out of the game before it even started. What's my prize?"

Collette laughed. "You want a prize after pulling me to the ground? Why do you deserve a prize?"

"Well, let's see. Someone did try to kill me. I took the brunt of the fall when I got you out of the way," he declared as he collapsed in the seat near her. "I even ended the game before the allowed ten minutes."

"I don't think there is a prize. However, if you do end up getting hurt in all of this, you should know my wrath will be spectacular to behold," she said. "I believe the only person with permission to hurt you is Arian, and even then, it's only a little."

Larent cackled. "So, if I allow myself to get injured, or get hit by a lucky shot, you'll tear down this castle and kick some-one's ass. Well, shit. I'm a lucky wolf."

Chapter Eighteen

Riken rested his head on his hand, elbow propped up on the long cherry wood table that took up the majority of the council room. Silently, and with an air of boredom, he observed the others in the room as they waited for Zephraim's arrival. Zephraim was about twenty minutes late so far, and while he had a right as king, it didn't stop Riken from planning to go find the other man, or have Rhoslyn do it, if he was much later.

Glancing around once again, he took in those in the room. The more unimportant nobles who tended to go with the crowd were ignored. So were several of the more moderate lords who could be swayed with fancy words or greased palms. None of those were the people he was concerned with. The real power players, the ones who could sway votes in his favor, were the ones he watched.

Lord Barris, the bright lord, the same age as Riken but seemingly so much younger, stood off to the right, an open friendly smile on his face as he spoke with the lesser nobles. Riken noted his eyes constantly flicked over to check on the two Mers who were standing against the far wall. It was a smart position, considering Elrick, Crobán, and their group were in attendance. Despite Riken's letter, Elrick had seemed insistent on pursuing the Merscale trade.

Riken gave a slight shake of his head. Lord Elrick was a moron if he thought he could leverage Barris through his Mers. Everyone knew Barris was fond of them, having been raised alongside them. Riken shuddered in disgust, unable to comprehend why Barris' father had done such a thing.

With another sigh, he looked at the door. Zephraim really needed to get here soon. Lord Crobán was eyeing him, and Riken had to fight to keep from rolling his eyes when the other man lumbered over.

"Riken, my boy," Crobán said with his usual exuberance. "You look quite eager to get started. I take it you have a matter of importance to bring up?"

Riken gave Lord Crobán a warm smile even as he gagged on the inside. "Nothing too important," he said casually as his hand moved to the stack of parchment on his right. "Just information on why we need the Merscale trade for our economy."

"Ah, yes," Crobán said with a nod. "That is a matter of discussion for today." He ran a thumb and finger along his beard, looking thoughtful. "As contentious as the matter is, I think there is reason to believe we can ethically engage in the trade again. I'm hoping His Majesty agrees."

"As am I." Riken removed his hands from the documents, a sign he knew Crobán would take as permission to take a look at them. They documented the kingdom's finances, both before and after the Merscale ban. "I have a few suggestions for how to do this in a manner that benefits both ourselves and the Merpeople. I just hope everyone will find it agreeable."

Crobán nodded again as he helped himself to the reports. A few moments of silent browsing and some nods indicated the older man agreed. Riken had to admit, for all of his faults, Crobán understood money. Fortunately, Riken did not have to further engage with Crobán as the chamber doors opened and Zephraim saw himself inside.

"My apologies for the wait," he said to the group. "I had matters to attend to."

Riken smoothly rose from his chair and bowed to Zephraim. "I hope everything is well, my king?"

"Indeed," Zephraim confirmed as he took his seat. He elaborated no further on what he had been up to, and Riken knew he would need to investigate. "Shall we get down to business?"

"Of course, Your Majesty," Crobán enthused as he and other nobles found their seats.

Zephraim waited for the group to settle, and without ceremony, began the meeting. "I know there has been question as to the direction of the King's Guard. Our former captain is presumably on the run with the traitor, and our commander, while not guilty of anything we know of, has questionable allegiances."

"Do you have any suggestions on how we can fix this?" A mousy voice asked from the other end of the table.

Riken felt dread climb down his spine. He had a feeling he wouldn't like this.

Zephraim motioned down the table, and as eyes turned, they found a beaming Lord Elrick. "Elrick has a history in the field, and he served my father well in prior skirmishes. He has the necessary skill and leadership qualities that are needed for the position."

Riken blinked several times. This … was horrible. Despite Elrick's experience, it was a well-known secret that Elrick had a tendency to vanish when a fight got too rough. Skill with a sword didn't negate his cowardice or his inability to plan.

Looking around, Riken noted a mix of celebration and skepticism. Crobán actually rose so he could clap Elrick on the back in congratulations. Lord Barris, on the other hand, wore

an expression of shock before schooling his expression into something neutral. Riken decided it was best to do the same.

"Tonight we will toast your new position, Elrick," Crobán announced, gaining cheers of support.

Zephraim chuckled and shook his head. "I'm happy to see I've pleased you all with this decision."

More affirmations were made, and eventually, Zephraim opened the floor for discussion. Riken waited patiently for the lesser nobles to voice their petty complaints or shower Zephraim with meaningless praise for his reign. For a moment, he was surprised that no one broached the topic of Mer trade.

Then, he caught Lord Crobán's eye. The plump man tilted his head in a way that suggested intention, as if Riken would be grateful. He would have to do something about Crobán and his people, eventually. They just didn't have the vision this kingdom needed, even if Riken detected no long-term threat from the man.

Finally, there was a lull, and Riken knew it was time. Standing, he bowed once again to Zephraim. "My King, noble Lords. If I may be so bold as to take the floor?"

"Of course," Zephraim invited. The slumping posture indicated Zephraim's attention had waned, and Riken would have to sell his idea. Riken looked around, noting that more than half the council was listening intently. The other half appeared ready to leave. He was surprised to note how intensely Barris watched him, but he pushed it aside.

"Gentleman, Coralia is on the verge of ruin." That caught people's attention. "Well, almost," he said with a sly grin causing some to laugh and others to nervously chuckle. From the corner of his eye, he saw Zephraim sit up slightly. Holding up his parchment, which Crobán had abandoned after the news regarding Elrick, Riken continued. "The king graciously allowed me to help him in small matters of the kingdom. Those small matters lead me to a very large issue. In my hand are the finances of the kingdom from five years before the traitor took the throne until now. The numbers are catastrophic."

He placed the paperwork in front of Zephraim and tapped the numbers he needed to review. "We are in this situation because Collette stopped the Merscale trade without something that could replace the same revenue. What this has done to our kingdom is unspeakable. Now I am not necessarily saying we need to go back into the Merscale trade. The reason the traitor, and some of the members of this council, voiced for ending the trade is sensible. But we must find something to replace it, and we must find it soon or our kingdom will be destitute." He held his hands out to allow for suggestions and waited patiently for someone to speak up and get the ball rolling where it needed to go.

"The trade is sensible," Crobán spoke in support of Riken. "Our society was too enmeshed in Merscale trafficking for the sudden end. Everyone suffered."

"Exactly," Riken said, giving Crobán a nod of recognition. "Everyone suffered, from our poorest citizens to our richest nobles, and I cannot come up with any sort of equitable alternative that will not take years to implement. We must return to the Mertrade, and in the meantime, slowly roll out something new." He gestured to the room at large. "What say this council?" The supportive cheers were almost unanimous. "What say our king?"

Zephraim wasn't as exuberant concerning the idea as he had hoped, but Riken detected thoughtful consideration. "I think my stance on the trade has never been so stringent as my sister's," he drawled, his fingers tapping the table. "Abandoning it presents legitimate economic consequences, which you have pointed out." He paused and tilted his head as he considered the parchment filled with numbers. "Still, I have concerns."

"Let us address them, my King. We are at your service."

Zephraim nodded, his sleepy gaze focused on Riken. "There were undeniable cruelties committed for the trade in the past. The world is changing, and such things are no longer acceptable amongst many of our people and our allies. How do you plan on addressing such a thing?"

The question was unexpected. Riken didn't think Zephraim had much interest in most political decisions. He would have to tread carefully. "I think we start by speaking with our local Mer population. The poor. The infirm. These groups naturally lose scales. We collect from them and go from there. I'm sure there are other things we could do as well." From the corner of his eye, he spotted Lord Barris attempting to speak, only to be silenced by the chuckle issuing from Elrick. Riken would have to talk to Barris when the pest wasn't around.

"Maybe," Zephraim said. "We'll have to have a solid plan in place."

"I agree." Riken pressed his lips in thought, not liking where this was going when an idea occurred to him. "I would, however, suggest we start allowing trade in small ways." He held up his hand to stop both Barris and Elrick from speaking. "Everyone is aware Barris's product is of the highest quality, and it's also reported to be ethically obtained. I would move to allow him to start trading again, as well as anyone else who can provide the product without harm." Lord Elrick moved to speak again, and Riken decided to let Zephraim handle his new mess.

"I think Barris and I should have a discussion on the matter," Zephraim said, cutting off Elrick before he could speak. "If that is amenable to you, Barris."

Barris nodded, giving Zephraim an open bright smile Riken knew made people feel like they had done something right. He needed to figure out how to weaponize that man against the other nobles.

Chapter Eighteen

"I am glad we were able to discuss this," he declared. "I hope we can figure this out soon. Our kingdom needs it." He was going to need Rhoslyn after this.

"Yes. We'll resume this discussion at the next meeting," Zephraim replied. "Any other business?"

To my Lord, My True King,

I write to you now wishing I had better news. The false King Zephraim is allowing for the trade of Merscales once more. He is starting small by allowing Pontus Bay to be the first, and only, to take back up the trade, but we know it will not end there. Already in Wildrun, there have been rumors of Mer children taken and families vanishing off the streets. I am sure Jayden has already advised you to call our people home, but I would urge you to spread the word, to let the nomadic tribes know they will be safe there. I have, through secure means, let the guard Cremisious Hawke know those he saves can be sent to our kingdom. I know in my heart he will do everything in his power to send them your way. May the seas bless us and keep us all. I remain your humble servant.

The letter remains unsigned.

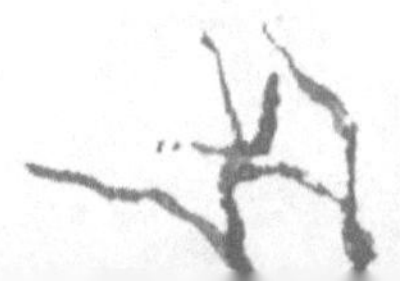

Chapter Nineteen

Crem stormed into the kitchen, soaking wet and fuming. Despite the late hour, he wasn't surprised to find Diana and two women he did not know still working. His expression was enough to drive the women from the room, though he said nothing. Positioning himself in front of the fire, he hoped to dry off as he flexed his hands into fists.

"Did they have you out in the rain?" Diana asked her husband as she brushed her hands on her apron. The countertop was covered in flour and dough, and Crem vaguely wondered why she was making bread so late.

"Obviously," he nearly growled in response.

"Why?" Diana asked, cocking her head to the side.

Letting out a heavy sigh, Crem tried to calm himself. As a younger man, he'd been prone to temper until Whyldon and Howle had knocked the tendency out of him. Besides, as angry as he was, none of this was Diana's fault. "The moronic child we are forced to call a king has made Lord Elrick captain of the guard. Elrick, in some asinine show of power, decided we needed to drill in the rain in winter."

Chapter Nineteen

Diana's eyes widened at the news, but she quickly shushed him. "People might hear you saying those things." She moved to check the spaces in the kitchen and seemed content to talk. "How have the others responded?"

"Five are threatening to quit outright, and I'd wager three more would leave if they did." The fire was doing Crem some good. He no longer felt the bone-deep cold, though he knew he'd be going upstairs to change before long.

"Conscription will be reestablished if people aren't careful," Diana replied. She sighed and stepped forward, nudging Crem so that she could check the contents of the cauldron hovering over the fire. Judging it sufficient, she grabbed the bundle of rags she used to avoid burning herself, and she moved the pot off the fire.

"I know," he said in agreement. "And now that I have a better idea of how things will be going, I'm going to go into the city and see about getting a few more families on their way." He ran a hand through his hair. "They're going to expect me to be upset about this, which means they'll be throwing accusations again and hoping something sticks. We'll need to stage another fight."

"I might really fight you if you don't stop trying to take all of this on your own shoulders," Diana replied. Hands going to her hips, she surveyed her husband. "You're going to kill yourself from exhaustion before an eye is ever turned towards me."

Crem chuckled. "What if I promised to go find Howle and make him handle some of this?"

"He's supposed to be doing that already."

"Yes, well…" Crem gave her a helpless shrug that told her all she needed to know about how good Crem was at allowing the other man to help.

"When I kill you myself, just remember this conversation," Diana said. Her expression softened, and she sighed. "Let's get

on with it. I still have to bring Agnes something to eat, and you need to change.”

“How is she doing?” Crem asked, his heart breaking for the older woman who had dedicated her life to raising and caring for Collette. Her close connection to the true queen had resulted in ill treatment from Rhoslyn.

“She’s worried, and that cow had her scrubbing floors all day,” Diana said, mouth pinched in fury. “Rhoslyn keeps threatening to throw her out of the palace.”

Crem shook his head. Agnes had served the royals with loyalty and love for decades. Of course, the scheming harlot would want to tear that down as well. “Give her my love, would you?”

“Of course,” Diana promised.

Crem nodded and took a breath, gathering up his rage over the current political situation and channeling it for what left his mouth next. He shouted in carefully chosen words, “This was a stupid, irresponsible mistake and will lead to our downfall!”

“You just don’t like it because you weren’t promoted,” Diana retorted, her voice raised and icy. “All you’ve done for weeks is complain, and you wonder why no thought was given to you.”

“Complain? Complain? I have been working double shifts for months. I’ve been the one doing the guard schedules, making sure everyone else gets breaks and proper rest. I’ve been doing my job. I should have been promoted over some lazy noble.”

“Like other people don’t work long hours?” Diana shot back. “What time did I get to the kitchens today? What time is it now? Quit complaining and be a man.”

“Really? That’s what you’re going to throw at me? I break my back for this kingdom, and you say I’m not a man?” He grimaced and gave his wife a look of apology. He hated raising his voice to her, even when it was fake. “Why don’t you just run off with one of these impotent lords, then? Maybe one of them will be man enough for you.”

Diana lightly swatted him, a playful move she could justify since no one could see them. "Fuck you!" she shouted all the same. "You can fucking sleep outside tonight for all I care."

"Sleeping in the barracks would be warmer than sleeping with you."

"Then don't hurry back," she replied.

"Fine, I won't." He reached out and took her hand, giving it a squeeze, then turned and stormed out of the kitchen. He passed a small collection of servants who had been listening. Good, they would gossip about the fight, and it would spread to all those occupying the castle.

After leaving the kitchen, Crem slowly trudged up the stairs of one of the many pathways leading to the upper level of the castle. He'd need to change and meet with Lord Elrick who had demanded certain officers provide daily reports at the end of the evening drills. It was a power play, something the lord did for pure pleasure. Crem would play along for now.

Clearing his head, he continued on his way, pausing in his stride only when he heard a very unwelcome voice from the next hallway. He stepped to the side, pressing himself against a stone wall, hoping to remain out of sight.

"Lord Barris," Lord Riken called out. "I hope I'm not interrupting anything."

Crem couldn't quite make out the rumbling, and Riken continued. "I have been trying to schedule a moment to speak with you, but it seems you've been unavailable as of late."

A moment of silence passed before Barris replied. "I've been rather busy in meetings with the king this afternoon. He was eager to form a plan to reintroduce the trade. Your impassioned speech was clearly inspirational." As always, the Golden Lord sounded cheerful, though perhaps a little impatient. Crem was reminded as to why he didn't trust either lord.

"So, things have moved forward, already?" Riken asked.

"Yes," Barris replied. "I imagine His Majesty will make an official announcement in the next day or so. In the meantime, I'm tasked with restoration efforts for my warehouses. With any luck, we might be back in production in the next week or so."

"So soon?" Riken sounded honestly surprised.

"Yes. I wrote to my people the moment the first part of the meeting was over. My word travels quickly, and my people work even quicker."

"Congratulations are in order. Please let me know if I can be of any assistance should anything pressing arise. I know the matter with Elrick is still tense." Riken's voice was dark as he mentioned the other lord.

"Thank you, Lord Riken. The help is appreciated. Lord Elrick has not been shy in his advances, but I … have been doing my best to handle it. I worry he will, once more, go after my people, especially once the money starts coming in." Barris sounded unsure but still overly upbeat.

"I will be there for you, however you need me," Riken said smoothly. When Crem glanced around the corner, it was to see Riken throwing an arm around Barris's shoulders as if they were old friends. Barris managed to conceal a look of discomfort.

"Come," Riken said. "Let's have a drink to celebrate your successes."

Crem stood for a minute before heading toward his and Diana's rooms. As he walked, he went through the conversation in his head. It was obvious Zephraim had approved the sale of Merscales again, news that had not been conveyed by Elrick. The trade allowance seemed limited if only Barris was involved, but it could, and likely would, grow.

He wanted to turn around, to inform Diana and have her get word to Howle. He wanted to forcibly remove the Mers from Quenall. And the Mother knew the anti-Mer sentiment would spread to others. This was going to turn into a cluster fuck quickly.

It was no longer a rescue mission, he admitted to himself. It was a rebellion.

Chapter Twenty

"So, do I look dashing?" Larent asked as he exited the washroom, wearing finely tailored clothing Arian and Nawalya had managed to put together since arriving. His jacket was a deep blue, trimmed in silver, and paired with matching trousers. The color told Larent who had been responsible for choosing his wardrobe, but he said nothing, knowing that it complimented the gown Nawalya supplied for Collette. They'd have to talk to the elf about choosing different colors if they stayed very long.

"You look very dashing," Collette confirmed, walking around him and straightening the seams and lines of his jacket and shirt. "You make a believable prince consort. I'd even say you were handsome, but we don't want that going to your head."

"Dashing is just another word for handsome, so it's going to my head either way." He adjusted the collar of the shirt. "Wearing this shows how much I love you," he said frankly, though the twinkle in his eyes could have meant he was also joking.

"Quit flirting with her," Nawalya instructed as she joined Collette's examination. "Remember to defer to Collette when questions are posed. You are a consort, not a king. It will be seen as disrespectful to come across as challenging or overly playful. Let her answer questions."

"Try to not speak unless necessary," Arian advised, causing Larent to laugh.

"Don't worry, Chuckles. I can manage."

"If not, next time we will tell people Nawalya is my husband," Collette determined with a smile.

Larent nearly snorted, picturing Nawalya dressed as he was now. He caught a displeased expression on Tolan's face. Now was not the time to bicker, as Collette had requested multiple times since arriving. Honoring her wishes was the least he could do right now. "I think Nawalya would make an excellent husband. She'd even offer her arm and everything."

Nawalya smiled and nodded. "Why be a husband if I did not intend to be a good one?" she asked.

Collette laughed. "I've no doubt of your ability to be a good husband. We can discuss all your skills when we are not expected downstairs."

"Brath will probably send someone to fetch you if you don't make an appearance soon," Whyldon agreed. "Are you certain you're both capable of attending tonight?"

"Yup," Larent confirmed. "I didn't actually get hit with an arrow."

"All the same," Whyldon said. He looked to Collette. "If anything looks suspicious—" he began, only for Collette to cut him off.

"We can handle it, Whyldon," she said and smiled at Larent. "Let's go. The evening promises to be a long one."

Larent acquiesced, noting the wariness threatening to break through Collette's demeanor. Her hatred of being confined to palace walls was palpable, and he silently swore that he

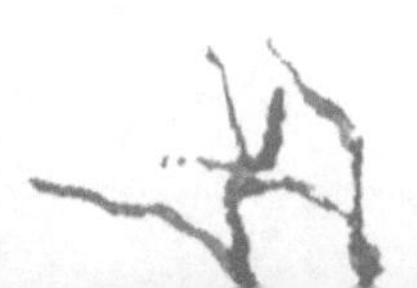

would do what he could to alleviate as much stress and anxiety as possible.

They left the room, walking down the corridor with a leisure they probably shouldn't have taken. "Here's hoping we can get through this quickly," Larent said.

"Nothing about these evenings go quickly," Collette replied. "Hopefully the food will be good."

"Hopefully so," Larent agreed. He looked over at her and offered his arm. "Did you sleep any last night?"

"About as much as I've been getting lately," she confessed. "Losing your kingdom, family, and being on the run aren't conducive qualities for sleep."

He leaned closer to her like a lover sharing soft words. "About as much, if less, than me? This is gonna be fun then."

Soon, they were entering the banquet hall which already felt overly swollen with people. Larent struggled to keep the look of abhorrence from his face. People were dressed in finery, laughing, eating, and drinking past the point of indulgence, and it was early enough in the evening that he wanted to cringe at the possibilities of late night.

"We could always make a run for it," he said to Collette as they stepped forward.

"I'll push you over if you start talking nonsense," Collette returned, casting him a playful smile.

Larent laughed, though he knew the sound barely registered in the roar of the room. "How about I spill red wine on someone, and we bolt?"

"I think you're just looking to create chaos," she said. A servant passed with a tray of wine; she selected two cups and handed one over to Larent.

"Life is chaos," he said as he accepted the wine. It smelled decent. He took a tentative sip, followed by a bigger sip. "The least we can do is have some fun."

Collette did not have a chance to respond, as they were approached by the increasingly familiar face of Lady Marine. "Oh, good evening, Your Majesties," she said, her voice tinkling in a way that reminded Larent of faeries. "I take it you're feeling better after the terrifying morning?"

"Good evening, Lady Marine," Collette said. "We are well, thank you."

"Lady Marine," Larent said, dipping his head as the woman stepped closer, almost invading his space. "Are you having a pleasant evening?"

"Of course," Lady Marine demurred. "We have been so pleased to have you here."

"We are pleased to be here," Larent said diplomatically, eying Collette. He felt so awkward. "The king is waving us over. We will see you later?"

"Of course," Lady Marine said. She inclined her head and dismissed herself.

Larent's nose wrinkled as he tried to rid himself of her smell. It was overly strong and chemical, like cheap perfume. "She doesn't smell right. There's want there, but also desperation and something else I can't identify." He stepped closer to Collette and leaned down like he was going to kiss her. Her scent immediately offered relief.

"Queen Collette!" Brath greeted in a hearty tone, interrupting the moment. "I am so glad you have joined us. I trust you are well-rested this evening?"

"I am, indeed," Collette returned. "Your palace is peaceful."

"I'm glad to hear it," Brath said, pointedly ignoring Larent. "It is my greatest desire that you be comfortable here." He offered Collette a smile. "Might I steal you away from your husband?"

Larent gave Collette a discreet nod, letting her know it was fine for her to go. "Enjoy yourself."

"Wonderful," Brath declared, extending his hand to Collette, who took it.

Larent watched Collette walk off with Brath, unable to suppress a low growl. He hated seeing Collette forced to walk off with that asshole, to see her force a smile onto her lips and play-act her way through the evening. He didn't understand how everyone else just ignored her obvious hatred of being here and going through the motions. And it wasn't as though they were new. She'd been unimpressed with court life long before they'd left Coralia.

He let out a sigh, wondering how he should occupy his time since mingling didn't appeal. Spotting doors that led to the balcony, he pushed that way through the crowd. Then he cursed when it was clear Lady Marine had followed him.

"Where are you off to?" Lady Marine said as she caught up with Larent.

Plastering a smile on his face, Larent turned to her, wondering if it was possible not to breathe until she left. "I was thinking of stepping outside to take in the view."

"Oh! I will join you," Marine declared. "There are excellent views from many locations in the palace. I know you will appreciate them."

Larent hid his wince. He did not want to go onto the balcony with her, but he couldn't see a way out. How did Collette do this? Offering his arm, he said, "I have seen many excellent views since we arrived, but they all fail to match up to my favorite view." He pondered if he could push the lady off the balcony and call it an accident, but he tossed the idea aside almost at once. Collette would be displeased with him.

"And what view is that?" Marine asked as she took his arm.

"Why, my wife, of course." He halted as they reached the balcony doors and turned to look at Collette. "She really is exquisite."

"Oh," Marine said, casting an exaggerated glance back at the queen. "She is a lovely thing. How did you meet?"

Larent momentarily froze. They hadn't discussed their backstory yet, and he knew this would be shared throughout the Azmarin court. Not taking his eyes off Collette, Larent began his tale. "It's not an exciting story. I'm the middle son of an unimportant lord and a bit of a scoundrel. I was escaping a jilted husband when I literally ran into her. After apologizing, I meant to keep running, but the moment I saw her I just… I was gone. I knew that she was my forever. I didn't know she was the queen at that point, but I still knew." He gave Marine what he hoped was a self-deprecating smile. "It took me a while to convince her, but I managed."

"Isn't she lucky to have caught your eye," Marine said. "I just hope she appreciates you, and your devotion, in the way you deserve."

"She does," Larent assured her as they continued out onto the balcony. The air was cooler than it had been earlier in the day, but he didn't mind it, not when layered in so many clothes.

"And you are happy?" Marine asked him, catching him by surprise.

"More so than I have ever been," he responded with a sincerity he couldn't have faked if he'd wanted to.

"Is she?" Marine asked. "Of course, I know the difficult time she is going through must be taxing. But do you think you bring her the happiness she seeks and deserves?"

Larent let go of Marine's arm and moved to lean against the wall, away from the railing of the balcony. "That, my Lady, is a trick question. I want to say yes. I believe the answer is yes with all of my heart, but you can never truly know if you make another person happy, not deep inside. The real answer is that I will do anything and everything in my power to make and keep her happy."

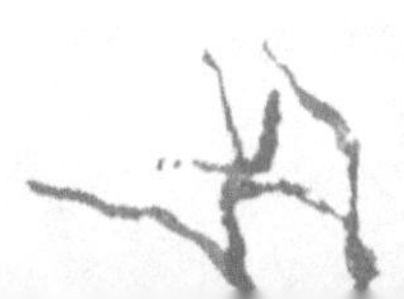

"And what is your lovely wife planning to do with her time if her efforts to regain her kingdom fail?"

Larent almost snorted at the question, but answered, his voice full of a confidence he truly felt. "She won't fail. Even if things don't go the way she plans, she'll get her kingdom back." What she'd do with it once she got it back was another question entirely.

"I'm sure there are paths back to what she wants," Marine replied. "It's really a matter of identifying what it would take and going from there."

"Exactly." He eyed her. This was not what he was expecting when she decided to follow him. He didn't have to wonder at her game for long, though. She was quite eager to share it.

"You know," Marine pointed out, deciding to join Larent on the wall. "As deeply devoted as you are to Queen Collette, surely you understand the assistance you can provide in her endeavor is limited."

"I know," Larent said, and he waited for her to continue.

"And you've stated that you truly care for your wife," Marine continued, pressing a hand against the deep pink of the bust of her gown. Larent wondered if she was doing this to draw attention to her breasts, which were ample despite her slender frame.

"I do," he confirmed. "More than anything."

"Then I think you would agree that King Brath is much better positioned to aid her in her goals. He has money. An army. Resources at his disposal…"

Larent couldn't help but laugh, though it was void of humor. He might have actually been offended if this facade had been real. "Lady Marine, are you trying to convince me to leave my wife or invite the king to join us? Either suggestion is rather … scandalous."

"I am simply suggesting that King Brath may be the better option for her in the long run," Lady Marine insisted. No blush came to her cheeks, despite the slight distress in her voice. He wondered what to make of that. "Not that you aren't appealing. You are quite handsome, and no one could question your motives when they see how you look at your wife. But the real question is, and should be, what is best for her in the long run?"

Larent gave the lady his most charming smile, one he knew drew people in and had them lower their guard, but his eyes held no warmth. "Lady Marine, may I ask you a question?"

She nodded. "You certainly might. I'm not opposed to questions."

He laid a hand on his heart. "Do you believe, in here, that it is more important to marry for love, even if it means you are poor but happy? Or is it preferable to marry for power, even if it means being miserable for the rest of your life?"

"I think the real answer to that question depends on what you hope to accomplish," Marine replied. "Certainly, Queen Collette might be happy with you, but she would never regain what she has lost."

Larent gave her a soft, sad smile. "Your deflection tells me everything I need to know. Without touching on the fact that women of your birth are taught their only worth is to marry a man of power, or worse, that they aren't worthy of real love, I will tell you a truth. Love, real love, and the happiness it brings is worth more and lasts longer than any kingdom or amount of power. Collette's situation should be used as an example of how quickly our circumstances change, of how fleeting power truly is." He let out a short laugh and shook his head. "She wouldn't let me step aside like that. She wants her kingdom back so she can protect her people. She's not going to give up the happiness she's made for herself to do that." Offering Marine a last pitying smile, Larent stepped away and moved towards the ballroom. He gave her a last look. "Everyone deserves to be loved, to be happy. Even you."

When he re-entered the ballroom, it seemed much hotter than when he left. Perhaps there were more people, or the cool air of the outside made it comparatively warmer. He might have to find an excuse to shed his jacket.

With those thoughts in mind, he barely made it five steps into the crowd before he spotted Collette. "Well, hello there, Freckles."

"Hello," Collette replied, looking relieved to see him. "Did you enjoy your conversation with Lady Marine?" she asked, a knowing smirk appearing.

Larent shrugged. "I simply gave her what I would call an educational lesson I hope she takes to heart."

"Dare I ask what it entailed?"

"I'll tell you the whole story when there are fewer people around," he promised. "She's suggested I leave you so that you can form a marital alliance with Brath. I told her about my philosophy on love. Hopefully, I didn't overstep."

Collette shook her head. "Granted, I didn't hear the conversation, but I know this world well enough to make an educated guess."

"So, you'd not be surprised to hear that, despite how much I absolutely adore you, it's not enough, I'm not enough, and I should step aside so you can marry your rightful husband, the king?" Larent asked. "How angry does she look?"

Collette looked over Larent's shoulder where she spotted Marine speaking with a group. Their gazes briefly locked, and Collette had to stifle a laugh. "I wouldn't say angry, but she's not happy. I wonder about her motivation."

"Someone put her up to it. The reason as to why remains a mystery." He shrugged and pulled at the collar of his jacket, hoping for a little air. "I'm afraid I might have earned myself a reputation of overly romantic sap."

"There is nothing wrong with being a romantic," Collette said. "I am, despite everything."

"I know," Larent confirmed, offering her his arm. "Just as I know what I said about your preference in choosing happiness is the truth as well."

"What led you to that conclusion?"

He leaned in close. "I enjoy watching you, or have you not figured that out yet?"

She looked up at him, doing nothing about the very short distance between them. "And in all your watching, what clued you into my desire for happiness over power?"

He gave her a soft smile, his lips barely rising, and leaned closer. "It's in the way you look towards the forest when you think no one's watching, the longing on your face. The way your shoulders tense when you speak to nobles demonstrates that you know how to handle yourself, but that you also hate it. The slight sigh you let out when Nawalya is able to go into the woods without an escort, but Whyldon insists you have one, is another clue. It's the way you speak of hunting, of camping, of riding a horse. It screams to me of needs that go unfulfilled." He shrugged as if to break the tension and moved away slightly. "Or it could just be my wolf side making shit up. Who knows?"

She didn't speak for several moments, leaving Larent to question if he'd gone too far, been too intimate with her. Only nights before there had been a moment where he was certain that they might have kissed. Lady, he was in over his head.

"You're not wrong," she finally said. "But I would also point out that Whyldon isn't the only one who thinks I need to be monitored. It makes me wonder how the lot of you trust me to run a country."

"I love that you think, after you win back your kingdom, we are going to up and vanish, leaving you handling everything on your own."

"That wasn't what I said, or the point I was making, and you know it."

"I know, but my point also stands. No one's going to be able to look at you sideways without sprouting knives from behind their backs."

"Just how long are you committed to sticking around after I am back on the throne?" she asked, turning to face him.

"How long do you want me to stay, Freckles?" he asked, his voice softening. Lady, she was beautiful. And he knew he shouldn't be thinking that.

"I haven't told you to leave yet, have I?"

He smiled. "I guess you're stuck with me forever, then."

"Good," she said simply.

Chapter Twenty-One

Head bowed, dark wavy hair obscuring her face, Nawalya moved quickly but efficiently through the palace, intent on investigating the attack on Larent's life. She moved carefully, though the efforts might have been wasted. Since arriving, she'd found herself and Arian effectively invisible. Arian loved to say the true state of any household, including a palace, was shown in how they treated the poor and those who were othered. It was obvious her presence, and that of Arian, was only tolerated at the palace because they were part of Collette's entourage. There was nothing to do about it. Instead, she had a job to do.

While Collette and Larent had attended different functions organized by King Brath, discreetly monitored by Arian, Whyldon, and Tolan, she had made her way through bedrooms, searching for information about just what Brath was thinking or planning. Tonight, while the visiting nobles attended the king's banquet, Nawalya intended to finish her search of the final rooms.

She had interest in a specific room, one belonging to Lady Marine. She let herself into the room, knowing the woman had been downstairs, batting eyelashes at Larent, no doubt. She'd made a good show of interest in Larent, even if it read false.

Marine's room was surprisingly messy, given how meticulous the woman was in style and dress. Perhaps her maid had not been by that morning, or perhaps they avoided her altogether. The layer of items littering every available surface seemed days in the making, casually tossed aside when whatever use it had became insufficient. Nawalya curiously picked her way through one pile, examining an expensive garment and shaking her head. She dropped the thing back where she'd found it.

Moving to the middle of the living space, Nawalya decided she would examine each area in small circles, eyes taking in every detail. She did this first in the living room and then the bedroom, though she noted nothing off despite the mess. Then Nawalya moved to the bathing area, nearly cheering in triumph as she immediately spotted the irregularity.

Standing before the vanity, she carefully moved all items from the left corner. The vanity was as cluttered as the rest of Marine's space, but the left corner was too perfect, too curated. None of the bottles were tipped over, nor was the area covered in remnants of spilled powder. Once the space was clear, she randomly knocked on the wooden surface, listening carefully for the hollow sound of a hidden compartment. She grinned when the expected noise echoed back. She cleared away more space, less carefully this time, searching for a latch or other mechanism to grant her access, and found a poorly hidden catch. A door to the hidden compartment popped open, causing Nawalya to smile in triumph, only for the smile to be replaced with a snarl. A vial of blackbane, badly brewed from the brownish tint, sat in the drawer.

Breathing deeply, Nawalya closed the compartment, leaving the poison against her better judgment, and put everything back in its place before leaving quickly. The poison wouldn't truly hurt Larent if he was the intended target. Shapeshifters weren't immune, but a badly brewed blackbane would cause days of horrific pain. If used on herself or Arian, it would render them unconscious. Collette or Whyldon… there was a high chance of death. She had to warn the others, and the kitchens needed to be watched.

She waited until the banquet was over to alert Larent and Collette, having decided barging into a diplomatic situation was unwise. Banquets had their usefulness, but diplomacy belonged to Collette alone. Nawalya stood in the shadows near the wing leading to Collette's rooms, popping out as the pair finally appeared well into the evening.

"Hello," she greeted, ignoring Collette's small jump. "I need to speak with you!"

"Nawalya?" Collette said, her eyes wide at the scare Nawalya had not meant to give.

"Sorry," Nawalya said in her soft, melodic voice. "I discovered a vial of poison in Lady Marine's room. I doubt she has it just in case an occasion for poison ever appears."

"Poison," Larent said, his expression a mixture of curiosity, amusement, and something darker. "We need to know what she plans on doing."

"We do," Nawalya agreed. "Arian and Tolan have assignments, but I would like to borrow Larent to see if we can force her into action."

"I hate being bait," Larent whined, looking at Collette. "Don't let her take me."

Nawalya rolled her eyes and smacked him lightly on the arm. "You will be fine," she informed him before talking to Collette again. "I do not think you should be with him for this, and while I will not tell you not to come, I would strongly

suggest you head to your room. If possible, do not eat anything the servants offer you."

"Report to my bedroom and behave like a good child," Collette summarized but nodded. "Will do."

Nawalya gave her a look reminiscent of Arian. "You are not a child. I know you are more than capable. If you wish to do something else, then please do so. I just wish you to be safe. I am not Arian and Whyldon.

"You are not," Collette conceded. "But we do know the response we will get if I do anything else."

"You should consider taking them to task when we leave here, physically if needed, so they understand you are a capable adult and not a helpless princess," Nawalya suggested before beginning to drag Larent off.

"I don't wanna go," he said reaching for Collette. "Collette, my love, sleep well and dream of me if the worst should happen."

Thankfully, Larent grew serious as Nawalya put distance between him and Collette. "What's your plan?" he asked softly.

"You are taking a walk around the gardens," Nawalya said. "If someone approaches you or questions you, say Collette is resting. It's late, they will believe it."

"Okay?" Larent said, prompting her to elaborate.

"I want to see who is interested in approaching you, or if someone will use your seeming isolation as an opportunity to strike. Nothing may happen, but between the arrow and poison, I'm inclined to think you being alone will prompt a response."

"I will continue to say I dislike playing bait," Larent said in a grumpy voice.

"Think of it less as bait and more like fresh meat," Nawalya smirked.

"Same damn thing."

"True, but this may be more fun than the banquet you just left, could it not?" Nawalya asked him.

Chapter Twenty-one

Larent snorted and glanced around before they reached the staircase. Somehow, he spotted Whyldon before she did. "Maybe we should ask Blue Eyes what he thinks about your plan."

"I dislike that nickname," Nawalya replied, giving him a stern look. "Just use his last name like the rest of us. It could be considered a nickname, after all."

"That's boring," Larent replied as they waved the man over.

Despite the late hour, Whyldon looked as handsome and alert as ever, and Nawalya was tempted to ask why he was up so late. She did not get the chance.

"I'm almost afraid to ask what the two of you are up to," he said.

"She is trying to get me killed. Help me," Larent whispered loudly, making grabbing hands at Whyldon. Whyldon just rolled his eyes.

Nawalya sighed. "I am sending him to the garden to see who approaches him. I am hopeful for an attempt on his life, but I am not trying to kill him."

"That shockingly sounds like you're trying to kill me," Larent said.

"Did something else happen?" Whyldon asked. "Or is the arrow the motivation?"

"I found poison in Lady Marine's room. I am assuming it is for Larent, given he is the only one to have been targeted, but I am not sure, hence, making it seem like he is strolling alone."

Larent made a face. "Tell her this is a bad idea, please."

Whyldon scratched at his beard. "I'm not sure it's the best idea, but if you are being targeted, I would like real proof."

"I believe this is the best way to gain that proof. Now that you are here, you can help me keep watch." Nawalya gave Whyldon a small smile. "To help make sure Larent is safe of course."

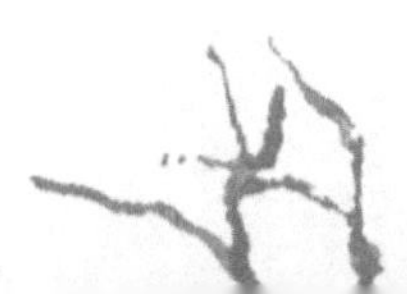

"Yeah, not because she wants to stare at you," Larent was cut off by a hard slap to the head.

"Let's get to it," Whyldon suggested, returning Nawalya's smile. Her heart practically fluttered in her chest.

Loose plan agreed on, the three walked down to the courtyard and found it seemingly empty.

Larent groaned. "I'll leave you two here and start my stroll." He gave them a salute, and undoing the buttons of his jacket, started at a leisurely pace through the yard, hands in his pockets as if he had no care in the world.

"I am slightly dreading the outcome," Nawalya told Whyldon as they moved to the shadows where they could keep an eye on Larent.

"I think we know he's been targeted," Whyldon said quietly. "And though this might cause some truth to turn up, what do we do with it?"

"Normally, we would eliminate the threat, by any means necessary. I do feel like Collette would frown on that, so in this case, we will expose the person and hopefully limit the future attempts."

"And if Brath is behind it?"

"Then we handle him. Discreetly."

Whyldon nodded. "I think Collette might be amenable when it concerns threats on those she cares about."

Nawalya snarled as she thought about the morning. "I believe if the king attempts to lay hands on her like he did at breakfast, we will not be the ones who handle him."

"It was not the first time it's happened," Whyldon pointed out. He paused in their movements as Larent did.

"Brath's lucky to still have his hands." Nawalya became quiet as Larent bowed his head.

"Lady Marine, what brings you to the courtyard?" Larent asked, his voice echoing through the night.

Chapter Twenty-one

"I needed some air," Lady Marine replied, her voice quieter than Larent's. "I thought you had retired with Queen Collette."

"I found myself unable to sleep, but my Lady was tired from the dancing, so I decided to let her get some rest. No need to bother her with my restlessness."

"How kind of you," Marine said, her voice cheerful. "Would you like company?"

Larent carefully and slowly led Marine closer to the shadows where Nawalya and Whyldon hid. "I don't think I will be out here for long, and I would hate for you to be bored with my company."

Nawalya whispered to Whyldon. "Of course, she would be the one to appear. Do you see the king anywhere? He could be watching from an upper window."

Whyldon shook his head as Marine spoke again.

"I would not be bored," Marine insisted, cozying up to Larent. "We had such a lovely conversation before."

Larent offered his arm. "Is there anything interesting about the garden a visitor should know?"

Nawalya nudged Whyldon to the next group of shadows as Larent began to walk, Lady Marine on his arm.

"Oh, the gardens are King Brath's pride and joy," Marine said. Here and there, she pointed out a particular plant or statue.

Nawalya let out a small curse as Larent and Lady Marine turned a corner, and several people came out of the banquet hall.

"This isn't good," Whyldon said. "We should leave the shadows and appear as though we are taking our own stroll."

"Well then, lead the way," Nawalya said, grasping his arm. Whyldon did as she instructed, and after pausing very briefly to examine the space, he led Nawalya along a more direct path, keeping their distance from Larent and Marine. Thankfully, they could monitor them, though Nawalya suspected the isolation had been intentional.

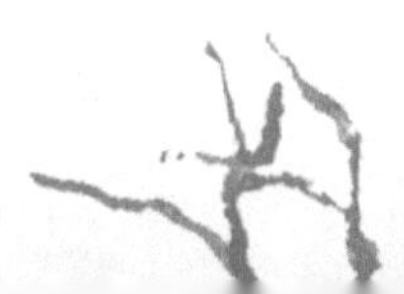

Turning another corner, the two pairs were in an open courtyard. Lady Marine broke away from Larent, taking several steps as she pointed out one of the elegantly carved statues. Larent looked on, though his shoulders tensed seconds before Nawalya heard the unmistakable sound of scraping stone. Looking up, she saw a statue, once perched on the ledge of the castle, falling towards the ground. She called out to Larent who, thankfully, had been observant enough to move out of the way.

Unfortunately, Marine seemed to have anticipated this, and she gave him an unnaturally strong shove back into the falling statue's path. Larent moved into a backward roll, narrowly missing the large, stone décor by millimeters. Unfortunately, he was struck by the flying debris, chunks of jagged stone ripping into his shoulder and forehead as the crashing sounds silenced in the night.

"Fucking shit balls," Larent muttered, his hand clumsily going to his head.

Lady Marine lay near him, having taken on more of the full impact. Nawalya had no concern for her. Hurrying to Larent's side, Nawalya paused briefly as she spotted two figures above them. "There are two men up there," she informed Whyldon, who nodded and went for help.

Tolan watched Collette and Larent as they ascended the stairs, arm in arm, heads bowed together. He didn't even notice his hand had come up to play with his necklace, an old habit he thought he had rid himself of. They appeared the picture of a perfectly happy couple. Jealousy flared each time he saw them together, and he hated himself for feeling so petty and petulant. His emotion-driven side wanted to scream at Larent for trying to take Collette from him, for depriving him of everything she represented in his life, but rationally, he knew this whole thing was a ruse meant to aid Collette in her quest.

Tolan knew holding Larent solely accountable for his feelings was unfair. In the beginning, Collette's ability to conceal her thoughts and feelings was enviable. Tolan thought she'd be singly determined to end her brother and take back her kingdom, but in the quiet moments when it had been just the two of them, she'd expressed her sorrows.

Collette had been quiet, sad, and acutely angry, but she hadn't shown it. By letting Larent distract her, she was feeding into the attention, or rather, avoiding the sadness and anger he'd expected since her arrest.

Lately, it felt as though Collette's mood had shifted, and she was embracing a novel approach to life. Her quiet sorrow had been replaced with jokes and laughter, and she seemed content to continue her days in the presence of their company rather than making consistent steps forward. This stop in Azmarin increasingly proved itself a waste of time. An attempt had been made on Larent's life, and Brath had avoided any serious discussion of providing assistance or formalizing an alliance. Did Collette not want to regain her kingdom? Tolan asked himself this question with increasing frequency.

He knew better, of course. Collette cared about rescuing her people from the horror that Zephraim's reign would bring. She loved her people too much to abandon them, but Tolan had started to suspect that she wanted to find a way to do that without being Queen.

Seeing Larent reach the door that would lead to their rooms, Tolan left the window ledge he'd been observing them from. He was supposed to be monitoring the kitchens since Nawalya's discovery of poison, but he paused when he saw Nawalya approach Larent and lead him away from Collette. Not wanting Collette to be alone in the castle and seeing an opportunity to spend time with her, Tolan headed to meet her, completely abandoning the assignment he'd been given.

She spotted him before Tolan made it to her, and Collette offered him a bright smile. "Hello," she greeted, her voice warm and welcoming despite the late hour. It was almost enough to wash away the uncertainty and hurt. Almost.

"Hello yourself," he replied, drawing closer under the guise of escorting her up the stairs. "Been having fun with Larent?"

"Larent is entertaining," she said, not quite answering his question. "What have you been occupying your time with?"

"Helping Nawalya and Arian with whatever tasks they deem important. We're still trying to find proof that Brath is behind the attack on Larent."

"Pinning blame is going to be a challenge, especially since so many eyes are on all of us," Collette replied.

Tolan glanced around, and seeing no one from his vantage point, he couldn't help but take the opportunity. "Not right now we aren't," he said as he backed her against the wall.

Her eyes widened in surprise, but her knowing grin only encouraged him to move closer. His arms went to either side of her body, and he left little room between them.

"I don't see anyone other than you," she shared in a whisper, meeting his gaze.

"I wouldn't care either way," he replied, ghosting his lips over hers. "I am tired of watching you with Larent. I'm tired of my empty bed and our stolen moments. I miss you." He kissed her, wanting to pour all of his love and affection into the movement.

"We might get caught," Collette warned, her voice a little dazed. She didn't seem to mind. Her arms were around him, pulling him flush against her.

"I don't care," he said and kissed her again, refamiliarizing himself with her taste and scent and trying to erase the numerous doubts he faced. Kissing Collette was always a heady experience, and for long seconds, he allowed himself to be absorbed by the moment. When that kiss broke, he began kissing along her jawline. "You're coming with me to my room while the others are busy."

"Okay," she easily agreed, tilting her head back for him, and he gently nipped at the exposed skin.

Tolan forced himself to pull away, then took her hand so he could redirect them to the room he'd been given. When they arrived, he locked the door behind them, leading Collette to the bed.

Collette resisted a lazy yawn until she was safely back behind the closed door of her suite. The late evening with Tolan had been necessary and intense, and part of her longed to crawl into her bed and happily doze until something pressing happened. She would have to make more of an effort with Tolan, knowing that their time in Azmarin had resulted in distance.

The door closed behind her, and she lazily stretched her arms above her head, issuing a quiet, satisfied groan. Her bedroom was illuminated by the faintest glow, a sign that the sun was rising before she'd have a chance to sleep. The day would be a long one.

"Nawalya," Larent's voice sounded from the interior, "if you brought more potions to shove down my throat, I will take back what I said about forgiveness. Besides, you should be looking for Collette."

"Why is Nawalya looking for me?" Collette called to Larent. She went to the bedroom and spotted him lounging on the bed, shirtless. His right arm and head were bandaged, and she could

see the signs of old blood that had soaked through. "What happened?" she asked, alarmed.

"It looks like we can call off the search party," Larent noted, looking up to meet her gaze. "Where have you been? We've been worried. Arian is ready to start stabbing and asking questions later." His eyes narrowed after he took a deep long breath. "Oh Lady, you stink of Tolan."

"You didn't answer my question," Collette pointed out, her lips pursed in annoyance. She did manage to not cross her arms. "What happened to you?"

"Hey, I'm fine. The statue barely grazed me." He held up his left hand. "Chuckles and Nawalya are overreacting, though not as much as Whyldon since they realized you weren't here."

"That tells me nothing, you know," Collette said. Sometimes it frustrated her that they collectively tracked her whereabouts. "Are you actually only grazed, or are you really hurt? It's hard to tell with head wounds."

"Someone tried to kill me again, obviously," Larent replied. "A statue was pushed. I got out of the way. Someone tried pushing me back in the way. The statue missed me, but the debris did not." He gave her an amused look. "Nawalya and Whyldon felt comfortable enough to make accusations after it happened. As soon as the finger pointing started, Lady Marine screamed Zephraim was behind my attempted crushing."

"That's ridiculous," Collette said.

"It is, but they've got their bases covered all the same." He shrugged. "Still, it was another thing for the others to worry about."

Collette sighed. "I will go find Whyldon. You stay here and think of new ways to tell me I smell."

"I said you smell of sex and Tolan. Normally, you smell of…" he paused, his voice going softer when he finally spoke, "wildflowers after a spring rain."

The change in tone caught her attention, and Collette was reminded of a night not so many days ago when she'd felt a pull to Larent. It was there again, only stronger. "Okay," she acknowledged. "I'm going to go find the others."

"Tell them no more potions," he complained.

"I'm going to insist on more," she called back as she walked out the door.

"Why is my wife so cruel?" he called back, causing her to laugh.

Collette's first stop was the suite of rooms given to the rest of the group. When she arrived, she noted the door to Arian's room was ajar, and she heard him speaking.

"Has anyone checked Tolan's room?" Arian asked.

"I haven't, but he is supposed to be helping in the kitchen to ensure they don't poison our food," Nawalya pointed out.

"I heard you were looking for me," Collette said, pushing the door open and stepping inside. She closed the door behind her. Arian paced the room, and Nawalya sat cross-legged on the bed.

"She lives," Arian said wryly.

"Apparently, even when I am with one of you, that is not good enough," she remarked in the same tone. "What happened to Larent? His explanation was very Larent in nature."

Arian glowered at the ground. "Considering Tolan was supposed to be elsewhere, you will forgive our worry."

"Collette did not know," Nawalya reminded him. She turned to Collette. "After we left, Larent and I came upon Whyldon. Together, we sent Larent off and followed behind him. Shortly after he started walking, Lady Marine approached him and pulled him to a more secluded area. There, a few of her servants pushed a large cat statue onto Larent from the third story. When Larent tried to move out of the way, Lady Marine tried to push him back into its path. Thankfully, she ended up more injured than Larent." Nawalya paused and took a breath. "As the lady

was taken away, she claimed to be your brother's lover, a convenient excuse, especially since I have heard she has never left this kingdom."

"How, exactly, is she supposed to be Zephraim's lover?" Collette asked, rolling her eyes. "Zephraim doesn't know we are here, even if he suspects this was one of the possibilities. It's a stretch of a story."

"She implied you were also a target, as she was being escorted away. I think she meant to add to the confusion and throw us off the trail of the person who instructed her to kill Larent," Nawalya said softly.

"No, I get that," Collette said. "But the claim is absolutely ridiculous under the tiniest of scrutiny. It would be different if Zephraim knew where we were, and Brath is smart enough to know we would see through the excuse." She contemplated the choice for a few moments. "I don't know what they possibly hope to accomplish with such a weak story."

"I think she panicked. She never believed Brath would have her arrested. Her eyes kept moving to him, and there was a desperate, betrayed look in them. Brath looked…" Nawalya paused to consider her words. "He was enraged to a degree that was inappropriate for what had happened. He also did not offer condolences or check that Larent was alright."

"Well, he wouldn't, even if he was not angry," Collette pointed out. "Larent is socially his inferior. Protocol would be to have someone check on his behalf."

"That he didn't even ask if Larent was okay when he's bleeding tells me he was less upset that Marine was caught and more upset Larent was not dead," Arian stated, his body tense and angry. "We will need to be on high alert, especially with the poison still in play and no one watching the kitchens."

"Tolan is free now," Collette said. "You could put him back on the kitchens."

"Oh, I am going to do more than that," Arian almost hissed. Pushing against the wall with tightly contained violence, he moved to leave the room, only to stop and do a tight turn to face Collette. "Here," he said, holding his hand out. "You have dinner with the king tonight. This should negate any poisons that are slipped into your food or drink." Once the note was in Collette's hand, Arian silently left the room.

"Do not mind him. He's worried," Nawalya said, shaking her head.

"I have grown accustomed to Arian's manner of approaching possibilities," Collette assured Nawalya. "He's right to worry, though. We should probably consider being ready to leave."

"I am already packed." Nawalya pointed to her bag by the door. "It is no coincidence poison waited in Lady Marine's room. I believe it was intended for Larent, given the attacks on him, but you still need to be vigilant with your food." Nawalya pulled out one of her daggers and held it out to Collette. "The dress you're wearing tonight has hidden slits to make reaching a weapon easier. I would feel better if you took this."

Collette accepted the knife and offered Nawalya a smile of thanks. "This is very well crafted," she remarked after examining it. She liked the weight of it in her hand and the ease with which her fingers wrapped around the handle. The design was elfish, perhaps from southern Galel if the flourishes along the handle could be trusted. The blade also showed some age, though it was well-cared for.

"Thank you. It was my mother's." Nawalya's voice was soft. "She would have liked you."

Collette gave her a gentle smile, touched by Nawalya's actions. So many people wouldn't have dreamed of handing over something so precious. "Then I will take extra care with it."

Nawalya nodded in acknowledgment and gracefully stood. "You have an important dinner with the king tonight. You should try to sleep. I can help you get ready when the time comes."

"That would be wonderful," Collette replied. "You are much better at doing hair than I ever could dream of being."

Nawalya smiled and nodded. "You are welcome to sleep here if you don't wish to disturb Larent."

"Larent is currently put off by the way I smell," Collette said without shame.

Nawalya let out a soft laugh, covering her mouth as she did so. "He would have said that about any of us. When injured, his wolf is more present to help speed up the healing. Sound, smell, and sight are amplified. If you returned to your rooms directly after intercourse, it would have been the strongest scent." Nawalya approached the door leading to her bed. "Feel free," she offered again, and Collette gladly laid down.

Chapter Twenty-Two

Getting out of the private dinner with Brath was impossible. Well, not exactly. Collette knew she could have told the idiot to fuck himself, gathered her people, and marched out of the palace, but even knowing they weren't going to get the support they wanted, it still seemed like a poor choice.

As there had been no way to negotiate an escort for this dinner, Arian, who had appointed himself her chaperone, could only follow Collette as far as the private dining hall. "We'll be on guard," Arian said as quietly as he could. "I'm aware you can defend yourself, but I don't trust Brath."

"I don't either," Collette said as they made their way through the corridors. She could tell they were moving closer towards Brath's quarters. The finery of the decorations drastically improved, and suddenly everything seemed accented with gold and jewels. Occasionally, she spotted items accented by shimmering Merscales. They turned her stomach. "But I want to hear Brath out before we pack up and try something else."

"Tell me you at least have a weapon on you," he asked.

"Of course. I always do," Collette said. "Did you think I was going to run off with three virtual strangers and not always have a weapon?"

Arian raised an eyebrow. "Consider what you just said, then ask yourself why I would check."

"We have to work on making you less friendly, Arian." They arrived at the door, and she scowled, feeling increasingly guarded. "Any parting advice?"

"I would say scream if you need me, but you'll more than likely try and handle any issues yourself so … be careful."

"Will do," Collette said. She gave Arian a short wave and watched as the elf made himself scarce. She very much doubted he would do anything but stay close, and Arian was good at staying in shadows and going undetected.

When she was alone, she was permitted into the inner parts of the king's quarters and shown to a dark table. It was made of rich wood, almost black in color. Again, she was reminded of the castle exterior made from stone found in a much more tropical environment. The table, like many of the surrounding furnishings, showed off intricate pieces of gold and gemstones pressed into the wood. She could make out no discernable pattern, and it struck her that the point was meant to boast rather than to enrich.

The surrounding tables were covered in lush, colorful flowers, still lovely to see, but quickly moving towards decay if the sickly-sweet scent was any indication. She might leave this encounter with a headache thanks to the fragrance. She ran her fingers along the back of the nearest chair as she looked around, thankfully detecting no glimmer of a Merscale. Brath was not a good person, but there were levels of evil.

She looked up as Brath entered the room, finely groomed and shallowly charming as always. He wore a vivid bottle green jacket, certainly meant to compliment his eyes, and his wavy blond hair had been pulled back into a ponytail. "Queen Collette," he greeted with a small inclination of his head. "You look stunning this evening."

Indeed, she thought as much. Another of Nawalya's dresses had been fetched from the safehouse, this a darker blue and more formal. She felt a little naked in the thing with her shoulders and arms bare for the world. Thankfully, her hair obscured a scar crossing her shoulder, but the one on her forearm was displayed—both remnants of a brief attack by a riding crop before she'd been crowned queen. The skirt of her gown was wider than she liked, though not restrictive, which was a concern she'd not had regarding her clothing until she'd been arrested. She didn't even have the luxury of wearing her mother's gold bracelet, which Tolan was still in possession of.

"Thank you, King Brath. A festive occasion warranted a festive dress."

"You wear it well," Brath said and motioned toward the table. "Please have a seat," he invited. "Wine? Beer? Something stronger? Nothing shall be denied."

"Wine will be sufficient," Collette responded. She took a seat in the designated chair and wasn't surprised to see an attendant at the table within seconds to fill her gilded wine glass.

Prompted, she lifted the glass, taking a moment to inhale the scent. She detected nothing alarming and took a small sip. The red liquid was sweet, more so than she'd expected, but the Azmarin tended to like their food and drink a little less savory than she did her own. "You have excellent wine," she complimented.

"I'm glad you like it," Brath said, finally taking his seat at the table, though not at the head where she expected him to go. Instead, he took up residence in the chair beside her, his posture relaxed. An attendant filled Brath's cup with the same wine, and Brath drank deeply. "It is made just outside of the

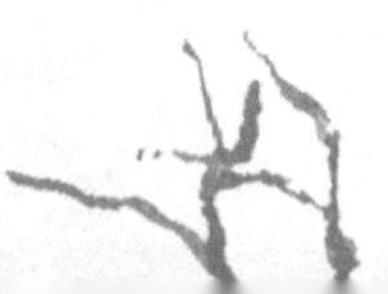

city. I appreciate having it available. I shall supply your party with a case before you depart. I'm hoping that time is far off."

"Are you committing to offering me aid in my pursuit, then?" Collette asked, knowing without a doubt this was unlikely. Brath had been disinterested at best during earlier discussions, and she was not inclined to believe his feelings had changed.

"I think there is still much to discuss," Brath replied, his answer not an answer at all. "Which I hope we can do this evening while sharing a nice meal."

"Of course," Collette agreed.

The first course, trays of fruit, bread, and cheese were delivered to the table, and the respective rulers were free to pick and choose from the items as they liked. Brath ate with more gusto than Collette, though she played the part of an interested guest well enough. She popped a piece of fruit in her mouth and chewed as Brath talked.

"I hope I am not offending you with this observation, but I'm still quite … uncertain when it comes to your pronounced marriage," he said as he picked up his wine. "This man, he is no one, is he not?"

"Why would you make such a statement about my husband?" Collette asked him, eyebrows arched, a feigned look of confusion on her face. "I would not marry 'no one.'"

Brath chuckled. "Not to suggest he is no one to you, of course. But what is it that this man provides you? He's no money. No army. No influence or power. I concede that he is objectively attractive, but I dare say it was not an advantageous match."

"I think we view marriage, and the definition of advantageous, differently," Collette replied. "I am quite fulfilled by my relationship with my husband. I find, too often, people in our positions do not have true friendships or connections with other people. We serve as tools for wealth and power rather than companions who bring a different sort of value to those around them. Those shallow, financially beneficial relationships come from the same types of people who ousted me from my own kingdom."

"And yet, had I been your husband, they'd have lacked the ability, would they not?"

"Perhaps," Collette allowed. "But even if we were married, I would not have permitted the continued sale of Merscales. I understand you have taken no such stance in your own kingdom, correct?"

"It is permitted," Brath confirmed. "But much more regulated."

"You are also in a castle built with resources from the Nereid Kingdom, are you not?" she asked, not deterred.

"Have you seen Merscales since entering my kingdom, Collette?" he asked.

"I have, Brath," she confirmed. "Not in the excessive way that once existed in Coralia under King Sargarus, but I've seen the glittering earrings worn by the ladies of your court, and the cuffs of your servants, even the very ornamentation of your extensive collection of baubles and art. Less adornment does not mean a lack."

"Merpeople are that important to you?" he demanded, his voice rising in volume. He seemed to realize his error, and when he spoke again, it was in a much calmer tone. "Merpeople are not the same as us."

"No, they are much less barbaric. I haven't heard one story of a Nereid or Alven or any other Merperson abducting humans to torture and maim for jewelry."

Brath's expression turned patronizing. "If the use of Merscale offends, I can do away with it. It is not as important to our economy as it was to yours. I dare say I can also do away with your husband just as easily, despite the difficulty he's given me in that task so far."

Brath paused, waiting for her to show her alarm, she was certain, but she deprived him. Larent had faced too many coincidental accidents since arriving for his pronouncement to be a surprise.

The king sat back, surveying her over his glass of wine. "You need to seriously consider the facts, Collette. Marrying me is the best offer you will get. You can have your kingdom back within weeks. You would not even have to lift a finger."

"Why are you so eager to marry me, exactly?" Collette returned, any amusement she'd had at the start of the conversation long gone. "We seem to align on virtually nothing, and you disregard matters I find to be of critical importance. That is before your confession that you've attempted to murder my husband."

"Don't misunderstand me, Collette. I intend to marry you because it is of political advantage to me. Your kingdom has valuable resources and riches that would make me quite happy to possess. Your father promised you to me; so as far as I am concerned, there is no question of your acquiescence to my claim. Frankly, if you want to have lovers on the side, I will not protest. You can even keep the half-elf my servant caught you with." He held a hand, as though emphasizing that his words were logical. "If you hadn't called your other plaything your husband, I wouldn't have to kill him. You cannot have split loyalties."

Collette let out a laugh. "You're ridiculous. This meeting is finished." She pushed her chair back and stood, only for Brath to do the same.

"You'll find I am quite serious on this matter, Collette," he said in a warning tone. "I am not a cruel man. I am offering you a throne. An army. A secure position in a world where you will have the ability to implement the changes you are seeking. All you have to do is follow the commands placed on you and submit to my authority as your husband." He grabbed her arms. "Willing compliance will get you much further."

Then he tried to kiss her.

Collette didn't plan on punching Brath, but somehow, it happened and right in the stomach with a force she'd not anticipated. The king gasped, surprised and in pain, as Collette stepped back. "Do not touch me," she said through gritted teeth.

Brath collapsed to the ground, struggling to breathe, his wine glass clattering on the stone floor. She didn't wait for him to recover or to call out for help. She knelt beside him, grabbed him by the hair, and slammed his head on the ground, knocking him out cold. She then rose and exited the doors she'd come in less than a half hour before.

Once in the hall, she was rejoined by Arian. "We have to leave," she announced.

"Is he dead? Do I need to finish the job?" Arian asked as he fell into step behind her.

"I punched him and knocked him out," Collette said as they walked. "He put his hands on me."

Arian halted, his expression dark. "May I kill him?"

She stopped as well, turning around to look at him. "Why?"

"He touched you in a manner that required you to react with violence instead of diplomacy. Is that not enough reason?"

Collette had not expected this reply, and she was so very tempted. "Were he anyone but the monarch of a very big kingdom, I'd agree, but we're better off with discretion." She indicated they should start moving again. "But thank you."

"I could poison him. That is a discreet manner of death," said Arian, a dangerous smile appearing on his face. "And you are welcome."

"If you can manage it after we're spotted outside of the city, have at it," Collette allowed. She wasn't issuing a directive, not when they needed to hurry.

"We can manage it," Arian said.

Soon enough, they were back at the issued rooms. She let herself into the suite, moving into the bedroom area. Immediately, she moved to shed the dress she'd borrowed from Nawalya and change into something less ostentatious. "Go alert the others," she called to Arian. "We might have ten minutes to get out."

"Will you be okay on your own?" Arian called back.

"I'm fine," she called back. "Go do what is needed."

Arian arrived in the shared suite of rooms minutes later, alarmed, but focused. "We need to leave now," he announced once the door was shut. "Collette assaulted the king for putting hands on her."

Whyldon emerged from the space allocated to him, his brows furrowed, and his lips pressed together in anger. "And he's still alive?"

"For now. I do not know the full details, just that we must leave," he elaborated as he grabbed his stuff. "She has given us permission to deal with him later."

"Good," Tolan decided. His hands flexed at this side near his weapon.

Nawalya moved to stand by Arian, something he was thankful for. "Larent, take Collette to the safehouse. Whyldon should go with Tolan. Arian and I will leave together."

Larent didn't hesitate and walked out.

Tolan looked like he wished to argue but instead turned to Whyldon. "Ready?"

Chapter Twenty-two

"Yes," Whyldon replied. He grabbed his own pack, and he and Tolan left the room.

Arian and Nawalya exchanged looks when it was just the two of them. "Do you think we need to create a distraction?" Nawalya asked in her soft, melodic voice.

Arian considered this but ultimately shook his head. "Larent will get her out in plenty of time. The rest of us are less noticeable." And if they found out that she was still in the palace, he would worry about creating a different distraction.

Making sure he had his bag and medical pack, he nodded towards the door. "Let's go."

The group arrived at the safehouse less than an hour later. Arian breathed a sigh of relief to see the other four had arrived. Getting out of the palace had been the more difficult part of avoiding retribution for Collette's assault on Brath. Escaping the city would be less challenging.

Arian settled back against one of the walls and observed the others while Nawalya settled on one of the beds beside Whyldon. Ever since the announced … encounter between the two, there was no separating Nawalya from Whyldon unless they could help it.

"They will expect us to leave the city right away," Nawalya announced, prompting everyone to look in her direction. "Likely, they think we will head into the forest and cross back into Coralia."

"That is the most logical path," Whyldon agreed. "And obviously one we will not follow. They are going to have people looking for her. Laying low and taking our time is the best choice."

"Correct," Nawalya said, her usually soft voice firm. "We can take our time getting away from the city. Other opinions, of course, are appreciated."

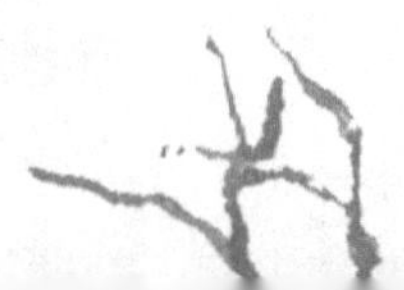

On the opposite side of Whyldon sat Collette. The guard captain was looking over her hand, presumably the one she'd used to punch Brath. Even from his spot across the room, Arian noted the slight redness along her knuckles, though nothing appeared cut or bruised. She'd likely suffer from stiffness and soreness, but nothing he felt compelled to intervene with.

"This isn't the most accommodating of places, but we can stay here for several days if needed," Tolan pointed out.

"I'm not opposed to it," Collette said, her lips pursed in impatience over Whyldon's examination, but didn't pull her hand away.

Arian rolled his eyes as Larent laughed, obviously amused by Collette's impatience with Whyldon. Arian didn't blame her.

"This place is set up for camping out for a few days," Larent pointed out. "All the same, I'd prefer finding an inn. We can move every few days."

"Staying here tonight is probably the safest," Collette said as she took her hand back. "We can use the morning crowds to relocate. The market isn't too far off."

"We have a plan then." Arian pushed off from the wall. "I am going to head out for supplies and listen to the rumors around the city so we may plan better for the coming days."

"Wait," Collette said, flexing her hand absent-mindedly. "Weren't you up all night keeping watch at the palace? You should let someone else go."

"Elves need less sleep than other races," Arian said, his tone slightly surly.

"That's bullshit, Chuckles," Larent spoke up. "And you know we all know that." He got up from his corner seat and approached the elf. "I'll go. You sleep."

"Seconded," Collette replied.

Arian glowered at both of them, but without argument, he moved to one of the beds.

"Not that one!" Larent said with a wince that told Arian all he needed to know about what had happened on that bed.

"Not in the safe room," Arian groused, finding another bed. He looked at Larent expectantly, and only sat when he got a nod.

"You already knew about Nawalya and Whyldon fucking in here," Collette said. "Tolan and Larent came running back acting like the world was on fire."

"Yes, but it is an added burden to know which bed." Arian's lip curled in disgust at the thought. "It means Larent can still smell it."

"And now I'm leaving," Larent said and disappeared out of the door.

"You two have to have sex elsewhere from now on," Collette informed Whyldon and Nawalya. "Larent is traumatized."

Whyldon's expression remained neutral while Nawalya gave a wide, soft smile.

"Rather than recount sexual escapades, perhaps we can go over what happened with Brath," Whyldon suggested.

"I would like the full details," Nawalya added.

Collette gave a dramatic sigh and nodded, though she shifted on the small bed so that she could lean against the wall behind her. "The short of it is, he considers me his possession because of the betrothal Sargarus arranged, which is unsurprising. We figured he would have a problem with Larent being my husband, and he has since we arrived." They all nodded.

"During our brief discussion, Brath confirmed he's been behind the attempts to kill Larent, and he still planned on seeing it through. He said I could keep Tolan." She looked at her lover. "We were caught by a servant, apparently." She glanced back towards the rest of the group. "In exchange for marrying him and letting him kill Larent, he offered an army, my throne back, and support to end the trade of Merscales.

Then he grabbed me, and I punched him. When he was on the ground, I knocked him out."

"I'm surprised you only hit him a few times," Whyldon said darkly.

"I have all of you to think about when I make decisions," Collette replied with a shrug.

Tolan put an arm around Collette, and she responded by resting her head against his shoulder. "I shouldn't have cornered you in that hallway," he said quietly.

Nawalya stood and walked over to Arian, pointed to his medical pack, then extended her hand, palm flat and facing up.

Arian pulled two vials out of his bag, considering them before holding them up. "Collette, would you prefer he suffers or goes quickly?"

Collette's eyes widened at the question, and Arian assumed she wanted to back off of the idea of killing Brath, but she surprised him with her answer. "It would be better for it to be quick, regardless of preference, wouldn't it?"

Arian traded a silent look with Nawalya. He then returned the vials to his bag and pulled out a third. This vial contained a thick, orange-yellow liquid, glowing vibrantly. It both attracted and repulsed.

Nawalya's smile turned deadly as she plucked the poison from Arian's hand. "His death will be quick, but it will not be painless," she declared. "We do not put hands where they are not welcome."

"Are you comfortable with this?" Whyldon asked Collette, another question that surprised Arian. He assumed the captain's anger made their plan the most logical path forward.

Collette hesitated, then nodded. "I usually wouldn't be, but now that he's been denied what he thinks he's owed, he's not going to be easy to deal with. Just imagine if he allies with Zephraim."

Tolan made a thoughtful noise. "Do we need to consider the removal of any advisors or others close to the king? I cannot imagine they were not involved in the plot to kill Larent."

Nawalya shrugged.

"We could do any number of things, but I suspect it will be suspicious should more than one person die," Arian pointed out and looked to Collette for her opinion.

"I agree with Arian. We can't go around killing people because of things they might do or have done. Especially with nothing more than suspicions. We know Brath has admitted to attempted murder. We know he passively backs the Merscale trade. He's also made it clear he believes I belong to him, and I greatly hurt his ego in rejecting him. We can reasonably conclude what his next moves will be. I can't support doing more."

"It's not as if they haven't killed indiscriminately before," Tolan pointed out.

Arian frowned. "You know very well what our vetting process entails. Have we made mistakes? Of course, but we are careful. Not to mention, I believe the blood of some of those mistakes is on your hands. We also don't just abandon plans because of jealousy."

Tolan looked away, refusing to meet Arian's eyes.

"If Tolan wants to start slinging mud, I am happy to indulge him," Nawalya said as she tucked the poison out of sight. "Maybe then we could get some answers about a few things."

"I find myself increasingly curious about this secretive dynamic between the four of you," Whyldon said, standing from the bed. Arian noted that Whyldon rarely remained still when talking, despite his calm demeanor. "Collette and I are constantly reminded of a long and mysterious history that exists there. Perhaps it would be better to know the whole story."

Tolan opened his mouth to object, but Arian held up a hand silencing both him and Nawalya. "There is not much mystery

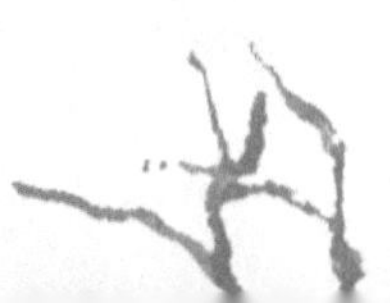

to it. Nawalya, Larent, and I ran into Tolan when he was much younger. Three decades ago, or so, I think. He was trying to create a life as a mercenary as well as an arena fighter. He was not doing well, and we offered to help him."

Arian looked to Nawalya for confirmation, and she nodded. Arian continued. "Tolan's past made him reluctant to trust elves. At first, that included Nawalya and me, so we made introductions, and Tolan connected with others like us. He made his way in the world. Through the years, if we encountered one another, he would occasionally work alongside us, and eventually, trust was built. Of course, he and Larent discovered they could not keep their hands off one another, and emotions developed. Larent would tell you it was love, and Tolan would argue otherwise. Tolan ended up badly hurting Larent either way, and obviously, they aren't together anymore." Arian paused to look at Collette, who had assumed a face of stoic curiosity.

"The next time we saw him was across a battlefield. Usually, which side a fellow mercenary takes doesn't matter. People have all kinds of reasons. Tolan happened to choose incorrectly on that occasion as he was on the side of a tyrant who killed the women and children we were fighting to protect. He implied he chose the tyrant based on where we positioned ourselves." Out of the corner of his eye, he noted that Tolan had his face buried in his hands. "Nawalya and I have moved past the event as we have since learned that was not his motivation. But that does not change the ever-increasing bad decisions he has made since. Truthfully, the only decision I've known him to make that couldn't be called a mistake, at least on his end, is his relationship with Collette."

Arian turned to look at Tolan directly. "Neither of us care if you and Larent fight, if you are a bastard, or get caught in the numerous personal issues you have. You will not, however, disrespect the work Nawalya and I do. I would say not to disrespect Larent, but then I would have to tell him to leave you alone, and that would be a spirit-blessed miracle." To Whyldon, Arian asked, "Any questions?"

Acting as if Arian hadn't just unloaded on Tolan, Nawalya moved back to Whyldon's side. "I am going to scout the castle. I will need to wait a day or two before I poison the king, but it will be best if I have a plan before then. I will be back quickly." She reached up and kissed his cheek. "Make sure Arian sleeps, please."

"Of course," Whyldon promised, kissing her once more before she left.

Nawalya beamed, then saw herself from the room.

Collette, meanwhile, remained next to Tolan, an arm going around him despite all the information Arian had shared. The elf wondered if she was comforting him out of habit, if she disregarded his point of view, or if she saw something redeeming in her lover despite the truth. Arian didn't ask, and instead took a seat on another bed.

Chapter Twenty-Three

To the King Zephraim,

In honor of our long-standing treaty, I wish to inform you that your sister, the disgraced former queen, has recently graced my court with her presence. While she unfortunately escaped after bringing harm to my person, the time she was here was quite informative.

Collette arrived asking for my help in restoring her throne. While I had no intentions of helping her, I did offer her my hand in marriage. This would have strengthened our alliance and allowed me to closely monitor her actions while you saw to the business of running your kingdom. To no one's surprise, she refused my hand, claiming she'd married a man named Larent Leassitor, a minor noble I've never heard of.

She also travels with a guard, Captain John Whyldon, an elf named Arian, another called Tolan, and an elvish woman called Nawalya. It is a small party, but their escape from the palace indicates we would be wise to avoid underestimating them in the future.

I do not know where they are headed, and I would advise keeping an eye on your borders and the ports. She seems to love the Mers, so that would be a good indication of a possible destination.

I wish you a happy and prosperous reign. Included is a belated wedding gift. Please give your wife my best. If there is ever anything I can do to assist you in the matter of your sister, please do not hesitate to ask.

Yours,
Brath Thancred, Emperor of Azmarin

Rhoslyn smirked as she watched a group of men engaged in a competitive bout of *jeu de paume*. The weather was warmer than the season suggested it should be, and she was happy to sit outside bundled up in her dark velvets and firs and enjoy the spectacle. The usually moody Zephraim grinned and laughed with delight with each swing of his racket, and she hoped his joviality would continue beyond the game.

Cheering echoes reverberated along the courtyard, drawing brief attention from servants and passersby who had not been fortunate enough to join a game with the royal couple. She looked up as someone entered her spectator's box.

"Put that there, Diana," she instructed the palace cook, who came bearing a tray of sinful looking pastries. Diana's expression remained neutral, much to Rhoslyn's amusement. The cook briefly glanced towards Rhoslyn, her honey blonde hair falling in tiny strands about her face. Rhoslyn found her pretty in a way that told her the cook held much sway with her husband, but the natural pout of Diana's lips made every expression seem impertinent. Rhoslyn imagined she would need to take a lash to the woman before everything settled as it should. "How is your husband?" she asked.

"He is kept busy with the work and duty bestowed upon members of the guard, Your Majesty," Diana replied, her tone as placid as her expression.

"Well, I should hope so. After all the disruption caused by the traitor and her dissenters, we do want to make sure His Majesty is well represented and protected," Rhoslyn replied in amusement. She waved her hand, dismissing Diana. She thought she caught the cook rolling her eyes, but she was in too good a mood to address it. At least, for now.

Turning her attention to the pastries, Rhoslyn considered her selection as Riken took a seat nearby. She smiled to herself, considering how well his blue tunic fit his broad shoulders. Truly, nothing he wore lessened his handsome features.

"You know," he drawled, keeping his gaze on the game before them. "I approve of every decision you've made so far, except for one."

"Oh?" Rhoslyn asked, glancing over at him. "And what is that?"

Riken dragged his eyes from the match to look at Rhoslyn, and like always, her breath caught in her throat when she was under that heated gaze.

"The cook," he said plainly. "She spies for her husband, who is working against you and Zephraim, and you know it."

"Oh. That's obvious," Rhoslyn replied with a chuckle. She paused to pick out a pastry with her long, slender fingers. "But keeping her close is useful, and I enjoy her subtle humiliation at being made to fetch."

"How is she useful?" he asked, long fingers tracing the line of the chair arm.

"What a question to ask your queen," Rhoslyn said before taking a bite of the small, delicate pastry. When it was chewed and swallowed, she continued. "I know she's untrustworthy and she talks to her husband. Possibly others. What has you so concerned?"

Riken raised an eyebrow. "Nothing other than possible betrayal, infiltration, and your blood spilling across your pillow."

"She is not one I would fear if it came to that," Rhoslyn assured him. "I have plans and keeping her close keeps her husband in line."

"Of course you wouldn't worry about her being the one to slit your throat," Riken said with a chuckle. He moved a few seats closer and selected his own treat from the tray. "Anything you'd like to share with your captive audience? Like how your husband is so calm, despite everything?"

"You know about Collette, then?" Rhoslyn asked.

"So, it's true the Azmarin king confirmed she visited him?" Riken asked. "And Zephraim is that calm?"

"He's rather furious, actually. But he has not yet decided what to do."

"And what have you decided?" Riken asked.

"I don't know what you mean," Rhoslyn said, a smirk still on her face. They were interrupted when Crobán approached, his face red and sweaty from his sporting endeavors. It was clear he would have preferred to observe rather than participate.

"Your Majesty," he greeted with an inclined head. "I hope you're enjoying the game."

"Oh, indeed," Rhoslyn replied. "My husband is quite skillful. You looked as though you were enjoying yourself well enough." As she and Riken had discussed in the past, their dislike and even disgust, of Crobán had to be overlooked. He knew too much and had been too useful in the overthrow.

"Indeed," Crobán replied, side-eyeing Riken for a moment before looking to Rhoslyn. "I hear that the traitor has been

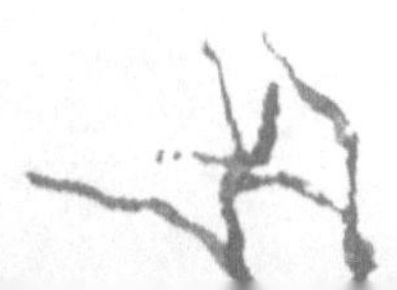

spotted. I hope that means she will be apprehended and brought to justice."

"Oh, I'm certain she will," Rhoslyn said, her head turned just slightly away from Crobán. His exuberant sports display left him smelling so ripe she thought she might need her own bath if he remained close by for much longer.

"I know it's illegal, but were my father still here, he might have some suggestions on what to do with the traitor once she is caught. Blood magic. Flaying. Use of the brazen bull. They all appeal," he said as he examined his nails.

"Riken!" Rhoslyn said, eyes widened in surprise. She playfully swatted his arm. "How terrible of you."

"Perhaps so," Crobán said. "But Collette is a woman who has earned punishment."

"Lord Crobán," Riken interjected. "Collette's skill in the woods is well known, even to those with little intelligence or observational skill. Azmarin is also a large country. Finding her might prove difficult." He looked at his nails as he spoke, though Rhoslyn admitted this was better than his usual treatment.

Crobán regarded Riken with a scowl. "Why don't you go get some wine to cool down, Garibald? The others will be finished with their game soon, and then it will be infinitely more difficult to quench your thirst." Her tone was light and friendly, and thankfully, he took her suggestion as it was given.

"That is a lovely idea, Your Majesty," Crobán said and slowly stood before waddling off. He was just out of earshot when Riken spoke again.

"How can you stand him?" Riken asked.

"He has his uses, and it is in our best interest to do so," Rhoslyn replied. "Besides, he was a staunch supporter of Zephraim."

"He would have supported anyone who financially benefited him, my love," Riken quietly reminded her. "He's still a useless lump, and you have better allies. You just have to let them off of their leash."

"Do my proclaimed allies have a problem with leashes?" Rhoslyn asked, one eyebrow raised.

He gave her a loaded look, then leaned forward and whispered in her ear, "I don't mind your dainty hands holding my leash, but we could have so much more fun if you'd just let me go." He grinned to himself before continuing. "I promise to beg for your permission first, if that helps."

Rhoslyn smirked at the response, though the rest of her expression remained politely interested. "It might be fun, seeing you beg."

"Only for you." A discreet glance around, and he gently ran a hand down her back. "I miss you," he said quietly. "I would hope you miss me too, unless you no longer want to play with your humble servant."

That did draw her attention, and she looked at him more fully. "You know I will always return to you," she quietly promised.

"Good," he whispered. "I would burn this world down for you, never forget that."

Rhoslyn might have forgotten herself, but the cheers from the players and the sounds of approaching footsteps prevented her from saying more. She plastered a smile on her face, a happy expression she wore whenever her new husband approached. "You played well," she complimented, laughing along as Zephraim hopped over the half wall to the spectator box to join her. Only then did he gather her up and kiss her deeply.

"I'm glad you were entertained," Zephraim said when the kiss broke. He was flushed from the exertion, but unlike Crobán, had emerged from the game with just as much appeal as he ever had.

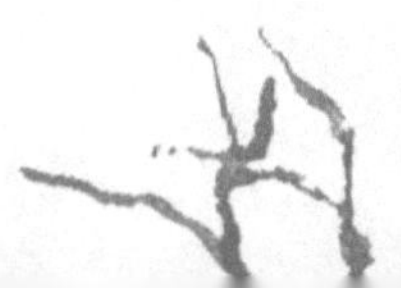

"You did well, my king," Riken added, not a trace of the prior conversation in his expression or voice.

"I'm afraid my skills in this game are lacking, Riken," Zephraim said. He took a seat beside Rhoslyn, his usually lazy posture on display for all to see. Even with Zephraim behaving more jubilantly than he had prior to their marriage, the inherent moodiness of his nature remained.

"You missed Lord Crobán," Rhoslyn informed him.

"Oh?" Zeph asked as he selected something to eat from the tray. "He seemed uninterested in sport today."

"It wasn't about the sport," Rhoslyn said. "He's heard about your sister's visit to Azmarin."

"All he's ever interested in is gossip. I think he lives for it more than he does food," Riken remarked.

Zephraim focused on his own treat, choosing bits from the selection that had earlier been presented to Rhoslyn. "I think Collette will realize she'll find no help now that she's left Brath's palace," he said.

"I would be happy to send my own people, just to check in on things, see what might be discovered," Riken offered as he grabbed a grape cluster from the offered food. "I was just talking about what possibilities await her once she is apprehended."

"If you wish to spend your time and money on the situation, you certainly may," Zephraim replied with a shrug. "She is near friendless and will run out of money and resources before long. She is not of concern, as much as I know you'd like to see her on the rack."

Riken nodded with a chuckle. "I have mentioned other options."

"With increasing gusto," Zephraim replied. "I believe you even said blood magic at one point."

"Do you plan on playing more?" Rhoslyn asked, offering her husband a chalice of wine which Zephraim accepted.

Chapter Twenty-three

"I thought I might retire until later," Zephraim said after a deep gulp of the red liquid. "Would my wife care to join me?"

Rhoslyn hid her face, pretending to blush in girlish embarrassment. Zephraim appreciated it. "I would go where my husband bids me."

Zephraim grinned and downed the rest of his drink before standing and offering a hand to Rhoslyn. "We'll see you later, Riken," he said and escorted Rhoslyn towards the palace.

She gave a brief look back at Riken, then directed her gaze forward.

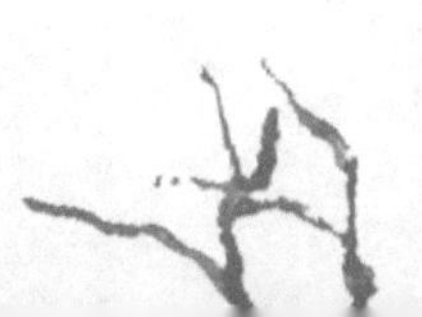

Chapter Twenty-Four

To the honorable majesty, King Brath,

I appreciate your notice of my sister's location in your kingdom. We were unfortunate in suffering her escape after she was arrested for countless atrocities. At your leave, I will dispatch soldiers to Azmarin in hopes of catching her. Of course, if you do so before we can, please see fit to dispose of her as necessary. I would not be surprised if she tried to rally your own people against you.

On another topic, I wish to extend my appreciation for your generous gift of wine and spices. Having such dear friends in times like these means quite a lot. I hope to extend my own friendship to you in any way that might be as appreciated.

Yours,
Zephraim, King of Coralia

Chapter Twenty-four

To the Nereid King,

It has recently come to my attention that my sister, the fallen queen, has been spotted in Azmarin. As I am sure you know, she professed being an advocate for your people, going so far as to host an ambassador in Quenall for a time before her arrest. It is my belief that she and her party might travel to your kingdom seeking sanctuary against the crimes of which she has been found guilty.

Please know that it is in the best interest of you and your people to apprehend her, should she appear, and either execute her, or if you cannot, hold her until Coralian representatives arrive. Choosing to support her claim to the throne would not serve your interests.

Yours,
Zephraim, King of Coralia

Jayden tilted his head slightly as he read the letter his cousin had handed him. The room spun, blurring the coral and tan colors of the decor together, and he considered he might have had more to drink than was wise. "Is he serious?" Jayden asked, reaching for his cup. He knew he shouldn't, but between Merscales being sold once more in Quenall and other parts of Coralia, and now this mockery from their king, more wine seemed like the best idea.

"I think so," Aphros said as he nursed his own drink. "The threats are … interesting to say the least. Still, some good came from this." He reached out for the letter once more, and Jayden passed it to him before refilling his glass.

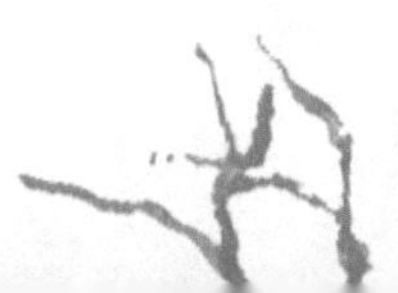

"What good are you seeing, cousin, because all I see is a spoiled man-child who thinks we should cower before him." With the threat, he could anticipate the Coralians would soon turn up in ships with swords.

Aphros gave him a smile. "We know she is alive, she escaped Coralia, and she's got a plan of some sort. That is more than we've known in months."

Even through the fog of drink, Jayden recognized the truth of Aphros's words, and he felt incredibly hopeful. Leaning on the table, he rested his forearms. "She does seem capable of keeping a cool head in a dire situation. And she has a very distinct sense of responsibility and priority. She thought to get me out of Quenall the night of the overthrow, after all." It still amazed him when he thought about it. There was a real possibility that he'd have been maimed and left for dead, otherwise.

He took another sip of wine. "I believe whatever she has planned, it may take time to bear fruit, but she will sit on her thrown once more. What it will take, what we will lose, and what she will sacrifice, I don't want to consider." He gave a snort. "It's hilarious that he thinks we would allow the Coralians on our lands."

"Of course, we would never permit such a thing," Aphros agreed. "But until this letter came, we could only wait for the possibility to come to fruition. Now we have been threatened, which means we can respond. And we know she is alive, which means we owe her support, and can likely count on the same from her."

Jayden regarded his king. "If it pleases, I would like to gather a team to look for her. I'm just not sure where to start." He paused and considered this option from another angle, even as he downed his glass.

"I have no objections," Aphros said. He took another sip of wine and sat thoughtfully. "We can assume things did not go well in Azmarin, no matter what her goal may have been. We can also surmise that someone high ranking reported her location to Coralia."

"I've heard rumors that Azmarin flies mourning colors," Jayden replied moving to reach for another bottle of wine, only to decide against it. "The timing is interesting, even if she ultimately had nothing to do with it." Somehow, he thought she probably did. "I will send people to Pontus Bay and have them work their way to Azmarin and Wildrun. We will see if we can find her, and if so, help to get her here." In Jayden's opinion, they owed her that much.

"That's as much as we can do until she makes herself known. Perhaps she is heading to us on her own accord. That would make this much easier," Aphros replied.

"It would, but this world is unkind. I hope, wherever she is, she is doing well."

"I have the same hope," Aphros said in agreement.

Chapter Twenty-Five

Days later, the group left the safehouse in the hours before dawn, traveling on foot towards the city gates. The plan, loose as it was, had them heading south, back over the Coralia border and into Galel. It was likely they would have to figure out where to bunker down until spring if they were not quick. If they made good time, it would be possible to catch a ship to the neighboring kingdom, Fyithas, or even the Nereid kingdom.

By midafternoon, they were strolling through the forest, enjoying the warmth brought on by the sun, and planning to stop overnight in the next village. After a short break while Larent went scouting, it was determined they'd arrive in another few miles. The time passed leisurely, with storytelling and jokes, and even a rousing debate on which group of elves made the best sort of weapons. Nawalya and Arian were both quite impassioned in this debate, even if they disagreed.

By the time they reached the inn and tavern, they had decided on staying in for the evening as the group was collectively starving. They settled at a table in a far corner, and soon found themselves provided with stew, bread, and a hearty helping of some sort of meat pie that smelled delicious. The ale and wine were plentiful, leaving Collette in a particularly good mood.

"Okay, so tell me," Collette said after swallowing a bite of food. She couldn't attest to the others, but her consumption of ale left her feeling toasty. "What were the three of you doing in Quenall?"

Surprisingly, Nawalya, Arian, Larent, and even Tolan froze. Exchanging glances and subtle changes in expression, Tolan looked away. Arian finally nodded to Larent, who grinned.

"That's a funny story. You see, we were there to kill Sargarus. When we found out he'd been dead for some time, we were there to kill you, if you were anything like the king. Thankfully, you weren't, so yay." He held up his hands and wiggled them. Clearly, the wolf was feeling his alcohol as well.

"You were going to assassinate me?" Collette asked, her tone and expression indicating the news delighted her. "That's amazing. Why didn't you?"

Arian, Nawalya, and Tolan just looked at Collette in surprise while Larent laughed. "I knew you'd react like that." He paused to catch his breath. "Because you aren't anything like your father."

"Ugh," Collette said with a look of disgust. "Don't call him that."

"Either way," Larent said, waving off the protest. "Now, you tell us something. Why the fuck was getting to you easier than getting to him? I know you can handle yourself, but we had so many opportunities to kill you that were not present when we tried to kill him."

"I didn't layer myself in personal guards is the short answer," Collette said after thinking about it. "And I didn't tell Whyldon to do anything about the three of you. It was also sort of obvious that Tolan knew who you were, and obviously, I trust Tolan. Not to mention, Larent, you're sort of terrible at being stealthy."

"I'm stealthy!" Larent insisted. "Besides, Nawalya is the one who outed us." Nawalya's cheeks turned red, and she looked down at her hands. He grinned and took a drink. "I still believe if she hadn't been so insistent on meeting Blue Eyes, we wouldn't have been outed for quite some time."

"I second that," Arian deadpanned, causing Nawalya's blush to deepen.

Larent laughed again. "She outed us so hard when you guys spotted her in the forest, and we won't talk about the dead body."

"What dead body?" Collette asked.

Whyldon sighed. "Arian brought a dead body to me one day at the castle. Sent by Nawalya."

"Why?" Collette asked.

Arian gave Nawalya a dark look. "A mercenary was sent to assassinate you. Nawalya killed him first, and then she decided I just had to bring the body to Whyldon."

"He had to get it from the courtyard to the war room without getting caught," Larent elaborated. "It was great, though not something Nawalya normally does, admittedly."

"Why was I not informed that someone was trying to assassinate me?" Collette asked, though she still found herself amused by all of this. "First, you three want to assassinate me because I might be as big an asshole as my predecessor. Then you change your mind, so some new guy shows up with the same plan and you stop him." She paused to sip from her ale. "In the meantime, I just get to play nice with the Almeidas. You all are unfair."

Larent laughed. "Hey, we told Whyldon. Also, we found a letter on him we couldn't link to any of the nobles."

"Please do not implicate me in this," Whyldon said with a laugh. "We couldn't definitively assign blame to anyone, but I had reason to suspect a certain family was behind it."

"But you *knew*," Collette insisted.

"I brought the body directly to him," Arian said with a small smirk. "He very much knew."

"That's why I sometimes call Nawalya "kitten," because she does shit like that," Larent said. He put his hands up as Nawalya's dagger appeared under his throat. "She hates when I call her that, as you can see."

Nawalya nodded and slowly withdrew the blade.

"You went back and forth on what you called me for a while," Collette said and finished her ale. Thankfully, the barmaid stopped by the table, refilled drinks, and promised more food in exchange for coin which was passed over. When they were alone again, Collette picked up on the conversation.

"Assuming the three of you might change your mind one day, and it's decided I do need to be assassinated, can I choose who does it?"

"Sure. It would be a matter of how you want to die," Larent said, pointing to himself. "I would slit your throat mid-seduction." Larent paused and pointed to Nawalya. "Poison." He indicated Arian. "Or given a fighting chance."

"Oh, very tough choices," Collette said, feigning deep thought. "Well clearly, I can't go for poison. That can take quite a long time, and it would be painful. I'd like to avoid a prolonged, tortuous death."

"For you, I would make it quick," Nawalya said softly. "While I hated the king, I could not hate you. Unless you decided to commit atrocities like your father, however, then it would last for hours."

"You forget, we probably wouldn't assassinate you now that we've shared a bonding experience. Not unless you lost your mind, and then all bets are off," Larent said matter-of-factly.

"It sounds like you're volunteering." Collette gestured to the group. "So, if you decide I need to be assassinated, I expect Larent to do it."

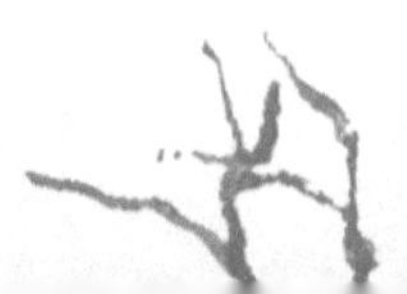

Larent held his hands up. "Nope, I'm out. It would be Arian."

"You wouldn't assassinate me, but you would be okay with Arian doing it?" she said, pressing a hand to her chest in an over-dramatic fashion. "Well, I'm offended."

Larent laughed. "I never said I was okay with it, but if we got to a point where you had to be taken out, I'd be too busy killing him." He jabbed a thumb in Whyldon's direction. "Lady knows Nawalya couldn't do it, and I don't know that I could kill you."

"I, on the other hand," Arian said, "would offer you honor in death and kill you knowing it was to protect the memory of who you had been."

"Why are we talking about your hypothetical death, exactly?" Whyldon asked.

"Good question," Tolan said under his breath.

Collette shrugged, raising her brow as she realized how quiet Tolan had been all evening. "They were potentially going to assassinate me. They might decide that needs to happen one day. Planning is a good thing. Besides, what else are we going to do? Some of us are drunk."

"Let me ask a different question," Whyldon said. His eyes crinkled as he laughed, and Collette knew he was enjoying himself almost as much as she was. "Are you planning on becoming assassination-worthy?"

"No," Collette said. "But we can never be guaranteed of anything. I could be cursed, or turn evil, or align myself with some shadowy force."

"And you think that's likely?" Whyldon asked with a snort.

"Absolutely," Collette said. "These three wanted to kill me, remember?"

"Yes, I am listening to the discussion," Whyldon confirmed.

"So, it is entirely plausible that something like a curse could happen," Collette said.

"Blood magic is always a concern," Arian said seriously. "And not just from one's known enemies. Piss off the wrong person, and they could decide to use it because they had a bad day, week, or year."

Larent drained his tankard of ale and thumped it down on the table. "We've dealt with that before, if you can't tell."

"If I am ever possessed by blood magic, just take me out," Collette said seriously. "I'd rather be dead than be used to hurt others." Her fingertips gently tapped against the bottom of her mug as she thought about the ramifications.

"It's the same for each of us," Arian responded. "We've heard there are ways to work around blood magic or to hinder it for a time, but killing the victim if you cannot kill the person who cast the spell is often best."

"You know, if one of us finds ourselves in a comparable situation, I could always write to Nana. She has the best ideas for how to handle that shit," Larent mused.

"No!" shouted Arian, Nawalya, and Tolan at once.

"Why don't you want to involve Nana?" Collette asked, intrigued.

"Nana Leassitor," Arian started before looking up at the ceiling. "Whom we all love and respect, is very … intense."

Nawalya and Tolan nodded while Larent just smiled. "She taught me almost everything I know and helped them refine their talents," Larent explained.

"She sounds lovely," Collette said and pointed at Larent. "I want to meet her someday."

"She'd adore you," Larent said brightly. "And it's possible you could meet her eventually."

"We don't want to drag people into this unnecessarily," Collette said. "Like this one guy I know, kept popping up in my private quarters in the palace. Next thing I know, he's on the run with me. Funny how that happened."

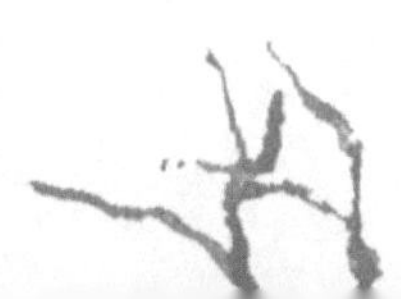

"Right, such a coincidence how stuff like that happened," Larent said with a grin.

It was hard for any of them to miss Tolan's glare as he rose from the table and headed towards the bar where they overheard him ordering more drinks. Collette was going to have to check in with him soon. It made her feel guilty for reasons she couldn't identify. Still, she looked back at Larent and opened her mouth to speak, only to be cut off by Whyldon.

"If you two start talking about assassinations again, I might carry it out myself and be done with it," Whyldon playfully warned.

"We could talk about assassination attempts that don't involve me," Collette pointed out.

"Oh," Larent said, looking at Arian with a grin. "Remember that one failed attempt?" he asked.

"Yes. One tends to remember when they fail to murder a king," Aria replied.

"What stopped you?" Collette asked, placing a hand on Tolan's thigh as he took his seat beside her. He offered her a weak smile, which made her want to know what was bothering him.

Arian raised an eyebrow as Larent laughed and Nawalya giggled. "You did."

"Me?" she said, then her eyes grew wide, and she looked at Whyldon. "I told you I saw an elf in the corridors, and you didn't believe me!"

Arian rolled his eyes. "You are still a gremlin," he directed to Collette.

"Collette has persisted in being herself," Whyldon confirmed, amusement dancing in his blue eyes.

"I love knowing that at the tender age of six, I spoiled your plans, Arian. You should have given me a dagger or an arrow or something, and I'd have likely gone away."

"I did not know that at the time, nor am I prone to giving weapons to children." He side-eyed Nawalya in a way that clearly stated handing weapons to youngsters would be her choice.

"In fairness, Whyldon didn't let me have weapons either," Collette said.

"That is more than likely for the best," Arian said, the corners of his lips pulling upward.

"It was," Whyldon confirmed. "She had more of a temper back then."

"Maybe she could have killed Sargarus for us if you had given her a dagger," Larent said with a laugh.

"You laugh, but she was better with a knife at six than many of the soldiers," Whyldon said. "Not so much arrows. She just thought they were pretty."

"You act as though I gave you a hard time, Whyldon," Collette protested as the barmaid came back around with a pitcher, having been previously summoned by Tolan. Collette declined further drink.

"You did," he confirmed. "Frequently."

All of them laughed.

Arian yawned and looked at Nawalya. "Are you still planning on heading back to the palace?"

Nawalya nodded. "Tonight proved sufficient exposure of our group far away from the capitol."

"We should call it a night, then," Whyldon suggested. "It is already late, and the distance is considerable."

Nawalya nodded, her dark hair brushing against her shoulders. "We had a late start this morning, so the travel will not be bad."

"I'll help you finish packing," Arian offered, and he stood from his seat, intending to follow after Nawalya. She gave the

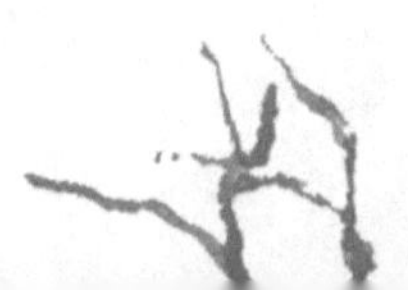

group a wiggle of her fingers in goodbye as she stood, then the two elves went upstairs, leaving the rest at the table.

"I suppose that's our cue to settle in for the evening," Collette said as she sat back in her seat. She looked at Tolan. "Are you ready to retire?" she asked quietly.

"Can we, please?" he asked, his mood mostly unchanged.

"Of course," she said, standing and offering her hand to Tolan. He took it, and the two left Larent and Whyldon to fend for themselves.

My Dearest Thomas,

Nawalya went off to kill King Brath tonight, and I find myself wondering what you would say if you were here. Would you condemn us for murder, or would you agree that we are doing the right thing? A part of me doesn't know if we are making the right choice, but Brath is a threat who is far too comfortable putting his hands in unwelcomed places. I wish you were here. I'm glad you are not.

Yours always,
Arian

This message, too, sat at the bottom of his pack.

Chapter Twenty-Six

Collette closed the door to the room she shared with Tolan. Except for the streetlights streaming in through the single window, the room was dark. Collette went to the dresser where an oil lamp sat. She lit it, and the room brightened considerably. Only then did she look at Tolan. "Okay," she began gently. "What's wrong?"

Tolan sighed, though his frustration remained in his shoulders and expression. "Nothing important. I just didn't care for the direction the conversation was going."

"Which part?" she asked, trying to understand. "It was just a bit of fun."

"Discussions about them planning on killing you and indirect snipes at my expense are fun?" Tolan asked. His hands balled into fists at his sides, and he closed his eyes as he took a deep breath. Yes, she was so much closer to Larent now and spent increasing amounts of time with him. Yes, his insecurities were rearing their head. But he didn't need to be mad at her. This wasn't her fault.

"I was having fun, and I was the butt of the assassination joke," Collette pointed out. "Even Whyldon laughed."

"It wasn't that funny. They are extremely good at what they do. Especially Arian."

"I'm aware," Collette said. "Nawalya is on her way to murder someone as we speak."

"And she's barely at Arian's level, having to use potions and such. Larent has to catch people off guard. He's not really a killer," Tolan said. He approached her and put his hands on her arms, not in the vice-like grip Brath had used, but gentle and concerned. "If Arian or Nawalya had determined you should die, you would be dead and there is nothing I could have done. They are better fighters, they would have been successful, and you were sitting there joking with them about it like it's okay they were considering killing you."

"Hey," Collette said gently, cupping his face with her hands. "Even if they were planning it before, they aren't now. I am safe."

Tolan stayed close, but he refused to look at Collette. Spirits, he didn't deserve her. "They approached me saying they had heard of a threat to you, that they were there to help. They used me, and lied to me, and I let them. I put you in danger."

"Out of everyone, you kept me out of danger long enough for us to be here now instead of me rotting away in jail or dead. Either way, you chose the option with the greatest chance of my survival," she pointed out.

"I allowed myself to be fooled. I happily went between them and Whyldon when I should have gathered the two of you up and told you everything I knew. If I had, maybe none of this would have happened," Tolan said.

"Maybe so, but nothing terrible has happened so far. I am alive, and I trust them. Should I not?"

Tolan put his arms around Collette, then rested his forehead against hers. He took comfort that her hands still held his face, that whatever shame he felt for himself did not come from her, no matter how much he deserved it.

Chapter Twenty-six

"Maybe? I don't know," he answered. "They are out for themselves often enough, but they have always tried to make the right choices."

"You believe I can trust them. Otherwise, you wouldn't have let me leave with Arian the night we left Quenall."

"I still should have done more." Hadn't Arian said something like that earlier, about his fuck ups and mistakes?

"You did," she insisted. "Why don't we try to get some sleep? The alcohol is demanding it."

"I'm not tired. Why don't you lie down? I'll stay here and keep watch."

She frowned, as he knew she would, but nodded and pulled him into a soft kiss. "Don't stay up too late."

"I won't," he said, his hand coming up to his necklace. Suddenly, he felt he knew what he needed to do.

Larent hated to admit their fun dinner had ended. He understood the reasons. Nawalya had a lengthy trek back to the capitol to dispose of Brath. There were many reasons the king deserved it, especially after he kept putting his hands on Collette. But, if Larent was being honest with himself, he wasn't upset because Nawalya would be gone for a few days. He was upset because of Tolan.

He had done everything in his power to monopolize Collette's time since they'd been back on the road, and it was starting to piss him off. She was with Tolan, and Tolan had zero interest in him, and he needed to be okay with their relationship.

For want of something that didn't involve sitting in his room alone, he decided to join Nawalya and Arian before she departed. He knocked on their door once before entering, only

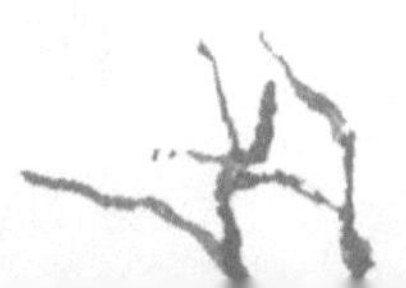

to find both elves bracing. "And what is going on here?" he asked them in surprise.

The two traded a look as if they were considering not telling him, as if they could keep something from him. They had tried before, to protect him, and it never worked out.

"Nawalya had a vision of you killing Collette in wolf form," Arian told him, voice flatter than normal.

Larent stared at Arian for a moment, then burst out laughing. "Pull the other one, Chuckles." He shook his head, unable to believe they would mess with him, only for the laughter to die as he looked at Nawalya. Her grave expression told him this was no joke. "Shit." His mind absorbed the information even as he asked, "How many times have you dreamt of it?

"Twice," Nawalya replied.

Larent felt relieved. Twice wasn't great, but it also wasn't bad. They had learned through trial and error that the more often she had a vision, the more likely it was to come true. Personal choice made a difference as well, so Larent was making the choice to not hurt Collette, no matter what. Even as he had the thought, another occurred to him. "We can't tell the others!" he blurted out.

"Why the fuck not?" demanded Arian. "Don't you think she has a right to know?"

"If we tell them, Tolan and Whyldon will take Collette and leave," Larent said, ignoring how desperate his explanation made him sound.

"Which would be the smart thing for them to do. If we are a danger to her…"

Larent cut Arian off. "We aren't. You know as well as I this is a possibility and not a fact. She's in more danger if she goes off with Whyldon and Tolan alone instead of staying with us."

Arian opened his mouth to argue, but Nawalya cut in this time. "He is right. Tolan and Whyldon are both skilled warriors, but Tolan is too emotionally invested to make smart choices where Collette is concerned and Whyldon too cautious."

Arian's caustic snort spoke volumes. "And you two are not emotionally compromised? You—" he pointed at Nawalya, "are worried about losing Whyldon."

Nawalya hung her head.

"And you," he directed at Larent. "Do I even need to say it?"

Larent looked sheepish. "That doesn't invalidate the fact that the more of us are with her, the better protected she will be. Also, if you two make sure I'm never alone with her..." He glanced at Nawalya, waiting for her to pick up the thread, which she did beautifully.

"I have only seen this outcome twice, with months in between the visions. I have been searching for it, and there is a low possibility of it coming true." She reached out and put a hand on Arian's shoulder. "Let us keep this between us for now. If I have the vision again, then we tell the others."

She gave Arian a soft, imploring smile that always got her her way, and Larent held in a cheer as he watched Arian crumple.

"Fine, but if this goes wrong, it's on your heads, whatever the consequences. Especially yours, Nawalya. I know we are all pretending not to know, but if she's killed, *Whyldon* will not be pleased." That said, Arian wordlessly left the room.

"What in the spirits is he talking about?" Larent asked, confused.

Nawalya just shook her head. "I will tell you when I return."

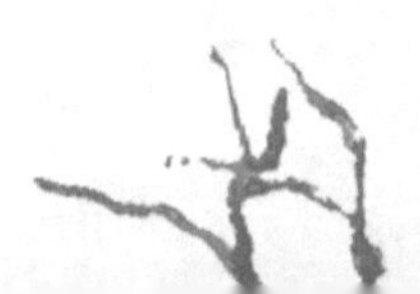

Chapter Twenty-Seven

Tolan sat in a chair in the corner long into the night, watching Collette as she slipped into a deep sleep. He'd thought about joining her, but sleep eluded him as his mind tossed and turned like a small boat on a stormy sea. As the hour grew late, the fire in the room burning to low embers, he came to the only conclusion he could. He was utterly useless to Collette.

He had always known this. He didn't need the voice in the back of his head, the one that sounded so much like his stepfather, or even Larent's random barbs, to remind him he had nothing to offer her.

Yes, he had been her emotional support, a shoulder for her to lean on, but increasingly that job seemed to be going to Larent. Nawalya was much more skilled at hunting than he was, and Arian was the better tracker. Whyldon was the voice of reason, and Collette could protect herself. That left him as the cook, and Collette didn't need a cook. She needed someone who could truly be an asset for her, for her kingdom, and really, there was only one way he could be an asset.

Grasping his necklace, his thoughts circled. This necklace was the only thing he had left of his mother and the only thing he had ever had of his unknown father. He didn't know the man's name as his mother was forbidden from speaking it after she had been forced to marry his stepfather. Honestly, he'd never thought much about the necklace until Collette had made a throwaway comment about it having the crest of L'orilan engraved upon it.

Not truly knowing what the emblem meant, he'd used his spare time in Coralia to research in secret and discovered something that might actually help Collette, something that might make him less useless, and he was going to take advantage of it right now.

Standing, Tolan quietly gathered his belongings, his thoughts continuing to run amok with self-loathing, anger, and determination. Looking over at the bed, a part of him didn't want to leave. He could so easily crawl into bed next to Collette, wrap his arms around her, and continue pretending he was worthy of her. But his thoughts continued to tell him he wasn't worthy, and she was the only one who refused to admit it.

Tolan gave a final glance around the dark room, wanting to make sure that he had everything he needed for his journey. *You're stalling*, his mind berated him. He knew there was nothing he'd need that he couldn't get along the way. He closed his eyes as he tried to force himself to do the hardest part.

Throwing his bag over his shoulder, he moved to the window but paused as the intricate gold bracelet on his wrist glittered in the moonlight. She'd gifted it to him as a token of good luck the day of the tournament, giving it no thought to pluck it from her wrist and hand it over. It was her mother's, a possession Collette prized above others, and just another reminder of how unworthy he was of her. He realized, then, that he had never let her announce their relationship because he had known that from the start.

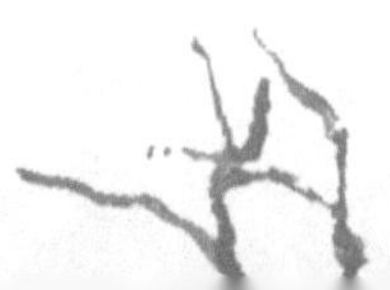

Setting his bag on the ground, Tolan walked back over to the bed, watching Collette sleep more peacefully than she had in weeks. He had to close his eyes again, trying to keep the prickling of his sinuses at bay. *This was the right thing.* He turned from her, removing the bracelet from his wrist with a speed that would prevent him from changing his mind. Gently, he placed it on the bedside table, an obvious spot for her to find it when she woke. Resolved, he went back to the window, grabbed his bag once again, and departed before he could stop himself.

Had he been in his right mind, had Collette possibly chosen that moment to awaken, he would have realized he was doing exactly what he had done to Larent. He was leaving in the middle of the night, with no word, and no explanation.

Chapter Twenty-Eight

Collette turned over, escaping the light streaming through the windows. It was early, and with Nawalya away, they would be lingering in the area for a few more days. She could sleep in a bit.

The bed was soft, the covers warm, and she was settling into sleep again when the thought that something was wrong hit her. She opened her eyes, realizing she was alone. Recalling last night's discussion with Tolan, she sat up, looking around the small room, hoping he hadn't slept in the chair in the corner. It was empty.

Her brows narrowed, and she got out of bed, finger-combing her hair, intent on looking for him. She had her boots on and was halfway to the door when she noticed her bracelet on the bedside table. She frowned and picked up the delicate gold rope. Putting it on, she surveyed the room again. It was empty of his things. Her heart stuttered at the possible meaning.

She left the room and quickly went downstairs, hoping that Tolan would be dining with the others. He wasn't, but she did see Arian and Larent eating a heavy breakfast. The thought of food was enough to turn her stomach.

Arian flicked Larent on the forehead. "If you do not stop pestering me, I will topple you from that chair, drag you into to the streets, and throw you into the largest pile of horse shit I can find," he threatened the shifter.

Collette rolled her eyes at the exchange but didn't address it. They were frequently engaged in bickering, and their easy exchange told her they weren't aware of Tolan's disappearance. "Have either of you seen Tolan this morning?"

Larent and Arian traded a look, Arian's more threatening before the two shook their heads. "No, but it is possible he awoke before us and is out on the town. Tolan has extraordinarily strong opinions about assassins and assassinations. It is the only line of work he refused completely," Arian said, looking on with concern.

"Yeah. He's all high and mighty about that part of our job," Larent chimed in.

Collette didn't think that was the case. He would have told her if he was going to clear his head. He also wouldn't have taken all of his things with him. "If he was angry, he would have said something to one of us, right?"

Arian shook his head, even as Larent said, "I wish. One time we had to assassinate this evil upstart to save a small village. Assassinating her saved a ton of lives, but he got all pissy and left for a few hours without telling anyone. It almost ruined the plan."

"He usually tells me," she said as dread spread through her chest. A reality she didn't want to embrace was sinking in, especially since she knew the presence of her bracelet was clear.

Larent and Arian exchanged glances again, and without a word between them, Arian stood. "I will search for him," he offered.

"I… I don't think that's going to help." She held up her arm to show them the bracelet. "He left this behind, and I think his stuff is gone."

"Fuck," Larent said. He pulled out the chair next to him and patted the seat. "It's still possible he's just out moping, Freckles. Let's give Arian a chance to check. He's a good tracker, after all."

Collette did take the seat beside him, leaning back, her arms crossed. She felt numb and jittery, and the posture kept it contained. Tolan had left. He was gone. It was the only thing that could have happened. Nothing else made sense.

"I will be back," Arian said before striding away, leaving Collette and Larent alone.

Larent patted her knee. "Try not to get upset just yet," he counseled. "He does hate assassinations. He's probably not too far off. Arian will bring him back."

"If by some chance Arian finds him, and he was trying to leave, why would I want him to bring Tolan back?" she asked.

Larent opened his mouth to respond, but he was stayed by Whyldon's arrival.

"Have I missed out on something?" he asked the two almost immediately, observant as ever.

It was Larent who replied. "Tolan wasn't in their room this morning. Arian is out looking for him."

Whyldon turned his attention fully to Collette, blue eyes narrowed in heavy concern. "Are you worried something happened to him, or do you think he's gone?"

She shook her head. "I know he left on his own."

Whyldon took a seat on her other side. "How do you know?"

"His stuff is gone," she replied in a hollow voice. "And he gave this back." She indicated her bracelet again.

"Did you two argue? Did something happen?" Whyldon asked. He had a tendency to get down to fact-finding when other options were lacking.

Collette shook her head again. "He was upset by the conversation last night, but there was no fight."

Whyldon was quiet for a moment, though he reached over and put a hand on her arm. "I am sorry," he told her gently. "I never expected this of him."

Collette snorted. Perhaps Whyldon had never been cruel to Tolan, but he had made it clear he hadn't approved of the relationship. "Since when do you like Tolan?

"I've never disliked him, Collette. In many ways, he reminds me of myself, but…" He sighed and shook his head. "I wondered about a lot of things. His insistence on maintaining secrecy about your relationship was one thing I worried about."

"Aren't you guilty of telling him it was for the best on numerous occasions?" she demanded.

"I am," Whyldon confirmed. "But he didn't have to listen. And if I am being honest, he's spent weeks moping. He clearly wasn't happy being here."

Collette abruptly stood. "I'm going out. I can't just sit here."

Larent straightened. "Do you want me to come with you?"

"I usually don't get a choice in being alone," she replied, feeling a little bad for being short with Larent. It wasn't his fault.

"I can stay." Larent shrugged, kicking his feet up.

"Given that we do not know for certain Tolan left of his own accord, is it safe for you to wander off alone right now?" Whyldon asked her.

Collette glared.

Larent intervened. "Let her have the time," he said, then turned his gaze on Collette. "You are armed, right?"

"I always am," she confirmed.

Chapter Twenty-eight

"See, she'll be fine, and if she runs into trouble, all she needs to do is scream and one of us will come running," Larent told Whyldon.

Whyldon sighed and nodded. "Be safe."

Before she left, Larent gave her a soft smile. "If you change your mind about company, we're here."

"Thanks," Collette said, turning from the table and walking out of the inn.

Chapter Twenty-Nine

Later that evening, Larent stood outside Collette's room listening to her pace. Arian had returned to the inn hours ago, unable to find Tolan or any clues as to where he might have gone. The lack of evidence had confirmed for them that Tolan had been intentional in his departure. Larent had a lot of strong feelings about Tolan, but hearing that he had disappeared again without talking to Collette had Larent hoping Tolan would stay away this time.

The news had sent Collette to her room, and she'd declined the evening meal, not that she'd eaten much else earlier in the day. He pondered the advice Arian had given, leaving her to have the space she needed because his own relationship with Tolan biased him.

However, a larger part of him, the part that cared for her as more than a friend, said he could put aside his own issues and help. Out of everyone, he understood what it meant to wake up alone, with the growing pit of dread in your stomach that you had been left, abandoned by the person you loved and whom you thought loved you in return. It was with that thought in mind that he knocked on her door.

There was a prolonged pause before she answered. "Come in."

Larent was surprised by the invitation, but he headed into the room, closing the door gently behind him before locking it. Looking at her, he could see how hard she was working to keep it together. She was hiding it well, but it was his job to read people. Not knowing exactly what to do now that he was with her, Larent just stood by the door for a minute before holding his arms out. "Do you need hugs?"

Collette shook her head, her arms crossed in what he assumed to be a protective stance. "We will be at this inn for the foreseeable future if I start hugging people now," she admitted.

"We have to wait until Nawalya returns, so this is the foreseeable future," Larent said as he slowly approached. "And, we don't have to tell the others, so you don't have to give them hugs, ever."

Collette gave a short laugh. "I'm trying to picture Arian hugging someone."

Larent grinned. "He gives the best hugs, but they are rare, and he is normally drunk."

"Perhaps I will be lucky enough to see one or both someday," she said with a poor attempt at humor. She sat down on the bed and ran her hands over her face. "I think I'd like to be drunk."

Larent perked up. That was something he could help with. "Cheap swill or expensive stuff?"

"Whatever," she replied, hands going over her face again before tangling into her hair. "I just can't feel this way anymore."

"Expensive stuff it is," Larent said. He could easily get her drunk until she was sick if she felt like it. It was the least he could do for her. "I'll be right back, okay?" he asked seriously, waiting for her reply before thinking about going for the door.

"Can I come with you?" she asked, looking up at him.

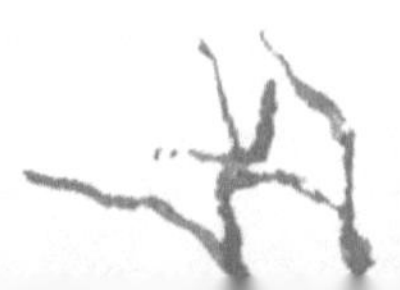

"Of course, Freckles. Whatever you want." He held out a hand which she took. He tucked her arm in his and led her out of the room.

"We have two options. We can purchase a couple of bottles and bring them back to the room, or we can stay downstairs. There are a few private rooms we could probably talk our way into."

"Up to you," Collette said. "I've made all the decisions I plan on making tonight."

Larent nodded and led her downstairs. The warmth of the tavern read as inviting even if it was chaotic with people finishing dinner and ordering libations. Larent sat them at the bar and ordered drinks. The barmaid returned, carrying two glasses filled with a deep red mixture.

"Ready for the best part?" he asked as the drinks were set down. Larent placed a hand on Collette's shoulder and had her lean back a bit as the barmaid pulled out a match and lit the drinks on fire. "Blow it out," Larent urged with a laugh before he leaned forward and blew his out, then picked up the pint glass, and started to chug it.

Collette followed instructions, blowing out the fire and then downing the red liquid. It was strong, a little sweet and spicy, the perfect combination of flavors to start the evening. When the glass was drained, she ran a thumb along the corner of her mouth. "I need another."

He wasn't surprised by the request, but he knew the drinks would kick her in the ass if she wasn't careful. Larent offered her an alternative. "How about I order us two more of those and a couple of bottles of their best whiskey? We can sit by the fire and drink?"

"Oh, you're trying to manage me," she teased, causing Larent to laugh.

"No, but I'd prefer not to get lectured by Arian if you get into a bar fight."

"Punching something sounds like the best way to spend the evening," Collette mused. "But if you insist."

"Well," Larent drawled. "Would you rather drink or fight? I can do either, but we can't do both. Not here."

"How bad do you think the lecture would be?"

"You'd get a severe lecture. I'd get stabbed."

"I suppose we're drinking then," Collette decided. "I don't want a lecture," she joked.

"And I don't want to get stabbed, well, not with a knife." He waved the barmaid over and ordered more drinks. "We will take the bottles elsewhere," he said.

The barmaid complied and made two more of the red drinks before grabbing whiskey bottles which she presented to Larent and Collette.

"Bottoms up!" Larent cheered. He blew out his drink and chugged it. Standing, he grabbed the bottles and grinned while Collette downed her second glass. "Let's go."

They first looked towards the fireplace, but Larent spotted a fire pit just outside. He motioned towards it, which prompted a nod from Collette. It was a bit chilly out, but Collette didn't seem to mind, so he settled on one of the logs surrounding the pit. Collette settled beside him, and he picked up one of the whiskey bottles.

"I should warn you. Those red drinks will hit us in about twenty minutes, then things will get fun."

"Good, I need fun," Collette declared and held up a finger. "No, I don't need fun. I need everything to stop being so fucking hard."

Larent gave her a sympathetic smile. "It takes a while, but you do feel better eventually. Or so I've been told."

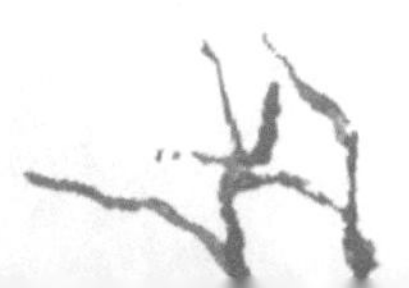

"Fuck that," she said. "I haven't felt better about losing my brother, or being arrested, or having my kingdom taken away, and now I must deal with Tolan's bullshit."

Larent nodded, opened his whiskey, and gulped down several ounces. "Fuck Tolan and his bullshit. Fuck your brother and that damn kingdom too." He handed the whiskey over to her.

"Fuck all those things," she agreed. She took a drink, then another. "And you did fuck my brother."

Larent choked on his whiskey, and he looked at her with surprised amusement as he used his sleeve to wipe his mouth. "How the fuck do you know about that, Freckles?"

"My brother has a reputation, and you're about as subtle as a house fire," Collette replied before taking a sizable gulp of the whiskey.

"I'm a spy!" he declared. "I'm very good at subtle. Just not where you are concerned."

Her mood turned melancholy, and she took another drink as she stared into the fire.

Larent frowned and shifted closer. "Let it all out, Freckles. Bottling this shit up will only make Arian drag you to a mind healer. And you've needed a good vent since we left."

"Why the fuck did he even come?" she demanded.

Larent took the bottle back and took another gulp, letting it burn down his throat. It gave him the courage to respond. "Because he does love you, and if he left because of any of the shit I said or did, I'm sorry."

"Leaving isn't love," she argued as they traded the bottle again. "Abandoning me like this is cowardly and selfish, and I'd have much rather known that about him before."

Larent closed his eyes, feeling guilty and responsible for her pain. He'd known who Tolan was. "I should have warned you," he said softly as he pushed the bottle towards Collette.

Chapter Twenty-nine

"I probably wouldn't have believed you, no matter what you had to say about him, until about twelve hours ago. I am so in love with him … and I just," she paused and brushed aside tears with the heel of her palm. "Fuck."

"If there is anyone in the world who gets what you're feeling right now, it's me. And fuck doesn't even begin to describe it."

She rested her head against his shoulder. "I don't know how I missed it. How is he so good at hiding who he is?"

Larent put his arm around her. "It's easy to overlook his faults because he does come across as devoted and loving. We ignore every sign he gives us because we want to."

"You're still in love with him?" she asked.

Larent leaned his head back. "No, but I do care about him. It's just not love. Not anymore."

She was quiet for a while, and Larent chose to not worry since her head still rested against his shoulder.

When she spoke again, she changed the subject. "You weren't lying about those drinks."

"I'm actually pretty honest, despite my job," Larent agreed. "Are you seeing strange colors yet?"

"Not yet," she said with a laugh as she sat up. "But I'm feeling pretty good."

"Good." Smiling, he grabbed the bottle and took a drink. "Tell me something. Anything."

He watched as she watched the fire, her expression less composed than he'd ever seen it before. Still, he didn't expect her answer.

"I don't want to be queen," she said, her tone matter of fact through the sadness.

"Then don't be. If that's not what you want for your life, then just fucking don't."

"I have to," she said with a sigh. Based on her relaxing posture and slight slur of words, she was feeling the alcohol.

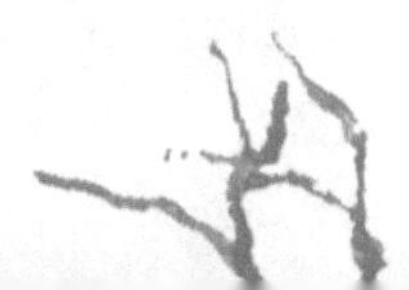

"I made promises. To the Nereid. To my people. And we both know Zephraim is going to be swayed into becoming just like Sargarus. I can't let that happen. We can't go back to that."

Now in problem-solving mode, which he could admit was probably hindered by his own whiskey consumption, he offered some ideas. "So, here's what we do. We take the kingdom back, execute those who orchestrated this mess, and we put someone else on the throne. That's a viable plan, and it keeps your promises if we find the right person. Arian would make a great king."

"Arian might kill you for suggesting that," Collette pointed out. "And as much fun as it would be to dream about him ruling, it's not nearly viable enough for me. I don't want to lose anybody else. That would happen in such an exchange. There's also the problem of finding somebody to rule the people. The people who want a crown aren't worthy of it."

"We could find someone like Thomas Fletcher. He would be good at the job. He has enough criticism of you that, surely, he has ideas of his own."

"I don't know that Thomas would want to," she said. "But that's a point in his favor. Maybe I could stand outside the palace and criticize him."

Larent almost spit out his drink at that image. "Oh Lady, yes! I would love that. I would, of course, defend you from Arian."

"You think Arian would go after me?" she asked with an intoxicated laugh.

"Not really, but he would pretend, so others don't get ideas." He gave her a soft smile, enjoying seeing her relax. "We could make a huge fucking production out of him coming after you."

"Oh, of course," Collette said, still laughing. "It's all about the show, after all."

"Honestly, that's all politics are—a huge fucking show. Tell me something else."

Chapter Twenty-nine

This time, she didn't spend a long time thinking. "I used to love it when you'd 'accidentally' show up in my chambers back at the palace. You spoke to me like I was a real person."

Larent frowned, though briefly. "You are a real person, queen or not," he said, wanting to know that she heard and understood him. He offered her a playful smile. "The first time we met, face-to-face, was actually an accident, but I'm happy I ended up in your chambers."

"So am I," she said simply.

"Good," he replied just as simply. "You're so much more than your title, and I'll always be here to remind you of that." He went for the second bottle of whiskey and took a long drink. "How are you feeling?"

She looked down at the gold bracelet she wore on her wrist, the one that had been worn by Tolan for weeks. "Devastated," she said honestly. "But drunk."

"Still no strange colors? Shit, you can hold your alcohol." He chuckled.

She laughed again. "What did you expect?"

"This shit has floored some of the biggest guys I know. I didn't know you'd last this long."

"It might still catch up with me," she said and shrugged. "Or maybe I'm magic."

"You're very much magic," he replied, his voice contemplative. "Tell me something else. Or ask me a question."

Her response was immediate. "I actually have magic. Healing magic, to be precise. Though it doesn't seem to do much about the alcohol." Her face scrunched up in consideration. "Pretty sure the colors are starting."

Larent hid his surprise well. Lady, she was spilling all of her secrets, and he was going to have to keep those secrets. "What good is it if it can't filter alcohol from your system faster than you can ingest it?" He laughed. "Tell me what you see."

"Lots of purple, I think," she said, then downed another gulp of the alcohol. "It's nice."

"Purple is a calming color," he said. "I feel like I should warn you. You might pass out soon."

"That suits me," she said. "Pretty sure I'm going to regret my decisions in the morning, anyway." She took advantage of his closeness and rested her head against his shoulder again.

"I'll take care of you. Don't worry about it."

"I'm not worried," she insisted. "You're here."

"I'm glad you feel that way, Freckles." He tried to ignore how the words made his heart flutter. She was heartbroken, and he had no right to do anything with his feelings. He stayed still, letting her drink and reflect for a few long seconds. Eventually, the sag of her body against him told him she'd lost consciousness.

Carefully, he shifted the whiskey bottles aside with one hand. Then he gathered her up in his arms, heading back towards the inn. Arian met him at the door, causing Larent to grimace. "How much shit am I in?"

Arian gave him a flat stare. "Depends. How much did she have to drink?"

"Two red flames and a little over half a bottle of whiskey." He looked down at her, checking to make sure she was still sleeping.

The elf sighed. "The potion is already waiting in the room, though getting her to drink it tonight will probably be impossible." Arian studied the queen's limp form. "Is she feeling any better?"

Larent shook his head. "She felt lighter, but no. She's not okay. She hasn't been okay for a long time."

Arian nodded. "I won't stab you for this, because clearly she needed a release, but didn't you just insist to Nawalya you wouldn't be alone with her?"

"I wasn't," Larent said, although he felt a little ashamed of himself. "You were watching, clearly, and we weren't far from the door."

Arian glared at him. "Get her upstairs."

Larent complied without further argument.

Chapter Thirty

Rhoslyn smiled to herself. She couldn't help but remember she had once been quite concerned for their future. There had been the question of Zephraim's motivation and endurance when it came to doing the work required of a king. He wasn't perfect, and the Mother knew he had so much learning to do. His main problems were not being harsh enough with their critics and implementing the changes they wanted. That would come with time. Riken had promised to see to it.

She entered the room, went over to the desk, and wrapped her arms around her husband's shoulders. "Working so hard, my love."

Zephraim gave her a sleepy smile, looking up at his wife with a slight turn of his head. "I'm trying," he said. "Riken counseled that I should follow up on my correspondence to our allies regarding Collette's whereabouts. Crobán did as well, come to think of it."

"A very good idea from both," Rhoslyn said. Slowly, and as though reluctant, she let her arms fall from Zephraim and stood beside him, silently encouraging him to work. "I know everyone is eager to show you their support."

Zephraim nodded and sighed, then tossed his quill on the desk. "Let me ask you something."

"Of course," Rhoslyn said.

"How do you feel about the Merscale trade? Truly?" He ran a hand through his red-gold curls. "I know economically and traditionally, our country has supported it. I also know Crobán, Barris, Elrick, and others are excited by the little trade I've agreed to allow."

"Are you not inclined?" Rhoslyn asked, eyes wide with innocent curiosity.

"Maybe?" Zephraim said with a sigh. "I mean, despite everything, Collette had a point. Mers don't deserve to be hunted down and maimed. It's—" he paused and sneered at the idea "—barbaric, and the allowance I've made may lead to worse treatment."

Rhoslyn made to look as though she was considering the idea. "I'm not saying that I disagree with you," she began after a moment, putting a hand on his forearm. "Of course, we want to be better than those who came before us. I just worry."

"What about?" Zephraim asked, leaning forward and putting a hand on top of hers.

"I think we both know how others are going to act, regardless. There was an underground economy under your sister," Rhoslyn said, giving him a gentle smile. "Is it not better to allow it, but with heavy regulation? I'm certain Riken would love to be of assistance in enforcing your edict while Barris oversees the daily operations. They are both kind, benevolent people with good heads for business, and Riken would make sure you were comfortable with everything."

Zephraim's lips pressed together in thought, and he leaned back in his chair. "I suppose that might work," he said after a moment. "But I would want to organize it so that we slowly tapered off trading in Merscales."

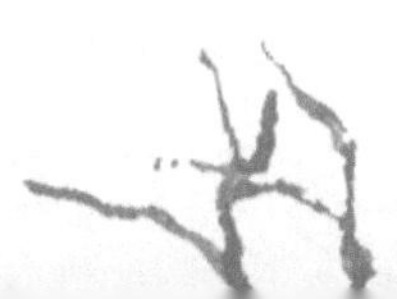

"Of course," Rhoslyn insisted. "I'm sure that is possible, and it will make all of those who lost fortunes under Collette's rule feel less robbed of their wealth." She offered her husband the saccharine smile he always fell for. "You are so smart, my love. It is amazing how quickly you resolved this."

"As long as you're pleased," Zephraim said. He gave her another smile then turned back to his letter with a sigh.

Rhoslyn took the opportunity to take a stroll around the office, something she did to prevent herself from running straight to Riken. Since he'd returned to court, Rhoslyn had developed many different tricks to help her see him. She paused by the bookcase, a fine old built-in that had been constructed under Zephraim the Wise three generations back. She ran fingertips along the spines of the books, pausing when she spotted an old bauble she remembered Collette playing with as a child. An old, worn opal set in gold.

It wasn't worth anything, or at least not much. She palmed it as she gave a short laugh. "We must have this office cleaned out for you, darling," she commented as she held up the item. "Collette's junk is everywhere."

Zephraim chuckled and looked over his shoulder to see what she had. "You're probably right. I didn't want to come in and start clearing everything out. I promise I will have someone help me sort things out."

"I will toss this for you, at least. I doubt it has any value with how callously she treated it." Rhoslyn pocketed the thing, intent on destroying it the first chance she got.

"Why don't we hold off on that particular item," Zephraim suggested, surprising Rhoslyn enough that her cheery facade fell. "But darling, you just said—"

"I know," Zephraim interrupted. "I do, but that was not just my sister's. It was her mother's. Queen Adora was always kind to me." He turned and held a hand out, a silent request for her to hand the item over. Rhoslyn had to comply.

"My apologies," Rhoslyn said, and she handed over the trinket without fanfare. "I shall let you work. I can have Riken come up to discuss the Mer situation if you like."

"Thank you," Zephraim said. He placed the opal on the desk and then picked up his quill once more.

Finding herself dismissed, Rhoslyn left the office.

Riken strolled the corridors, bored out of his mind and increasingly resentful of Zephraim's behavior. If he were honest with himself, and Riken knew he was honest when it counted, the source of much of his displeasure with Zephraim revolved around Rhoslyn.

It wasn't fair, having to share such a magnificent, brilliant woman with someone who lacked ambition and pride. Someone who was proving to be a less ambitious and decisive ruler than the person they just ousted. Rhoslyn deserved a husband who would complement her skills rather than hinder her.

He flexed his hands in and out of fists as he walked, contemplating how to address the situation. It was not as though they could just have another uprising. Not so soon after the last. Still, he needed a plan, one he could work on over the next few weeks.

He looked up as he heard steps and smiled as he spotted the woman he loved, though the smile faded into an expression of concern as he took in her look of fury. Her cheeks, usually colored soft pink, were splotchy and red in her anger. "What—"

"You should go dispose of my husband," she snapped.

Whatever Riken had expected her to say, it wasn't that. However, he was willing to complete any task she demanded of

him, including regicide. "I shall do it right away, My Goddess," he responded, eyes gleaming.

Rhoslyn took a deep breath and closed her eyes, an action she took when she needed to calm herself. Riken approached her, wary of being too affectionate in the open where anyone might see. "What happened?" he asked in a gentle, quiet voice.

"He dared to admonish me for suggesting he rid the palace of her things." Her temper flared again. "As though I am some tedious, disobedient child."

Riken frowned. "He admonished you? Because you want to remove a stain from this castle?" Riken's eyes darkened. "How do you feel about being a widowed queen?"

Her response was whispered, having gotten control over her spurt of anger, but it was heated. "I think he should be reminded of what I do and have done for him. He would be off getting drunk in a tavern with my idiot brother were it not for me."

Riken put a hand on the small of Rhoslyn's back and gently led her further into a corner so their talk could be more private. "As much as I would love to remind him who put him on his throne, we cannot. He can never know about Wrenn." He sighed when she nodded in agreement, not liking that this was not a problem with an immediate resolution. "Perhaps I have a different idea on how to handle our king's attachment to his sister."

"Which is what?"

Riken considered his idea before we spoke. "The item in question, what was it?"

"Some stupid brooch that has lived on a shelf for literal years. Supposedly, it belonged to Collette's mother, which explains why it looks like it's been beaten half to death."

Riken paused again. He knew well Zephraim's attachment to Queen Adora. She was one of the few who had treated Zephraim with any care as a child. This would need to be handled with more care than he originally thought. "I preface this by reiterating that I do agree with you, but I am reluctant to go heavy-handed. Zephraim valued Queen Adora, as did others. I can speak with him, let him know that his approach with you was quite hurtful." He offered her a smile. "He'll simper and grovel at your feet, which should amuse you."

"That doesn't fix the problem," she reminded him.

"Admonishing you for any reason is a problem in need of address," Riken corrected. "But to your point, I will speak with him about the necessity of clearing her from this castle. He listens, especially when more than one person advises him of appropriate action." Riken quickly glanced around, then cupped her face. "Would that make you happy?"

A genuine smile emerged, one that always caught him off guard. "It would," she replied.

"Good," he said. "I would do anything you asked of me if it would bring that smile to your face." He gave her a near lecherous grin. "Now, what would you say to the two of us going and finding a way to help relieve some stress?"

"And tell me, what stress do you need to relieve?"

Riken gave her a pointed look. "He had his hands all over you at dinner last night, in front of everyone, as if he truly has a right to you. It took everything in me not to do something, to mark you for myself, and send him on his way."

"We should do something about your possessiveness, my love."

"And what, pray tell, should we do?" He backed her against the wall, his hands resting against the stones on either side of her body.

"That, my love, is entirely up to you," she said with a heated look. "It is *your* possessiveness."

"Then we will do nothing, as it is not a character flaw," he replied, his lips hovering above hers for a moment before he stepped back. Rhoslyn made it all too easy to get carried away, and they were in public. Instead, he held a hand out to her.

She looked at it, a teasing smile on her beautiful face. "I don't know," Rhoslyn replied. "You've already pulled away from me. What's to say you won't do it again?"

"Oh, you want me to take you here?" He waved a hand to emphasize the corridor, even though it was currently empty. He closed the distance once more, pressing himself against her so she could feel his want. "I can do that." He leaned down to kiss her.

A small gasp of delight left her lips, though it was quickly silenced by his kisses. Her arms went around him, silently encouraging more.

Riken grinned against her lips. "Come back to my rooms with me. As much as I am ready and willing—" he ground his hips into hers "—I don't want to share you with an audience."

Rhoslyn opened her mouth to speak when the distinct clearing of a throat sounded from behind them. Riken whipped around quickly, his body hiding Rhoslyn from the sight of Garibald Crobán. Crobán looked more triumphant than Riken had ever seen him before, and without thinking, his hand went to the hilt of the dagger he wore in his belt.

"Good afternoon, Your Majesty," Crobán began, bowing to Rhoslyn with all the usual respect he gave her. "And you, too, Riken," he said, not bowing this time as Crobán outranked Riken in title. "I am pleased to see you found a way to entertain yourselves, given the terrible weather."

Riken palmed the dagger but did not put it away. "The turn of the weather has made it hard to attend to our normal outdoor activities, yes, but we make do where we can." There was an edge to his voice, and he stepped away from Rhoslyn so that she might better see and speak.

"I can see that," Crobán replied. "Though I might suggest such activities be held in more private quarters. Our king is very soft-hearted, especially about his dear wife. It would be quite a shame for him to catch wind of such treachery. Especially with your admittance newly reinstated."

Riken threw his head back and gave a full body laugh at Crobán's words. "You throw the word treachery around so easily, and yet last night at dinner with Lord Elrick, didn't you say you were thinking of needing to do 'something' about Rhoslyn?" His question sounded jovial, but his eyes spoke to the true depth of his rage. "I believe you called her high-minded and uncontrollable. I wonder, if I were to take that to the king, do you think he'd doubt my word?" Riken looked at Rhoslyn. "What say you, Your Majesty? Should we go see our dear king and tell him Lord Crobán is trying to blackmail you with lies in order to control you?"

"If I were to blackmail our queen," Crobán insisted, eyes narrowed in deep suspicion, "it would not be with what I just witnessed."

"I think certain people believe they know more than they actually do," Rhoslyn replied, looking straight at Crobán who had the good sense to look down. "I have been kind to you, Garibald. I've made sure His Majesty has listened to your concerns and made decisions to your benefit, and you try to plot against me?"

"I would never..." Crobán protested.

Riken snorted. "You do, and I'm not the only witness. I suppose you're feeling left out, or perhaps insulted that you did not become her confidante when she became queen. So, you started stirring whispers of treachery."

"I don't like traitors, Garibald," Rhoslyn said icily. "You should know that I will do anything it takes to protect myself, and this kingdom, from such a threat. You might ask my brother."

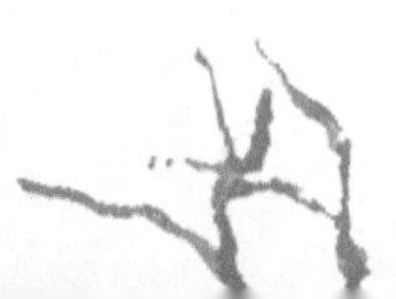

"He is dead, Your Majesty," Crobán stammered as realization dawned. "I could not possibly."

Rhoslyn turned her gaze on Riken. "Handle this, or I will."

Without hesitation, Riken advanced on Crobán, ignoring his pleas. He took hold of the older man's jacket collar, roughly pushing him back towards the window.

"Please!" Crobán begged. "There is no need for this!"

"You're a threat, and after what happened to my father, I eliminate all threats," Riken said. Without warning, he pushed the man out of the open window, giving him no more thought despite the terrified cries and the meaty thud of Crobán's body hitting the ground below. "We should flee," he said to Rhoslyn.

"We should. Let's go down. I'll go outside as though on a walk and discover him," she said quickly.

"Lead the way," Riken said.

Rhoslyn moved to the staircase with a speed she rarely used, her mind alert and watchful for others passing by. Thankfully, they made it to the ground floor without detection, and she held out a hand. "I'll go out first and discover the body. Then you come rushing when I scream. If you can, find some other occupation before. Something I can interrupt."

Riken nodded but couldn't resist saying. "I adore you, you ruthless, cunning woman."

"Only adore?" Rhoslyn replied but gave him no time to answer. Instead, she strolled into the corridor, leaving Riken to wait for her cue.

He schooled his features into something more pensive and began a casual stroll of the corridor. He gave a servant a distracted smile and slight nod, only glancing towards the door Rhoslyn had gone through moments before once the servant passed. Further down the long hall, he passed one of the guards, who also received a nod. The boy was young, likely untrained, and Riken reminded himself that he needed to get his own men into the castle.

Taking another breath, he paused as if to say something to the guard when Rhoslyn screamed. Doing an about-face, he sprinted to the door, only to notice the guard wasn't following.

"That sounded like the queen!" Riken shouted at the boy. "Follow me and do your job," he growled out as he pushed the door open. Racing into the garden, he skidded to a stop. Rhoslyn had collapsed on the ground and was wailing with horrified grief. No one could doubt her sincerity or tears. He would have to applaud her later.

Adding to the scene was the sound of the young guard vomiting behind him. More screams erupted as castle residents scurried outside. Gathering himself, Riken moved to Rhoslyn's side, lowering himself as if to block her view of the mess that Crobán had made. "Someone fetch the king!" he shouted as he pulled her against him. "The queen is in shock." He made sure to chastely hold the queen against him, a sign that no one could mistake for more.

The next several minutes passed in a frenzy. Servants, nobles, and other occupants of the castle appeared. When Zephraim came down and saw Crobán's body, his face became pale and strained.

"Riken," he said to his friend. "Help the queen somewhere less stressful."

"Of course, my king. I will take her to her chambers post haste."

"Do what is needed. I will be up as quickly as I can," Zephraim said. He did take a moment to kneel and check on his wife. "I will be with you as soon as I can," he promised her softly. Just as quickly, he was back on his feet and off to deal with the catastrophe.

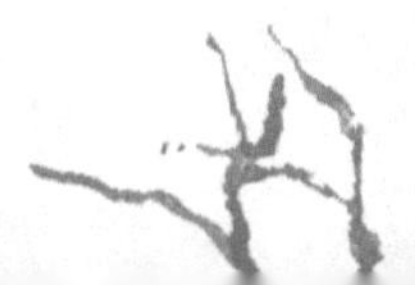

Riken helped Rhoslyn stand, going so far as to put a steadying hand around her waist. "Come, let us get you someplace safe."

Rhoslyn nodded and clung to Riken as though she could barely manage without him. "Thank you," she murmured through her continued tears.

Riken hurried her up to her chambers as quickly as he could, glaring at anyone who dared look at her sideways. Once in her room, he released her long enough to lock the door before pinning her up against it and kissing her hard.

Rhoslyn's arms went around Riken instantly, her returned kisses as hard and desperate as his. "Fuck me," she commanded.

"As you command." He pulled her up his body and pushed up her skirts. Her legs wrapped around him. His hand reached beneath and found her core, his thumb caressing it while his index and middle finger entered her. "Fuck. Already wet and ready for me," he rasped.

"Always for you," she replied in a breathless voice that showed how much she needed him.

"Undo me," he said hoarsely.

Rhoslyn loosened her grip from around Riken's shoulders, and with a little adjustment, quickly undid the lacings of his pants. Then she helped herself to his erection, freeing it from his clothes and stroking it several times.

Riken groaned, closing his eyes so he could enjoy the feel of her soft hand caressing him. It was good, but not what he wanted just then.

Pulling back, he gripped his cock and guided it inside her, moaning her name as he buried himself deeply inside her inviting warmth. He had to rest his forehead against her shoulder for a moment, her name on his lips, as his hips set a brutal pace.

Rhoslyn moaned with each hard thrust, her need for him palpable in the way she held onto him, as though he were the lone tether to the world.

"I love you with every part of me," Riken shared before claiming her lips in a possessive kiss.

"I love you," Rhoslyn replied, her voice pitched in the way it always was right before she fell off that cliff of pleasure.

"Come for me, love," he growled, and her body shuddered with pleasure. Riken had to stop himself from biting down on her shoulder as he followed after her a few hard thrusts later. They were left breathless and loose-limbed, though Riken didn't release her just yet. "You were amazing," he whispered, kissing her again.

"You always are," Rhoslyn whispered in return. "And not just like this."

"You are a goddess, and I wish I could worship you at all times," he said and sighed. "I do not want to let you down."

"I don't want you to," she admitted, soft and vulnerable with him in a way she could not be with others. "Sometimes I wish we could leave here and do anything else in the whole world."

"I know," he whispered. "One day, though, things will not be as they are. I promise you that."

"We have to give him time to fail," Rhoslyn said, and Riken nodded. As much as he hated it, Zephraim had to prove incapable. Only then could he decisively act.

He carefully separated from her and lowered her to her feet. They were already pushing the allotted time they had. "I made a bit of a mess of your hair," he playfully pointed out, surveying her, his eyes darkening with desire. "May I make a request, Your Majesty?"

"What request is that?"

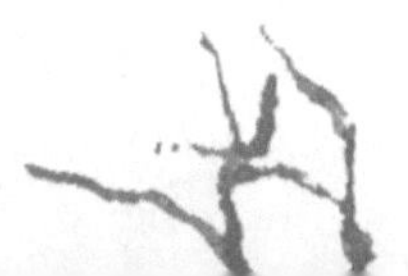

He gave her a wicked smile. "Clean up everywhere but there," he said, fingers brushing the line of her skirt that led to her core. "I want you to have a reminder that you are mine."

"Oh, there can never be any mistaking that," she promised.

He kissed her hard, running a hand through her hair. "Go clean up." He stepped away from her and righted himself.

By the time Zephraim arrived in Rhoslyn's chambers, she'd pulled herself together from the quick, heated round of sex. She'd situated herself in a comfortable chair in the corner of the room, adopting an expression of shocked grief. Riken sat across from her, sword on his lap as if he had been guarding her the entire time. He stood as Zephraim entered the room, sheathing his sword as he did so.

"How are you?" Zephraim asked, going to Rhoslyn's side. He knelt beside her, taking her small hands in his.

She looked up, her eyes round and wet with tears. "This keeps happening," she said in a meek, quiet voice. "First Wrenn, and now Garibald. This has to stop, Zephraim."

Riken kept his face neutral as he watched her work. She truly was amazing, and he would tell her as often as he could going forward.

"I know it does," Zephraim said, breathing out a deep sigh of helplessness. "And I promise I will find a way to stop it. Is there anything I can do for you right now?"

Rhoslyn shook her head.

"Okay," Zephraim replied. "I am going to speak with Riken, but call for me if you need anything."

Riken rose from his chair and bowed deeply towards Rhoslyn. "We will not go far, Your Majesty. I will make sure there are guards in case you need anything." Another nod and Riken turned to Zephraim before both men left the room.

They did not make it far down the hall before Zephraim spoke. "Crobán was pushed, though I'm sure that's obvious."

"It was," Riken agreed. He paused as they passed a window, and he shook his head. "You might consider bars or some other form of security," he suggested, a thoughtful expression forming.

"Perhaps," Zephraim said with a sigh. "That's two murders within these walls in less than a year, and this time, my sister isn't around. So, who do we blame? He was pushy, but Garibald didn't have a lot of enemies. People liked him."

"People tolerated him," Riken corrected quietly. "He was opinionated and caused several of the lords and ladies great discomfort. I am sad to say I did not care for him much myself." Riken's voice was thick with regret. "I may have an idea of who killed him, but no honest proof. I have had something on my mind all day and considered coming to you with it when Rhoslyn screamed."

"Speak of it."

"You are aware that I have people in the castle to help keep an eye out for possible threats, correct?" Riken said, looking down in a show of shame.

"I am," Zephraim said, giving his old friend a half smile. "I may be new to this role but I'm not blind."

"I have never thought you were blind, my King." Riken paused again. "Lord Crobán has been acting … off lately, so I've had my people keeping an eye on him. Last night, he was overheard being very open about his unhappiness with the way the Queen has been treating him as of late. Apparently, my arrival has ruined some of his plans, especially since he believes… believed her marriage to you could be directly attributed to him. He seemed to be hoping she would be more malleable, and he would have influence over you through her."

Riken chuckled as though the thought was ludicrous. "No threats were made, but he did say he would have to do something about it sooner rather than later. As the meal progressed,

he became intoxicated, and he said he knew the guard Cremisius Hawke was unhappy with the status quo. He rambled about leveraging his pretty wife against him to help get his plans on track.”

“You think Cremisius Hawke was behind this?” Zephraim asked.

“I do,” Riken confirmed but couldn’t tell if the king believed him or not. “It seems obvious that Cremisius took offense to the idea, and he reacted poorly.”

“We’d have to have something solid if we went after Cremisius Hawke,” Zephraim said. “He’s toed the line from what I know. He’s also popular amongst most of the guards, and he was close with Collette and Captain Whyldon.”

“I know. My people have been trying to keep up with him for weeks now, but he’s neither done nor said anything that could be construed as wrong.” He stopped in their walk. “He has fought vocally with his wife about being unhappy with several things in the kingdom. I will admit he hasn’t been watched as consistently as I would like, but he is our best suspect unless Lord Elrick or another lord became upset with Crobán.”

“If it was Barris instead of Crobán out there, I’d suspect Elrick. They’ve been fighting for weeks.”

“That is very true. Perhaps I should set someone on both before it escalates more than it already has,” Riken suggested.

“Perhaps,” Zephraim said after a moment of contemplation. “But keep a close watch on Hawke going forward. His wife, too.”

“Of course, my king.” Riken gave Zephraim a small smile. “How are you doing with all this?” He waved a hand in the direction of Crobán’s body.

“I’m not sure,” Zephraim confessed. “Death is always terrible, even when it is warranted, and I’m not aware of anything he’d done to warrant being pushed from a window.”

Riken placed a hand on Zephraim's shoulder, squeezing slightly. "We will find out who did this, and we will bring them to justice."

"I know we will," Zephraim said. "If this has ties back to Collette, we have a lot of work ahead of us."

"Given that our top suspect is a supporter of her, we may need to tread carefully," Riken agreed. "But let's not worry until we have more proof. You have enough to worry about."

"Like my newly traumatized wife," Zephraim said. "I should go tend to her. We should talk later, though. I have other matters I wish to discuss."

"Of course. Would you like me to send a message to Crobán's family while you see to our Queen?"

"Yes, thank you. His family will want to know as soon as possible." Zephraim let out a frustrated breath. "If I am needed, I will be with Rhoslyn."

Riken bowed and watched Zephraim walk back to Rhoslyn, wondering if he could get away with a second murder today.

The light streaming through the window roused Collette. Well, not the light. The pain licking at her temples woke her, and the light just made it more acute. She groaned and threw her arm over her eyes to block it, briefly contemplating the quickest method of death.

From beside her, a deep, sleepy chuckle sounded, unmistakably male. Something was pressed into her free hand. "Drink this. It will make you feel better. I warn you, though. It tastes like ass."

"Laughing at me is treason," Collette mumbled, not even caring that Larent was clearly next to her in the bed.

Larent chuckled again. "Arian gave me a nice, long lecture last night. I'll gladly take the beheading if it means avoiding more of that."

She sat up with another groan and looked at the bottle in her hand. Without questioning the item, she pulled out the stopper and quickly drained the remainder, scowling at the taste. "Why is it so disgusting?"

"Arian does it on purpose, I think," Larent said, keeping his voice low. "Thankfully, it should start working in a minute or two."

"Arian is an ass," she declared as she fell back on the bed. As bad as her head hurt, she wasn't feeling sick, which was positive. Looking over at Larent, she noted that he was shirtless, but she felt too sick to address the strange lack of boundary. Besides, he wasn't bad to look at.

"Yeah, but we love Chuckles," Larent replied. "When the potion kicks in, let me know and I'll get you food and water."

She could feel her headache slowly retreating, which brought other things to mind. Things she didn't want to think about. Why had Tolan left her? "I drank way too much last night," she said after a few minutes of blissful silence.

"Not really," Larent insisted. "I mean, maybe I shouldn't have gotten you the second cocktail, but we had fun." He shifted so he was facing her. "Feeling a little better?"

"I guess," she replied. "I don't feel like the sun is trying to kill me anymore."

Larent laughed. "Good. In that case, I will be right back." He got out of bed, slipped on his shirt, and left the room. Collette chose to get up, noting that she was thankfully a lot more dressed than he'd been.

Her hair was still in the braid she'd worn the day before, and a quick glance in the mirror showed that her hair was messy. She undid the cord binding it at the end and was unraveling her hair when Larent reappeared with a tray of food and water.

"Greasy food," he announced as he sat the tray in front of her. "No idea what it is, but the owner's wife swears by it."

Her hair finally loose, Collette began eating, and for the first few minutes, she thoroughly believed that the innkeeper's wife deserved to be honored for the meal. She finished half the plate before she'd had her fill and offered the rest to Larent,

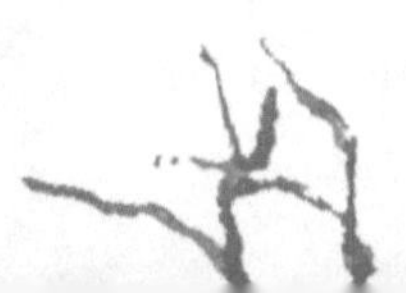

who seemed happy enough to finish it. In the meantime, she poured herself a large glass of water from the pitcher on the tray. She drank several long gulps, then put the glass down on the bedside table.

"Do we know when we expect Nawalya to return?" she asked, rolling her shoulders in a stretch.

"Not really," Larent said through a mouthful of food which, thankfully, he'd covered with a well-placed hand. "The travel alone will take a couple of days. Getting into the palace… who knows? We're in no hurry, though. It's safe here."

He finished up the food and got up long enough to move the tray outside the door. Then, he returned to the bed, getting under the blankets. "It's cold in here. You should get back under the covers and let me steal your body heat."

Collette glanced at the fire, which was still burning well enough, but complied and got back in bed. He was right. It was warmer there, and she didn't object when he wrapped his arms around her and pulled her close.

"I hope she gets back soon," Collette said. "I want to get moving again."

"She'll be back when she's back," Larent replied. "It's not like they are going to think we're hiding out in random villages, enjoying nights of drinking."

"I think you are looking for excuses to stay in bed," she half-joked.

"That's partially true," he agreed. "But honestly, if we were going to have problems being here, it would have happened already."

"Things change quickly," she pointed out. "And we're down two people until Nawalya returns, so we have fewer eyes than normal."

"But I'm comfortable, and it's warm, so I think we should stay here until someone shows up to remove us."

Chapter Thirty-one

Collette sighed but stayed where she was. "I'm giving you ten minutes, maybe. Then we are going to be responsible."

Larent laughed. "You don't want to be responsible, and you know it."

She scowled remembering all of the stupid confessions she'd made the night before. It made her heart sink, knowing she'd been so stupidly honest. "That's not the point. Or our priority."

"Why isn't it the point or the priority?" he asked as he rolled over on his back, dragging her with him so her head was pillowed on his chest, his arm tucked under her. "What you want should always be our priority."

"We were on the road a month before you, Arian, and Nawalya even asked me what the goal was, and that was at my prompting."

"We were kind of busy putting as much space as possible between us and your whiny brother," Larent pointed out, looking down at her.

"It doesn't negate that the three of you, and Whyldon, were making plans for me without consulting me," she said. "The 'Do we go to the Nereids or Azmarin?' debate didn't involve me until I pointed it out."

"We explained and apologized, but you can throw that one around as much as you like." Larent laughed, which infuriated Collette a little. But not as much as his next words. "You're cute when trying to start an argument with me, but I think you know I'm not the arguing type."

Perhaps it was the word "cute" that set her off, and the accusation she was trying to start an argument didn't help. None of it was great in light of the fact that her heart was broken, and she honestly didn't know how she was supposed to move forward. All she knew at that exact moment was that she was getting up. Which she wordlessly did. She looked around the room long

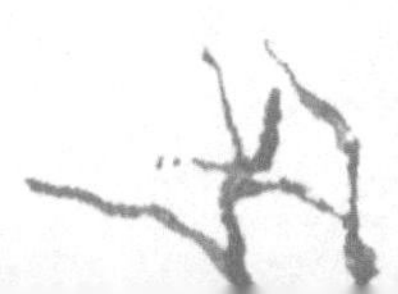

enough to locate her boots, something she would need if she planned on walking very far. Spotting them near the bedside table, she grabbed them, and without stopping to put them on, she left the room.

"Shit, I'm sorry," Larent called out from behind her.

Collette heard his footsteps quickly close the gap between them. Somehow, he not only caught up with her, he managed to block her from descending the stairs. They were locked into a position where she looked down at him.

"I was trying to distract you and keep your mind busy, and I did a shit job. I've never been great at comforting people, and this is more difficult because I know I felt the same way when Tolan did this to me. I should have gone with my gut and told you I would be a comfort fuck whenever you needed one, but that seemed like the wrong thing to say or do." He gave her a winning, if nervous grin, clearly hoping this burst of sincere vulnerability would help.

"He left you without saying a word?" she asked, addressing nothing else Larent said.

Larent winced and slowly nodded. "Yes. Our situations are slightly different, but yes."

"Why didn't you tell me? Before I mean."

Larent looked away. "I think I hoped it would turn out differently for you. He admitted to loving you, which he never did with me. I was just a warm body with a sense of humor. I believed it would be different for you. Admittedly, I was worried you wouldn't believe me."

He was right. She might not have given a harsh response, but she wouldn't have heard the truth. She'd been so accustomed to building Tolan up and defending him, she'd have brushed aside such a warning. She reached out and put her arms around Larent and hugged him. "I'm sorry," she whispered.

"You have nothing to be sorry about, Freckles," he said as he returned the hug. "Let's go back upstairs, and we can talk some more if you want."

"Sure," she agreed. She relinquished her hold on him and took the short trip back to the room they'd vacated. She settled in one of the chairs, while Larent sat on the bed, looking at her.

"Ask your questions," he prompted her with a smile.

"How long were you and Tolan together?"

He paused, looking down at his hands. "That's a complicated answer, and largely dependent on whom you ask. We knew each other for nearly a decade before we spent any real time together, and even then... I used alcohol as an excuse to kiss him for the first time. Eventually, I told him I loved him. He didn't say it back, not ever, but he did things to make me believe it was reciprocated. To this day, if you asked him, he'd probably say we were just two friends who enjoyed each other's company and fucked sometimes."

Collette let out a breath. Larent's tone was light, but the bitterness seeped into the words. Tolan was not, and could not be, the person that she thought he was. "He's such a shitty person," she decided. "You deserved better than that, even if he didn't feel the same way."

Larent shrugged. "We both deserved better."

"We do," she agreed, leaning down to finally put on her boots. "Are you ready to head back?"

"Unless you'd rather stay and have sex, or cuddle, or ask me the other question that's been on your mind for months now," he said, trying for humor that didn't quite reach his eyes.

"I think we will have days and weeks ahead of us to talk," Collette said.

"But will we have the privacy to fuck?" he asked with a cocky grin. He stood and walked towards the door.

"You couldn't handle me," she replied as she joined him.

The two descended the stairs in much better moods. The lower gathering room was already crowded with other patrons lining up for breakfast and enjoying the warmth of the hearth. Collette was happy to leave through the front door when she spotted a familiar face.

Larent paused, a smile blooming when he realized why Collette had paused. "Oh shit!" he exclaimed, laughing excitedly. "The Lady loves me. Truly, she does."

"We should go say hi," Collette said, her expression mischievous.

Thomas Fletcher sat at a small table, a bowl of steaming porridge at his side as he browsed a pamphlet. He only looked up when Collette's shadow fell across the table, and though his expression showed alarm, good humor replaced it. "What a small world we live in."

"Hey, Blondie. How goes it?" Larent asked before making a face. "That nickname doesn't work at all."

"I'm alive, so that's something," Thomas replied. "You two look decent for having been on the run."

"We've been staying at an inn that provides warm baths," Larent replied, his voice near giddy. "Glad to see you alive, but I know someone else who is going to be both happy and horrified to see you."

"Ah, so you didn't split up?" Thomas asked. "I supposed that was the safest."

"We did, very briefly in the beginning," Collette corrected. "But I want to know how in spirit's name you ended up here?"

"I was smuggled out of the city by Cremisius Hawke and a man named Rion. A furrier, I gathered from our time together."

"Rion smuggled you out?" Collette asked.

"He did. We parted about two weeks ago," Thomas confirmed. "Oh," he said and began checking the pockets of his coat. Eventually, he found a sealed letter and handed it to her.

"I promised to deliver this if ever we crossed paths. I thought it was impossible, but here we are."

"Who's Rion?" Larent teased. "Secret husband I need to be worried about?"

"He used to be one of the King's guards," Collette explained as she broke the letter's seal. "And one of mine in the first year I ruled." She skimmed the letter. As always, Rion was brief, but the words made her smile. When she was done reading, she tucked the letter away for safekeeping.

"I'm jealous of that smile," Larent said in a mock-serious tone.

"Don't blame you," Thomas said as he picked up his spoon and took a bite of his food. "Rion is an interesting man. He had lots of stories about his fair queen."

Collette snorted. "I can only imagine what bullshit he concocted."

"Now I want to meet him to hear all the stories," Larent said, pulling out the chair next to him for Collette. "I bet they were all true and horrible."

"Oh, no doubt," Thomas agreed, swallowing a mouthful of porridge. "I might have been kinder in my assessments of her had I known them."

"I thought you enjoyed your critiques of me."

"I did," Thomas acknowledged. "And I always tried to be fair."

"The day you called her a whore was a bit much," Larent said as he waved over one of the workers so he could order food and drink. "But usually, I enjoyed your ranting."

"We all did," Collette said. "Perhaps one day I will tell you how close you were to the truth about certain things."

Discussions paused as drinks and food were delivered to the table. Larent handed over some coins to the girl.

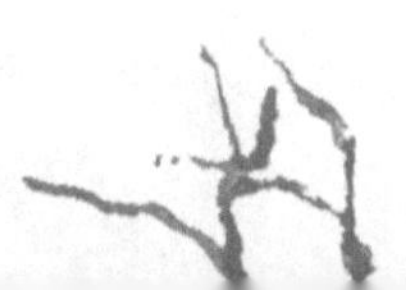

Alone again, Collette spoke. "How is Crem, since you mentioned him?"

"He was running himself ragged, trying to get those in danger out of the city when I last saw him," Thomas said. "I asked why he stayed, and he said he and Diana will be the last to leave."

"Fuck," Larent breathed.

Collette shook her head. "That sounds like Crem. He should know they'll have eyes on him."

"And they do," Thomas confirmed. "The best I can tell is that they are waiting for him to give them reason to arrest and execute. Right now, they have no proof."

Larent just raised an eyebrow. "They'll let him run around for a bit before they do anything. See if they can get him on trumped-up charges."

Thomas nodded in agreement. "They are in a tenuous position and have to appear as though they are doing things correctly and justly. An overthrow doesn't grant permission for seeming injustice or anarchy."

Larent snorted. "Don't take this personally, but you being here is going to make shit really interesting."

"Is that so?" Thomas asked.

Larent turned to Collette. "How many times since we left Coralia has Arian mentioned Thomas?"

She shrugged in response. "I don't know. A few times, I'd guess, but not to me."

"And that is why shit is about to get interesting. He doesn't talk about people who are … important." Larent's grin truly grew when, from behind them, came a familiar voice.

"Oh fuck."

Eyes wide with anticipation, Collette looked back to see Arian.

Thomas, on the other hand, experienced a genuine smile. "Well, hello."

Arian's mouth worked silently for a moment before he finally said, "Hello, Thomas. Are you… Are you in good health?"

"I suppose so," Thomas replied with an air of amusement. "I could ask the same of you, but you look well."

"I'm well." Arian paused, then reached into his pack and pulled out a potion bottle. "You look tired from traveling. Take this. It will help." He turned to Collette and Arian. "Nawalya sent word. She was successful. I'm going to inform Whyldon." He turned to go, then looked back. "You are more than welcome to join our group, Thomas, but you might be safer not traveling with us."

Thomas, who was palming the potion bottle, grinned. "That's more of a plan than I had," he said. "I will join."

Arian gave a tight nod and fled without another word.

Larent busted out laughing as soon as he was gone. "I am so glad you're traveling with us, but let me say now, I am so sorry."

"That sounds ominous," Thomas observed. "But I've committed. Going to see the thing through."

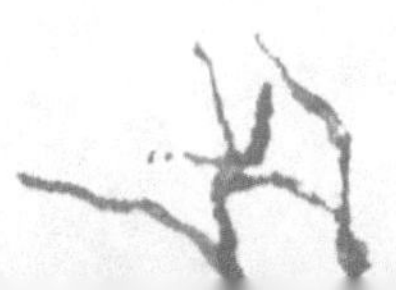

Chapter Thirty-Two

Morning was coming. Foggy darkness lingered in the streets as Nawalya walked towards the inn. Three days had passed since her mission had been completed, and she'd managed the trip quite quickly on her own. She liked the quiet streets of this little town, and had they not technically been in hiding, she might very well have asked to linger. That was not possible. In the next day or so plans needed to be made, and progress towards those plans observed.

She entered the inn, finding the space empty, except for the innkeeper and a young woman who might have been his daughter or his wife. The innkeeper wrote in a notebook while the woman ran a rag across the counter. As she sank into a chair at one of the inn tables, pleased and exhausted, she couldn't help but reflect on the mission. Getting back into the castle had been far too easy, as had accessing Brath's quarters. She'd waited for him, lacing his evening wine with a potent poison with no remedy. Hiding in the shadows, she'd smiled gleefully as he'd swallowed the drink, and though his death was quick, she'd intervened to keep him silent as he spent his last painful moment choking and gasping for help that did not come.

When it was over, she took her time leaving the castle, and she was pleased with the initial accusations that Lady Marine must have been behind the death. It was a conclusion she had not anticipated, although logical after what she'd openly done to Larent.

Nawalya knew, even now, that she would never tell Whyldon about her decision to stay and verify what she'd done. She had felt it her duty to do so, and she didn't like taking chances.

When the young woman approached, Nawalya asked for food and drink. She smiled in anticipation as a dish consisting of bread, eggs, and cheese was placed in front of her along with a sizable tankard of beer. "Thank you," she said in her soft voice.

When Whyldon joined her a few minutes later, Nawalya offered him a warm smile.

"It is good to see you, even if you haven't been gone long," he informed her as he took a seat. "Arian said you were successful?"

"Yes, I was," she confirmed, laughing softly. She wished to hug him in greeting, but she sometimes found asking for physical contact a difficult thing.

"Good," Whyldon said. "He was far too physical with Collette." He smiled up at the barmaid as she brought him his own portion of food and drink and picked up the tankard for a long sip. When they were alone, he asked, "Did you pick up on any news while you were there?"

Nawalya's smile vanished. "No plans of pursuing Collette, which surprised me given that she physically accosted Brath. There were other rumors, which may just be rumors." She tilted her head and considered Whyldon. "I know he was very physical with Collette, but I'm still surprised that you are okay with what I did."

Whyldon gave a soft shrug. "I told you what I have done in my past. This is no different."

Nawalya nodded, knowing that both were guilty of regicide. It was a similarity she had not expected, even with the kind of work she did. Looking over at Whyldon, who was eating, she considered the possibility of telling him about her visions of the wolf and Collette. He deserved to know, considering the actions he'd taken and the choices he'd made on the queen's behalf, but he'd leave with Collette. The thought of losing him now terrified her. So, she decided to focus on the rumors.

"If the rumors are true, Zephraim may reopen the labor camps Sargarus used," she said. "It also seems like the Merscale trade might be reinstated based on what I overheard in the marketplace."

Whyldon's lips pressed together in a thin line. "I had hoped for better from him," he said after a moment. "Either way, we've got to figure out our next steps." He sighed and shook his head. "I have news for you, while we wait for the others."

Nawalya tilted her head again, prompting him to continue.

"Tolan is gone," Whyldon began. "And Thomas Fletcher has joined us."

Nawalya, admittedly, didn't hear the second part. Her reaction to Tolan's departure was instantaneous and without thought. One moment, she was sitting and enjoying the time she had with Whyldon. The next, she was standing, her chair laid on the ground, and she was heading towards the door. She wasn't as good a tracker as Arian, but she was confident she could find Tolan. Whether or not he was alive at the end was still a question.

"Arian already went after him," Whyldon called after her. "It's no use."

Nawalya whipped around to face him, ignoring the curious looks from the two workers. "I'm not going to find him. I'm going to kill him."

"Nawalya," Whyldon said gently. "That is a fruitless effort, and we both know it."

She stalked back to the table unhappily but did not sit. "He won't have made it far, even traveling alone. It would take me maybe a day to track him, and he would be dead before he knew what happened." She was angry, even though she knew this was not Whyldon's fault. "Twice now, he has done this, Whyldon. I understand his issues. We've talked about them extensively in the past, but this is ridiculous, and I am past done."

"I understand," Whyldon assured her. "I do, and I only know bits and pieces from what has been shared or what I have overheard. He is not worth the effort. We know better than to trust him in the future, and no one can argue that."

Nawalya sighed, knowing he was right, but she didn't want to admit it or let go of her anger. She picked up the chair, then she decided to crawl into Whyldon's lap for comfort, and thankfully, his arms willingly went around her. "I should have let Arian kill him last time. But I knew it would upset Larent."

"I would think he and Collette would be quite upset if something happened to Tolan, no matter what he's done."

"They would get over it," she mumbled into his neck.

"I don't think so," Whyldon said. "Larent still harbors feelings, years later. Collette, I am afraid, will do the same."

"Apparently love is hard to push aside once it catches you. I am thankful to have avoided romantic entanglements before now."

"They can be challenging," Whyldon confirmed quietly. "I have been married, and I had an affair with a woman who I was certain was the great love of my life. And I have met you."

Not bothered he had much more experience than her, or that there had been other prior loves, Nawalya still looked up at him curiously. "May I ask, what happened to your wife?"

"She died giving birth," Whyldon replied. His tone was matter of fact, but she could hear the pain that came with the confession. "The baby followed after."

The child was something she had not known, and Nawalya cuddled in closer, hoping to comfort him. Again, the wolf flashed in her mind. She had only had the vision twice. There was no point in telling him unless she had another one. "I am so very sorry for your loss." She paused, and then asked, "How did you get entangled with Collette's mother?"

Whyldon sighed. "I don't feel comfortable speaking when we are so public, but I can summarize. After my wife died, I joined the army for a combination of reasons. Eventually, my skill and capability in the field led to a security appointment for the royal family," Whyldon said reflectively. "I often found myself alone with Adora because she was every bit as adventurous as Collette. She liked riding, strolling through the gardens, all things her husband and his detail hated. So, the duty was left to me."

"She sounds like she was an amazing woman."

"She was. She liked to argue about everything," Whyldon said with a soft laugh. "But she was never as strong as she needed to be, not when married to a man like Sargarus. Collette was two when Adora became ill. She never recovered."

"I cannot even begin to imagine the strain being married to such a monster would cause," Nawalya said. "I also do not believe he would have married an overly strong woman. The risk of her turning on him would have been too great." She shook her head. "I am sorry for her death, for both yours and Collette's sake." Taking a deep breath, she asked, "How did you do it? How did you manage to work for him and not become a monster yourself?"

"I had someone to protect," Whyldon said. "I'd have left service long ago had that not been the case."

"What made you join in the first place?"

Whyldon took longer to answer this time. His brows furrowed, his jaw set, but he eventually answered. "I think, at that time, Sargarus's sadistic tendencies weren't as obvious. He wasn't openly doing anything other leaders weren't. When the differences became more pronounced, I couldn't leave Adora behind. And then Collette was there."

"I have a very hard time seeing Sargarus as anything other than evil. That man changed the course of my life in such a terrible way."

"I know," Whyldon said with a nod. "What he did to you and to Arian… It's still not widely known. A farmer from Galel wouldn't have known about it."

"It was well hidden, what he did to us. Had we not survived, no one would have ever known," she admitted.

Whyldon began to speak but was interrupted as Collette approached and joined them at the table.

"I hope I'm not interrupting something. Your expressions aren't a sign of things going badly in the capitol."

Nawalya shook her head. "Things went as intended. He is dead."

"Good," Collette determined. "It's what he deserved."

"I'm surprised to see you down here," Whyldon commented, his expression full of concern.

"I was threatened by one of our remaining travel companions."

Nawalya studied the young woman, not liking what she saw. There was a sadness, and a harshness present in Collette's demeanor that she was unaccustomed to. "Do you wish for me to intervene?" Nawalya asked.

Collette shook her head and sighed. "No. He wasn't wrong. I can't dramatically hide away in my room until we decide to leave."

"There is nothing wrong with that if it's what you need," Nawalya said. "Larent did worse in your position."

"Larent is a lot more dramatic than I am. Even more so since Thomas showed up," Collette said. She looked towards the bar, catching the eye of the young woman who was already pouring more drinks.

Nawalya was about to respond when what Collette said fully registered, and a very amused smile bloomed on her face. "Thomas is here?"

Collette nodded. "Whyldon didn't tell you?"

Nawalya gave Whyldon an apologetic look. "The other news you gave me was a distraction," she said softly before turning back to Collette. "Is Arian hiding from him?"

"From what I understand," Collette confirmed. She hummed with appreciation as food and drink were presented to her and went straight for the beer. "It's sort of funny, Arian's reaction. He stood right over there," she gestured at another table, "and told him he was welcome to join us."

"Of course he did," Nawalya said with a sigh. She got up and returned to her seat so she could finish her own break-fast. "Arian lacks skill when it comes to personal matters. Their exchanges will be fun to watch."

Collette waited long enough to swallow a mouthful of eggs before responding. Nawalya noted that her appetite was good, which seemed positive. "Thomas has been amused by his behavior so far. I'm just not sure that amusement comes with infinite patience."

"Let's hope they can figure out how to be around one another for the long-term," Whyldon said.

"Arian has no issue slipping a knife into someone's back, but true affection frightens him," Nawalya replied.

"I say, let Larent encourage Arian. It will be good for a laugh," Collette said.

"Larent's idea of encouraging romance is not… It will not work for Arian." Nawalya made a thoughtful noise as she considered options.

"I'm not exactly pro-relationship myself," Collette said, "but I think if Arian decided what he wanted with Thomas, he could be happy."

Nawalya nodded. Collette was correct in her assumption; she just didn't say that Arian was better at ruining things for himself than he was at assassinating people.

"Ohhh, are we talking about Arian?" Larent said as he straddled the chair next to Collette. "Did we get to the part where he killed his last romantic partner?"

"We were also talking about you, in fairness," Collette said, looking over at him. "But mostly Arian."

"Of course you were talking about me. How could you not?" he asked. Nawalya found herself intrigued by Larent's lingering gaze on Collette. Larent must have noticed her watching him because he spoke again. "Arian crawled out of a window to avoid Thomas."

"That's a bit ridiculous," Whyldon said. He sat back in his chair, surveying Nawalya. "You and Larent clearly want us to ask about Arian's last relationship."

Nawalya and Larent exchanged glances, but Nawalya decided to provide the details. "It wasn't a relationship exactly," she explained, playing with the ends of her hair as she thought about it. "Well, it was the beginning of one. We were on a mission to save a village from Lord Barris' father and his forces. The man betrayed us for coin. We lost the village, and Arian killed him for it. It devastated Arian. So yes, his response to

Thomas is ridiculous, but given what has occurred in the past, it's understandable."

"I don't know why any of you are shocked by this," Larent said as he picked off Collette's plate and jabbed a thumb at Nawalya. "This one had us deliver a dead body to her love interest, and I've had to be drunk to confess my feelings before. We aren't the picture of healthy and happy."

"And Whyldon and I are?" Collette asked Larent with a half-sarcastic smile.

"You very much are," Larent joked.

"Asshole," she said and playfully nudged him.

Larent nudged her back. "He'll get over it in a day or two. Arian is nothing if not efficient, and he does want Thomas around. It will work itself out, or I'll lock them in a closet."

"Lock them in a closet together," Collette said.

Larent blinked at her. "I mean, okay. Give me ten minutes?"

"Do not listen to Collette, please," Whyldon implored.

Collette looked at Larent. "That's also treason."

"Sorry, Blue Eyes. It's treason to not do as she says."

"Don't tell Whyldon when you're doing it," Collette suggested. "Less fun that way."

Larent looked right at Whyldon, grinning widely as he said, "I won't say a word to him."

"I wonder how this plays out," Whyldon said, shaking his head.

"Badly," Nawalya said.

Chapter Thirty-Three

Arian sat on the windowsill of his room looking out at the bright town, berating himself for inviting Thomas to join their group then actively and notably avoiding him. His behavior was ridiculous, and he needed to move past it for the sake of the group, if nothing else.

He was happy Thomas was there, and the unsent letters at the bottom of his pack proved it. At the same time, he was very concerned. Thomas could take care of himself. He'd proven that in the confrontation with the guards. He'd also proven that he held a cavalier attitude towards danger. Arian did not want him in danger, a fact that hadn't changed since Thomas had helped him deposit the bodies of the guards with so little care. His feelings had further solidified when he helped replace Nawalya's quiver and arrows when she had an episode.

Arian would not lie to himself. It had been months since they'd last seen each other, and yet, he still thought about the other man's smile, his courage, and more often, the only kiss they shared at the fletcher's house.

Sighing, he rested his head more firmly on the windowsill. Thomas was a distraction but one he wanted around. He just wasn't sure where to go with their relationship or if he wanted one at all. A knock on the door drew his attention from his musings. "Enter," he called, not leaving his spot.

The door opened, and Thomas stood in the entryway. He expected the other man to come into the room, but Thomas remained where he was, leaning against the doorframe. Arian noted that Thomas had tied back his long blond hair.

"I'm starting to think you didn't mean it when you invited me to tag along, Arian. If that is the case, I can make my departure."

Nothing harsh or accusatory existed in Thomas's tone, but the words left Arian feeling guilty. He hung his head but did not rise from his seat. "I did mean it," he insisted, knowing his words were inadequate.

"You might have," Thomas allowed. "But from my perspective, you've done what you could to avoid me. Larent even reported that you climbed out of a window to avoid me. It makes me wonder where you plan on hiding when we're on the road."

Arian sighed again, feeling his cheeks burn with embarrassment. "I will not hide any longer." He stood and moved to the center of the room, still struggling to meet Thomas's eyes. "I am sorry if I made you feel unwanted."

"I don't know that unwanted is how I would describe your behavior," Thomas said, his expression still curious and amused. "Regretful seems more accurate."

Arian blinked, confused as to why he would be regretful. "I … do not understand."

"Perhaps I'm wrong, but you seem less pleased to see me than you did in Quenall."

Arian shut his eyes. "I am not regretful that you are here or that you will be traveling with us. I am concerned you will be in more danger than if you traveled alone. I'm also concerned that I will not be able to protect you."

"You shouldn't worry about protecting me," Thomas said. "You are escorting our fugitive queen. That is what you should be worrying about."

"I find that I cannot help but worry about you. I have worried about you since we left you in that damned kingdom." Arian finally looked up, meeting Thomas's gaze. He knew he didn't deserve for Thomas to believe him.

"I got out alive, didn't I?" Thomas asked with a surprising grin. "I'm not nearly as helpless as all that."

Arian liked his smile, a fact that shouldn't have mattered just then. "I do not believe you to be helpless." Arian thought of how jovial he had been with the guards who so wanted to hurt him. "I do worry you underestimate danger, however."

"The fact that I didn't cower in fear when I was being assaulted doesn't mean I underestimated the threat."

"True," Arian conceded. He didn't bother to point out that Thomas had egged them on.

Thomas straightened from the door. "I've not eaten yet, so I will leave you to hide." He gave a short wave, then he closed the door behind him.

Arian sighed, knowing this whole thing was a disaster.

Chapter Thirty-Four

Riken strolled down the hallway towards the council chambers, dressed in the dark finery he preferred. Although he was not officially in mourning for Lord Crobán, he knew the expectation of respect was there, even if most agreed Crobán had been gluttonous, absurd, and motivated by money. As he approached, he knew he was going to be late, but the spectacle he and Rhoslyn planned on creating would be more than worth it.

He was soon joined by Rhoslyn, dressed in the dark blacks and purples reserved for mourning nobility. She was beautiful, and he only kept his hands to himself because of the servants.

He bowed to her and asked with a small smirk, "Are you ready, Your Majesty?"

"As always," Rhoslyn replied with a definitive nod.

The servants opened the doors. Riken schooled his face but had to fight a smile as the doors fully opened into chaotic yelling Zephraim was obviously unable to control.

The two stepped inside, drawing no attention. Riken turned to Rhoslyn and bowed, then pitched his voice high enough to be overheard by those closest. "I apologize, Your Majesty. The members of this council are normally more well-behaved than this. Had I known they were acting like animals, I would have come in to prepare the way."

"Indeed," Rhoslyn said, surveying the room with a critical eye. "Surely, there will be some civility now that I have joined."

"One would hope," Riken replied.

They stood watching as Zephraim tried and failed to bring the room to order. As the scared nobility shouted about his lack of action towards their safety, that there were rumors of Mers and elves plotting against them, that the old queen was behind Crobán's murder, Riken took note that only Lord Barris was seated, looking utterly bored by the entire thing.

"Can we all quiet down? The queen is present," Riken said, his voice carrying over the low roar of the room. Some in the room did quiet down, though whether it was out of respect for Riken or for Rhoslyn, it was hard to say.

Zephraim shot the two a thankful smile and rose to offer his wife a hand, which she accepted. He walked her to the appropriate seat.

Rhoslyn smoothed a hand along her skirt once she was seated and surveyed the room with an impassive expression. "I feel as though I should ask what has led to all of this animosity. Surely, this is not the way we behave in front of our king?"

"I believe they may be shaken by recent events, Your Majesty," Barris offered with brightness. Riken almost purred, knowing that was the only opening she needed.

"Recent events," Rhoslyn repeated. "There are so very many, I wonder as to which you refer."

Barris had opened his mouth to respond when Zephraim moved to stand as if to end the conversation. Riken interjected. "I think he is referring to the death of our dear friend, Lord Crobán."

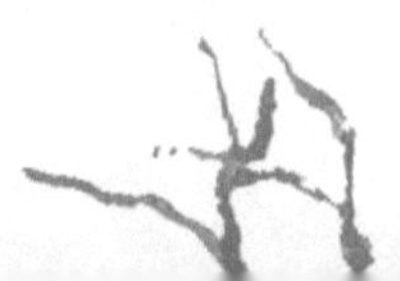

"Ah," Rhoslyn said with a nod. "What a sad tragedy that Crobán is dead, especially knowing that the traitor is likely behind it."

Silence fell in the room. "You… you think the queen did this?" asked one of the nobles. Riken didn't know his name, just that he was unimportant and used to hanging on the coat tails of others.

Rhoslyn's eyes narrowed. "You dare to give her that title? After all she's done?" Even Zephraim frowned in response, clearly agreeing with the question.

Riken moved in to save the cowering noble. It would be nice to be owed a favor. "I am sure he misspoke, Your Majesty. No one in this room supports the traitor. Right?" He addressed the room at large, and immediately the others were tripping over themselves to agree.

"I should hope not," Rhoslyn said, her chin held high as she looked around the room. "How easily such titles are thrown around. That woman killed my brother, and now Lord Crobán, and yet, she somehow manages to have followers."

"I do not understand how she could be behind this," said the same lord, obviously not having the brains to stop when he was ahead.

"You should hold your tongue and consider how you address Her Majesty," Zephraim warned the noble. "We know the traitor was spotted in Azmarin in the company of elves and received no assistance. Coming back here and going after her enemies would be a natural progression of her treason."

Riken was impressed with Zephraim's leap of logic. After all, Collette was many things, but a murderer was not one of them. Keeping quiet, Riken observed the room as Zephraim's words struck the chord they needed. Fear and anger rose amongst the nobles.

Chapter Thirty-four

Elrick was the next to speak. "It seems to me we must address the support until we can get our hands on the traitor."

Riken raised an eyebrow, thrilled beyond measure with how this was going. He didn't dare to look in Rhoslyn's direction for fear of giving something away. "What support would you like this room to address?" Riken drawled.

"Our citizens who still show support to the traitor. Who else?" Elrick replied with a smirk.

"And what would you have us do? Continue to throw them in jail until our prison is so overpopulated, we have to start mass-beheading in the town center?" Riken looked down at his nails. "I thought we were past such things."

"We need to consider less violent means of dealing with dissenters," Rhoslyn interrupted, once again drawing eyes on her. "No one in this chamber disagrees with my dear Zephraim's rightful place on the throne. In a short time, he has accomplished so much, and all of it to the benefit of the kingdom. Still, transition is always difficult, especially when a vocal minority means to cause strife."

"I think we can all agree that there has been quite a lot of strife, Your Majesty," Riken replied. "Prison is not the answer, as it taxes our already injured economy." He went quiet, though subtle changes in his expression suggested he had a thought.

"You have suggestions?" Elrick demanded of him.

Riken nodded, though he made sure to allow uncertainty to show on his face. "I know we abandoned the use under Collette's rule, but…" he trailed off, wincing a bit. "Reopening the labor camps is an option. It would allow us to empty the prisons while putting those who are found guilty to work for the good of the kingdom."

"I'm not sure it's the best idea," Zephraim said, his reluctance evident in his tone.

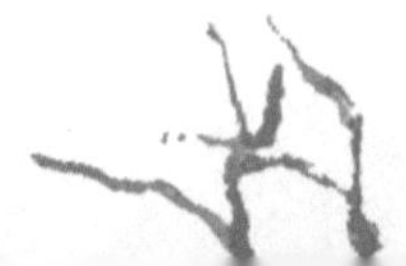

"Perhaps not," Rhoslyn replied. "But prison is not a deterrent, and you can hardly execute people for being angry about Collette."

Riken nodded. "I completely understand your reluctance, my King, but our queen is right. The labor camps are our best option, unless you have ideas of your own." Riken leaned forward as if to hang on Zephraim's every word. He doubted the other man had something to present to them.

"I've actually been engaged in communication these past few days with the Nereid kingdom," Zephraim said, meeting Riken's eyes. He leaned back in his seat, and Riken briefly wondered if he'd crossed a line. "Despite the possibility of Collette being behind what happened to Crobán, it does not mean she has not reached out to the Nereid for their assistance."

Riken opened his mouth to comment when another lord butted in. "How does that help us with the problems here and now? How does that protect us or deal with the problem? Unless you're suggesting we ship our criminals to them?" He knew immediately that this was the wrong thing to do.

"Communication with the Nereid helps because we have to know what, if any, resources she has," Zephraim shot back. "We are dealing with a traitor, elves, and dissenters, but what if she's wrangled herself an army?"

Riken noted several in the room did not look happy. He once more tried to say something only for Barris to speak up. "And what have the Nereids to say, my King?" He sounded genuinely interested.

"They have been rather elusive in their responses," Zephraim replied. "Thus, there is no confirmation to report, but involvement seems likely."

"Then I think we need to resort to labor camps even more," Rhoslyn cut in. "If nothing else, we need dissenters away from Quenall."

"Once again, our queen speaks the truth. It is obvious you are hard at work to prevent more deaths, but we need a solution now," said Riken. "The labor camps in Wildrun may have been abandoned, but they are still well maintained. I can have them set up in a week's time. If it pleases the king, we can even discuss changes to make them more humane. I'm sure the queen would lend her voice to this as she is known for her many works of charity."

A glance towards Zephraim confirmed he was unconvinced, but when he nodded, Riken let out a breath of relief.

"As long as they are humane and the labor is proportional to the crime, I'm willing to proceed," the king said.

"I will ensure it, my king. You have my word." His eyes flicked to Rhoslyn, noting the triumph in her eyes.

"Good," Zephraim said and rose from his seat. "I have things to attend to. You are all dismissed." He cast a dangerous gaze in the direction of the lord who had questioned him, but he said nothing before leaving the chamber.

Riken rose and walked to where Rhoslyn sat. He saw that Barris left quickly behind Zephraim. They would need to talk again and soon. Riken offered his arm to Rhoslyn. "Is there anywhere I can escort you, Your Majesty?"

"I think something a little more relaxing than a room of complaints would be nice," she replied, rising and taking his arm.

"I will proudly escort you to your destination." He waited until they were out of the chamber and a good distance down the hall before saying, his voice low, "You were amazing." If others hadn't started filing out of the meeting room, Riken might have shown her just how amazing she was.

"So were you," Rhoslyn replied. "Though I was surprised by Zephraim."

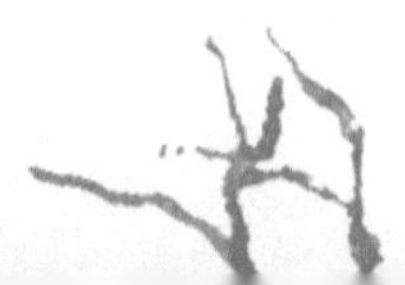

"As was I. I was sure he was going to shut us down again." Riken sighed. "He is being stubborn on topics I assumed he agreed with."

"His attachment to his sister is starting to show with the distance."

"It is, and his views are leaning more towards hers as well." Riken sighed and shook his head. "It always seemed like his ideas were more on our side of things, but now I am … unsure." He looked to Rhoslyn for answers and guidance on where to go next.

"We will watch him and act as needed," Rhoslyn said gently. "We have time."

Riken nodded. In this, he would follow her lead. "What of those lords who spoke against him?"

"Kill them."

Riken's eyes darkened at her words. "I will handle it."

Zephraim,

To say I was amused by your barely veiled threats would be to suggest that you are justified in the use of the title "king" when writing to me. Nothing you say or do is of concern to me. Once the true ruler of Coralia returns, and she will return, she will deal with you in the most appropriate way.

Aphros, King of the Nereid

Zephraim slammed a hand on his desk, infuriated by the response from the Nereid as well as the way the council meeting had gone down. Why was everything such a chore? Why did his council struggle over matters of no importance? As he slouched back in his chair, Zephraim could not help feeling resentful towards Collette.

Chapter Thirty-four

This was all her fault. As the world seemingly crumbled around him, she was out there, causing trouble, seeking assistance, doing everything she could to undermine his rule. And what made it so bad was that she'd run off with people in an effort to hurt him more than she already had.

Then there was Riken. Riken, who made a show of deference and respect, but every word he said dripped with a near indetectable amount of doubt and sarcasm. He would have to do something about that soon. For now, he needed decisive action. Something that would put him in a more secure place.

He rose from his desk, having made a decision about an idea that had been planted in his mind months ago. Perhaps he'd known all along that things would come to this. That he would have to dabble in things he'd wanted to avoid. Leaving his office, he knew he would eventually venture up to the next floor, to offices that had not been used since before Sargarus had died. His collection of books, including one in particular, lived there, though his items had been abandoned to collect dust for years.

First, he stopped by another set of chambers that had belonged to him before he'd been king. He needed hair, and though he first thought of collecting something from Collette, clearing out her things weeks before meant finding a personal item would be more difficult. The fact that he'd already had a plan that came to him so simply only told Zephraim he was doing the right thing.

Going to his dressing area, he found an old hairbrush, one holding a few strands of russet hair. He left without giving the room another thought and headed upstairs. The office was as he expected to find it, thickly coated with dust. The windows had been covered by thick curtains, and Zephraim pulled back a few so that he could work.

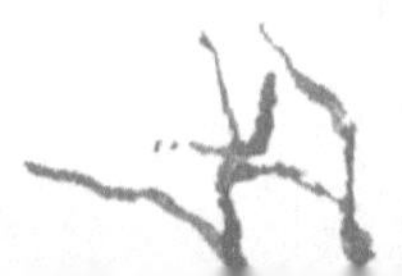

Soon, Zephraim had a fire going in the fireplace, a cauldron bubbling merrily along. He leaned against the desk, eyes browsing an old piece of parchment, so fragile that it threatened to tear along the folds at the slightest movement.

He tossed it aside, and went to the cauldron again, staring at the foaming bright blue contents. Collette had not only teamed up with his former lover, but it was reported they had married. "I bet they were together the whole time," he grumbled to himself as he considered his sister and Larent. It wasn't the only thing that bothered him, but it was what he focused on. "She's been making a mockery of me. Running around, trying to garner support from our allies."

As he spoke, he retrieved the hairs. Unceremoniously, he dropped the fibers in the cauldron, and the blue foam grew darker. Perfect. It was working. He stirred the contents clockwise twice, and then counterclockwise three times. "He probably told her everything I ever shared with him. She and Larent probably sit around laughing about it now." Just like Riken and Rhoslyn…

He shook his head, not sure why the thought crossed his mind.

The dark liquid slowly turned red and thick, soon resembling the color and consistency of blood. Now was the time. Spooning the liquid into a cup, Zephraim stared down at the contents, considering his next action. He raised the chalice to his lips, but then paused. If he did this, if he possessed Larent and killed Collette, there was no going back. The thought almost stayed his hand, but another surge of anger pulsed through him. So, Zephraim downed it, ready to deal with the problem directly.

Chapter Thirty-Five

In the weeks following their self-imposed exile from the Azmarin Empire, winter settled into the land. Every day brought a new layer of fluffy white snow, making travel toward Coralia slow and tedious. Every day, they had to start later and end earlier because the weather made their usual travel schedule impossible. They'd also spent more time within villages, meaning more opportunity to be spotted, to have things go badly. Arian scowled every time he thought about it.

The plan since leaving the capitol had been to travel south to Galel before pivoting east toward Pontus Bay. From there, they'd charter a ship to the Nereid Kingdom. They had only slightly more hope of success upon arriving, but it was a plan.

Still, as they walked the path along the tree line, trying to make it to the next village by nightfall, Arian felt obligated to voice his thoughts. "We may need to consider lodgings for the next month if the snow gets worse."

Collette, who was walking close behind him, was the first to respond. "What, you aren't happy to continue this trudge through the snow?" She pulled her heavy coat more closely around her as the wind picked up but made no complaints.

Despite the heartache she'd experienced at Tolan's abandonment, Arian was surprised to note how much of the loss she'd kept to herself. It wasn't healthy, but Larent insisted she was fine, and he was helping her handle it. Arian didn't want to know what the wolf meant.

"Arian hates snow," Larent informed her.

"I wouldn't exactly say any of us are fans of the snow or the ice sheets," Thomas pointed out. Regretfully, he had positioned himself back with Nawalya and Whyldon. Arian wanted to do something about their distance, but he didn't know what. He supposed Thomas's continued presence and jovial attitude might be a good sign. Then again, the practiced, careful distance suggested Thomas was upset with him. Arian more than understood why.

"But have you ever gotten so upset by snow that you actually tried to stab it?" Larent agreed with a chuckle.

Arian shot him a look. "That is not what I was doing."

"So, what exactly were you doing?" Thomas asked, and Arian found himself trying to avoid getting too excited.

Looking down to hide his reddening cheeks, Arian said, "There was a storm coming and no shelter. I was contemplating the idea of digging out a safe place."

"With his knives," Larent added, laughter barely contained.

"That's kind of sweet, even if I don't think the snow would have provided much shelter," Thomas said.

"If you build it right, and add ice for support, you can outlast a bad storm without freezing to death," Arian explained. "But you're right. It's temporary." He shuddered a little as the blast of wind died down, hopeful they would soon reach the village. A fire and warm stew sounded inviting, and a quick glance at the rest of the party confirmed they felt the same way.

"I'm not saying trying to make a shelter was a bad idea," Larent said, his arm going around Collette's shoulders, no doubt a gesture meant to help keep her warm. Arian was continuously surprised by Larent's subtle care for the queen. He had expected more blatant professions of love. He was also surprised to note that Collette leaned into his embrace, and Arian had to wonder how their relationship was going to turn out. "I'm saying we should have used the available shovels rather than your knives."

"We are back to him stabbing the snow for being cold?" Collette asked.

"He would sleep through the winter if he could," Nawalya said with a mischievous grin, prompting Arian to shrug.

"We should be in the village soon," Whyldon said to the group. "It looks like this weather may pass in a day or two, and we can progress from there. At some point, we will need to decide where we will be bunking down for the next few weeks. Unless we manage to travel three times the distance we've been averaging, we aren't going to be able to get a boat for several weeks."

"Not until spring, at least," Larent agreed.

"That sounds about right," Whyldon said. "We could stay in the next village indefinitely, but I think traveling further into Galel makes more sense. It would be easier to go without notice."

"You mean I shouldn't insist that you start using my title in public even though we'll be back on the land I'm supposed to rule?" Collette joked.

"I know you're joking, but I feel like you're going to make Arian's head explode by saying that," Larent said with a laugh.

"Your head will explode first," Arian said flatly.

"We need Larent to stick around for entertainment," Collette insisted.

"He is only entertaining for you," Arian replied.

"Someone has to fill the role, Arian. I would be sad otherwise."

"Thomas can entertain you with political arguments," he argued, resisting the urge to glance back at the other man. Thomas would probably appreciate not being ogled.

"I could," Thomas replied and shoved his hands in his pockets. "But I doubt that I would stay in good graces for very long."

Arian was tempted to offer his gloves to the fletcher but doubted Thomas would accept them.

"In that case, I could always tell the story of how Arian and I made our way to your escape house the night I was arrested," Collette suggested. "Everyone would be entertained by that."

"You're lucky I can't stab you," Arian called back to her.

"Stabbing Freckles would be treason," Larent replied before looking down at Collette. "You have to tell us, you know."

"Should I tell them, Arian?" she asked, gaining a noncommittal grunt from the elf. "Arian was tasked with concealing me halfway to the safehouse because we came upon some guards. Can anyone guess his method?"

Arian kept his gaze forward, refusing to take part in the conversation. He knew Nawalya and Larent would laugh, and Collette wasn't telling the story maliciously, but he didn't have to add the joke was at his expense.

"Tell us," Larent encouraged.

"He pressed me up against a wall and pretended to fuck me," Collette said. "It worked. We went unobserved."

Larent choked on air so hard Nawalya had to slap his back to help him catch his breath. "Oh, Lady. Oh shit," he managed between coughs. Then, laughter burst forth, and he actually stopped walking, which brought the group to a halt.

"You're both lucky none of the guards asked to join you," Nawalya said with a smile.

"They would have died, had they," Arian mumbled.

Chapter Thirty-five

Larent opened his mouth to say something that would more than likely piss Arian off when he suddenly winced. Breathing deeply through his nose, he pressed the heel of his palm to his temple.

"Headache?" Arian asked. Without waiting for an answer, he swung his pack around and sorted through the contents until he handed over a bottle. Larent took it and downed the greenish liquid without complaint.

"You've not been taking care of yourself" Nawalya lectured. "When we settle for the evening, you're getting a good meal and sleep."

"Yes, Nawalya," Larent complained. He handed the empty vial back to Arian, and once it was packed away, the group resumed their journey.

Chapter Thirty-Six

They arrived in the village before nightfall, and thankfully, there were enough rooms at the lone inn for everyone in their group. A change into dry clothes and a warm meal by the fire lifted their spirits considerably. Whyldon raised a hand for refills on drinks, and he watched in amusement as Larent and Collette argued. Clearly, the potion, the food, and some rest had rejuvenated him.

As alcohol flowed, the group indulged. Collette's indulgence had been a little more noticeable in the weeks since Tolan's departure, and that combined with her dynamic with Larent often resulted in playful banter like this. Whyldon was happy to let her do whatever brought her some joy.

That evening, Arian seemed less inclined to watch where the current debate was going. "Are you two planning on getting drunk?" he asked, an eyebrow raised.

"No," Collette insisted, her eyes bright and her cheeks flushed with the drink she'd already consumed. "But Larent seems to think he can out-fight me, and that I cannot stand."

Arian gave them a flat look while Nawalya perked up. "I know you won't listen, not while you've both been drinking, but no brawling is allowed."

"It's not like we're drunk, Arian," Collette said, then amended, "Well, I'm not. I can't speak for him."

"And Mother knows we can't have you challenged," Thomas said, hiding his amusement. Somehow, he managed to not get a look from Arian for the comment.

"I'm good. You know it takes more than two drinks," Larent said before looking at Thomas. "That's treason, you know."

"Why is everything treason, suddenly?" Whyldon asked, hoping to sway Collette and Larent away from their prior argument.

"Because we said so," Larent said and took a large swig from his mug. "But it's not treason to state the fact that I'm a better sword fighter than you," he said, pointing at Collette.

"Then let's see your skills," Collette said, her expression playful for all its challenges. "I promise to avoid making you cry."

"You mean, let's test your skills. I've got this in the bag," Larent retorted with a wink.

"Let's go," Collette said as she rose from the table.

Larent grinned, sprang to his feet, and ran upstairs to grab their blades. Whyldon sighed, happy he didn't stumble at the very least. Nawalya stood while Arian hung his head, and then looked at Whyldon. "I do not see this ending well."

"Nor do I," Whyldon confessed. "But I don't see a way of stopping them without causing a huge commotion."

Arian sighed. "Let us make sure they don't kill themselves then."

Larent came back downstairs with the swords minutes later and handed over the one belonging to Collette. They decided to conduct this demonstration outside, so they all filed out to watch.

"Are we sure we want this to happen?" Whyldon called out to them. "Larent is physically bigger and stronger than you, Collette."

"I have better footwork," Collette called back. "That closes the gap nicely."

"Wait, why do you assume you have better footwork?" Larent asked even as he brought his sword up.

"I've seen yours, and it is lacking," Collette replied.

"She is right. You need more practice fighting as a human," Nawalya said from where she stood beside Whyldon.

"Boo, both of you. My footwork is fine."

"Then show us," Collette said. She rolled her shoulders and lifted her sword. "I'll let you strike first."

"Nope. Ladies always go first." He moved his left foot back slightly and rebalanced himself.

"That's almost insulting," Collette replied. She began a slow circle, knees angled in the slightest of bends. Even in her slight state of intoxication, Whyldon noted her careful study of her surroundings, and he was not surprised to see her take the better starting position with ease. Indeed, she was slighter than Larent, but the careful movements and confidence in her ability made her forward lunge and the overhead swing of her blade all the more impressive.

Larent blocked Collette's first swing, brows rising seemingly in surprise at the strength she put behind it. He pushed back against her sword, trying to get her off balance.

Collette's footing helped her pivot out of the way, and once her feet were grounded again, she lunged. "You're quick," she observed.

"I try," he said with a shrug and parried her thrust.

She moved back, blocking his sword with her own. "Bend your knees more," she instructed. "They are too rigid."

Larent didn't argue. He just bent his knees and lunged again.

"Better," Collette complimented, the effort of blocking his attempted blow maximized by the slight change.

"Okay, you two have demonstrated enough," Whyldon interjected.

"Have we?" Larent asked as he faked going left and then went in on the right.

"I'm having fun," Collette said, dodging the last swing.

Larent took a few steps back, studying her the way she'd studied him. "Me too."

"Still," Whyldon said. "You're taking real swipes at each other. This is how someone gets hurt or killed."

"That only happens if we aren't paying attention. This is really just practice, which I know I need," Larent replied.

"You're both drunk," Whyldon pointed out.

"Five more minutes and I will end this," Arian declared.

"Not drunk. Slightly inebriated." Larent moved to Collette's left and went for her legs.

"That was good," she complimented and jumped out of the way with a laugh. "You can fight, too, Arian. You don't have to be left out."

Larent grinned at Collette then risked a glance at Arian. "We don't want him joining right now."

"I'm going inside," Whyldon declared. "When you two slice each other up, I hope Arian will stitch you back together."

"There will be no stitching up," Arian said darkly.

"I swear," Collette said with a sigh. "We're making them mad, Larent. We need to stop."

"We've attracted an audience," Larent said softly as he moved in closer. "Especially that creepy guy who kept watching you at the inn."

"He was looking before we came out here," Collette said as she tossed the sword into the snow. "Whatever. I'll be good."

Whyldon winced. He and Arian had managed to cross one of her boundaries again. Unfortunately, Larent was the one to address it.

Larent looked around and gave her a mischievous grin. Dropping the sword, he grabbed her hand and started for the nearby woods. "Run," he exclaimed and dragged her off toward the trees.

Arian cursed and moved to follow them only for a small, calloused hand to stop him. "Let them have fun," Nawalya said softly.

"Nawalya is right," Whyldon said. He knew Collette would be angered by further interference. He collected the discarded weapons.

Chapter Thirty-Seven

Larent ran with Collette until they were a good walk away from the tree line, laughing loudly and slightly out of breath. "That was fun," he shared, pleased with himself for coming up with a way to lighten her mood. He was going to have to directly intervene with Arian and Whyldon, it seemed.

"It was," Collette agreed as she looked around, though Larent knew the darkness would obscure her view. "I think we've bought ourselves some trouble from Arian."

"Oh, fuck him. I get that he's worried, but you need to be able to have fun sometimes," Larent bemoaned.

Collette sighed and shook her head. "Seriously, I have lost my patience with the overprotective bullshit."

Larent chuckled, lowering himself onto the slightly damp ground that, thankfully, wasn't completely covered with snow. "I get it. I also get why they're worried, but they really do need to back off so you can breathe."

"I'm about three seconds from saying goodbye and going off on my own," Collette retorted. "It's not funny. I've told them to leave me the fuck alone countless times, and they haven't listened." She'd remained standing and crossed her arms over her chest. He didn't blame her. He could see the tension in her shoulders and sitting down wasn't going to relieve it.

"You can't leave without me, Freckles. Just remember that," Larent gently teased.

"I'll take you with me. I'm not an inconsiderate fuck like some people."

"You better, or I will hunt you down, and tickle you until you can't stand it." He held up his hands and made a tickling motion.

"Ugh, I hate tickling. You are not allowed to ever do that, or I will like someone else better."

"Good thing I'm over here, and you're over there. Apparently, I'm too old and out of shape to even roll over. You're safe."

Collette smirked. "Is this the part where you want me to argue you're young and strong and virile?"

"It might be fun to hear the argument, but no. I'm honestly just being lazy. Though, I have to agree my footwork was awful. I rely too much on my shifting in a fight."

"Practice is always good," Collette replied. "You seemed surprised by my skill when we were sparring."

"You are deceptively strong, but I knew you'd be good. You've been training since you were five from what Whyldon implies. I was more surprised by how unfamiliar I've become with a sword. It's a trap my Nana warned me about."

"Fuck, if I had your abilities, I'd rely on them, too," she said gently, finally taking a seat beside him. "But we'll get you sorted if that's what you think you need."

"Thanks." He gave her a soft smile. "It was almost impossible to shift while I was working in your castle, and as Nana loved to say, 'A shifter who relies too much on their powers doesn't live to be two hundred.' She would know since she and Pops might be the oldest shifters alive."

"Part of your castle problem came from making up excuses to run into me, you know," she said, giving him a playful push.

He grinned. "Yeah, you're right."

"You are lucky I didn't shove you off a balcony. I normally would have if I'd encountered some random stranger in my quarters."

"You probably should have, but I didn't mean to end up there that first night," Larent said.

"You did mean to the subsequent times, though."

"Every other time but the chapel," he admitted. He turned his head to look at her. "Tell me something."

She sighed, leaning back on her hands. "I am very frustrated with Arian and Whyldon, even though I understand their motivations and would probably be the same way in their shoes."

He made a thoughtful noise as he considered other options. "I bet if you threatened Chuckles with a knife, he would finally get the point."

She shook her head. "I don't like making threats I wouldn't see through."

"You could stab him a little bit. He wouldn't mind," Larent said. "You could also appeal to Nawalya. Give her some tears and you can weaponize her against them."

"I also don't use fake tears, nor am I particularly good at conjuring them," she said. "Actually, I'm not really great at the real thing, either."

That was no surprise. She'd never cried, to his knowledge, about the insurrection in the kingdom, and she'd barely shed a tear over Tolan. "Neither is Nawalya, which is why I suggested it. Crying children, especially, sets her off the most."

"You don't get much opportunity to cry, or much encouragement, when you're in my position."

Larent nodded, understanding her burden. It explained how she could so easily put on a brave face when she'd been hurt

so badly so many times in the past months. "Tell me something else, or ask me a question."

Collette was quiet for a moment before she asked a question. "Why a wolf?"

Larent thought about that for a moment, unsure at first of how to answer. "Shifters can take any animal form, but only one will feel right and make you complete and whole. A wolf feels right."

"Why does a wolf feel right for you?" she asked.

He snorted. "Nana says it's because I have a need for family while still trying to prove I can go it alone."

"Tell me more about your family," Collette prompted.

"I was given to my grandparents at two. My parents, well my mom, didn't want a shifter child. Nana and Pops are great..." He shrugged, his words trailing off. "I met my parents again when we were adults. They had no clue I still existed. It is what it is."

"I'm sorry," she said. "I know it's not a wonderful feeling."

"It's alright," he said in a sullen tone. Then he smiled and cast his gaze toward her. "Ask me something else."

"You always want me to ask things," she observed. "What specifically would you have me ask?"

"Nothing or anything. I just like talking to you," he admitted.

"Okay. What do you want in life?" she asked. "I've told you what I want. It seems fair to ask the same of you."

"I haven't thought about it too much, but a farm sounds nice. Something like what my grandparents had. It was an easier life, but I didn't appreciate it when I was younger."

"That sort of life sounds amazing, honestly. Simplicity with hard work. Peaceful existence."

"It was fun growing up, but as an older teen, I hated it," Larent confessed with a wry smile. "I couldn't wait to go on adventures, but as I've gotten older, I've missed it."

"Then I hope you have it for yourself one day. Or whatever else would make you content."

"If I live long enough, I might want that. What makes people happy changes as they grow. Maybe in a few years, I'll want to be a baker. Whatever I do, it'll make me happy. Now you tell me something."

"If you do decide on becoming a baker, I will visit you, but I won't eat your bread," Collette shared with a laugh.

"Ah, why not?" he asked with a fake pout.

"I've eaten your cooking. I love you and all, but I have to be honest about your skills lying elsewhere."

His heart beat a little faster at her words, even if she didn't mean them the way he wished. "Yeah, I'm a terrible cook. I've gotten Chuckles sick twice, and he will not let me touch his potion equipment anymore."

"That is probably very wise on Arian's part. Although, as specific and deliberate as he is about his potions, he probably wouldn't let you cook, regardless." She shrugged. "We didn't have a lot of potions going on in the palace. Sargarus hated magic and magic users. Potions fell under his approval."

"So, he never knew about your gifts, I take it? Other than me, does anyone else know?" he asked.

"Tolan," Collette said. "And Whyldon, of course. He was the one who recognized I had them. It's not like healing abilities are super flashy or anything."

"Wouldn't know. You're the first person I've met who has them. For all I know, you have to sing or your hands glow green for the magic to work," he teased.

"You don't want me to sing. I promise," she said with a smile. "And my hands don't glow. They do get quite warm though, and a little tingly."

"Tingles are always fun, depending on the tingles. I bet you sing well. I sound like a dying bird." He laughed.

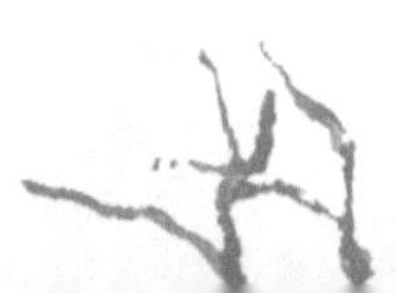

"I sound like an already dead bird," she said, laughing now. "I did not know how bad I sounded when I was a little girl. I used to make Whyldon and the other soldiers listen to me while I gave impromptu performances."

"I bet they clapped and still cheered you on, though."

"They did with the help of spirits. Honestly, younger me was a lot like current me. Foul mouth and all. I think the poor singing was probably viewed as a positive thing because being musically inclined was deemed an appropriate skill for a princess."

"When I was young, I decided I was a sheepdog, and I was gonna help with the sheep. Nana and Pops thought it was great until I also decided I was no longer human." Larent shot her a playful grin.

"Why did you do that?"

"I was ten, and we had these three dogs that were just so amazing and had an easy life. No chores or baths, just whatever they wanted. I decided I was going to be a dog and live like them. It made sense at the time."

"It makes a certain bit of sense now, honestly," she said. "Sans the bathing thing. Bathing must happen."

"Young Larent believed three things as if they were the word of the Lady." He held up a finger. "Nana made the best pies in the world." A second finger went up. "Pops was the strongest person in the world." A third finally went up. "And baths were sent from the evil one."

"Okay, so now I have a new question for current Larent."

"Go for it."

"What three things do you most believe in now?"

"Family isn't always blood. Evil only prevails if we allow it." He looked down at her. "And you are the best of us," he said.

"How do you reconcile that last statement with your frequent encouragement for me to abandon my quest as queen?"

"Simple. I know you won't. Even if it would be better for you, you won't. That's just who you are," he said with genuine, if blunt, honesty.

"And if I did?"

"Honestly? I would be stupidly pleased because you would be putting yourself first for once." He took in a breath. "Changing topics. How did you not inherit the king's prejudices? From what I understand, the previous five kings all held the same beliefs."

"Relatively speaking, King Zephraim the Wise and Queen Censha were peaceful," Collette said. "Of course, I was not alive during their reign, but they were praised for their kindness and benevolence. How they produced Sargarus is a mystery."

Larent considered that. He'd always thought about most of the Coralian rulers in one way: evil. He supposed, realistically, that Collette's viewpoint was probably more consistent with most people. Conquests and war were constant themes throughout history, and those themes could be found in every country. "The only thing I recall about that period was the loss of the fairies. Because of that, I've always questioned how good Zephraim the Wise could be."

"I did say relatively," Collette replied with a sigh. "I've never thought there was a justification for cruelty or treating others with disdain and hatred."

Larent said, "I wonder if madness runs in your family."

Collette shrugged. "Sargarus isn't my father. So, if madness is the explanation, I won't inherit it."

Larent looked at her, eyes wide in confusion. "What?" he said.

"Sargarus is not my father," she repeated. "I thought that was obvious."

Larent shook his head. "Why would that be obvious? You're the queen. He was the king. You inherited the title from him."

She surveyed him with an expression of amused surprise. "How have Nawalya and Arian figured it out, but not you?" She pointed to her jaw. "Come on. This is obvious. As is my hair. I have all the freckles, I just don't have the blue eyes."

Larent sat up, studying Collette in the dim light of evening. "No," he said as he realized that she did resemble the guard captain. "How did I miss this?" And if she was, in fact, not the heir of Sargarus, she really had no moral obligation to continue on her path. She was doing it because it was the right thing.

He shook his head. "The magic comes from Whyldon's line, then?"

"I don't know," she said. "It might, but I don't remember my mother at all, and I've never been in touch with her family."

"Have you asked Whyldon? Does he even know you know?"

"He does not," Collette admitted.

"Why haven't you talked to him about it?" Larent asked. He didn't know how he'd respond in a similar situation, but he knew he was a curious person who would likely seek answers.

"How do you bring it up?" she asked seriously. "It wasn't safe back home."

"It's safe now," he pointed out.

"Is it?" She asked. "Obviously, I trust you, Nawalya, and Arian. And Thomas, strangely. But what we are trying to accomplish… If more people knew, I'd have no legitimate claim. Besides, he hasn't brought it up either. He may not want to."

"Not sure why he wouldn't. Seems weirdly out of character for him, unless he truly believes you don't know." No one had been so diligent in making sure she remained safe on this trip, but Collette was right. If the connection somehow became widely known, she could have more trouble.

"Who knows," Collette said.

"If I was sure it wouldn't kill you, I'd bet you a bowl of my homemade stew he thinks you don't know."

"And we are back to the fact that as much as I love you, I'm not eating food you make," she replied, teasing him.

"Which is why I said if it wouldn't kill you," he said with a laugh. He couldn't help but look at her lips, something he instantly knew he shouldn't have done.

"Arian would be very mad if I died of your cooking. I would still be afraid of Arian even if I were dead."

"Oh, don't worry. If I accidentally got you sick, I would kill him and run." He moved so he could more easily face her, her mouth tempting him further. He tried to ignore it. "I feel like we've had quite the rambling conversation. Granted, I've been a bit distracted."

"Care to share why?" Collette asked.

Larent made a face like he was considering telling her, then crooked his finger. "Come closer and I will." Once she was close enough, he whispered, "Your mouth may be the most distracting thing I have ever come across. I very much want to kiss you." He knew he shouldn't. It had only been a little over a month since Tolan left, but he just couldn't help himself.

Surprisingly, Collette didn't move away, but her eyes widened at the confession. He was certain she'd laugh him off or back away. She didn't.

"Why don't you?" she asked.

"With everything going on, I wasn't sure you'd want me to," he quietly said, his eyes slowly going to her lips and back up to her eyes.

"I want you to," she confessed.

"Well then..." Reaching out, he pulled her closer, and his lips softly brushed against hers.

"I hate to interrupt, but the others have made some interesting decisions," Thomas said.

Larent growled in frustration.

Collette sighed and shot a look at the fletcher, who now stood between some trees a couple of feet from them. "What kind of decisions?"

Thomas looked up at the sky, clearly unhappy to be reporting the news. "Nawalya overheard the man from the tavern tell his companion who you are, so naturally, she, Arian, and Whyldon decided it had to be dealt with."

"That's not good," she said begrudgingly, though she stood as did Larent. "How does he know who I am?"

"I have no idea, and they are trying to figure it out." Thomas motioned to the west side of the clearing. "You should find them if you start in that direction."

Larent nodded. "That means they are going to do whatever they need to get information from them." He looked to Collette. "Do you want to go check on how they are doing or stay away?"

"If this is happening on my behalf, I might as well be there," Collette replied.

"I agree," said Thomas. "I understood the need to kill Brath, but I'd hope you'd have concern over possible torture."

Larent winced. "Please tell me you're not squeamish about shit like that?"

"It's not being squeamish to point out that Collette needs to determine what lines she's comfortable having crossed in her name," Thomas said frankly.

Larent wanted to laugh, even though he understood Thomas's point. "We are going to do whatever is necessary to keep Collette safe, and by extension, make the world better. A little torture in exchange for peace is nothing."

"Really?" Thomas replied, eyebrows raised. He looked at Collette. "Do you condone this?"

"Try having your race hunted to near extinction, or watching your family getting butchered, and say that to me again, pumpkin," Larent interrupted.

Thomas exchanged looks with Collette, a look of disapproval on his face. "This blood will be on your hands, Collette." He stepped back, and Larent knew Thomas wouldn't be joining them. "I'm packing up our belongings. I'll be at the tavern when you're done." With that, he turned and walked away.

"I like Thomas, and I understand where he is coming from, but he's going to have to rethink some things if he plans on staying around long term," Larent said. He lifted his head slightly and took in a deep breath, picking up the scent coming from the west. "He was right. They are this way." He offered a hand to Collette but was disappointed when she didn't take it.

"He wasn't wrong," Collette said as they began walking.

"Maybe not," he relented. "But sometimes, you have to do unsavory things. We have firm lines we won't cross, but we've done things that keep us up at night, Collette. It doesn't change the fact that sometimes, the hard thing has to be done." He came to a stop, checked his surroundings, and then motioned them forward. "This way."

"Justify the unsavory thing we're about to witness," she said.

Larent looked down at her, brows furrowed, and turned his gaze in the direction they walked. He stepped forward a bit as the underbrush grew thicker, knowing he saw better in the darkness. "Just because Thomas immediately jumped to torture doesn't mean things will get that far. We aren't monsters, even if we aren't good people."

"But you don't deny it's a real possibility," Collette replied. "That's why Thomas had a point."

Larent laughed and opened his mouth to say something when a scream ripped through the air. "I guess they did go for torture," he muttered as he hurried their steps.

The concealed area Arian, Nawalya, and Whyldon had chosen was a mess. A short, stocky man lay on the ground, bound with his hands behind his back, at his knees, and his

ankles. The stench of urine wafted through the air, and a cursory glance at the man confirmed he was frightened.

The other man, the one who had been noted at dinner, was strung up between two trees. He was shirtless and covered in fresh lacerations. Nawalya stood in front of the man, twirling her knives and humming happily.

Arian paced nearby, his face contorted into livid fury, his hands curled into fists. Whyldon sorted through packs presumably belonging to their hostages.

"Who. Hired. You," Arian growled out.

"I don't know!" cried the bound man. "It was up through a proxy. We never met the man who wanted it done."

"You sure you still want to be here?" Larent whispered to Collette. Her expression was grim and disapproving, and there was no attempt to hide her feelings.

"Thomas was right. This is on my hands now. No point in being a coward."

He almost felt regretful, but he knew there was no walking them back. "Maybe you should make some inquiries." Larent motioned her forward, something else she did not argue.

"Someone explain," she called out in a commanding voice Larent had only ever heard when he'd been spying at the castle. A voice he associated with anger. Great.

Arian nearly jumped at the sound. Clearly, none of them had noticed the scene had grown by two. The elf turned to stare at Collette like she wasn't really there. Nawalya offered her a beautiful smile, and Whyldon only looked up in brief acknowledgment before resuming his task.

Taking a deep breath, Arian spoke. "These men are part of the group that was hired to kill you in Coralia. They were minions of the man Nawalya had delivered to Whyldon."

Collette frowned. "What has been said?"

Chapter Thirty-seven

"Very little," Arian gritted out. "They don't know much about who hired them and have implied they were considering finishing the job."

Collette turned to the men. "You realize your employer is dead?" she asked them. She nodded in Nawalya's direction. "She took care of him all by herself. Tell me why you should receive better treatment."

The man strung up spit, badly, in Collette's direction. "I hope you die, bitch," he replied, earning himself another deeper cut from Nawalya's dagger.

"You should be nicer to our queen," she said in a sing-song voice and twirled her dagger again.

"I don't know anything!" the bound man cried out. "I swear! I just met with the proxy. I had nothing to do with this!"

Arian unsheathed his sword and held it to the man's neck. "Describe the proxy." Unsurprisingly, the man went silent despite his cries.

"I've already decided what we're doing with him," Collette said then pointed to the man who had spit at her. "Help me make my mind up about you."

The man on the ground seemed convinced he was safe, at least for the time being. "He… he always wore black pants and a blue dress shirt with a white undershirt. I n-never really saw his face."

Arian and Nawalya exchanged looks, and a subtle nod of Nawalya's head had Arian pressing the blade against the man's neck. "That tells us nothing," Arian said.

"Wait!" The man sobbed, his words broken. "He had a hawk or owl crest on the button of his sleeves."

"That sounds like one of Lord Elrick's men," Larent said. He'd spent enough time bedding Lady Elrick to have taken in a few details. "He's the bird guy, after all."

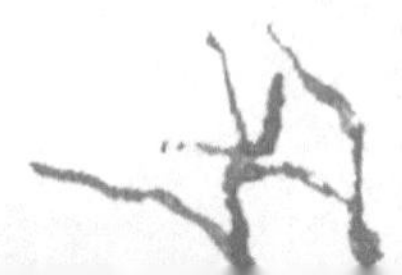

"It does," Collette confirmed. "Is there anything else we should know? Think very, very carefully before you answer."

The man opened his mouth, then shut it with an audible click. "No," he said firmly.

"He knows something more," Nawalya sang.

Collette took a breath through her nose and looked back at the man who'd been strung up. "Kill him," she said.

Nawalya grinned and happily slit the man's throat, further splattering herself in blood.

Collette looked back to the man on the ground, no sign of regret or hesitation in her expression. "Do you feel like sharing your secret with us yet?"

"I hope whoever claims the bounty on your head makes it slow and painful," the bound man growled, his venomous tone a departure from his earlier tears.

"You know, that person might be lucky," Collette conceded with a pleasant smile. "But that doesn't help you here and now, does it?" She approached the man and knelt down so that they were eye level. "It's just us and you, now. You have a choice to make, and trust me, no matter the consequences, I will sleep well tonight."

The man leaned forward enough to respond. "You were a weak queen who cared more about others than her own race. If not for these freaks, your head would be on a pike where it belongs. You'll get nothing more from me."

Collette smiled again as she straightened. "I'm almost disappointed you took this route. But insulting my family cannot stand." She looked to Arian and Nawalya. "Have fun." She turned away from the scene and walked back in the direction of the tavern.

Nawalya made a face of pure glee. "That means I can slice you up like I did your friend!"

Arian grimaced at Nawalya's words. Lady, sometimes it bothered Larent as well, the joy she got out of killing. "We will get no more from this one," Arian decided, and he made quick work of beheading the man rather than dragging it out.

The elf pushed his hair back from his face when he was done. "Did you find anything else in their packs?" he called out to Whyldon.

"Nothing other than more confirmation of what we already know," Whyldon replied. "We need to get this cleaned up." He went to gather supplies to create a fire. They would burn what they could and bury the rest.

"I should go check on Collette," Larent determined, only to be stopped by Nawalya.

"Give her space," she said. "She was forced into an unexpected situation." She looked over at Arian. "You go back to the tavern," she told him. "Make sure you're packed up and take care. We'll finish cleaning."

"Thank you," Arian said softly before he headed back.

With just Larent, Whyldon, and Nawalya, they started the tedious process of cleaning up. "You know she's angry," Whyldon said as he stoked the fire.

"Yes, but is she angry at us or at the situation?" Nawalya asked honestly. She and Larent were cutting down the man who had spit at Collette.

"Both, I think," Whyldon said after a moment. "We should have waited on her before we did anything."

"I don't regret what we did. I would do it again, but you are correct," Nawalya agreed.

Larent made a face as he mulled over the question in his head. He still believed that getting information from, and then getting rid of, the two men had been the wisest choice. It had been the only real choice. But he couldn't deny that the actions had hurt Collette.

"I will talk to Arian about this," Nawalya decided.

"Might I suggest that the three of you make more of an effort to listen to what she's been saying?" Larent added. "She isn't used to people making decisions for her, or being coddled, and the more it happens, the angrier she gets." He gestured in the direction she'd walked. "In case no one else sees it, she's barely keeping it together. Stuff like this isn't helping."

Nawalya looked down. "If we do not do better, she may break. I don't know what will happen if she does."

No one wanted to dwell on the possibility, especially when Larent knew their reasons had grown beyond ridding the world of the possible threats that came with Zephraim on the throne.

"We will do better going forward. As much as we can," Whyldon said. "For now, let's finish cleaning. We don't have long before sunrise, and we need to be well away from here."

Chapter Thirty-Eight

ollette arrived back at the inn, jaw set, and eyes narrowed. She was infuriated by what had happened, by the lack of choice she'd had in the brief torture and eventual murder of the two men. She'd wanted to scream, to demand to know what they were doing, but what would have been the point? The actions taken before she'd arrived dictated how they had to proceed and how it had to end. There had been no safe way to turn back, and nothing she could do to change it. Even now, as she collapsed at one of the tables, she was seriously contemplating leaving.

She ran a frustrated hand through her hair, feeling like the fun sword fight with Larent had happened years ago instead of a couple of hours. She growled in frustration as someone joined her at the table, but she schooled her emotions as she saw it was Thomas.

He sat himself at the table, placing a mug of ale in front of her. "I take it you didn't like what you found?" he asked her.

"I did not," she confirmed. She straightened her shoulders and let out a sigh before picking up the mug.

"If you want to talk about it, I'll listen," he said sympathetically. "If not, I managed to gather up everyone's supplies, so we can leave as soon as the others are ready." He surveyed Collette for a moment. "Assuming you are amenable to traveling with us after tonight."

"That's still the plan," Collette said. She took a sip from her mug, not really tasting the drink but appreciating it all the same.

"Good," Thomas said, offering her a smile. He leaned forward, resting his arms on the table. "Tonight was awful, and I know you are angry. Don't let it stop you from moving forward."

She offered him a cursory smile. "I'm going to keep doing what I've been doing," she assured him. "It's my obligation and I am fully capable of continuing on this path."

"You're unhappy, though," Thomas pointed out. "And not just about tonight."

"I think you'll find my happiness is rarely the priority."

Thomas waved, and Collette looked back toward the stairs, spotting Arian. He'd changed since Collette saw him in the clearing, perhaps because he'd been splattered in blood.

Hesitantly, the elf walked toward the table and lowered himself into a seat. He looked as though he wanted to say something, his jaw working and pausing, but he remained silent.

"What?" Collette asked him, brow raised. "Feel free to speak."

Arian shook his head. "I was just going to ask if we were ready to go."

"Once the others are back," Thomas replied, offering his companions a knowing grin. "That isn't what you were going to say, though."

Arian paused, his expression considerate and careful. "I am aware that you are upset and have every right to be," he directed to Collette. "I acted without thought for your choices and feelings. You are in charge of this, not I." Arian closed his eyes for a moment. "Once I knew what they were planning, I reacted on impulse. It will not happen again, but if you cannot continue with us after this, I will accept that."

Collette kept her eyes trained on her mug of beer. Arian seemed more aware of how she was feeling than he'd let on. He was so task-focused, it could be easy to overlook the person he actually was, which was, perhaps, why Larent was such an advocate for him. The thought made her decision easy.

"I'm not leaving, but if any major action is taken in my name without my consent, I will leave and not look back," Collette said, meeting his gaze.

"It will not," Arian promised, bowing his head. "But I do wonder if you would not be better off without us," he admitted softly.

"That is ridiculous," Collette said, her response purposefully blunt.

"Is it?" Arian asked. "I worry what being around us is doing to your moral center. Larent is not wrong in how he describes you or us."

"You're still being ridiculous," she replied. "I can mind myself well enough, and I can speak my mind when I think we've crossed lines."

"You may be one of the most capable women I have ever met, second only to Larent's Nana, who I personally witnessed gut someone with a needle," Arian said thoughtfully.

"Good," Collette replied. She let out a breath. "I suggest moving forward since dwelling on it will just make me angry again."

Arian nodded. Thomas rose to get the elf a drink, and the three were found in quiet contemplation when Larent returned.

"Oh, a waiting party," he said cheekily as he joined the party. "I feel special."

"Of course you do," Collette said with a snort. Her beer was drained, but they would be leaving soon, so she decided she was done for now. "Are the others far behind?"

Larent shook his head. "They are waiting for us in the clearing." He made a vague gesture over his clothing, and Collette remembered the splashes of blood.

"Our bags are ready," Thomas said, motioning to the pile beside him. "Shall I go and settle up?" He rose from his seat without waiting for an answer and went to speak with the innkeeper.

"Do we have a destination?" Collette asked.

"Same stop we were planning on before," Larent answered. He started distributing travel packs to everyone "Assuming that there isn't a reason to change."

She shook her head. "No, but things change quickly. It's possible those men were not alone. The next village isn't far."

Thomas rejoined them. "Let's go," he prompted, and they left the inn.

Chapter Thirty-Nine

Passing back into Coralia came without a problem. The ground was covered in snow, and most of the people they'd expect to encounter in warmer weather were safely tucked away in their homes until spring. Travel was safer because of that, as even Arian was less insistent on secure travel.

They'd opted to settle in for the evening near a clearing, though that had meant wood needed gathering. Nawalya and Whyldon volunteered for the job, and Thomas thought it would be a while before they returned. He chuckled as he helped Collette set up the tents for the evening. They didn't often use them, but the weather required they have more of a shield that evening.

"Okay, I know we're thinking the same thing," Larent said as he cleared away snow so they had an area to build a fire.

"I'd hope everyone present knew what they were planning," Collette said. "It was sort of obvious."

Thomas chortled as Arian rolled his eyes and went back to sharpening his sword.

Larent wiggled his eyebrows at Collette. "Want to 'collect' firewood, too?"

"Not in this weather," Collette responded with a smirk. "It's fucking cold."

"No worries, Freckles" Larent insisted. "I will bring a blanket for you. I'll make sure you stay warm."

Collette snorted. "I'm not getting naked in the snow, no matter how warm you say you'd keep me."

"That's not a strong no," Thomas joked. He straightened, surveying his work on the tent and judging it sufficient for the wind. "Just a delay until the weather is better."

Larent cackled. "One of the tents is finally up," he said, pointing to one belonging to Nawalya. "Maybe while we're having fun, Chuckles and Thomas can have some fun as well."

Arian growled at him.

"When Arian stabs you, I'm not helping," Collette replied.

"Maybe he could stab Thomas instead," Larent replied with a suggestive smirk.

Rolling his eyes, Arian stood. "We need timber for the fire. I will collect some since Nawalya and Whyldon are otherwise occupied." He didn't wait for a response, nearly sprinting into the forest.

Collette straightened and shot a glance toward Thomas. "You probably should go with him," she said before tossing one of the tent stakes at Larent who ducked out of the way.

Thomas considered not following Arian into the woods. Still, the part of him that didn't back down from curiosity and conflict forced him to follow after the other man. The trees were bare and brown, and Thomas thought it likely during the summer, the dense foliage would make it more difficult to travel through the forest.

After some searching, he finally came across Arian, who had an armful of dry wood. Thomas found himself looking forward to the warmth of the evening fire. "I was sent after you," he informed the elf.

Arian gave a wry chuckle. "Payback, I assume."

"I'm fairly certain Larent wants alone time with our queen."

Arian paused at his words. "Perhaps we should head back. There is no telling what he might talk her into."

"He's had plenty of opportunity when it's been just the two of them," Thomas pointed out. "And she's opinionated enough to not let Larent cross any lines." He closed some of the distance between himself and Arian.

"You'll notice we do not often give them a lot of time alone, just in case," Arian replied. He sighed and shook his head, leaving Thomas to wonder what other unspoken motivation Arian held.

"Are you that unhappy being alone with me for even a few minutes?"

Arian's posture went rigid. He added another piece of wood to his pile. "I do not mind being alone with you."

"Are you certain? You've been incredibly distant with me since I arrived. I'm still not sure you actually wanted me to take you up on the offer to join the group."

Arian focused on his wood collection. He opened and closed his mouth several times, shaking his head now and then. Finally, he responded. "I am glad you are traveling with us. Sincerely, I am. You offer a different opinion than most of us, which is needed. You are unafraid to call out our mistakes and have been a great support to Collette." He paused again, not looking at Thomas. "I cannot deny that you are a distraction. It's best that I keep my distance while we work to win back her throne. I've done enough things that could be considered mistakes since we left the kingdom."

"What kind of distraction am I, exactly?" Thomas asked.

Arian almost dropped his sticks, his whole body tensing again. "Ask another question," he replied, his voice deeper than normal.

"I have asked the question I meant to," Thomas said.

Arian gave a deep sigh. "I find myself watching you when I should be doing anything else instead."

"Then what is the problem, exactly? I've not been shy about what I feel, and it's obvious that you feel the same."

Arian's shoulders slumped. "As of this moment, it is, but a distraction means mistakes, and mistakes mean someone could die. I will not have that happen. I will not lose you or anyone else during this mission."

"You are the only member of this group that seems to take that burden full on," Thomas commented.

"We all have our roles. This is mine. Nawalya may be better at thinking on her feet than I am, but preparing and protecting belongs to me."

"I'm hearing excuses, Arian," Thomas said. "You believe you have to protect everyone even though none of the others take the burden on for themselves. Look at what they are doing now."

Thomas could see temper rising in the elf's face. His brows were narrowed, and the corners of his mouth turned down.

"It's different," Arian insisted. He stepped away from Thomas.

"How is it different? Because you want reasons to justify distance?" Thomas asked.

"Because people don't die when Larent and Nawalya make mistakes. Whole villages aren't wiped out when they make an incorrect decision!" Arian nearly shouted. "Their mistakes do not cost lives, Thomas."

He tossed the wood from his arms and leaned against one of the trees. Thomas noted the glassy look of Arian's eyes before he covered his face in his hands. He closed the distance between the two and put his hands on either side of Arian's face. "You put far too heavy a burden on yourself."

Arian's breath caught at the moment of contact, but he did nothing to end it, instead letting his hands fall to his sides. "It is a burden I have chosen. I cannot hand it off to someone else."

"It's a burden you could share," Thomas said quietly. "You will burn yourself out if you keep this all to yourself." He brushed a thumb across Arian's cheek, resisting the urge to kiss him. "I know you are busy with your distractions and your burdens, and I know you are not in a place to do anything about what is between us. Just know, we are each other's destiny. My backing off and giving you space isn't me giving up."

"How are you able to state that so easily, knowing the things I have done?"

"Because I know you, and even when I have disagreed with your choices, you did not make them lightly."

Arian shuddered, then rested his head against Thomas's shoulder. "I am a monster, Thomas."

"I don't think you're a monster," Thomas replied. "You could never be a monster in my eyes." He smiled as he felt Arian's hands rest on his waist.

"I am," Arian argued. "I have done horrific things."

"I know," Thomas replied as his thumb continued to stroke Arian's face.

"I do not understand how you can look past all of that and find me worthy when I cannot do so myself."

"I think you judge yourself more harshly than others do," Thomas replied simply.

Arian closed his eyes and allowed himself to tilt his face into Thomas's hand.

More might have happened had a spindly man not come running by, a trail of blood just visible on his forearm.

"That's not good," Thomas commented from where they were concealed.

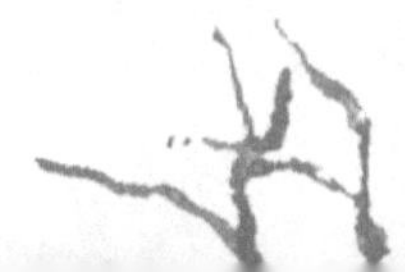

Arian visibly started and flinched as a scream for help rang through the air. "Oh, Spirit!" he exclaimed softly before he took off running.

Chapter Forty

Crem looked down the dark alley at the men accompanying him. Barely detectable in the inky darkness of late night, all of the men were dressed in grays and blacks to further conceal themselves. Like the rest of the group, Crem wore a domino mask, hoping to obscure his identity should someone get close enough to detect him.

Leaning forward slightly, he looked at the roof of the building several houses down where three others waited. His eyes darted to an adjacent side street where more waited. Their leader, an older man named Howle, signed their readiness, and Crem gave a brief nod of acknowledgment.

In total, he had eighteen men for the rescue mission, a scant number that might easily be outnumbered within minutes. Eighteen had to be enough, though. Too many people were relying on their intervention. Too many could die if they failed.

The group waited in complete silence, even the younger, more impatient members of their party. The minutes ticked by, and slight fidgeting detected in the others stirred up anxiety in Crem. The whole evening already felt off, as though something wasn't quite right. The odds were against them, and the thing they continuously waited for slowly drained confidence. This wasn't good. Not at all.

The only reason he stayed was because of the mysterious letters, letters that had not led him astray so far. Surely, he could continue trusting them.

The light creak of a wagon wheel almost evaded Crem's notice, but the whispers and accompanying footsteps of the guards did not. So far, his latest secret letter had been right. That meant the five emerging wagons sneaking through the city in the middle of the night were filled with elves, Mers, and other "dissenters" of all ages, even children, all bound for the labor camps.

Holding up a hand, Crem signaled for the men to hold. He began counting the guards he could spot, not knowing if others were within the wagons or hidden in the various nooks and crannies of the city block. Howle was doing the same from the other side, and he held up two hands and then two fingers toward Crem. A dozen counted guards. To be safe, Crem thought they should double the number, and he signaled as much back to Howle.

They waited for the line of wagons to fall between the three units of men, the most advantageous position they could reach. As this fifth wagon creaked past, Crem gave the attack signal.

The first wagon was overtaken by the elves who descended from the rooftops. The group from the alley took the second and third. Crem's group rushed out, he and another man swarmed the fourth wagon while the other three took the fifth.

Surprisingly, and despite the time of night, the dozen or so guards were all they encountered. It alerted Crem to a possible trap, but he had no way of stopping to worry. People needed rescuing.

He found the lock to the wagon door, peering inside the small, barred window at the scared faces hidden inside. "I'll get you out," he shouted, then ducked as a swinging fist came at him from the side.

In a fluid motion, he landed a punch into the soldier's stomach, and the man fell to the ground. Crem kicked him a few times, then found a ring of keys on the man's belt. He extricated them and quickly worked through the set before finding the key that fit the lock. Once opened, the lock was tossed aside, and he pulled the door open. "Hurry," he said to the former prisoners and moved out of their way so they could flee.

He tossed the keys to the men at the next wagon. "Get the wagons emptied!" he ordered the group as Howle ran over. Speckles of blood showed one more of the guards had been taken down.

"Elrick and his men are here," Howle announced as he shook his shock of long silvery hair from his face. "Ten men are with him."

"How many does that leave us?" Crem asked.

"We still have everyone we brought," Howle guessed. He looked around, his lips moving in silent counting. "I'd guess less than twenty total. My team took out a few of the guards. It looks like the same happened here."

Crem nodded as he spotted the older lord in the distance, a little more fragile and corpulent from age, but agile enough with a blade.

"We have to hurry," Crem said to himself, wanting the wagons emptied before more conflict arose. He turned to check on the progress, spotting people fleeing from two more of the wagons. Three wagons in total. They might just have a chance.

Howle departed to help with the remaining wagons, leaving Crem to face Elrick, who'd closed the distance between them. The lord swung his sword, the accuracy and strength surprising. Crem barely blocked the blow, receiving a shallow cut to his side for his distraction.

"I'm surprised you're actually fighting," he taunted the older man as he went on the defense, waiting for another opening.

"Unlike you, I actually deserve my rank," Elrick shot back as more fighting erupted amongst Elrick's soldiers and Crem's men. The shouting and sounds of swords and fists quickly filled the air of the otherwise quiet city.

"That's a lie and you know it," Crem yelled over the noise and dodged a swing. "You were present when the false king needed a warm body to fill a role."

The fourth wagon opened, and more escapees fled the scene. One to go.

"You'll hang for treason!" Elrick called back. He shouted an order to his men as a family managed to disappear into the night, but no one gave chase as they were surrounded by Crem's fighters.

"I'll rid the world of you on my way out," Crem promised, taking the quick distraction to knick the other man's arm, enraging Elrick.

"You better hope your wife had the sense to get out of the palace," came Elrick's growled threat.

Crem's expression grew dark at the veiled threat, and as he moved toward Elrick with no concern for his safety. Elrick must have felt the threat as he called for his men to surround Crem.

Crem took a deep breath, centered himself, and took in the group of soldiers. He recognized faces, like Borin and Rulf, that had been so reckless and cruel for no reason. The others were younger, third and fourth sons of ranking lords who needed a way to earn money. They had little training and discipline. "What, too cowardly to finish this yourself?" he taunted Elrick.

The words prompted the men to lunge at Crem. The youngest guard, regretfully, he dispatched with little effort. The darkness of night kept him from fully confirming it, but he was certain the man was dead. A second went the same way, though this time Crem continued hearing the soft groans from the ground.

He wanted to check on the boy, but a punch to the jaw from Rulf prevented him. Crem stumbled to one knee. "You could only win by cheating," he spat out, tasting blood.

"That's still winning," Rulf said with a cackle as Borin moved closer, kicking Crem over with his boot. With the former guard commander grounded, he and Rulf moved to make the killing blows.

Crem closed his eyes, thanking the Mother that he'd told Diana he loved her before going out. He expected death, but instead, he felt the warmth of freshly spilled blood splash across his face. He opened his eyes, taking in the dazed look coming from Borin, who had an arrow jutting out of his neck. Crem sat up and saw a blade cross Rulf's throat, spurts of his blood dotting everything around him. Body after body fell to the ground, leaving Crem confused in the haze of gore and fighting.

The responsible party, who he first thought was one of his own men, turned out to be someone completely new. Dressed in solid black armor composed of leather and metal, Crem knew this man would be wealthy. His head covering included a mask, though Crem had never seen anything like it before. The only trace of skin he saw was the opened mouthpiece, and the man was smiling playfully.

"Looks like we arrived just in time," he said to Crem before motioning to a new group of people dressed just like him. "Kill the rest," the man, his voice unnatural and cold as he strode toward Lord Elrick.

The lord's eyes widened, surprised by the intervention. Even as Howle moved to Crem's side to help him off the ground, Crem couldn't help but watch the stranger smoothly cover the distance between himself and Elrick. His sword rose

into middle position, his stance amply communicating that there would be no quarter.

The stranger did not speak as he quickly disarmed Elrick. The quiet certainty of his movements made even Crem wary of the figure, even as other guards fell by the quick movements of the stranger's companions.

It was terrifying, if Crem was being honest, and he wanted nothing more than to be gone from here, but his body didn't seem to want to cooperate. "Any idea who that is?" he quietly asked Howle.

"None," Howle said with a shake of his head.

Crem watched as the mystery man pushed Lord Elrick into a kneeling position. From a distance, Crem thought there was fear in Elrick's eyes. The black-clad figure leaned down and said something too low for Crem to hear, but whatever it was, Lord Elrick's face changed from fear to rage, his mouth opening to retort, only for the stranger's sword to suddenly be pushed through his chest. Crem watched with some small satisfaction as Elrick coughed up his own blood and life drained from him.

The man withdrew his sword as Elrick continued sputtering and coughing, giving him no mind as he turned back toward his companions. "Get the last wagon open," he commanded. "Dawn is coming, and they need to be out of sight when this mess is discovered."

He strode back to Crem and Howle, stopping only to clean his blade on the body of one of the fallen guards. "I apologize for our late arrival. I didn't know it was a trap until it was too late to send another letter." He looked back at the fallen body of Lord Elrick. "They are going to pin this on you, you know. We should get off the streets so we can discuss our next move."

"Who the hell are you? Why should we trust you?" Howle growled.

Crem didn't think now was the time to argue, but he didn't disagree with the statement either.

"My men and I are hardly going to unmask in the middle of the street where someone might be able to identify us to that joke of a king. How about we get off the street first?" The man's lips quirked up. "If it helps, I think I can recite the contents of every letter I've sent you while we walk."

Crem didn't think the man was serious, but the stranger started his recitation. He didn't even make it through the first letter before Crem motioned for his people, who had finished freeing the other civilians, to follow. He signaled Howle discreetly, a command to meet up at their secondary hideout. Howle turned his attention to their men and quietly gave orders for them to stay behind. The group disbursed, and Crem and Howle motioned for the stranger to lead the way.

More of the letters were recited as they walked, a good distraction from the pain Lord Elrick's cut caused him. Finally, they arrived at the small warehouse at the end of the merchant block. Crem started cursing up a storm.

"Fuck, Howle, I need paper. My wife needs to know what happened. Shit, I don't—" he paused and growled in frustration. "I don't think she will be able to leave safely."

Howle firmly gripped his shoulder. "I'll get ya paper, but she's a smart one. Your plan to make her look innocent was a good one. She'll be fine."

"If it helps, I left one of mine behind to keep an eye on her," said the stranger. "They will extract her if needed."

Crem turned to demand to know who he was, but the stranger and his men were removing their headgear. Crem was left speechless at the sight of a grinning Lord Barris surrounded by Mers.

Chapter Forty-One

Once the tents had been erected and a space cleared for the fire, Larent had excused himself, leaving Collette to her own devices.

Collette sat on a rock, leaning back on her hands, and turned her head. She lacked the sensitive abilities Arian and Nawalya had, or Larent's heightened wolfy senses, but she was aware that the heavy, sprinting steps from the distance didn't belong to anyone in her party. The running clued her into the possibility of danger. She sprang to her feet, eyes peering into the distant tree line, waiting for the appearance of the would-be attacker.

And she was … almost disappointed as he came into view. Lanky and sallow, the older man stumbled into the snowy clearing, a tarnished broadsword perched on his shoulder, a stupid placement for a man who was running.

He spotted her halfway across the clearing, and an evil little smile crept up his face before he launched himself at her, sword held high. She laughed at the absurdity of the situation, but planted her feet and withdrew her own blades, ready to take him on.

She let him have the first swing when he was in reach, easily ducking out of the way despite the slippery snow. "You made a big mistake, my friend," she told him. "Last chance to turn around."

He responded by swinging again, missing her entirely and losing balance. He managed, just barely, not to fall, and he growled when Collette laughed at him.

"You started this," she reminded the man. She took a step back, her position ready when he lunged again. She avoided the sword and drug a dagger across the length of his forearm in a fluid motion. She didn't like to kill if it could be avoided, and she hoped the warning cut would be enough to scare him away.

"You bitch!" the man screamed at her, looking at the slash on his arm in horror. It was shallow, though the blood would be scary for someone not expecting it.

"Look at you! Big man with a big sword you can't swing, and now we're name-calling," she mocked. "You want to use that big sword on me, don't you?"

"You'll be lucky if that's all I do," the man snarled.

Collette laughed in response. Larent emerged from the tree line, and perhaps the sight of him made her less cautious than she should have been. "You got this, Freckles?" he called out as he strolled closer.

"We're just playing," she called back, knowing better than to let her eyes leave her attacker, skilled or not. "Aren't we?" she asked the attacker, further infuriating the man, if his decision to run at her full tilt, blade aimed at her center, was any indication. Thankfully, the lack of subtlety in the movement was more than enough to have her easily dodging the latest attack.

"Maybe you should consider training him instead of playing with him. He really could use the help," Larent responded.

"That might have been possible had he not started calling me such terrible names," she called back. As fun as the taunting

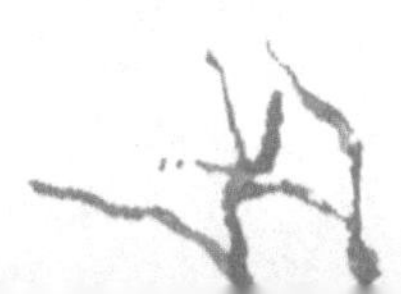

had been, this was getting old. "Are you done, yet? You can admit defeat, maybe even walk away if Larent feels generous."

Larent tilted his head. "I don't know. Maybe he can go if he tells us how he found us. Or maybe I'll just gut him." He gave a feral grin to the man, the wolf beneath begging for release.

The man held the sword aloft, alternating between pointing it at Larent and Collette. "I could gut her if you think this is so funny," he threatened.

"No, you couldn't," Larent stated. "You're holding the sword wrong. You're overreaching, and you're broadcasting your movements. She has years of training; I could bind her hands and she'd still win this fight."

"And that's without getting into the fact that you're not capable of handling your weapon," Collette taunted.

"He doesn't look capable of handling anything." Larent followed his statement with a glance up and down at the man. "We have several companions who will be here any minute, and they won't play with you. They will just kill you. One might torture you. You sure you wanna stick around for that?"

Collette hoped the man would do the smart thing, even if she had no worries about facing him. Unfortunately, he made the sad choice to sprint toward her again, which made her all the more inclined to end this. She dodged out of the way again, glaring.

"You want to kill him or should I?" Larent growled.

"Lunge at me again, and I'll cut your fucking heart out," she warned the would-be assassin, her temper flared. Unphased by the warning, he tried to strike again.

"Oh, dear Lady," Larent sighed. "You're terminally stupid, aren't you?" he said to the man. He rolled his shoulders, knowing he was going to intervene. "Mind if I handle this?" he asked Collette. "I'll hold him down, you rip out his heart, and I'll eat it as a snack."

Chapter Forty-one

"By all means," she replied. "I'm done playing."

"Perfect," he replied, his grin turning deadly. He took a step forward and shifted into the large black wolf, now on all fours, his teeth glinted in a dangerous snarl, and Collette expected him to make quick work of the assassin.

But something was wrong. Very wrong.

Collette wasn't sure what it was at first. The wolf's mere existence appeared to be a struggle, the smooth musculature of his wolf form jerked and shook, and the rigidness of his muscles was evident even beneath the thick, black fur. She took a step back, unsure of what to do.

"Larent?" Collette said, her words clipped in worry.

The wolf stepped closer to Collette, shoulders tense and eyes locked on her. Eyes that were red, intent. Eyes that didn't belong to Larent.

Blood magic. Someone was using blood magic on him.

"Shit," she breathed out, afraid. She took another step back as he gave a warning growl. Then he leapt at her, and this time, Collette had to try to avoid being struck. She just made it, having dropped and rolled out of the way. Quickly, she forced herself to her feet, her knives abandoned on the ground.

The wolf circled, stopping in front of her, deadly teeth on display. He growled, low and dark, and she knew he planned to strike again. The assassin took advantage of the standoff, long sword raised as he ran at Collette.

She jumped out of the blade's path, the sharp object narrowly missing her. Larent's wolf followed, but the struggle of his pursuit showed that he was fighting the magic, and the pace of his steps showed a losing internal battle.

The next time the wolf jumped toward her, she was not so lucky. She avoided the worst of the attack, rolling out of his range before lifting back to her feet, but long claw marks slashed across her side. They didn't hurt at first. Only once the

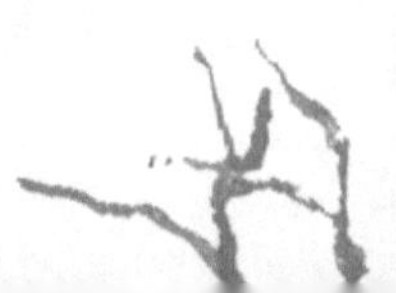

dark blood soaked through her shirt, and she noticed the droplets falling into the white snow, did the intense stinging alert her to how seriously fucked she was.

"Shit," she said under her breath, her eyes darting back and forth between the attacker who was grinning victoriously, and the wolf who would never have harmed her of his own accord. She gingerly pressed her fingers against her blood-soaked side, wincing a little at the pain and trying to decide her best course of action.

Larent was the more dangerous problem, though avoiding further injury from him made the would-be assassin more dangerous than he should have been. It wasn't like Collette could outrun either now that she was injured.

Larent's snout lifted, sniffing the air, her flowing blood drawing his attention. His red eyes turned to her again, bloodied claws gripping the ground. He was resisting, or trying anyway, and with her having no clue when the others would return, she knew there wasn't much choice in her next move.

Of course, debating her options distracted her from the attacker, and almost too late did she note he was coming at her from the side. She prepared to fight him, knowing she was likely going to die if she wasn't extremely lucky.

Luck was on her side. Collette's proximity to Larent brought the man to a halt. He seemed to contemplate an attack and shifted his weight back and forth. Now was her chance.

"Larent," she said, glancing back and forth every few seconds between the two. "Larent, I know this isn't you. You aren't doing this. I know you're in there. I can help you. I just need you to keep fighting it, just a little longer, okay?"

She held out a hand, knowing that the physical request to stop did nothing, but it grounded her a little. Slowly, and without taking her eyes off the wolf, she knelt to retrieve one of her daggers, aware that the cowardly attacker stood close.

She rose as quickly as she could, the pain licking at her side as blood flowed, wet and sticky. She'd fix that when she could.

The retrieval of one of her weapons prompted another attack, this one a little more successful than the others. With Larent near unpredictable, the easiest path of avoidance was blocked, and she physically didn't have it in her to fully avoid the assassin's attack.

The tip of his blade finally met its mark, penetrating her abdomen and conjuring a growl of pain. The wound felt shallow but one she hadn't needed. Emboldened by his successful blow, the attacker raised his sword to strike again, only for Collette to harshly push him back with the hand not holding a dagger. He grabbed at her arm, though his grip was slick with his own blood, and he only managed to catch her by her mother's gold bracelet, ripping it off as he stumbled back. Her ability to fight back must have scared him because he was gone almost as quickly as he'd arrived. That suited Collette. Now she just had the wolf to contend with.

She turned her attention back to Larent, ignoring how light-headed she was feeling or the pain she was in. She needed to help him. "Let him run," she forced out. "He'll tell people he's killed me." If she didn't act quickly, the story would be true. "I'm going to approach," she told him in a voice that wasn't as strong as before. "Keep fighting. Fight like you've never fought for anything else."

The wolf vibrated with the effort of staying put, issuing a whine of pure pain.

She took slow, careful steps forward, and eventually, she was close enough to place a hand on his furry head, stroking the dark fur, giving him something more to focus on. Perhaps helping him would give her the strength to stay awake while she bled out.

Instead of trying to staunch the flow, she put her other hand on his head, cupping the place just beneath his ear. She closed her eyes and took a deep steadying breath, focusing. She'd never used her magic for something so serious, and from her readings, she knew countering blood magic was challenging under the best of circumstances. "I probably can't break this," she warned. "But I can buy you enough time to shift back."

Her hands grew warm on his fur, and there were the small, tingling vibrations she'd nearly forgotten about. She hadn't healed anyone in so long, she'd forgotten how hot her hands could get or how powerful the magic felt flowing through her body. She could feel her magic flooding into Larent and the strength of the blood magic fighting for control. It was dangerous and red, though she got no closer to discovering its truths.

Larent managed to slowly shift back into his human form. Collette noted that he was pale, sweaty, and shaky. She could do no more for him now.

"Heal yourself," he rasped out.

She nodded and sank to her knees, ignoring the wet cold that penetrated her trousers. Pressing a hand to her stomach and covering the stab wound, she tried very hard to stop the bleeding. Her hand grew warm again, but her power was weak. She didn't have much time.

Larent rolled onto his back. He groaned with pain and forced himself into a sitting position. He looked around for Arian's bag, but Arian rarely left it behind. Crawling to Collette, he moved so she could rest against him.

"Tell me something, Freckles?" he asked in panic as he surveyed all the blood.

"I think I'm pretty close to knowing what dying feels like," she replied with a short, bitter laugh, the dark humor only alleviating some of her panic. Her trembling hand left her stomach and moved to her side. She was positive she could make the bleeding stop. But somehow, she knew she was too late.

"Arian! You pointy-eared fucker, I need you!" Larent screamed. With luck, someone in their group was in hearing range. "You're not going to die, Collette. I won't let you. Tell me something else."

"You're my favorite person," she answered. She was off her knees, managing to hold herself up with an arm, and her four wounds no longer bled. The blood loss, however, she just couldn't fix. "Even when you use my actual name."

"And you're my favorite person," he replied, his voice raspy with emotion. Tears fell down his cheeks, his eyes scanning her as though he desperately wanted, but didn't know how, to help. "Your name is beautiful." He put his arms around her body, offering her physical support and holding her close. "You can't die on me. You can't," he whispered. "Tell me something else."

Crashing sounded in the distance.

"I'm trying," she whispered, her vision blurring around the edges. She reached up with the hand not covered in blood and brushed away a few of his tears with her thumb.

"Please," he begged. "Please, keep your eyes open, Freckles." He let out a sob. "I love you. Don't leave me…"

She opened her mouth to respond, but this time she couldn't. Her hand dropped from his face. The connection she'd been holding onto severed as the fuzzy, dark edges around her vision grew. As everything faded to black, the last thing she heard was the sounds of Larent's screams.

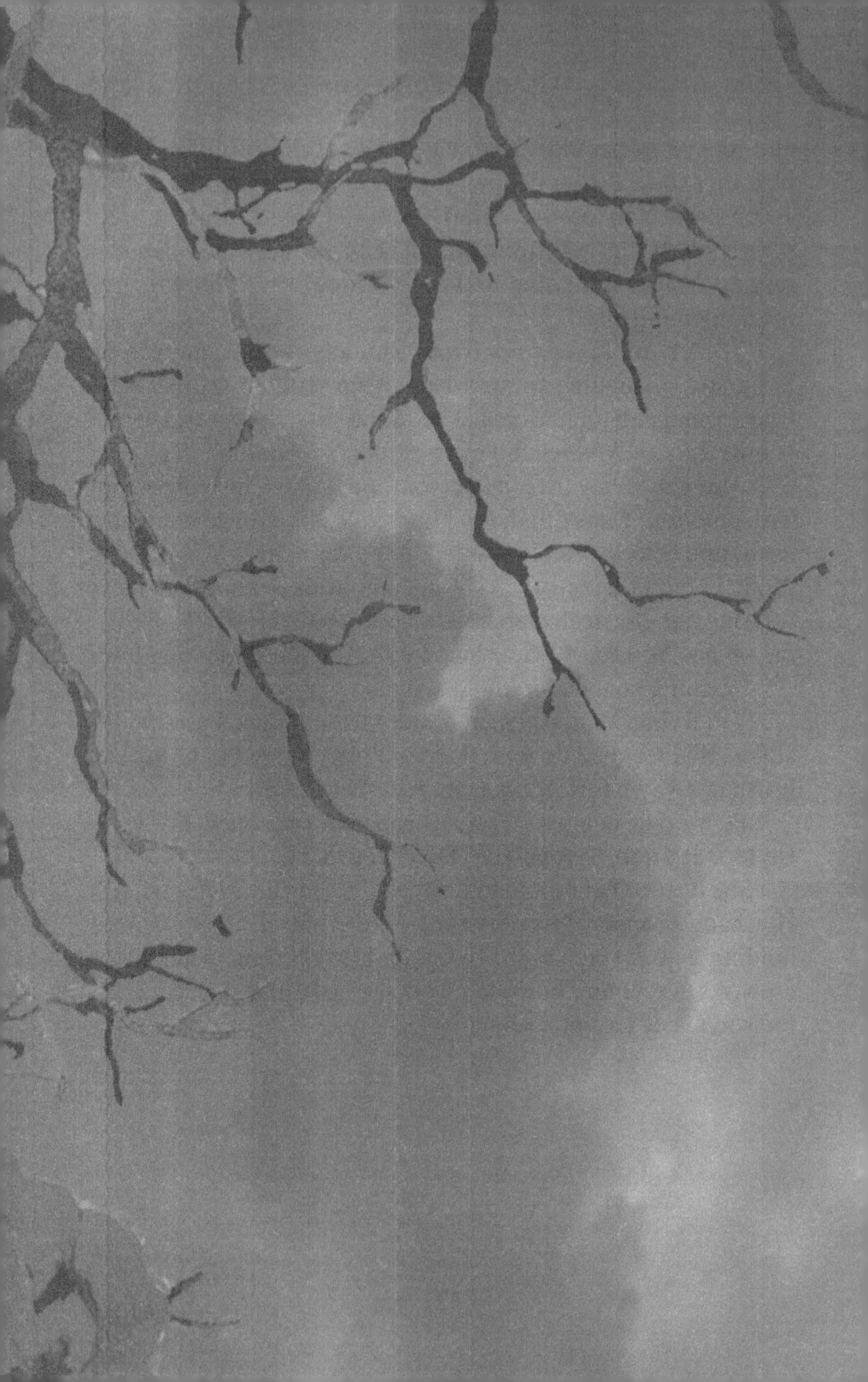

Book Club Questions

1. Tolan struggles with self-worth and general worth in helping Collette. What do you think motivates these feelings?

2. Why do you think Tolan left? Would you have done the same?

3. Why did Nawalya, Arian, and Larent decide to hide Nawalya's vision? Was this the right decision? Why or why not?

4. Collette mentions that she doesn't want to be queen. What moral and ethical responsibilities does she have? Is she obligated to be queen?

5. Regicide is discussed in this book. Did Whyldon do the right thing when he murdered a king? What about Nawalya?

6. Collette is faced with moral dilemmas over regicide and torture. Did she respond appropriately? Why or why not?

7. Should Collette consider Larent as a viable romantic partner? Is he good for her? Is he better for her than Tolan?

8. Did Larent do the right thing when he claimed to be Collette's husband? Were there other options?

9. Crem works against the Crown while leaving his wife vulnerable in the palace. Do you agree with his actions, or would you have done something different?

10. Were you surprised by the role Lord Barris plays in the last chapters? Do you think he can be successful? What are his motivations?

11. Despite his efforts, Zephraim seems ineffective and uninterested in being king. What advice would you give him?

12. Rhoslyn is clearly in love with Riken, and she is unable to inspire Zephraim to be the sort of leader she wants him to be. Should she stay in her marriage, or should she pursue a different path?

13. Riken is involved in adultery, murder, and possible genocide. Is he evil, or is he trying to rectify the problems brought on by King Sargarus and Queen Collette?

14. Is it wise for Aphros and the Nereid to support Collette in the event they find her, or should they focus on self-preservation?

15. Arian's mental health struggles often present as moody, distant, and closed off. Do his struggles justify his behavior toward Thomas?

Author Bios

Kate D. Jenkins enjoys writing fantasy, Sci-fi, and romance as much as she enjoys reading them. She lives in a small town in Idaho with her autistic teen who is her whole world, her parents, and between them, four dogs and eight cats. When not hanging with her son, she loves gaming, especially first-person shooters and asymmetrical horror games she can play with friends. She's a K-pop enthusiast and harbors a secret love of K-dramas and Anime, much to her mother's displeasure, as she's slowly being sucked into them with her. Her favorites tropes are currently enemy-to-lovers, there was only one bed, coffee shops, time travel fixes it, and soul mates/soul identifying marks. She is hopeful one day she can talk her co-author into writing these with her.

Morgan A. Moreau is a lover and writer of all kinds of fiction, including fantasy, history, crime and mystery, and modern-day stories. She embraces the Ariel aesthetic, especially when it comes to her vivid red hair and mermaid tattoos. She continues growing her *The Little Mermaid* collection on a regular basis. She lives in Alabama with her dog, though she makes frequent trips to visit her niblings. Her current passions include higher education, animal rights, and watching the 1995 *Pride & Prejudice* at least once a month. In addition to her current literary loves, Morgan is a fan of vampires, pirates, and superheroes, and she hopes to incorporate this into future works.

A sneak peek from the upcoming sequel, *Legends of Coralia: Hope and Ashes*.

A scrawny man sat at a table, surrounded by people, food, and drink. They laughed and talked, and roared on occasion, none of which would have caught anyone's attention had the scrawny man not held a simple gold bracelet between two long, pale fingers.

The sight of the bracelet reminded Tolan of the night he'd abandoned his lover. He'd placed the golden trinket on the pillow next to Collette, having carried it with him since the day of a jousting tournament when she'd handed him the item as a favor. His blood ran cold as he contemplated the possible ways the bracelet—her bracelet—was now in a random roadside inn.

"Took this off of her before I left," the man bragged to a group of fellow drinkers. He laughed heartily and twirled the golden trinket around his fingers a couple of times before it clattered to the table. He laughed again at the sound and swiped it up before others could grab it and pass the thing around.

"And we're supposed to believe you took out the queen?" a man bellowed with disbelieving guffaws.

The scrawny man chuckled again. "In truth, I did have some help from a wolf," he admitted before throwing back a large gulp of his drink. "But she is gone."

Without thinking, Tolan moved quickly toward the table. He grabbed the spindly little man by his shirt and slammed him into the bar top. "Say that again," he growled.

The man seemed to not have expected backlash. He dropped the bracelet again, unable to retrieve it, and looked up at Tolan, visibly frightened by the man's height and physique. "W-what do you mean?" he stammered out.

Tolan pulled the man off the bar and slammed him against it hard. "You just bragged about murdering Queen Collette with the help of a wolf. I want the whole story. Now."

"The, uh, wolf did most of it," the man replied, his eyes wide with fear, his complexion growing paler with each passing second. "His claws are what got her."

"I'm running out of patience," Tolan warned. Somehow, he was managing to keep his fear from surfacing, perhaps because he wasn't convinced the man could have possibly taken her out.

"I don't know what else to say," the man pleaded. "It was dark, and the wolf was huge. Bigger than any wolf I've ever seen."

"Was he with the woman when you got there?"

"Yes," the man replied, his voice quavering. "But he wasn't a wolf at first."

More books from 4 Horsemen Publications

LGBT Romance

AJ Buchannan
Orchestrated Love

Eskay Kabba
Hidden Love
Not So Hidden
Signs of Affection
Deeply Devoted to Him
Honest Love
A Plane and Simple Connection

Lucas LaMont
Roman's Reckoning: Type 6
Mikaél's Moment: Type 6

Stephan's Resurgence: Type 5
Anastasia's Arrival: Type 6

Stormie Skyes
Check Yes, No, or Maybe

V.C. Willis
The Prince's Priest
The Priest's Assassin
The Assassin's Saint
The Champion's Lord

Fantasy

D. Lambert
To Walk into the Sands
Rydan
Celebrant
Northlander
Esparan
King
Traitor
His Last Name

Danielle Orsino
Locked Out of Heaven
Thine Eyes of Mercy
From the Ashes

Kingdom Come
Fire, Ice, Acid, & Heart
A Fae is Done

J.M. Paquette
Klauden's Ring
Solyn's Body
The Inbetween
Hannah's Heart

Lou Kemp
The Violins Played Before Junstan
Music Shall Untune the Sky